THE HOUSE OF CAIN

The
HOUSE
of CAIN

Arthur·W·Upfield

London Times Literary Supplement : "It is a remarkable and original story, told with ability."

Dustjacket from the 1929 Dorrance edition

THE
HOUSE OF CAIN

by
ARTHUR W. UPFIELD
Author of ''The Barrakee Mystery,'' etc.

DENNIS McMILLAN · SAN FRANCISCO, CALIFORNIA

1983

Originally published 1928 by Hutchinson & Co., Ltd., London
Reprinted 1929 by Dorrance & Co., Inc., Philadelphia

ISBN 0-9609986-0-8

Dennis McMillan
1353 4th Avenue
San Francisco, CA 94122

UPFIELD'S PRE-OSTEOMANTIC NOVEL

I DON'T know about you, but I'm grateful to Dennis McMillan for the publication of this long-lost novel. *The House of Cain* first appeared in 1928 in England, made a little splash, was reprinted in the U.S. in 1929, then sank into that dark and cold ocean which lies beyond the literary North Pole. This ocean is called The Great Publishing Oblivion—among other things.

The House of Cain has been as rare and unobtainable as Arthur Upfield's other very early novels, *Gripped by Drought, A Royal Abduction,* and *The Beach of Atonement.* These are so "hidden" that many otherwise knowledgeable rare bookdealers have not even heard of them.

Though few have known about the above-named four, some readers, myself among them, have been enchanted by Upfield's series about an Australian Outback detective named Napoleon Bonaparte. "Bony" for short. I discovered these about fifteen years ago and started collecting them. And rereading them for the sheer pleasure of it. I now have all the Bonys, twenty-nine, I believe, and treasure them.

I also obtained from a second-hand bookdealer Upfield's biography, *Follow My Dust,* written by Jessica Hawke in collaboration with him. This was published in 1957 by Heinemann, England.

Follow My Dust tells much about Upfield, though not enough and even lacks a bibliography. In fact, I had to go to Steinbrunner's and Penzler's *Encyclopedia of Mystery and Detection* to find the year of Upfield's birth, 1888. I still don't know the day and the month.

What happened in A.D. 1888? Well, Jack the Ripper leaped into fame, and Lord Greystoke, a.k.a. Tarzan, was born. "Casey at the Bat" was published. The first typewriter stencil was introduced in London. The *National Geographic* magazine began publication. The first successful electric trolley cars went into service in Richmond, Virginia. The first Chinese railway opened. The first patent for a pneumatic bicycle tire was awarded. Brazil's slaves were freed. Nickel

1

steel was invented in France, and the first commercial aluminum was produced in Pittsburgh. *Looking Backward,* Edward Bellamy's classic Utopian novel—an example of science-fiction—was published.

All this and much more happened in 1888, but no one except the immediate family noted Arthur Upfield's birth. His grandfather and father were drapers, and he was born in Gosport, which is on the west side of Portsmouth Harbour, a seaport and naval base of Hampshire, and about seventy miles southwest from London by road. Despite this nautical environment, Arthur did not want to go down to the sea in ships. His desire, though he did not then know it, was for that ocean of rock and sand and thin soil within the coasts of Down-Under. Because of circumstances I won't go into here, Arthur was raised mainly by his grandmother and her sisters, but there is no evidence that this environment harmed or aided him. He was, however, probably allowed more scope to exercise his imagination there than he would have been in his father's house. At the age of fourteen or fifteen he wrote a 120,000-word novel, a science-fictional tale of a voyage to Mars. It's safe to assume that this was inspired by his readings of Verne and Wells and others of the host of science-romances flourishing then. This novel has been long lost. Just as well, I'm sure, though I'll admit I'm curious about it. Was it purely derivative or did it have sparks of originality, of Upfieldisms?

If Arthur had not done so poorly in school and been so lacking in business sense, and if he had not then been shipped off to Australia by his father, we might have had another Edgar Rice Burroughs or E. E. Smith. I, for one, am glad that he shipped out. I would have been less rich, as far as enjoyment goes, if "Napoleon Bonaparte" had not been invented.

Because of space limits, I won't go into detail about the youthful Upfield's life in the Outback after his arrival in 1910. Suffice it to say that he roamed through that vast terrain as a working tramp and gained a superb knowledge of the wild land and its more or less wild people, including the aborigines. He was gone from his adopted country for a while during World War I and was present at the horrible debacle of Gallipoli. His biography scarcely mentions what must have been a deeply traumatic experience.

Upfield met a half-aborigine policeman, Tracker Leon Wood, and he used this real-life person as the model for the fictional Napoleon Bonaparte. The first Bony novel was *The Barrakee Mystery.* He sent it to a literary agent, an honest one, for criticism. The agent gave him some very good advice about rewriting it, and Upfield was intelligent enough to take the advice. He set the novel aside for a while, let it cool, and wrote the book at hand, *The House of Cain.* This was a straight thriller; it lacked Bony. But the reader acquainted with the Bony novels will see in *The House of Cain* the seeds of the latter and better books.

However, it's not necessary that this be read just for comparison purposes. It is enjoyable in itself. Though somewhat old-fashioned in several respects and though its characters are like those in other slick novels of its time—not pulpish, slick, mind you, there'a a big difference, with the weight of superiority in favor of the pulps—*The House of Cain* is an interesting mystery, and some of the characters are a cut above cardboard. It's also evident even in this early work that Upfield has been in the Outback, soaked it in, as it were, and he's not describing it after a brief visit or after reading about it in some library.

There's also something Doc Savageish about it. The flavor is very slight, but the theme that crime might originate in a lesion of the brain and that, if the lesion is excised, the criminal is cured, is right out of the Doc Savage novels. Except that Upfield did it first.

Now. To a theory of mine, if the reader will forgive me.

Napoleon Bonaparte was found shortly after his birth in the arms of his dead mother, slain under a sandalwood tree. Apparently, the mother had been killed by her tribesmen for the sin of bearing a child by a white man. Why the baby was not also killed was a mystery, but the tribesmen may have thought that it would soon die unattended out in the great waste and bake.

The baby was found just in time, however, and raised in a mission school. Named Napoleon Bonaparte, the half-aborigine grew up to be handsome, blue-eyed, and very intelligent. He became a famous detective inspector in the Queensland D.P., eventually got married, and had handsome intelligent sons whom he sent to college.

It's my theory that this hybrid of two peoples and cultures, Bony, was the illegitimate son of Arthur J. Raffles. Raffles, if you don't know, and you might not if you're young, was the infamous English gentleman-burglar of the late nineteenth century whose exploits were narrated by his admiring sidekick, Harry "Bunny" Manders. (E. W. Hornung agented these stories.) Raffles began his criminal career while quite a young man in the Outback. (See "Le Premier Pas," a short story in the collection, *The Amateur Cracksman.*) For many years, Raffles was so famous that a "Raffles" meant a debonair gentleman criminal with a high code of ethics—for a burglar.

While Raffles was in the bush country, he had a brief affair with a black or half-black woman and shortly thereafter returned to England with the police hot on his trail. The fruit of this mating was Bony, who inherited not only his father's good looks and courage and light eyes but his genius. The son, however, used this genius on the right side of the law.

While you're thinking about this, enjoy Upfield's pre-osteomantic novel, the now available, brought-to-you-from-exotic-lands-at-great-expense-and-travail novel, *The House of Cain.*

—Philip José Farmer

CONTENTS

CONTENTS

THE HOUSE OF CAIN

CHAPTER I

THE LUCK OF WEDNESDAY

EVERY one in Melbourne is acquainted with the *Tribune* Building: all the world knows the story of Sir Victor Lawrence, its owner, the man who rose from printer's devil to Prime Minister, and in between somehow amassed a gigantic fortune in journalism. To-day he is not Prime Minister: he makes Prime Ministers, as a famous Earl of Warwick made kings.

When the editor-in-chief of Sir Victor's most important paper, *The Daily Tribune,* entered his private office on the top floor of the huge building, he found the "power behind the throne" seated with his feet on the roll-top desk, a cigar held firmly between his thin, strong lips, and his hat tilted at a dangerous angle on the back of his round bald head. It was eleven-thirty, and Sir Victor had but just dropped in from a theatre.

"Ah, Sherwood! take hold of a chair and a cigar," Sir Victor said in clipped tones. "The 'Forthcoming Marriages' column was most interesting this morning—most interesting." A meaning smile accompanied these words.

The other, a slight, handsome, but tired-looking man of thirty-nine, drew a chair to the left of the desk, indicating with a motion of a long-fingered white hand that he preferred a cigarette.

"Is there anything in the *Tribune* that escapes your eyes, Sir Victor?" he asked quietly.

Sir Victor lowered his feet, removed the cigar from his mouth, but continued to balance his hat carefully. His smile broadened to a grin—a regular schoolboy grin—when he said:

"Only the leading article. Why should I waste time in

reading the articles of a man who knows my mind better than I do myself?"

There was an implied compliment in the speech which brought a slight flush of pleasure to the face of the younger man. The Birthday Knight went on:

"So you have set the day for the seventeenth, eh? A Wednesday! I always think Wednesday the luckiest day of the week. I was married on a Wednesday. I trust that the years will bring you the luck that one Wednesday twenty years ago brought me."

The little bald-headed man, who looked much like a retired ostler, held out a plump red hand. His small brown eyes glistened with friendly humour.

"Thank you!" Martin Sherwood said quickly, gripping the plump red hand. "Already, I think, my good fortune has begun."

"Then doubtless you first met your future wife on a Wednesday. You did? I am glad to hear it. Still, I must say, your notice doesn't give us much practical information. Nor, indeed, much time to prepare for the mighty event. To-day is the eleventh, and you are to be married on the seventeenth. You do not say at what church."

"My doctor forbade me most strictly to do so. He insists on the affair being kept quiet so as to avoid the worrying details and the excitement of a fashionable crush. My doctor, I fear, is a bit of an alarmist."

"He may not be, Sherwood—he may not be," Sir Victor murmured, studying the pale face and the abnormally large, dark eyes gazing unwinkingly at him. "To be blunt, you are looking rotten. Your trip to Europe will make a new man of you—the sea and your wife will assure that."

"I believe a long rest will do me good."

"I'm sure of it. I've worked you to death, my boy. I've been the Old Man to your Sinbad. For a space you leave the *Tribune* a power in Australia. It will be difficult for Moplett and me to keep it at the level to which you have lifted it. I shall be obliged to read Moplett's leaders in proof."

"I feel you may place thorough confidence in Mr. Moplett. With him in my chair I shall not be missed."

"You will be missed by me. I shall have to read his leaders," groaned Sir Victor, half mockingly. "Your article to-day emphasizing the absurdity of the Victorian Minister's trip to America to learn how to run railways was, I fear, unduly severe. Granted, our railways are run splendidly; yet we can always learn. We are getting behind the times, Sherwood. The *Tribune* wants modernizing."

"Sir!" gasped the scandalized chief editor.

Again the schoolboy grin.

"I mean it!" he said, contradicted by the grin. "When you get to London, you spend a couple of hours in Fleet Street, and see how they run newspapers there."

"But the *Tribune* is recognized as the most advanced paper in the Empire," Sherwood protested. "Surely you are joking?"

"I never joke, my boy. If the Minister for Railways wants to learn how to run trains, we want to know how to run a newspaper. The State, or the people who finance the State, pay his first-class expenses for the knowledge. The *Tribune* shall pay all the expenses of your honeymoon for the knowledge how to run a newspaper."

"Sir Victor, this is both most wonderfully generous and—pardon me—wonderfully foolish of you. I doubt sincerely that the *Tribune* can be improved upon."

"We are never too old to improve, Sherwood. You take your six months. Stop worrying. Give that fine brain of yours a rest. Forget that I ever rode on your back; that I shall ride there again immediately you return." Sir Victor rose to his feet. His round face was beaming when he held out his hand for the second time. In his left he held an envelope.

"I shall be disappointed if my wife and I are not invited to the wedding. We promise to keep time and place to ourselves, Sherwood. This cheque will go towards your expenses. Put in for the balance when you return. Good night, Sinbad, and Wednesday's good luck to you!"

Martin took the proffered envelope and the outstretched hand of the man who was one of his dearest friends.

"You shall have the invitation, Sir Victor," he said warmly. "I will carry your simile further, and add that if I am Sinbad your weight was extraordinarily light. Good night!"

When Martin Sherwood reached his own office it wanted but one minute to midnight. The issue of the paper for Friday, the twelfth, had been "put to bed," and the sound of the machines in the basement had become a thunderous roar. A small clock on his desk struck twelve silvery chimes while he donned his greatcoat, for it was early September and the nights were cold.

For a moment he surveyed his workroom, his eyes wandering over the familiar objects, mute witnesses of the strenuous evolution of his brilliant leaders, and of the tireless energy directed to many other departments of his darling paper. Then, with a sigh, as if he foreboded strange happenings ere, if ever, he should occupy that room again, he passed out into the corridor, closing the door softly behind him.

At the main entrance to the Building an ill-formed, crooked-featured man, in the dark uniform of a hall-porter, opened the swing-doors to let him pass. Martin mechanically nodded his thanks and went through to the pavement, where at the curb was waiting his single-seater run-about. The porter reached it first, however, and opened the door.

Again Martin nodded, but this time, looking into the man's eyes, he was struck by the joyous light within their jade-green depths, revealed by the arc-lamp close by.

"Why, Hill! how is it I find you on duty at this hour of the night?" he asked in surprise.

"I come back 'arf-hour ago, sir. Kinda felt I couldn't sleep till I told yous the news."

"News! News is my job, Hill. What is it?"

"It's a boy, sir. Arrived this afternoon, 'e did."

Martin stared at the hall-porter with a puzzled frown.

"I'm a-trying to tell yous, Mr. Sherwood, sir, that I bin made a father to-day," Hill explained, his voice trembling with emotion, his whole attitude that of a man who, having imparted tremendous news, is dashed by the flat reception of it.

Martin smiled with sudden understanding—a smile that lit up his haggard face and brightened his dull, tired eyes. Its spontaneity, its sympathy, made Hill hardly coherent. Without giving Sherwood time to speak, he rushed into a flood of words.

"When I think o' what I was, sir, a thief and worse, a gaolbird, a man wivout even the respect of 'is feller-thieves— when I remember the time I was like a lorst dorg, and now orl this love and joy wot you and Miss Thorpe brought into me life, I feel I orter go down and kiss yer boots." Then, without a pause and striking off at a tangent, he added: "'E's got blue eyes like 'is movver—strike me dead if 'e ain't!"

"Well—well—well," Martin said, in his quick way, whilst climbing into his car, "I'm very glad, Hill. Really I am. I feel sure Miss Thorpe will be the same. She will want to visit your wife to-morrow, I know."

Hill, whose world was bathed in wonderful colours and filled with indescribable music, saw a thin, white hand held out to him. He hesitated, then rubbed his right hand vigorously on his trousers, and, snatching at the proffered hand, shook it with sudden abandon.

"Good luck, Hill! I told you honesty *was* the best policy, didn't I?" he heard his idol murmur when the car slid off from the curb.

Martin drove slowly along Collins Street and turned into Elizabeth Street. Even at so late an hour the pavements were dense with promenaders and people hurrying from cinemas and restaurants to tram and train. Making a second turn into Flinders Street, he pulled up outside the Flinders Hotel.

Passing through the vestibule, he nodded absently to the clerk on night duty at the office, and then, following a ground-floor corridor, paused outside a door at which he rang the electric bell. Almost at once the door was opened by a uniformed maid, who with a smile of recognition stepped aside to admit him.

"Miss Thorpe in, Bessie?"

"Yes, sir. She is expecting you."

That had been his question and this her answer every midnight during the past six months, excepting Saturdays and days preceding holidays. The question and answer had become almost a ritual. The girl's taking his hat and coat had become almost automatic.

Martin, stepping across the small hall, opened the door of the drawing-room of the suite and passed within, closing the door softly behind him. For perhaps ten seconds he remained a statue; his eyes alone on fire with life, searching with never-flagging interest each feature of the woman standing before the fire.

There are pretty women, there are handsome women, but Austiline Thorpe was a woman splendid. In repose her face was remarkable for its sculpturesque beauty; now, in meeting the gaze of Martin Sherwood, it was flushed to a breath-catching loveliness. Few are the mortal men fortunate enough to see such a face with such a look upon it for them alone.

Her deep green evening dress contoured a perfct form. But that and the gleam of her white arms held out to him in welcome were but dimly seen by Martin, absorbed in the glory of her eyes, the colour of bronze, flecked with red.

Always thus did she hold him spellbound at the door, homage unconsciously given, a tribute to her perfection.

"Austiline!"

"Martin!"

Slowly they drew together. Caressing white arms rose about his neck, whilst her curving lips throbbed to the pressure of his own and white blue-veined eyelids momentarily veiled the splendour of her eyes. Then quite suddenly they were raised again, and for one exquisite second the soul behind them swept aside all physical barriers and leapt forth to meet his.

"Man! you are very tired," she whispered. "Those horrible machines are killing you."

A smile of infinite tenderness stole over his features.

"The killing is suspended for six months."

"Your leave at last? Come, sit here, and tell me about it after your coffee."

She might have been a sympathetic nurse, and he almost an invalid. The subtle gentleness with which she guided him to a great arm-chair—the only masculine piece of furniture in the room—there to arrange sufficient feminine cushions for his comfort, was really an art inspired by a wonderful love.

Sitting close opposite him, she drew beside her a silent waiter on which was a silver coffee apparatus. At his side she placed a cup of fragrant coffee and a small plate of sandwiches.

"Not another word till you have drunk at least half your coffee," was her command.

Again he smiled, this time at her mock firmness.

"Sir Victor——" he began.

"Half your coffee—*please,*" she entreated.

For fully a minute they regarded each other, the barriers of their souls withdrawn. Not for a fraction of one second did their eyes waver, not even when he took occasional sips from the cup.

Then, at long last, her eyelids fluttered and she drew a deep sigh. When again she regarded him the innermost barrier of the thousand guarding her soul was up again.

"Better?" she asked, taking the cup and refilling it.

"I *was* tired," he admitted. "Your coffee is wonderful."

"Then you may tell me now—about Sir Victor."

"It is only half an hour since I left him, both glad to give me leave, and sorry to have me absent," he explained with his habitual rapidity. "He remarked that he had always considered Wednesday a lucky day. I told him you and I met on a Wednesday. He read this morning that we were to be married on Wednesday, the seventeenth."

"That *was* nice of him."

"Yes!" Martin agreed. "He is a dear old chap, Sir Victor. He expressed but one regret at losing me for six months."

"And that?"

Sherwood laughed softly, watching her select a cigarette, put it to her mouth, light it in three small puffs and then insert it daintily between his lips. This was a nightly act of return homage she never omitted to perform.

"He said that he never bothered to read my leaders because they only expressed his own thoughts. While I am away, he says he will have to read Moplett's leaders in proof before publication. He gave me the impression that leaders bored him."

"That was not quite so nice of him," she said with brightened eyes. "Surely he must know how brilliant are your leaders, that every day he has something of you, that wonderful something which is the only thing you cannot give me?"

"On the contrary I felt flattered," responded Martin with a smile. "Really, it is a splendid compliment when the active owner of a newspaper relies so implicitly on his editor, who, he says, expresses his views better than he could himself."

"Ah! I think I see. Sir Victor, I apologize. What next?"

"After saying that he never read my leaders, he referred to my leader in to-day's issue chastising the Victorian Government's waste of public money in sending a minister abroad to study railways when our own are run so well. He disagreed with me."

"What! After his 'splendid compliment'?"

"He said that travelling abroad for experience was a good thing for our railways. I am to visit Fleet Street when in London and learn how to run a newspaper."

"Martin!"

"Yes; and the *Tribune* is to pay our expenses in the same way as the people pay the expenses of a minister due for a holiday."

"I don't think I quite understand."

Sherwood smiled again.

"It was Sir Victor's way of giving us a wedding present. Here it is, in this envelope."

Leaning forward, he chuckled and said, while she opened the envelope he gave her:

"Evidently, Austiline, you did not read my leader in to-day's issue any more than did Sir Victor. My leader for to-morrow's deals with the tram versus bus question."

She laughed at that, a delicious gurgle of mirth. And then, on reading the slim pink form she took from the envelope, her eyes widened.

"Oh, Martin! A cheque for one thousand pounds!"

"Didn't I say he was a dear old chap?"

"You did, and so he is! A real nobleman, in spite of what the snobs say about him."

"Better still, my chief is a great man, one of the sort that make history," Martin added.

"Indeed he must be," she said slowly, replacing the cheque in its envelope and returning it. "But you are a great man, too, Martin. That brain of yours is wonderful, but you work it inhumanly. Martin dear, you are like a prodigal farmer, who takes all from his land and puts nothing back. Now, for six delicious months you are going to fallow that mind of yours. You are going to give it the complete rest it has needed so long."

He sighed, making a slight movement which indicated that he was prepared to stretch himself luxuriously even at the mere prospect of rest.

"What other news have you, Man? Like your machines, I am hungry for news."

"Hill saw me to my car to-night. He appeared unduly excited. I think I reminded him that honesty *was* the best policy."

"Hill! At the Building at a quarter to midnight!" Austiline exclaimed. There was little in the routine of the *Tribune* staff that was not familiar to her.

"Yes. He was so anxious to tell us that his wife had presented him with a baby-boy this afternoon."

"Oh!" Her eyes softened.

"His ugly face was transformed. It was amazing."

For just two seconds her moistened eyes held his, and then, turning her head slowly, she gazed thoughtfully into the fire.

Woman-like, she spoke quite away from her thoughts when she said:

"There is good in the worst of us. I knew there was good in him."

"There is," he agreed. "Yes, he wanted to be decent all his life, and knew not how. He wanted to be good in gaol, and even more so when you spoke to him on Princes Bridge the day after he came out for the seventh time, without a reference, with no prospect of honest work, only the prospect of gaol again in the future."

"But it was you who found him work, became his friend, his ideal, almost his god. It was you who with friendship, firmness, and encouragement eased the itching of his fingers to steal. It must be dreadful to be alone in the world, without love, surrounded by indifferent or hostile people."

She shuddered faintly, then burst out:

"Martin, I must go to Mrs. Hill's to-morrow."

"I told Hill you would," he asserted, rising to his feet. "It is getting late."

"But you haven't told me when your leave commences," she expostulated, herself rising.

"Sorry! I forgot. It *has* started."

"Really! Oh, I'm so glad! To-day is Thursday, or rather Friday morning. And Wednesday—*next* Wednesday, Martin!"

"One hundred and thirty-two hours," he said, his voice trembling. "Oh, Austiline! I love you so!"

Again she was in his arms. The moments flew, the while they were locked within the Gates of Paradise, which are beyond the rainbow. When they drew apart and moved towards the door, she asked him:

"Monty comes to-morrow—doesn't he?"

"Yes, at one-thirty. I will bring him here at four o'clock, if that will do?"

"That will be nice," she assented, squeezing his arm. "You shall drink afternoon tea with me. I feel so sure I shall like him."

"Monty! Like Monty! He is the most wonderful chap in the world. He has but to smile at a——"

She stopped him abruptly by placing a hand gently against his mouth. Then, bending towards him, she whispered:

"The most wonderful man in the world but one. *You* are

the most wonderful man in my world. You, Martin! You, my—Man!"

"And you are my own far more wonderful Woman!" he whispered back, drawing her to him.

And, while he drove slowly to his home along the magnificent St. Kilda Road, he murmured repeatedly to himself the words:

"To-morrow, at four o'clock."

CHAPTER II

TO see Monty Sherwood once was to remember him for life. To remember him was to remember power, cleanness, dependability, all compacted in one human form.

On the morning of the second Friday in September he lounged at ease, a solitary occupant of a first-class compartment of the Bendigo-Melbourne express. Before the events to be related in this story the world outside the triangle formed by the towns of Broken Hill, Coolgardie, and Darwin was ignorant that in one man was epitomized the spirit of the vast country mapped as Central Australia. To inquire of any one within that triangle who was Monty Sherwood was automatically to label oneself either a new-chum or a fool.

To see him walk gave the sense of pleasure one receives while watching a good dancer. To see him ride an outlaw horse was to obliterate for ever any chance of again being thrilled by a cinema cowboy or a competitor in the Olympia Horse Show.

If you have not yet seen his picture in the Press, imagine a man standing six-feet-two in his socks, huge of chest and narrow of hip, with a face, clean-shaven, like Atlas: power in the jaws, iron determination behind the grey-blue eyes, and yet, strange to say, a wistful gentleness about the mouth.

Any man proud of his manhood admired Monty Sherwood on sight. As for women——! The girl at the bookstall at Castlemain Station had watched his approach with wonder and not a little misgiving; but when he smilingly asked for a newspaper her nervousness vanished, and he left her with a memory of some wonderful vision.

To this man from the semi-desert of Central Australia the houses, now crowding together outside the carriage window to become the city of Melbourne, were imposed upon his mind much as the famous Wembley Exhibition imposed itself on the mind of many a child.

17

From the silences of untrodden spaces he was being whirled into the hurly-burly of a human ant-heap. An electric train flashing past made him start back, and then laugh at himself for shying at such a trifle. Interest sprang into his eyes at sight of half a score of great dray-horses feeding on a small plot of ground beside a tall factory building; for they were well-conditioned, well-groomed, and he was a worshipper always of the king of animals. The masts and funnels of the ships at the wharves near North Melbourne brought back to him scenes of days when he and thousands of splendid men had embarked on that voyage from which for so many there was no return.

Quite suddenly he found himself out of the train at Spencer Street Station, shaking hands vigorously with his brother Martin.

"Well, Lazarus, how do?" he cried joyfully, his voice remarkably musical for so big a man. His tanned face beamed while he pump-handled the thin white hand—beamed until he saw the slight look of pain in Martin's eyes. "I'm sorry, old boy," he said softly; "I always forget that blasted gas."

"Quite all right, Monty," Martin assured him, in his quick way of speech. "Only you keep forgetting that powerful grip of yours. Had a good trip?"

"Fair . . . fair. Nothing happened much, bar one beautiful argument with a card-sharp who was skinning a mug t'other side of Maryborough. He got quite rude. You know what happens to rude fellers when I'm there, don't you?"

Martin laughed out gleefully and stooped to pick up Monty's suit-case, leaving his brother to carry a huge brown-paper parcel.

"Your civilizing methods are somewhat drastic, Monty, but undeniably effectual," he said, whilst they moved with the crowd towards the exit. "Where are you stopping? No room at my digs, I'm afraid."

"No matter. The first pub. we come to will do."

"Then let it be Spencer's Hotel, across the road there. It is fairly expensive, but I expect you have plenty of ready and they welcome your sort. Mind this tram!"

"I'm thinking it's the tram that will have to mind me," Monty returned, when the antiquated cable-car had rumbled past. "They call this the Murder City, don't they? What do they murder 'em with—guns or trams?"

"Both. Here we are, and there is the office."

It was five years since Monty had been in Melbourne—five years of action, hardship, and incessant toil since last he had dined in the grill-room of Spencer's Hotel. He knew where to find the office; but, turning suddenly to Martin, he said in what was meant to be a whisper:

"Say—isn't she a bonzer!"

He referred to a girl-clerk sitting at the desk. She heard him, knew he referred to her, and accordingly tried to freeze him with a look. Unfrozen, the big man strolled over to her desk, and, leaning against an upright, smiled down upon her. Martin, watching, saw the ice melt like snow in a furnace beneath the glow of Monty's smile, and marvelled as he always did when women invariably responded to his brother in that way. He heard Monty say:

"Miss, I'm in town for just a week. For seven whole days I am a millionaire. I want the best suite of rooms in the hotel."

"Yes, sir," she said sweetly. "The second suite on the ground floor is vacant. Bedroom, bathroom, sitting-room, and drawing-room. Will you please sign here? George," turning to a waiting page, "show this gentleman to the Corner Suite. Thank you, sir!" This to Monty, who smiled his thanks and wondered what he was being thanked for.

And, when he followed George and was followed by Martin, the young girl at the desk gazed hard at a calendar without in the least seeing the rows of white figures printed thereon.

The page-boy led them to a suite of rooms which, if not quite so lavishly furnished as those at the Flinders Hotel occupied by Austiline Thorpe, were equally well situated. Martin was surprised at his brother's choice, having expected him to be satisfied with a single room. The big man, turning on the page, said:

"Your name George, eh?"

"Yes, sir," replied the youth, keen as a knife-edge, and superbly conceited.

"Well, you hop along to the bar and bring me half a dozen bottles of the best beer stocked."

"Beer, sir!" exclaimed the genuinely astonished boy, whose clients invariably scorned so common and vulgar a beverage as beer.

"I said beer, son," the big man stated gently. "Spotted

Cats, High Balls, and Corpse Revivers look pretty, but I want a *drink*."

"Yes, sir," agreed George respectfully.

"And please don't 'sir' me. I'm not used to it. If you must honour me with a title, 'mister' will do."

"Yes, sir."

"Hell!"

"Yes, sir," the youth replied politely, and withdrew.

When the door closed they both laughed. Then occurred individual action which made it conspicuous that one lived in a city and the other in the very Back of Beyond. Martin sank into a wickedly easy chair with refined grace and at once produced a cigarette-case and a silver matchbox. Monty, however, divested himself of coat and waistcoat, after which striding to the mirror over the mantelpiece, he removed his collar and tie. Then, heaving a deep sigh of relief, he rolled up his shirt-sleeves above his elbows, and, diving into his trousers pockets, brought to light a pipe of great age and much decrepitude, a plug of black tobacco, and a clasp-knife.

Martin gazed at the pipe and laughed again. The answering smile which dawned upon the rugged features of Monty might well be described as sheepish, thence to broaden into genuine amusement, accompanied by a long, low chuckle.

"Remember the days of long ago when, as a very young man on the Dad's station, I persistently refused to wear a collar?" he said slowly, chipping at the tobacco-plug. "You and me were squatter's sons, Martin, and it was expected of us that we should wear collars to be different to the common men. I am afraid I sadly disappointed the old Dad more than once."

"In some little things, Monty, perhaps. But in things that really mattered the Dad was very proud of you."

"The Dad was a generous man. I would to God he and the mother were alive to-day. But to revert to collars. Somehow the damned things always did strangle me. I like to feel the wind nipping at my arms and chest, to be able to move my head without hindrance, and my arms without the rustle of starch. Then I feel free. I love freedom, old son."

"You have it. You're a lucky man, Monty."

"Because I always appreciate my luck. I love life."

The big man lit his pipe and then, leaning back in his chair, regarded his brother with the interest accumulated by five years of separation. His look was returned by one of unfeigned admiration.

Between these two existed a bond of sympathy unusual between brothers. Each was the antithesis of the other in physique and in mentality, holding in common but one characteristic. No one ever would have guessed that they came from the same stock, had not both the same trick of using their eyes when amused: the same twinkle—to use an approximate word—which spoke a language easy to understand.

They were descendants of grim, dauntless pioneers—not the so-called pioneers who came to Australia in the post-discovery days to take up fertile lands in the abundantly-watered coastal districts and draw free labour from the convict establishments; but pioneers worthy of the name, who pushed out into the waterless desert, battled with the blacks and the elements, planned, suffered, laboured for years with their own hands, to find reward in success, contentment in beautiful old age, and wonderful happiness in the love and devotion of two such sons as these.

Bolting buggy-horses had killed old man Sherwood in 1910. Monty, a young man of twenty, became, in the interests of his mother and Martin, then at college, the manager of a three-thousand-square-mile cattle-station north of the McDonnell Ranges in the Northern Territory. Mrs. Sherwood died a year later, adding to Monty's responsibilities. Came, three years afterwards, the Dreadful War. Monty enlisted. He was the sort of man that nothing could keep back, so he sold the station, invested the capital, and departed on the Glorious Adventure, leaving Martin to shoot skywards like a rocket in the great *Tribune* Building.

During the war years he and Martin did not meet; but Martin was in France in 1917 and back in Australia again the following year, struggling against the effects of gas.

The war interlude made little difference to the younger man's meteoric career. His sojourn in man-made hell left outwardly no effects to speak of, but it coloured his mind with visions of a world as it should be and a sense of bitter shame at what it is. The Australian loves progress and hates stagnation. With the *Tribune* as a standard he led thousands. The multitude, as is the way of multitudes, sees the standard but is unaware of the bearer. Yet he is content.

Monty, however, was affected by the war very differently. Even the freedom contained within a three-thousand-square-mile holding was as nothing compared with the freedom, disciplined freedom, of those epic years.

While millions of others returned to their chains of humdrum existence he retained his wings, and lived like a god. Back to his beloved bush he went, to find it gripped with drought.   He bought three thousand store cattle at ten shillings a head. He was laughed at and told he would never get them to a railway; but he drove them north into the very wilds, and shepherded them with the help of two blacks for eighteen months; then struck the railway at Bourke in New South Wales and trucked them to Sydney.   He lost only seven beasts, but he made a profit of twenty-eight thousand pounds.

Followed then a prospecting expedition which resulted in the discovery of the Yellow Mount: making millionaires of five sharks and adding but fifty thousand to his fortune.

Possibly Fortune smiled on him because he did not value money; which is not to say that he threw it away, but that his needs were simple and that much money had not the same meaning to him that it has to most of us who love luxury and pleasure. Not for anything would he discard his disreputable pipe and purchase a new one.

"How   old   are   you?"   came   the   somewhat   surprising question from Martin.

"You know I am forty-three," Monty replied chidingly.

"Have you ever been in love, Monty?" the younger man asked soberly.

"Hell! No," energetically.

"That seems marvellous to me, Monty; because, in all my experience, I have never met a man who attracted women as you do. And you're the first man I've met who attracts other men quite as much as he does women."

"What is all this butter leading to?" demanded the big man with a broad grin.

"Only this," Martin continued: "that, in spite of your masculine charms, you have reached forty-three years of age— by no stretch of imagination could you be guessed to be more than thirty—without having been captured by a woman; whereas I, who look forty and make a poor figure of a man beside you, am in love with and am loved by the most glorious woman under the Southern Cross."

"You take it from me, old stick-in-the-mud," the other interjected, shaking his head protestingly at his brother's self-depreciation: "women may smile at me—I see so few that I cannot help smiling at them—but they don't admire bulk, brute strength, and bushman's ways.   Here's George with a sniffter."

When the page had silently withdrawn, after having given a respectfully disapproving glance at the big man's bare arms and neck, Monty leaned forward in his chair and said:

"Martin, old lad! Tell me the old, old story up-to-date. Every word of it. Forget your letters to me about her. I want it first-hand."

The younger man's answering smile vanquished the tired look and made his face almost beautiful.

"I met her about twelve months ago on Princes Bridge. There was nothing so conventional about our meeting as an introduction," Martin began.   "It happened that a poor wretch just out of prison was nearly run down by a motor, and, in his effort to escape it, crashed on the pavement at our feet as we were about to pass.

"The fall broke his ankle, and she and I rendered common assistance.   It was then she learned that Hill—that was his name—was just out of prison, was without money, without work, without friends.   Austiline was then renting a bungalow at St. Kilda, and insisted upon having the man taken to her home.

"We must have fallen in love even while we looked in consternation over the figure of Hill sprawled on the pavement. I remember so well the sudden light that came into her eyes. My own, I know, were blazing.

"From chance acquaintances we became friends. We found we knew the same people, and—afterwards, Monty—were introduced as formally and as properly as even the dear little mother could have wished.   I asked her to marry me six months ago."   And then, when he handed the big man a photograph taken from his wallet, he said with simple dignity: "I am a very happy man, Monty."

Monty took the photograph and studied it intently. He saw a picture that made him suck in his breath, a picture of a face whereon was indicated beauty of mind as well as beauty of feature.   The eyes gazed at him with fearless trust, the lips though inviting were parted like the petals of a rosebud, and the broad forehead proclaimed an intellect above the ordinary.

"Here," mused Monty, "are Beauty and Brains combined. Knowing Martin, I expected nothing less."   Aloud he said quietly, making reference to the soldiers' favourite game of two-up, "It seems to me, old scribbler, that you're heading 'em pretty well. I know her name is Austiline Thorpe; but who is she?"

Martin smiled.

"That I knew you would ask," he said. "Her people, I understand, live in a Hampshire village where her father is rector. She writes books, and came to Australia in the first instance for local colour."

"Writes books, eh? Don't think I have ever seen her name on a book-cover."

"You wouldn't Monty. She writes under the name of 'A. E. Titchfield'."

"What!" the big man exclaimed. "The books about wilful maids and he-men who bounce 'em about empty shacks in the Canadian wilds! 'A. E. Titchfield' your girl! Well, I never!"

"It's extraordinary, I know," Martin admitted. "That is why I cannot understand why she loves me when there is a man in the world like you."

"I can!" asserted Monty. "Any woman who knows any-thing about he-men with hair on 'em knows enough to miss 'em by a mile."

"That was her explanation of the problem when I put it to her. You must for ever keep her pen-name a secret, Monty, for this reason. The first book she wrote, called *The Heart of John Strong,* was an enormous success. Austiline admits that she was flattered. She wrote two more with even greater success. She created a new type of story. But when she grew a little older she lost her girlish admiration of he-men, and wrote a book—I have read it in MS.—a really wonderful book, but entirely different from the he-man type. The publishers would not risk the financial loss they estimated would occur if it appeared under her own name, and prophesied the utter ruin of 'A. E. Titchfield' if that name appeared on its cover. Austiline seems to think she is doomed for ever to go on writing of—to use your own words—'wilful maids and he-men with hair on 'em.' She says she would die of shame if the public got to know she was 'A. E. Titchfield'."

"There's nothing to be ashamed of," Monty remarked emphatically. "There is a something about her books which makes you read 'em right through, and then send for more." He returned the photograph, adding: "Your Austiline is a lily in a paddock full of daisies. She is the kind of woman who would lend elegance to fur, and not become elegant by wearing fur. I'm mighty glad I brought those skins."

He jumped to his feet with surprising agility in so large a man, and, pouncing on the big brown-paper parcel, broke the cord as easily as a woman breaks cotton, and, ripping open the paper, literally kicked out over the carpet a mass of dark silver fox-skins.

"You see five dozen of the finest fox-skins ever brought out of the back country right here under your nose," he cried with excusable enthusiasm. "They are the pick of nine hundred pelts Wall-eyed Jack and I caught this winter. Not knowing what's in fashion now, I thought it a good idea to allow your future wife to decide how she'll have 'em made up. The finished articles are to be my wedding present to her. She'll want furs if you are leaving directly for England."

Martin said nothing just then. He could not speak. He knew the value of fox-skins and was no mean judge of them. He knew that his brother could not have selected a finer five dozen out of fifty thousand pelts, for each was a perfect match to the rest in colour, texture, and length of fur. Such a parcel as it stood was worth a hundred guineas; when made up by expert furriers the skins would represent at least four times that amount.

It was a royal gift. When Martin rose to his feet his eyes were shining, and, holding out his hand, he said with unwonted slowness:

"You always were a damned good sort, Monty!"

CHAPTER III

THE SHADOW

LATER in the afternoon the brothers Sherwood walked up the wide granite steps leading to the vestibule of the Flinders Hotel, the one wrapt in a lover's reverie, the other revelling in the sensation, so remote from his everyday life, of the jostling crowds along the sidewalks and the ever-flowing river of traffic in the streets.

The Flinders Hotel is probably the most luxurious and, therefore, most expensive caravanserai in Australia. Nevertheless, because of or perhaps in spite of these characteristics, its guests are exceedingly cosmopolitan: wealthy squatters, famous writers and travellers, island planters and members of the army of wanderers over the continent who, when they do make holiday in the cities, live at the millionaire rate as announced by Monty Sherwood to the desk-girl at his own hotel, are always to be found there.

Yet of all visitors there the most important appeared to be Miss Austiline Thorpe. When Martin Sherwood called during the daytime, and that was often, the manager himself regularly received him with beaming politeness, immediately deputing a page to escort him to Miss Thorpe's suite. The dapper little man with the eyes of a bird was issuing from his private office when the two men entered.

"Good afternoon, Mr. Sherwood!" he called out briskly. Then, coming forward: "What a wretchedly dusty day it is, to be sure. Good afternoon, sir!" This to Monty.

Each made acknowledgment with a nod and a smile. Martin said:

"It's the sort of weather we could well do without, Masters. This is my brother, Monty, come out of the Back of Beyond to be my best man on Wednesday."

"Ah! Delighted to meet you, Mr. Sherwood. I was informed that you were coming down for the affair. Your brother is a lucky man, sir, extremely lucky. I only wish I

26

were a young man; but please don't give me away to my wife. You know what wives are, or perhaps you have yet to acquire experience of their little peculiarities?"

"I am confiding to you all the arrangements for the reception and breakfast, Masters," interjected Martin, with bright eyes.

"Imagine yourself Aladdin and me the genie, sir," replied the little man, half-French, half-Australian. "You have commanded, and I have obeyed to the very last letter. Henri, my brother, and the most wonderful *chef* in the wide world, I was obliged to take into my confidence. Not another soul besides my wife knows of the coming event. I know, it is in my blood that my brother will out-Henri Henri. How many guests are you inviting?"

"One gentleman and two ladies, with the addition of Mrs. Masters and yourself."

"Sir, you are magnificent," cried the manager, piloting them along the corridor leading to Austiline's suite. Monty grinned, but was unobserved. The far more Frenchman than Australian rattled on: "Be assured. Do not worry. Everything has been planned. Henri has a headache through smoking too many cigarettes. For three nights he smoked them, one after the other, but he has been victorious, and has created a new sauce to go with the fish. A sauce of superlative delectability. I tasted it. It was superb. Yes——"

They had halted outside the door leading to the Blue Suite occupied by Austiline. A faint yet distinct report reaching their ears stopped Masters' flow of words.

The three men looked at one another, first in bewilderment, then in alarm.

"Sounded like a gun," drawled the big man.

"Yes. And from inside the suite," Masters agreed, applying his finger to the bell-button.

"God! Will no one come?"

"It'll be all right, Martin," Monty assured his brother, who was trembling visibly, his eyes wide with horror, his face like paper.

"We must let ourselves in," Masters announced firmly. "It is against the rules of the establishment, but I fear something has happened."

With a skeleton-key he opened the door, revealing a small, neat hall, which in turn gave entry to three rooms. The doors of these rooms were shut, but it was the centre one that Masters tried to open, knowing that it was the drawing-room. It was locked. When he tried to insert the skeleton-key it was found that the door-key was on the inside.

"Better burst open the door. Let me lean against it," Monty suggested.

"Wait! Listen!" Masters urged.

Quite plainly they heard some one breathing: a whistling, catching breathing. A sharp knock brought no response or cessation of the breathing.

"Dear me! I don't know what to make of it," the little manager exclaimed.

"Nor I—with the door shut. Stand away!" came Monty's voice, strangely metallic.

Against the pressure of his massive shoulder, an effort which under normal conditions would have aroused admiration, the door splintered loudly and flew inward, the lock being torn out. Upon the threshold they stood as still as those confronted by Medusa's head. For there, on the floor in the centre of the room, was the stark figure of a man lying on his back, one leg drawn up, one arm grotesquely bent under his body. Blood welled slowly from a small wound exactly in the middle of his forehead. And, looking down at him, was the tenant of the suite dressed in walking costume. She was swaying to and fro on her feet, and her right hand clutched what Monty recognized to be a .22 calibre five-chambered revolver.

The room, decorated in light blue, was sumptuously furnished. A man's hat and gloves lay on the mahogany table, over which was spilled a vase of flowers. The large French windows were wide open; the curtains billowing out over the deep veranda.

"Great heavens, Austiline!" burst out Martin, springing to her side and slipping one arm round her waist. When she made no reply, not even raising her gaze from the prostrate figure, he added softly, coaxingly: "Austiline dear! Tell me! What has happened? Who is this man? What has he done?"

She seemed neither to see nor fear him, her wide, horror-filled eyes centred upon the still white face and the slow trickle of blood. That the man was dead was too sure. No human being could survive such a wound. While Monty knelt beside the body the little manager slipped out into the hall and barred the front door. On his return the big man nodded approval.

"Austiline, don't you know me?" Martin implored.

"Please let me take that weapon. Come, dear! Come, dear, sit down in this chair."

Very slowly she raised her glorious eyes, now stark with horror and set in ivory. A momentary flash of interest came into them when she saw Monty, but instantly her gaze sank again to meet the rising hand holding the revolver.

The eyelids flickered. The expression of horror gave place to one of bewilderment. Came then a deep-drawn sigh, a slight shudder, a stiffening of her body.

"Is he dead?" she whispered. Then she added, apparently seeing her promised husband for the first time: "Martin! thank goodness you are here. This is terrible."

"Tell me, dear! How did it happen?" he urged distractedly, waiting in torture for her answer; the others no less agitated.

"He—he came here to demand money—hush money," she cried in sudden hysteria. "I knew he was coming. I had been to the bank to draw treasury notes, and he was here when I got back, standing beside the table. I tossed the money on the table and commanded him to go. I was expecting you, and didn't want him here when you came.

"He was just about to pick up the notes when someone behind me fired. I turned and saw a man locking the door. He rushed forward and seized the bundle of notes. Then he said: 'You're well rid of him, Miss,' and, holding out the revolver to me, I took it. He went out of the window. I don't remember your coming, Martin. Martin—Martin dear—I feel so sick. Get me some water, please."

"I will, but first sit down, Austiline"; and, after practically forcing her into a Chesterfield, he turned—to find Monty at his side with a tumbler of water faintly discoloured with brandy.

Austiline Thorpe drank deeply, and then sank back as though strength had deserted her. Martin, on his knees before her, held her hands in his, his face the colour of hers; his eyes, big and blazing with terrific mental excitement, searching each one of her features.

By common impulse Monty and the little man turned and wandered over to the open French windows. Masters caught and drew in the billowing curtains, an act giving uninterrupted view of the wide veranda guarded by a railing of wrought-iron. The veranda or balcony was level with a narrow strip of carefully-tended lawn, beyond which, six or seven feet lower, was the pavement. Masters was about to step out when Monty gripped his arm, whispering:

"Jumping nannygoats! Look at the tracks."

Masters, an indoor man, first looked across the wide thoroughfare, and then intended leaving the apartment to glance along the veranda both ways, as though he might see the murderer escaping into one of the many rooms fronting it. But the giant was a bushman. His first act was to observe the ground, in this case the veranda floor, for tell-tale tracks.

It was covered with fine red dust. The close-set iron railing protected the carpet of dust to a great extent from the high wind which was blowing from the hotel across the street. It was not a multitude of tracks on the dust which had made him softly exclaim, but lack of them. There was only one set of tracks, and they had been made by a cat. The tracks were almost smothered, and to Monty's trained eye it was quite evident that they were at least an hour old. The absence of human tracks affected the two men like a blow.

"It's a dark world, Masters," murmured the big man.

"I cannot believe it. Miss Thorpe must—mon Dieu! This is terrible."

"We've got to believe it," came Monty's hardened voice. "If there was a man in the room who fired the shot, where is he? He didn't leave by the window, else he would have left tracks there on the veranda. And it is unlikely that he jumped across to the railings, because the distance must be at least ten feet. He may have just managed—it is a remote possibility—to escape from this room and hide in one of the others, and then left by the front door while we've been in here. Go and see if the front door has been unbarred."

Left alone, Monty Sherwood allowed his thoughts to race. He was coldly, deadly calm. The situation required clear thought and decided action; life or death might hang on his doing the right thing quickly.

It was natural and human for him first to consider how the corpse could be hidden from the eagle vision of the law; and that idea was discarded not because such an act would be legally wrong, but rather because criminal history has proved beyond the shadow of a doubt that the chances of successfully concealing a body are about one in a thousand.

The second idea, equally natural and human, was to invent a chain of lies to satisfy the law that the corpse within had materialized through a justifiable act on Austiline's part.

Half a dozen such chains occurred to him. But, casting one swift glance at the still tableau behind him, one penetrating look at Austiline's lovely face, his shrewd character-judgment obliged him to condemn this second idea also. Austiline was a woman doubtless capable of tempestuous passion; capable also, possible, of sudden violent action under terrible provocation; yet incapable of lying superbly.

Then how account for her statement that the man was shot by a second man who escaped by the window? How account, if that were true, for the absence of human tracks? Her overwrought mind probably created the second man, a creation so vivid that the situation had stamped it upon her brain as truth. But suppose that there had really been a second man; suppose that she had spoken the unvarnished truth: how had the man escaped from the room?

Now, Monty's respect for the law was profound. Voracious novel-reader though he was, his experience of police action in Central and Northern Australia had taught him that the average detective is by no means the fool many novelists imagine him to be. Having reached the decision that Austiline might have spoken the truth, he felt confident that men far more expert at such problems than himself would discover how the murderer left the room.

But a man's reasoning follows the line of his own mental composition. It never occurred to him that anyone having scrutinized Austiline's face and heard her story would doubt the truth both of her words and of her facial expression. It did not occur to him that, being the brother of her *fiancé,* he was naturally biased in her favour; and that others would examine the situation with the coolness of a vivisectionist testing a new variety of death on a rabbit.

When Masters rejoined him, his jaws were clenched grimly and his eyes were sombre.

"The door is still barred," reported the little man softly. "I have searched the other two rooms thoroughly, and have discovered no intruder. They are lighted by windows like this one, and open out on the same veranda. There are no footprints on the dust in front of them. Only those of the cat."

The big man sighed and pursed his lips.

"It beats me," he said simply.

"You think as I do—that she shot him?"

"I don't know. Yet I doubt that she did."

Masters looked up sharply.

"Then you have a theory?"

"Wish I had."

"But, my dear sir," Masters expostulated, "Miss Thorpe's story won't hold water. Did she not say that the man escaped through this window, and did not you yourself state that no man passed out as there are no human footprints on that dust?"

"No matter," came the stubborn answer.

"I fear—but oh! I do so hope that the detectives will believe her innocent. I must ring up the headquarters at once."

For the second time Monty grasped his arm. He said earnestly:

"Could we not agree to say nothing about Miss Thorpe being found by us holding the revolver?"

"Tiens! No! Of what use to lie to these law-hounds?" Masters returned, throwing up his white, podgy hands. "Nothing will benefit any of us but the truth. The smallest lie will but injure Miss Thorpe. I must go. I will not use the telephone here. It will but alarm the lady. Mon Dieu! My hotel! I shall be ruined!"

"Damn your hotel!" Monty breathed. "Damn the wind and the dust! It is going to be awkward for Austiline for an hour or so, but they'll probably find the man or the way he got out." And then, for the first time in his life, he doubted himself and his reasoning.

Supposing they did not discover what he hoped they would? Supposing they examined only the surface facts? Supposing they concluded that Austiline was a liar, and therefore a taker of life?

Martin! Poor old Martin! Suddenly he found his brother at his elbow.

"Has Masters gone for the doctor?" Martin inquired.

"Yes—and the police. This is going to be an unpleasant business, old lad."

"It's horrible. I am afraid Austiline is going to be very ill," the younger man said quickly. "The wedding will probably have to be postponed. Will it be necessary for us to say that we found her holding that gun?"

Monty Sherwood blinked at the appealing look in the anguished grey eyes. He wondered if Martin doubted Austiline, even before he discovered or was told of the absence of the vital tracks; or merely wished to obscure any fact which might delay his wedding. Knowing what the police would discover, realizing that any attempt he made to ruffle the dust carpet would be futile and bring suspicion upon himself without in any way helping Austiline, he decided to be perfectly frank. Yet he could not bring himself to announce this decision just then. To gain time he said:

"What are the other two rooms of this suite?"

"A reception-room and a bedroom with a small dressing-room and bathroom beyond."

"Then why not take Miss Thorpe to the bedroom, away from *that?*" the big man suggested. "Try and calm her, so that she may answer the police questions coolly and collectedly. All of us must be like that, old son."

Martin agreed with a nod and rejoined Austiline, over whom he bent affectionately while speaking. Without replying, she arose and allowed him to half-lead, half-support her from the room. Monty, through half-closed eyes, watched them go, feeling an utterly new sensation, that of despair.

Never before had he found himself in so helpless a mental *cul-de-sac*. Even then the police heads were doubtless listening to Master's agitated report; even then the hounds were being unleashed. Time! Had there only been time! If Masters had not entered the suite with them, Monty felt that he could have done something . . . at the least have supported Austiline's story by sweeping the veranda clear of dust, or, better, have supplied the missing tracks by means of borrowed boots. Now there was nothing to be done but wait inactively for crawling Nemesis. And waiting under such circumstances was a nightmare.

Martin found him slumped down on the settee, his brows knit, his eyes closed. The younger man felt as if his brain were being hammered into a million separate pieces with a noise equal to ceaseless crackling thunder, in the tumult of which he struggled to collect his thoughts. A strange apathy was stealing over him, deadening the noise in his ears and softening the flare of strange lights before his eyes. Even while he stood beside the table regarding his brother he felt himself losing the power to think.

From Monty his eyes moved slowly to the chiffonier set against a corner of the room, there to rest on a tantalus which Monty had taken from the cupboard. Like a sleep-walker, he moved over to it, and poured out half a tumbler of brandy with a hand that shook so badly that almost as much again was spilled on the shining walnut surface. The glass tapped against his even teeth so loudly that Monty looked up. But the brandy, shooting through his body, rose to his head and swept aside the noise, the lights, and swamped the feeling of lethargy. With quick steps he reached Monty's side, and, bending forward till their eyes were level, said:

"What do you think about all this, Monty?"

"Think! What is there to think?"

"Monty, you know. I can see it in your troubled face. You know more about this ghastly affair than I do. What passed between you and Masters at the window?"

"We were discussing the tracks left on the dusty floor of the veranda."

"Why discuss them, Monty? Tell me, please."

"Very well, then. But you must brace up," Monty sighed. "Your girl said that the man who shot that feller escaped by the window. Unfortunately, she made a mistake there, which is going to be bad. No man crossed the veranda—only a cat walked along it within, at the least, an hour."

The brothers stared fixedly at each other, the big man still slumped on the settee, the other still bent forward, their faces level. Martin read plainly in the grey-blue, narrow-lidded eyes Monty's doubt of Austiline's story. Yet, because he was past feeling anything, because his brain was numbed by the recurring noises in his head, he showed no recoil from what must have been a stunning blow. To him Monty's voice was very distant.

"Steady, old lad! Here comes the Nosey Parkers."

CHAPTER IV

INTO DARKNESS

MARTIN SHERWOOD straightened up and faced about when the hall door was opened by Masters, who led within three men.

One of the three was obviously a policeman; the other two might have been members of any profession. The younger brother knew them all. To them he was equally well known as editor of *The Daily Tribune,* as well as an influential and greatly respected member of society.

The man who carried a small black bag stepped at once to the dead man and made an examination that was not unduly prolonged. Silently the others watched him. Not till he pushed aside the spilled flowers and began to write at the table, as though the incident had lost all interest for him, did the taller of his companions speak.

"Murder or suicide, doctor?" he inquired, in a low, unemotional voice.

"Murder, undoubtedly. No powder-marks."

"Humph!" The detective-sergeant languidly laid his raincoat over the back of a chair, his silver-mounted walking-stick he leant against the chair, and his hat and fawn-coloured gloves he placed on the seat of the chair. Then, with long-fingered, well-manicured hands, he absently patted his sleek hair and gracefully sank into the only masculine article of furniture in the room—Martin's especial chair.

"Now, Masters, as you communicated with headquarters, tell us please, your version of this affair," he said, in what was nothing else but a purr.

Fluently, but strangely without excitement, the little hotel manager described how he, with the brothers, had been obliged to force an entry, and what had met their astonished gaze when the drawing-room door had been splintered inward by Monty's shoulder. Then, warming up, he exclaimed:

35

"It is the very worst thing that has ever happened at my hotel. It will do it a great deal of harm."

"That cannot be helped. It's done," came the dispassionate voice of the detective-sergeant. "About what time did you hear the shot fired?"

"I noticed the time was exactly four o'clock when I left my office and met these gentlemen. It must have béen about three minutes later."

"It is well to establish the exact time. Your telephone-call to us was made at precisely twenty-six minutes past four. How was it that you did not ring us up sooner?"

"I hardly know. Time seemed without measure. Miss Thorpe appeared as though in a trance, and it was a few moments before she could be induced to give up the revolver. Then I searched the other rooms for the man Miss Thorpe said she saw."

"Humph! Miss Thorpe! Where is she now?"

"In the next room," replied Martin. "Naturally she is much upset. She will see you when you wish."

"Better make sure, Highatt." At which the policeman who looked his part went out into the hall and, first barring the front door, knocked on that indicated to him. Being invited to enter, he merely replied that he wanted to know if she was any better from her shock, and on hearing an affirmative returned to the side of his colleague.

"I understand, Mr. Sherwood, from a private source, that you are to be married to Miss Thorpe?" was the indolent detective-sergeant's next query.

"Yes; we are to be married next Wednesday."

"Unfortunate—I mean this affair is unfortunate. Have you anything to add to Mr. Masters's testimony?"

"No. But hadn't a hue and cry better be raised for the murderer?" Martin said with accelerated quickness. "Time is so precious in this case."

"Quite so, Mr. Sherwood," was the gentle rejoinder. "But let us fully understand the case before we act. Have *you* anything to add, Mr. Montague Sherwood?"

"Nothing."

"Very well. We will now examine Miss Thorpe. Ask her, Highatt, if she will be so kind as to come in here."

The subordinate did as bidden. During the ensuing silence Martin, suffering an agony of apprehension, searched the face of the detective-sergeant for the slightest indication of his thoughts so successfully veiled behind an almost vacuous mask. Upon the entrance of Austiline they rose to meet her, each of them regarding her in a different light, but each and all experiencing a thrill of admiration for her beauty and carriage. She had discarded her hat, but still wore her outdoor costume.

Her eyes had lost all trace of hysteria, but seemed unnaturally wide and bright, two burning orbs in an ashen face. That she was suffering mental torture was evident at least to the shrewd police-surgeon; that only a powerful will enabled her to rise superior to feminine weakness, and terror was evident also.

Torn between his loyalty to her, his love for her, and the prosaic assertion of his brother Monty regarding the absence of the tracks that would have corroborated her story, Martin went to meet her, and with almost pathetic devotion escorted her to the settee, where he made her comfortable with cushions and then stood beside her facing the examiner. Thus, he hoped, his nearness to her would lend her strength.

"I think, Miss Thorpe, it would be much better if you were to tell us in your own words exactly what has happened here," said the now seated indolent one, with a slight smile intended to be reassuring. "It is so much easier than telling it by answering questions."

She recited her story in practically the same words as before. She spoke simply, without hesitation, her eyes fixed intently on the face of her questioner. Almost as intently as she regarded him Monty gazed at her: and, quite suddenly, as though a searchlight had lit up his mind, he saw that she spoke the truth, that her story was based on real facts and was not the creation of a bewildered brain. A flood of joy surged over him, and Martin, noticing his face, wondered.

"I do not remember anything that happened from the moment the man disappeared out of the window until I discovered Martin—I mean Mr. Sherwood—at my side. I did not hear them knock, nor did I hear the door being forced," was her concluding statement.

"This man—will you describe him, please?"

"I—I don't think I can. He was just an ordinary-looking person."

"Humph! Was he tall or short, thin or fat?"

"He was neither, just ordinary."

"Well, what sort of clothes did he wear?"

"Oh! a dark suit—dark blue, I think."

"Did he have any distinguishing marks about his face?"

"I did not see his face properly. He wore a black silk handkerchief which concealed the bottom half of it."

"Ah! And what sort of a hat did he wear?"

"A soft hat, I think! I don't really remember."

The senior detective appeared to ponder on those, to him, possibly unsatisfactory answers.

"I believe you said just now that the intruder fired from the door there. That you did not see him fire. Will you kindly stand just where you were when the shot was fired?"

Austiline did as requested, taking a position between the table and the door. The examiner stood where the corpse had been discovered. It had since been removed, and now lay covered with a sheet behind the open door.

"I am taking the place of the man who was shot—am I right, Miss Thorpe?"

"Yes," in a whisper.

"You are certain you stand now where you did then?"

"Quite."

"Did you, by any chance, feel the passage of the bullet— say, a puff of displaced air against your cheek?"

"I don't think I did."

"Thank you. Pray be seated, Miss Thorpe."

It was Martin again who attended her, and whilst thus engaged the detective jotted memoranda in a notebook.

Monty frowned. He had been standing directly behind the detective-sergeant when the latter had taken the position of the murdered man, and he alone of the spectators guessed what the notes were that were jotted down. He had seen the object of the recent questions and the conclusion the detective-sergeant had drawn from the answers.

For Austiline Thorpe had stood in direct line between the detective and the door, and any one firing from the door must have been a very expert shot indeed to have missed her and hit the intended target.

"This weapon, which you say the man thrust into your hand, was, of course, his own?"

"No; it was mine."

"Indeed!" The detective-sergeant permitted his eyebrows to go up the fraction of an inch. "Are you not aware that it is an offence to have a weapon in your possession without police permission?"

"No; I am not aware of it."

"Why, then, did you purchase it?"

"Well, you see, I live alone in these rooms. My maid lives elsewhere in the hotel. There are so many burglaries—and I became nervous."

"The dead man—what was his name?" came the next politely spoken question.

"Peterson," was her answer.

"What was the hold he had over you?"

"Oh! I cannot, I cannot tell you," she burst out.

"It would so simplify matters if you would," said the man coaxingly.

"No, no! I cannot—indeed, I cannot tell you."

"Well, well; I won't press you. But how much money was there in the roll of notes?"

"Two hundred pounds."

"Two hundred! Quite a large sum. What were the denominations?"

"They were five-pound Treasury notes."

"Ah! And from what bank did you draw them?"

"From the Bank of Commerce."

"Have you any idea of the precise time?"

"Oh! I don't know. I got there just before the big doors shut."

"Humph! three o'clock." Her interrogator seemed to ponder over that, gazing steadily at his immaculate shoes, whilst his audience watched him anxiously. His expression was still blandly uncommittal when, looking up, he said:

"Now, as far as we can make out, the murder occurred at three minutes past four, which leaves approximately one hour unaccounted for. What did you do between the time you were at the bank and your entering this room?"

"Really, I don't know," she admitted. "I must have walked about in the street. I dreaded to meet Peterson. He always filled me with loathing."

Again the detective-sergeant wrote in his elegant notebook. Then, rising, he motioned Highatt to the windows, saying:

"Please allow me to examine the balcony."

They watched the two human bloodhounds stroll to the fatal windows, saw them thrust forward their heads to examine the dusty floor with keen, observant, trained eyes. They heard whispered conversation—an ejaculation. The doctor was called to them, and then the hotel manager

Monty began to walk slowly to and fro across the room, his hands clasped behind him, his head sunk upon his mighty chest. Martin, turning, faced the wall so that none should see the agony writ so plainly on his ghastly face. As for the woman, she looked at them alternately with puzzled eyes. Of them all, she was the least perturbed, in spite of her serious position; for, so she thought, her ordeal had been left behind.

The tiny clock set on the writing-desk in a corner ticked with accentuated loudness during these minutes of suspense. From without came the rumbling roar of the traffic and the passing crowd. A caged cockatoo somewhere near shrieked defiance. A camera clicked thrice, followed by the sound of a steel tape being unwound. To the brothers an eternity elapsed before the party on the balcony and at the windows returned to the centre of the room.

Monty, ceasing to pace the room, saw the bland detective-sergeant nod to the other man, who came and stood beside the seated woman. That action, simple enough yet so significant, made the blood rush to his face and his great hands clench into formidable fists.

"Miss Thorpe," said the silken voice, "I regret that it is my most painful duty to arrest you on suspicion of causing the death of the man Peterson. I have to warn you that anything you say may be used against you as evidence."

"Arrest me!"

"My God!"

"Jumping nannygoats! you're a fool."

"So I have been called before, Mr. Sherwood. Will you, Mr. Martin, kindly procure the lady's outdoor things? By the way, Miss Thorpe, where is your maid?"

In the comparative silence that followed, Austiline rose to her feet with slow, deliberate action. Her leaden lips were parted as though her breathing had stopped. When she spoke her voice trembled a little.

"I—I—Oh! my maid is away for the day," she said, then, turning to her lover, went on pleadingly. "Martin! Martin! don't let them take me to prison. Oh Martin! it will spoil *our* Wednesday."

Martin's lips moved, but no sound came from them. For a second or two she waited, then to Monty said:

"You're Martin's brother, Monty, aren't you? Please, please, tell them not to take me away. They have made a

mistake. Indeed, they have. I did not kill him—I couldn't
—oh! I hated him, but I did not kill him."

At no time in his life had the big man come nearer to losing
his self-control and running amuck. Only by an effort did
he curb his almost overwhelming desire to smash the
policeman, pick up Austiline with almost the ease he would
exert in picking up a child, and run—run north by west, run
for ever and a day, so long as he got her safely away from these
men who would drag so fair a flower into a sewer. He groaned
aloud.

"Masters! go and get a car—a closed car," the detective-
sergeant snapped, in astonishingly altered tones. "You,
Mr. Montague Sherwood, stand back. The consequences will
be serious if you interfere with me in the execution of my duty.
Highatt, get the lady's hat."

"Martin! Martin! do something," was Austiline's cry.

"Madam, pray calm yourself," urged the doctor, a kindly
soul, slipping to her side and placing his hand supportingly
under her arm.

She did not see him. Her great bronze-brown eyes were
fixed beseechingly upon the deathly face of her lover, standing
with his brother, looking back at her with eyes that were
clouded, almost void of expression. His voice was a mere
echo; his words an echo to those of the doctor.

"It will be all right, Austiline. Everything will turn out
all right in the end. We will do all we can, old Monty and I."

"But, Martin, I didn't kill him. You of all men know that
I really couldn't do such a thing. They cannot take me from
you when I didn't kill him. You don't believe I shot him, do
you? Do you, Martin? Oh, Martin dear! don't desert me
now, now when I need you, when I want you for my very
life."

She broke off when Highatt interjected:

"You hat, Miss Thorpe."

Ignoring the proffered headgear, she held out her arms to
the horror-stiffened man, who could now neither move nor
speak, and who would have collapsed had not Monty held
him to his feet. When she spoke again, her voice was harsh,
even metallic. The moisture in her eyes vanished, giving
place to a look of unutterable pain, which in turn was replaced
by the light which must have shone in the eyes of Ste. Jeanne
d'Arc when the English led her to the stake. Her voice was
steady and her words liquid clear.

"I am disappointed, Martin. I have made a mistake. I thought chivalry still existed."

Taking her hat, she walked then to the mirror over the mantelpiece, pinned it to her hair, snatched the vanity-bag from the attentive Highatt, and dusted her face with powder. Turning about, her eyes met those of the detective-sergeant in a haughty stare, a stare which banished for a fraction of a second the look of vacuous boredom. She said:

"Do what you think is your duty. I am ready."

She and her sinister escort left the room—left Montague Sherwood supporting on his left arm the senseless body of his brother Martin.

CHAPTER V

MARTIN SHERWOOD lodged with an old lady and her widowed daughter occupying an old-fashioned house off the St. Kilda Road. They were, or had been, people of some standing, the deceased husband of the old lady having been Chief Commissioner of the Victorian Police, whilst the daughter's husband had died heroically in France. They belonged, however, to the masses whom the Dreadful War had impoverished, and were glad to be able to augment their diminished income by letting the two best rooms of their villa.

The editor of the *Tribune* thought himself fortunate to obtain rooms in so homely a *ménage,* whilst the ladies considered themselves as fortunate in having Martin Sherwood as tenant. The relationship of these three people had become much warmer than the usual commercial bond between landlady and paying guest: Mrs. Montrose coming to regard the young man quite in the light of a son; while Mary Webster and Martin treated each other in the simple affectionate manner of brother and sister.

To them all the coming separation occasioned by Martin's wedding was a matter of personal regret, quite aside from the financial aspect. The old lady was visibly affected, to the real surprise of her daughter. Unable to leave her invalid-chair without assistance, it was her wish that the wedding should take place from her house; but her daughter was against it, fearing that the excitement would be too much for her.

The ladies were occupying what they called the back-parlour, Mary Webster reading the paper aloud as was her habit after the clearing away of their light dinner, when they heard a car stop outside the garden-gate and the door-bell ring a moment afterwards.

"That's Martin come home in a hurry for something," the

invalid announced in her soft, clear voice. "Did not his six months' leave begin this morning?"

"Yes, mother," agreed the daughter, in a voice the very echo of her mother's, leaving the room. But, on opening the door, she was not surprised to see a stranger; for she had not forgotten that Martin had his own key.

He was a huge man, this stranger, a man who appeared to fill the landscape. Mary Webster, by no means a small woman, was obliged to look up at him, and for the fraction of a second their eyes met and searched the depths. He instinctively removed his felt before speaking.

"Does Mrs. Montrose live here?"

"Yes."

"Then, of course, you know my brother Martin?"

"Yes, he lives with us. You must be Mr. Montague Sherwood?"

Monty nodded. "That is my name," he said. "I am glad I found you. Are you Mrs. Webster? Yes! My brother has mentioned you often in his letters to me. He has had a great shock and is very ill."

"Dear me! Where is he?"

"Out there in the car. He is quite unconscious. You see, Mrs. Webster, I've heard what a lot you and your mother think of him, and—well, to be plain, I don't like private hospitals. I thought——"

"Go and carry him in at once."

It was a command given by a pretty woman not much over thirty years old; a woman whose eyes were suddenly bright with concern, with compassion. She watched Monty striding to the garden-gate, subconsciously admiring his grace, and quite consciously admiring his strength when he returned with Martin in his arms, exhibiting less exertion than that of a lesser man carrying a sheaf of wheat.

"Bring him this way," she ordered, turning and going before him into a cool, spotless bedroom. With deft fingers she laid back the bedclothes and produced a pyjama suit.

"Put him to bed, Mr. Sherwood. I must go and reassure mother."

"What is wrong?" asked Mrs. Montrose sharply, when her daughter rejoined her.

"It's Martin, mother. He has been taken ill, and his brother Monty brought him in a car. He is putting Martin to bed."

"What's the matter with him, do you think? Measles, scarlet fever, or what?" the old lady demanded, regarding Martin Sherwood as a delicate boy, as was her wont.

"I cannot say. He doesn't look as though in a fever."

"Well, well! Send for the tyrant Goodhart. He can't cure me, but he may Martin. And then make hot plenty of water: he'll want poultices, linseed poultices, perhaps."

"I'll get Mr. Sherwood to go at once," Mary decided, and, passing along the short passage, found Monty waiting for her.

"Do you know what caused the shock to Martin?" she asked him anxiously.

"I do," he replied grimly. "I've had a taste of it myself."

"Had I not better telephone at once to Miss Thorpe at the Flinders Hotel?"

"She won't be in, Mrs. Webster. Miss Thorpe has been arrested."

"Arrested!" she gasped.

"That's so," he said, fingering his hat. "Where can I dig up a good doctor?"

"Dr. Goodhart is our doctor," she explained. "Martin always goes to him. He lives a little way along the street on this side. You will see his name-plate."

Monty left almost at a run. Mary returned to her mother, who regarded her with bright, beady eyes.

"Well, what now?" she demanded, with the imperiousness of chronic invalidism.

"Mr. Sherwood has gone for the doctor," the younger woman said, vigorously poking the fire unnecessarily, so that the astounding news of Austiline Thorpe's arrest would clear from her face.

"You know more than you say," came the accusation. "Well, well; possibly you think it is for the best. That must be the tyrant now. Tell him before he goes that I wish to see him."

Dr. Goodhart was a second edition of Mr. Masters, small and bird-like. He took life so seriously that he never smiled. He was brusque to the point of rudeness. Yet these two drawbacks to a medical man were amply balanced by a keen brain and profound knowledge of modern medical science.

"Good evening, Mrs. Webster," he barked in a deep bass voice which threatened to crack an antique Chinese plate that decorated the hall. "What have they been doing to this wretch?"

"You had better see him, doctor."

"See him! Of course I'll see him. That's what I left a good dinner for. Lead on, Mrs. Macduff."

Twenty minutes later, he was addressing Mrs. Webster and Monty in Martin's small study across the passage.

"Mental shock. Collapse. I fear brain-fever," he barked. "He'll have to receive very careful attention. I advise a private hospital."

"He is going to stay here," Mary Webster said firmly. "You can send a nurse, and I'll do all I can to assist her."

Monty looked at her gratefully. The doctor replied briefly but comprehensively:

"Well, it will be a long and trying job. I'll send a nurse from the Home. Might have to send a second later. You are taking on more than you can manage, but it's no use arguing with a woman. When you find the job getting beyond you, let me know at once."

"How long do you think he'll be like that?" Monty asked.

"No telling. Perhaps for weeks. He's been working too hard. Too much mental work is worse than too little physical work. He's a bundle of nerves. Called me a fool. No news that—but I'm still walking about. I'm going to finish my well-earned dinner now. Compliments to Mrs. Montrose. Back in an hour."

"Very well, doctor. What can I do in the meantime?"

Looking up at her, he grunted. His voice, perhaps, was a little less harsh when he replied:

"Nothing, my dear," and, laying one finger on her arm, added: "You're a good woman, Mary Webster."

Thus it came about that, when Monty returned to his hotel late that night, he left Martin Sherwood in the hands of three very capable people.

Early the next morning, the big man was visited in his bedroom by a constable who handed him a summons to attend the coroner's inquest the following day at ten o'clock. Several hours later found him seeking permission from the prison authorities to interview Austiline Thorpe—permission readily granted when he made himself known. The detective-sergeant, who had charge of the case, happened to be in the office.

"Good morning, Mr. Sherwood," he said in what to Monty was becoming a hateful voice.

"Good day-ee!" Monty drawled, slowly examining the immaculate form from highly-polished boots upward. When he met the other man's eyes he feigned a start of surprise, saying:

"I think I have met you before. Ah! yes, I remember. You have not yet been reduced to a constable, I see."

"No. Why should I be?"

"For being such an old emu as to arrest Miss Thorpe. I wonder no longer that there is such a lot of crime going on in Melbourne."

The detective-sergeant winced, yet his voice was still silken when he replied suggestively:

"It's surprising, though, the number of people I've had hanged."

"I don't doubt it. You'd have an infant hanged for killing a navvy with a blacksmith's hammer," the big man returned swiftly, at which the detective-sergeant laughed good-naturedly, thereby raising himself quite a number of steps in Monty's estimation.

"How is your brother to-day?" inquired the inspector to whom Monty had made application for the interview.

"He's just the same, I saw him an hour ago. He is still unconscious."

"It is a very unfortunate affair," the inspector remarked. "He was to be married next Wednesday, too."

"It is not too late if only you would switch the detective-sergeant here on to the real murderer of the blackmailer," Monty said hopefully.

The two officials observed him keenly. The inspector leaned forward over the table at which he sat, speaking earnestly:

"Mr. Sherwood, listen to me. Mr. Oakes, here, is considered one of the foremost detectives in the Commonwealth. I have been in the Police Force nearly forty years, and those years have given me a wide experience of crime, the evidence of crime, and the production of evidence of crime before a judge and jury. I don't think Miss Thorpe stands the ghost of a chance of acquittal. What makes you think she is innocent?"

"Her face."

"A beautiful one, no doubt, but beautiful faces seldom influence judges and juries," the inspector went on. "I think I may say that not one member of the Victorian Police Force does not heartily sympathize with your brother. Every one of us owes him a debt; for, through the paper he edits, he obtained reforms and better conditions for the Force than our associations would have got in twenty years. On that account, when he recovers consciousness, please tell him what I have said, and assure him that what can be done for Miss Thorpe's comfort up to the very end of her trial will be done. I cannot console him further. I wish I could say I believed in her innocence."

Monty found Austiline Thorpe not in a prison-cell but seated at a writing-table in a plainly-furnished but comfortable room. Rising to meet him, she smiled wanly and held out her hand.

"This is a queer place for two people to make acquaintance in, is it not, Mr. Sherwood?" she said, her low, sweet voice reminding him, strangely enough, of a nursing sister of an English hospital in which he had had occasion to stay during the war.

"We're living in queer times," he replied gently. "Say, I wish you would cut out the 'mister.' You've no idea how titles of honour annoy me."

"Very well! Then I shall expect you not to annoy me in that way either. Won't you sit down. . . . Monty?"

"That's better," the big man returned, with an irresistible smile. "I've come first of all to apologize for not killing that detective-sergeant when you turned to me for help. But it wouldn't have helped any to have made a fuss."

"I can see that now," she agreed readily. "I feel so ashamed at having thought any one could have prevented my arrest. I suppose Martin hasn't forgiven me yet for speaking so hatefully as I did?"

"Fact is, I don't think Martin heard you," Monty said slowly. "He is very ill."

"Ill! Monty—how ill?"

At once she was alarmed: fear, anxiety, concern, flashing into her compelling eyes. She leaned a little towards him, her lips parted, her breath caught, to await his answer.

"The doctor who saw him when I took him home fears brain-fever," he told her, realizing it were kinder to tell her the truth quickly. "He is being well looked after by a nurse and Mrs. Webster."

"Brain-fever!" she echoed. "Oh, Monty! Is he so ill?"

He nodded, his powerful face troubled.

"When you left your apartment yesterday in company with the detective-sergeant, I found that I was holding Martin up on his feet after, most likely, he had lost consciousness for some moments. He is still unconscious, but the doctor hopes when he comes to that he will be all right."

"Oh! I knew, I felt, that our happiness was too splendid to last," she cried brokenly. "Poor Martin! If only we had never met, he would have been spared this."

"Martin always was a good fellow," Monty declared earnestly, adding, with intent: "He's a damned better feller for having loved you."

The little swear-word had the effect the shrewd Monty desired. It banished emotion that threatened to overwhelm her; and, though he did not know it, gave her a tranquil sense of his protectorship, as of a masculine stronghold to which she could cling.

"Monty," she said, dabbing at her eyes with a handkerchief, "I am glad to have met you. You gave me just the medicine I needed."

He smiled broadly at that, saying:

"A feller in a book once said that women and horses were much alike temperamentally. I understand horses. I suppose, Austiline, you'll permit me to barge in on your defence?"

"Quite what do you mean?"

"Well, I mean as regards employing the best legal brains to show these fools that they've got the wrong man—I mean woman."

"You don't believe, then, that I shot that man?"

"Me! Course not."

"Thank you, Monty," she said softly. "I'm not nearly so much afraid now."

"No need to feel afraid whatever," he told her. "A fool and his prisoner is soon parted, you know. Have you engaged an attorney yet?"

"Yes; I sent for my solicitor this morning. Then Sir Victor Lawrence, Martin's chief, visited me about ten. He tried hard not to let me see it, but he believes I did shoot Peterson. In fact, he said, in a roundabout way, that every blackmailer should be shot on sight, and the killers absolved by Act of Parliament."

"Must have had some experience of them," Monty said with a broad smile. "I'd like to see a feller blackmail me. His mother would think he had turned into a parrot when I'd done with him. I saw Sir Victor when he visited Martin. Fine old chap! Says he's going to change the constitution to get you off. If faith in himself and string-pulling can do anything, the constitution will be changed all right."

"Still, he believes me guilty of murder."

"He called it justifiable homicide."

"He believes me guilty," she insisted.

"Well, somehow, when I come to think about it, I cannot wonder at a lot of people believing that," he said slowly. "You see, the dust on that veranda does not bear out your story, for one thing."

"Then you aren't speaking the truth when you say you do not believe I did it?" she accused him, a little fiercely.

"But I *am* speaking the truth," he rejoined. "Fact is, I happened to study your face when you were telling your story to the detective-sergeant. Martin was beside you and didn't. I don't think he doubted you, even when he made me tell him about the dust on the veranda."

"You talk in riddles, Monty. What have Martin's doubts and convictions to do with dusty verandas?"

Monty started and looked hard at her. So she had not been told of the absence of human tracks outside her windows. He said slowly, as gently as he could:

"You said, didn't you, that the man escaped out of the French windows to the veranda?" She nodded. "Well, it was a dusty day, you remember, and dust lay thick all along the veranda floor. There were the tracks of a cat there an hour old. But there were no tracks of a man."

Her face whitened a little. Partly rising from her chair, her fingers gripping its arms until they showed as white as her face, she said, little louder than a sigh:

"No tracks!"

He shook his head.

"Could he not have got away without leaving tracks?"

"Not by the window and veranda, Austiline. It's got me beat."

For a moment they remained gazing fixedly each at the other. Suddenly she sank back into her chair, and, falling forward over the table, buried her face in her arms.

"Then I am indeed lost, lost, lost!"

Her voice was almost a wail, so utterly abandoned did she become. The big man patted her gently on the shoulder, himself feeling, but not showing, emotion.

"You buck up, Austiline. I know you're guiltless; you know, yourself, you're innocent. There's a bit of a fog about just now, but we'll all win through to the sunshine beyond, never fear. Then we will look back at the fog, and know that our tribulations were but dreams."

Suddenly he saw himself regarded by tear-drenched eyes. She took his hand and pressed it warmly, like a little child clinging to its father's hand in a lone dark lane.

"You're a big man, Monty. Thank God, for sending me a *big* man!"

CHAPTER VI

BENT NOSE

IN the Coroner's court Austiline Thorpe maintained a calm, detached attitude under the fire of questions aimed at her. Dressed in a navy blue tailor-made costume, relieved with white silk only one shade whiter than her cheeks, she faced the ordeal with serenity almost regal.

Monty, who was called to relate the finding of the woman alone with the dead man, holding her own revolver from which one cartridge had been discharged, thought he never had seen so lovely a woman, nor one so spiritually superior to her surroundings. Not even when the Coroner committed her for trial did she weaken, but passed from the public stare as she had come before it.

Coroners' inquests very often overstep their function. The nominal duty of the court is to inquire into the death of a person supposed to have met with an untimely end. The actual procedure of the court is to accuse a person of murder, drag in confirmatory evidence, and then the Coroner usurps the office of a qualified judge to mark that person with the brand of Cain or declare him or her innocent.

Naturally the public read about the case in the newspapers. The killing of Peterson was made a matter of keen public interest. Immediately the evidence at the inquest was published, the public agreed with the Coroner that Austiline fired the fatal shot and judged her guilty. What a farce—common at any rate in Australia—is a trial when, from evidence given at a Coroner's court, the Judge and each member of the jury have quite made up their minds long before the trial opens!

Little interest was taken in the dead man, because little was known. He had arrived in Melbourne from England some six months before his end, and had resided at a boarding-house at Brighton. Because Austiline refused to disclose the nature of his blackmail, the public refused to believe him a blackguard of the worst type, and acclaimed him as a kind of martyr. Her trial was looked forward to with a sense of gloating over revenge to come.

During the three days that elapsed before the magisterial proceedings took place, the big man was permitted to visit her daily. At each visit he found her cold, reserved, and resigned. Even his cheerfulness could not revive a spark of hope.

"They will hang me, Monty, and bury my body in lime," she said. "I don't mind dying, if die I must—but my dear old father and mother! they will die, too, of horror and shame."

Three times daily he called at the house at St. Kilda for news of his brother. They would not allow him to see the patient, but from Mary Webster he learned that Martin was constantly delirious and continually raved about his *fiancée*. Dr. Goodhart was worried, and practically lived at the house.

No additional evidence was given at the Magistrate's court. In spite of Sir Victor Lawrence's willingness to go surety for any sum, in spite of the police raising no objection to the prisoner receiving bail, bail was refused.

"By George!" the little newspaper knight roared at Monty. "I'll—I'll break that stipendiary magistrate as you would break a straw. Martin kicked him severely last year over one of his sentences, and now he's put the boot on in return. I'll get Moplett to jump on him with both feet in every issue of the *Tribune* till he's off the Melbourne map."

And from that moment, illogically and without reason, this warm-blooded man, generally so keen a judge of character, joined forces with the bushman as a firm believer in Austiline's innocence. And the refusal of bail rankled in other minds also, for three days afterwards the magistrate was nicely caught exceeding the speed limit by an unusual number of police witnesses.

For Monty the days and weeks following the magisterial hearing were filled with foreboding and wearing anxiety. Austiline's solicitor briefed Sir Henry Winter, Victoria's premier advocate, who, after reading the brief with a clear mind, for he said that on principle he never read reports of coroners' inquests, promised that he would do his very best, but——

The defence he intended to raise was that Austiline was truthful in her statements both to the investigating detective-sergeant and to the Coroner. He intended calling witnesses to prove that Monty had jumped—a standing jump from the windows—the ten-foot wide veranda without stepping on the floor. This the big man had done, but only at the third attempt.

During those dark days Martin grew steadily worse. Dr. Goodhart almost despaired for his life; would, in fact, have done so had not his natural optimism forbidden it. Monty invariably spent an hour with old Mrs. Montrose, who came to regard him as the emblem and shining example of manly perfection. Delighting in his quaint aphorisms, charmed with his unusual frankness, the old lady awaited his comings with happy anticipation and submitted to his goings with regret. There was no reason to doubt that Mary Webster was similarly affected, if not more so. The invalid was not sure about Mary, but was discreetly silent.

It wanted but a fortnight to the day fixed for the opening of the trial when Monty first noticed the gaunt man with the crooked nose. Walking along Collins Street to his hotel, the big man was jostled by Bent Nose, as the man afterwards became called. Monty was not the sort of man who could be jostled easily, any more than an Atlantic liner could be jostled easily by a steam-launch. The jostler fell back, muttered an apology, picked up a letter he had dropped, and hurried away.

Although engaged on an entirely different case at the moment, Detective-Sergeant Oakes observed the incident with keen interest.

The next afternoon it was with something like a start that Monty discovered Bent Nose sitting next him in a cinema which he patronized when his feet ached from walking the unaccustomed pavements. Having but half-a-crown in his pockets, he gave himself over to the questionable and rare pleasure of having them picked. But Bent Nose behaved irreproachably, much to the bushman's disappointment.

Again out of doors after the show, the big man crossed the road to Collins Street, intending to proceed to the Café Australia for afternoon tea with a friendly little woman he had met there casually before. He was thinking of her, and wondering what there was about him to make some people think that he and his money were so easily sundered, when, feeling in his pocket for his pipe, he pulled out with it a letter.

Puzzled, he looked the letter over. It was sealed but unaddressed. How it came to be in his pocket he could not

make out. Frowning, for an honest man hates mystery,
Monty edged into the doorway of an art-shop, where he
broke open the envelope and drew out a single sheet of cheap
writing-paper. He read:

"Martin Sherwood has been a good friend to me. Sir, I
am grateful, and will prove it. He should get well when the
good news is published. Destroy this without fail and
menshun me only to him.

"BENT NOSE."

"You have had bad news, I fear," remarked a silken voice;
and, looking up, Monty met the inquisitive eyes and the
bland smile of Detective Oakes.

"Excuse me one moment," Monty drawled; and, taking
care that the detective could not read the note, he reread it,
committing it to memory. Then, with a smile fully as bland
as the detective's, he struck a match and joined his mentor in
watching it burn slowly to an ash.

"A feller in a book once said: 'A wise man never writes
a love-letter; only a fool keeps them'," he observed coolly.

"Yet a fool is sometimes a wise man, and occasionally a
wise man is a fool, Mr. Sherwood. How is your brother?"

"Crook—very crook. He has one chance of pulling
through."

In spite of the betraying twinkle in the big man's eyes the
detective said:

"I am glad to hear he has even one chance. What is it?"

"That of your gaining a little horse-sense and looking for
the killer of Peterson."

The detective-sergeant laughed outright. Monty, joining
him, found the sensation queer, for he had not laughed for
days.

"Doing anything?" he asked.

"Nothing much, Mr. Sherwood. I was just wandering
round looking for a man with a bent nose."

"So! That should be easy in this crowd," Monty said
without turning a hair. Suddenly he pointed to a passer-by.
"Here, see that one. His nose is like a triangle. Perhaps
that's him." Then he laughed again, and Oakes felt not a
little admiration for Monty's coolness.

For be it stated that, after the jostling incident, Oakes had
searched the Rogues' Gallery, where he found a photograph

of Bent Nose, whose real name was William Hill. The accompanying docket gave Hill's history fully in detail and concisely in official prose. Why did the ex-thief, who then was quite a respectable citizen, earning an honest living as hall-porter of the *Tribune* Building, take such extreme pains to introduce a letter, evidently a message, into Monty's pocket when it would have been so much simpler to have spoken to him? Why, when the letter had been discovered—he was convinced it was the same dropped by the ex-crook the preceding day—had Monty been so careful to destroy it? He was sure that the incident was connected in some way with the murder.

Luck had favoured the detective that day. Coincidence or luck plays a tremendously important part in human affairs, especially in the field of crime and its detection. It was only by the merest chance that the detective-sergeant had seen the big man paying for a seat in a cinema at the box-office at the entrance.

Unaware of Monty's aching feet, he was mildly surprised that the bushman of one country could be thrilled by the romantic cowboys of another; but his surprise became less mild when he observed Bent Nose immediately follow the big man inside. For two hours he waited with trained patience for the next act in this drama of real life.

Reasoning, while thus waiting, that the ex-chief would impart his message orally within the cinema and thereby have played his part, Oakes decided to observe Monty when he reappeared and see how he would play his. It was the kind of game that Oakes liked, and liking it had raised him high in the respect of both his superiors and the criminals. Indeed he regarded his profession as a game, confiding once to a friend that if all criminals became honest he would quickly die of boredom.

"I am afraid you will never believe that black is black and not white," he murmured, his precisely folded raincoat over one shoulder, his dainty walking-stick tapping his immaculate shoes topped by white-lined black socks.

"Maybe not, but I do believe I have a raging thirst," came the drawled reply. "I was on my way to afternoon tea when you rudely butted in."

"May I not accompany you?"

"You bet! I'm honouring the Café Australia. Let me pilot you through this crowd. You might get lost."

A few minutes later they entered the comfortable tea-room with its subdued lights, its thick carpets and its luxurious chairs; whereupon the friendly little woman, who was waiting impatiently for Monty, hurriedly rose and vanished into the ladies' room, on catching sight of his companion. As a matter of cold fact, the ingeniously introduced note had banished her from his mind, and he was now inwardly chuckling at the thought of the solitary half-crown in his pocket, and the prospect of making the detective pay for the tea. . . .

Mrs. Montrose enjoyed the joke no less when Monty confided to her his adventurous afternoon. She was immensely pleased to be his confidante, to be let into the secret of Bent Nose and his strange communication. It gave her food for reflection for days during those hours she sat alone in her invalid-chair.

Mary Webster walked with him to the street gate when he took his leave that evening. The afterglow burned faintly above and blurred the outlines of the taller trees in the Botanic Gardens across the road. The distant roar of the city accentuated the stillness and peace of that warm spring evening.

It was "Monty" and "Mary" with them by that time; but, if Mary was becoming to look upon the big man as a god, he regarded her merely in a brotherly way, with a little more affection, perhaps, than he had had for any woman. At the gate she laid a cool hand on his arm, saying:

"I am beginning to be afraid for Martin."

"So am I, Mary."

"He keeps calling so for Miss Thorpe. It really is heart-rending. Dr. Goodhart says he will pull him through, but I am beginning to doubt it. Oh, Monty! If only they would allow Miss Thorpe to come to him. I feel sure her presence would relieve his fever."

"That's likely enough," Monty agreed heavily. "But she is fast behind iron bars, Mary, and when I suggested the visit to Inspector Watkins he said he would do his hardest to bring it off. But he failed, and we can only hope. I'll call again in the morning, Mary. Good-bye!"

"Good night, Monty!" she said, but only the "shadow" crouched against the brick wall on the further side heard the soft sob when she turned to the house.

Monty, striding to the tram-stop, did not notice the said "shadow," nor did he realize that he was closely shadowed all that evening till he reached his hotel about eleven o'clock. It was, perhaps, lucky for him that he *was* shadowed, and that the "shadow" spent the entire night in company with the night clerk of the hotel, and therefore could prove that Monty returned to his rooms and stayed there until nine o'clock.

CHAPTER VII

HIDDEN FORCES MOVE

AT midday the big man arrived in a motor-car at the house in the walled garden. Mary Webster, expecting him, and hearing the car stop, hurriedly left the house and met him in the garden. She saw beneath his arm a roll of newspapers, in his eyes the dancing light of excitement, on his rugged face a broad grin of delight. In her face he saw traces of tears, and at once became sympathetic.

"Why, Mary, has anything happened?" he asked with unusual quickness.

"Yes, Monty; I have both good and bad news for you. Let us sit in the summer-house and exchange our news, for I see you have news, too—good news, by your face."

She led him to a little rustic shelter built in the shade of a giant almond tree, and then when they were seated she said softly, a tremble in her voice:

"Martin has regained consciousness, Monty, and Dr. Goodhart says he will quickly get better. Martin is sleeping now, such a beautiful, peaceful sleep."

"Thank God for that!" the man said fervently. "But what is your bad news?"

"Oh, Monty! you must prepare yourself for a blow," she said, her hands clasped over her breast, her blue eyes wide and misty. Unconsciously he squared his shoulders, saying:

"I'm used to blows, Mary, but I like 'em quick."

"When Martin became conscious," she said slowly, "Dr. Goodhart and the nurse were with him. The first thing he asked for was light. The nurse raised the blind, letting in a flood of sunlight, and again he fretfully asked for light. The fever has left him quite blind, Monty."

"Blind!" The big man stared at first uncomprehendingly, and then leaning towards her, added in a whisper: "Did you say 'blind', Mary?"

And then her hands went up to meet her lowered head, and

instinctively he patted her heaving shoulder, whilst she cried and he looked vacantly out into the garden. Blind! Martin blind! The thought was terrible, realization a crushing blow, almost as crushing as though Martin had died. Slowly the numbness of his brain wore off, and the soft sobs of the woman beside him soothed him with their compassion. He thought they were for Martin, and suspected love. He didn't understand that they were more for him, and suspected not love for himself.

Silently he gave her time to regain composure. How strange, he thought, that ever since he came to Melbourne there had been little else but women's tears, and one unpleasant shock after another—shocks which left him helpless, to fight against effects—him helpless, who all his life had overcome difficulties and dispelled dangers. He felt as though chain were added to chain to fetter him—he who so loved freedom. When her sobbing ceased he said gently:

"Does he know that he is blind?"

"Yes—they got me to break it to him," she said, still hiding her face. "Oh, Monty! it was awful, but he was very brave and, thank God! very tired. He held my hand, oh! so tightly, till he fell asleep."

"What does Goodhart think?" was his next question.

"He can give us little hope. He says the fever has paralysed the optic nerves. To-morrow he is bringing an eye specialist to see him."

He sighed deeply and was silent. If only Martin's blindness and Austiline's misfortunes were clothed in flesh and were men, what happiness it would have been to have flung off his coat, rolled up his shirt-sleeves, and punched them into nothingness! But they were like imps of sulphuratted vapour from the nether world who jeered at him and his strength. He heard her say, with more composure:

"What is your news, Monty?"

"Rather startling," he replied. "Austiline has broken gaol."

"Escaped!" she breathed. "Are you sure, Monty?"

"Dead sure. When they counted the prisoners this morning, Austiline was reported missing."

"Tell me—all you know."

"That's what I came for," he assured her, fumbling in his pockets abstractedly. "Would——"

"Of course you may smoke," Mary told him, guessing his wants.

"Thanks, Mary! I kinda feel I want steadying." Adding, when he had lit his venerable pipe: "Oakes came to me when I was still in bed this morning. I was duly surprised at his early visit, and offered him breakfast. Lord! the man's inhuman. To see his face, empty of expression like a colander of water when he had such momentous tidings, was wonderful. Quite casually he let out that the gaol had been raided: three wardresses drugged, a warder on a watch-tower almost strangled to death, Austiline lowered out of a window, the prison-wall partly demolished with explosives to assure an easy get-away, and a powerful car ready to drive up to the breach, pick her and a man up, and whirl them away."

With traces of tears still evident on her fresh young face, her eyes fixed on him, and her lips parted, Mary Webster remained wordless. Not for anything would she have interrupted him.

"I would have engineered the raid myself if I had had the brains of the feller who did," he went on. "Not having the brains, it was left to him to carry out without a hitch the most daring goal-raid ever attempted. And the feller who had the brains to do it will have enough brains left to keep Austiline out of goal for ever.

"Can you guess what the detective-sergeant said? He said, as calmly as though he asked me to pass him the salt: 'I am really very pleased that the raid *was* successful. It will give me much pleasure to lay my hands on the perpetrators in one way, and much pleasure also in another way if Miss Thorpe is never recaptured. Officially I am against murder, but privately my sympathy is entirely with killers of blackmailers. Blackmail should be made a capital offence.'

"I don't understand Oakes," Monty went on. "He is the very first man to baffle me. One minute he gives you the impression that he likes getting people hanged, and the next that he likes having people murdered. Quite a casual sort of feller, Oakes, and I think I shall end up by liking him."

"It is extraordinary!" she said, her mind engrossed with Austiline's rescue. "Whoever could have done it, do you think?"

"I have no more idea than Oakes," Monty admitted. "I told him, though, that if he were successful, I should pay for their defence, just to give him some idea how pleased I was. Things were looking very black against Austiline, and I had given up hope that she would be acquitted. I think Martin loves her very much."

"So do I," she said more brightly. "Do you know, I have never seen two people more wonderfully in love than she and Martin. I feel sick with sorrow for them."

"Well, I don't feel exactly in heaven," was his seriously meant comment. "I only hope Austiline isn't rash enough to try to see Martin. If she does she will be caught for sure. This house is being watched."

"Watched! By whom?"

"There is absolutely no need for worry, Mary. Naturally the police think it quite probable that Austiline will visit her sick lover, and they daren't leave any loophole unguarded. However, I do not think she will come. The people who helped her to escape will point out to her the danger."

"Yes; but, on the other hand, Austiline knows that Martin is very ill. She might dare anything to reach the side of the man she loves. I know I would. If only we could get word to her that he is recovering—just that and no more!"

For several moments the big man smoked without speaking, wondering how such knowledge could be conveyed to Austiline Thorpe. Then suddenly the frown between his half-closed eyes lifted, and he said:

"I think I'll go and see Sir Victor Lawrence. Perhaps he would have a notice published in the *Tribune* to the effect that Martin was on the high road to health."

"That's an idea, Monty! And let them say that Martin's friends have no longer any cause for anxiety. Austiline will see that, or some of her friends will show it to her."

"Mary, you can see farther beyond a brick wall than any woman I know," the bushman said, rising to his feet. "I'll go along right away and fix that little business. I'll 'phone you every half-hour to hear if Martin has wakened. I must talk to him as soon as possible afterwards."

They parted outside the summer-house, she watching him stride to the gate where, turning, he waved his hat. The curtains of her mind were held back at that moment, and, had the big man seen the expression in Mary's eyes, he would have——

But, not having seen, he hurried to the city, and in the *Tribune* Building he saw Sir Victor, to whom he made the suggestion formulated by Mary and himself. Sir Victor chuckled.

"Sherwood," he said, "I believe you'd make a very fine pirate."

"Like the Irishman, I'm agin the law when it's up against my friends," Monty admitted.

"I admire Miss Thorpe," the knight said emphatically. "I have met her on several occasions. I should feel very much annoyed if she fell into this booby-trap arranged by our perspicacious police. The news of your brother's recovery shall be broadcast, and as plain a hint as possible given that Mrs. Montrose's house is watched."

"Thanks!"

"No need. What do you think of this gaol-raiding stunt?"

"It's beyond me. Never dreamed Austiline had so many friends."

"Nor I. Like yourself I am a good pirate at heart," remarked the little man, lighting a cigar and closing an eye. "If we can only delay Austiline's capture, something may turn up in her favour."

"Then you think she will be caught?"

"Most certainly. I hear they have sent for Johns, the crack Sydney detective. When he and friend Oakes run in double harness things generally happen."

"Then I shall have to take a hand in the game myself," Monty said lightly. "Have the police got a clue yet, do you know?"

"I don't think so. If you call again about six I may have something to say. We've got some smart men on our staff. So long!"

Leaving the Building, the big man telephoned Mary Webster from a public call-office, and, learning that Martin still slept, sauntered along to Elizabeth Street and thence to Little Burke Street, where he entered a shooting-gallery. The "shadow" was puzzled at Monty's choice of recreation. He did not know of the bushman's passion for firearms, the one surviving enthusiasm of boyhood, nor had he ever before witnessed a display of skill such as he observed when he pushed open a little way the street door of the shooting-gallery.

The proprietor of the gallery greeted Monty effusively, recognizing in the big man his very best patron. It was a fairly large place. On one side was the usual array of bottles on wires and tiny coloured balls poised on the tips of little fountains of water. There was also what looked like a cannon, through which the marksman fired at a target at the further end, a small bell ringing when the bull's-eye was hit.

But these methods of sport were ignored by Monty, who often shot a fast-flying crow with a revolver, or brought down an eagle-hawk with a high-powered rifle. With the further end of the gallery as a protective background he had induced the proprietor to hang a bottle from the ceiling by a string. Standing on one side, the man swung the bottle in a descending and upward curve whilst Monty, standing back some twenty paces, broke it with a revolver. This he did gradually. His first shot smashed the lower half of the bottle, the second left only a portion of the neck. The next six shots were spent in severing the twine just above the bottle-neck. The seventh shot was successful. Turning to the admiring proprietor, he said :

"I'm getting old, Jacobs. Soon I'll be taking to carpet-slippers and a smoking-cap. Tie on another bottle and swing it faster."

This done, and the bottle swung till Monty had severed the string above the neck at his second try, enabled the big man to say : "That's better." He went on to ask Jacobs, a little lithe man of forty, rat-eyed, and with every action of feline quickness, to find him two pieces of cardboard, each one foot square. Neither of them observed the "shadow" peering at them through the narrow slit between door and frame.

The cardboard produced, Monty fashioned one piece with his tobacco-knife into a rough outline of a human head, seen from the front, and the other into a profile-shaped head. With a stub of pencil he marked in eyes, nose and mouth. Then, with hammer and nail he affixed the full-faced head against the wall.

Jacobs looked on curiously. The second piece of cardboard, representing a head in profile, Monty affixed to the top of a long broom-handle, and the handle he stuck into a bucket containing some of the sand with which the floor was covered.

He was careful to place the profile head about four feet in front of the full-faced one nailed to the wall, and then, stepping back, took up a position some sixteen paces distant, at which, looking at the heads, he saw the nose of that nearest him almost in line with the left cheek of that attached to the wall.

"Come here, Jacobs," he ordered, "and look under my arm at those heads."

"Yus ; I see 'em."

"Now Jacobs, if you felt like corpsing a man with a gun," the big man drawled, "would you fire at him from here, with a second person almost directly in the way, as that profile-shaped head is there?"

"Well, being as 'ow I'm streets behind you in shooting, I don't think I'd risk it."

"What would you do, then, if you thought your enemy had a gun also, and could use it?"

"I 'ardly know. Perhaps I'd 'ave to risk 'itting the other bloke," opined the accommodating Mr. Jacobs.

"But as the other feller didn't have a gun and was not expecting any one who did have one, what would you say about the marksmanship of a man who would risk shooting the person in line and place a bullet very neatly through the forehead of the person beyond. Like this!"

Monty's weapon rose and cracked, and they saw a faintly discernible hole in the centre of the forehead of the head against the wall.

"I'd say 'e is the kinda bloke I don't like seeing in 'ere. 'E breaks too many bottles," Jacobs replied with emphasis. Whereupon Monty grinned, gave the little man a one-pound note, and gained the street.

At five o'clock the boys with the evening papers were rushing through the streets, yelling like maniacs. Monty secured a paper in Collins Street, and read it while drinking tea in the Café Australia. There was no friendly little woman to interrupt. His paper was issued from the .*Tribune* Building, and when he found a half-column devoted to Martin's illness he chuckled; for there, almost in plain English, Austiline was warned not to attempt any visit to her lover, who was now almost quite recovered.

"It is evident that something amuses you, Mr. Sherwood," said a softly bland voice, and Detective-Sergeant Oakes dropped into a vacant chair beside the bushman.

"Hullo! you here?" exclaimed Monty, smiling broadly.

"Yes, I followed you in," was the unabashed admission. "I think you owe me a tea."

"You may be right."

"I am sure I am. Tea and muffins, please."

Again the big man chuckled; and when, having beckoned a waitress, he gave the order, he said, giving the detective-sergeant the paper:

"Read that, my dear Sherlock!"

Detective Oakes sighed on returning the news-sheet, and thoughtfully poured himself a cup of strong tea.

"You have crushed but one of a fair number of hopes," he said without a smile, without a frown, as though he had said: "I always take two lumps of sugar with my tea."

"I'm going to crush a few more in the natural course of events," he was told with superb confidence.

"Ah! I am informed that you are trying to establish the possibility of Peterson being shot from the doorway, with Miss Thorpe almost within direct line."

"Were you now? What do you think of my shooting?"

"I am informed also that you are a very excellent shot."

"Too right. I could have murdered Peterson with the utmost ease. What a pity I was outside the locked door and in company when the shot was fired. What joy would you have found in having me hanged! My poor old immaculate sleuth! I am quite sorry for you."

"You have need to be," murmured the detective-sergeant. "How is your brother to-day?"

"Better, much better," Monty said soberly. "The fever has left him, and at present he is sleeping, a good healthy sleep. But—the fever has left him quite blind, so Mrs. Webster tells me."

"Blind! Good God!" For the first time Monty saw the vacuous mask drawn aside, and the real Oakes regarding him with genuine dismay. "What a dreadful thing! But surely there is a possibility of the sight being recovered?"

"Goodhart doesn't think so. He is getting an eye specialist to see Martin to-morrow."

"We will hope that Goodhart is wrong," the detective said, the mask once more in place. Then: "I have had to have your friend with the bent nose arrested."

"What for?"

"Suspicion of being implicated in the gaol-raid last night. I suppose he told you about it in his written message yesterday?"

Monty regarded his friend-enemy with twinkling eyes. He said in his inimitable drawl:

"If you were to drink your tea without milk you wouldn't get such queer ideas. Believe me, cow's milk is a brain-destroyer. I never drink milk, which is why I play poker rather well—bluff-poker, I mean."

CHAPTER VIII

A T seven o'clock the big man learned from Mary Webster that Martin had just wakened: he promptly jumped into a car, and less than half an hour later was deposited at the garden-gate. Mary met him in the hall, looked up at him mistily with her hand laid encouragingly on his arm, and, without speaking, motioned him to the open door of Martin's room.

When Monty entered, the nurse rose from a chair and softly withdrew, closing the door after her. A lamp on a table beside the bed shed soft radiance on the sick man's wasted face and dark-ringed eyes gazing upwards with a terrible blankness. The bushman, inured to the rough and granite-hard corners of life, who all his days had fought because it was his nature to revel in fighting and overcoming men and material difficulties, bent over Martin and kissed him on the white brow. Then, sinking into a chair beside the bed, he grasped the thin white hands.

For nearly ten minutes they remained without speaking. Then with, to Monty, surprising calmness, Martin said:

"What was the Dad's favourite Biblical character, Monty?"

"Job," promptly replied the big man.

"I am a reincarnation of Job."

"Maybe, but you know why the Dad liked Job, don't you, old lad?" Monty said gently. "No matter what trials the Lord put on Job, Job kept on smiling. So did the Dad. When the blacks speared his cattle, when the bush-fires destroyed them and miles of fencing with 'em, when drought and disease came, the old Dad kept on smiling. What's good enough for Job and the old Dad is good enough for us, eh, Martin?"

"It is going to be very hard," almost whispered the patient.

"It is," the big man agreed. "The clouds have gathered and the sky is black, but the sky won't be black for long. It never is. Have they told you Austiline has broken gaol?"

"You mean escaped?"

"That's so."

"That looks like the first rift in your stormy sky, Monty. How did it happen? They say I've been unconscious for weeks. Tell me all that has happened since that awful afternoon."

The big man did so with a flow of quaint bush dialect that helped to lift Martin's despairing spirit out of the Slough of Despond.

"This evening's papers describe the raid as the most audacious in the annals of crime," Monty concluded. "It appears that the wardresses in the women's wing of the gaol were permitted to take in coffee and cakes from a near-by restaurant for a meal they had at midnight. No one can say how the drug was got into the coffee—the feller who took it to the ladies swears he knows nothing about it—but he's been arrested all the same.

"We don't know by whom, but Austiline was aroused in her cell, dressed, and lowered out on a landing-window by a rope into the courtyard surrounding the building. As the only main entrance is guarded by half a dozen warders, and as the outer wall is twenty feet high, with four feet of unmortared bricks on top of it so that to scale it means bringing down a ton of bricks, the gentry on the raid blew a part of the wall down. The warder on guard in the look-out tower was scientifically dealt with by a feller with strong arms and hands; but, even while being squeezed into insensibility, he saw the wall blown down, a man and a woman run across the yard, out through the breach, and enter a powerful car which drew up for just enough time.

"If ever I meet the feller who engineered that little picture-play, I am going to ask him to shake hands. If there is one thing I admire more than any other, it is Brains with a capital B."

"Publicly I should denounce the scoundrel, but privately, Monty, I should—I should take his other hand. What does friend Oakes think about it?" inquired Martin.

"Wish I knew," the big man replied regretfully. "I told him I could play bluff-poker pretty well, and at that he smiled as though I were a kid telling a Test Match player that I could play cricket rather well."

"Have you met Sir Victor?"

"Yes, old lad. We are father and son. We——"

"What is his opinion, please?"

"Says he is sure Austiline will be recaptured. He told me they had sent for Johns, the big Sydney 'tec."

"Ah! He'll work with Oakes. They make a formidable team. What is your opinion, Monty?"

"Oh, judge and prosecuting counsel and third degree expert! my views are without value," Monty said half-mockingly.

"Nevertheless, I should like to know them," came the gentle voice.

"Well, as I told Mary, I reckon that the feller clever enough to kidnap Austiline out of such a gaol is quite clever enough to keep her out. This evening's paper is roaring about the inefficiency of our police and the number of murderers still at large. It said also in another place what a terrible fine bloke you are, and how glad the whole staff was to know of your complete recovery from illness."

"But I am not completely recovered yet, O my brother!"

"To the outside world you're full of energy, you are engaged in writing a brilliant series of articles, you are much annoyed to know that the police are watching this house, and you decline to see any friends. At least, that's what to-night's paper said. And, being editor of a paper, you know perfectly well that newspapers never tell lies."

"You are not joking?"

"Not this once, old son," Monty went on. "You see, Mary, being a woman, reckoned that Austiline, daring everything, would visit you, knowing how desperately ill you are. We had to warn her or her friends that the police thought as Mary did: so I went to Sir Victor, who promised to fix it. He fixed it all right, much to our heroic sleuth's annoyance."

"What next?"

The big man described his observation of the detective when he got Austiline to take her former position exactly, and the inference which Oakes drew from the fact that she was almost in line between him—in Peterson's place—and the door. Then he described his shooting experiment of that afternoon, and his recent conversation with the detective-sergeant at the café.

At this point the nurse entered and motioned him to leave, which he did a moment afterwards, promising to see Martin on the morrow.

The gaol raid captured the imagination of the entire

Australian public. It would have terminated as a nine days' wonder had Austiline been recaptured; but it was prolonged much beyond that time, and the brilliant Johns-Oakes combination was helped or hindered by countless enthusiastic amateurs.

Reports poured on the police from people who swore they recognized the fugitive in places as far apart as Geelong and Broome. One man declared that she was a stewardess on a ship sailing to America and that she disembarked at San Francisco—resulting in much money being spent on cablegrams. But all to no avail. Austiline Thorpe remained hidden "in smoke."

Days and weeks passed with horrible monotony to one man most of all. Martin Sherwood recovered strength but slowly. In one respect the loss of his promised bride was of great benefit to him, because it kept him from brooding too much over his devastating affliction.

Sir Victor Lawrence was a constant visitor. He was one of the few such visitors to whom the popular editor of the *Tribune* at first was restricted. Although less constant, Detective-Sergeant Oakes was also a frequent and welcome caller. As Monty had stated, he was a baffling character. It was undoubted that his private liking for both Martin and the big man was sincere; it was undoubted, too, that in his official capacity he was as inhuman as Joubert in *Les Misérables*. His armour of vacuous indifference was always perfectly worn, being pervious only to the beady-eyed, sharp-tongued, yet lovable, Mrs. Montrose. Invariably she turned him inside out. Reading him as an open book, she dragged out of him the clues he and Johns had found, their deductions from them, their hopes and their plans; praising him one minute, scolding him the next, tactful always, making him fear her and yet regard her with respectful affection.

Hill, alias Bent Nose, with several others, they were obliged to release from prison, since nothing could be proved against any one of them. The detective-sergeant had decided to keep his eye on Bent Nose especially, and was both mystified and angry when Bent Nose disappeared from human ken, not even his wife knowing his whereabouts, or pretending that she did not know.

And then came Christmas Day, and with it the breeze which began to blow away the black clouds of Monty Sherwood's imagined sky. The breeze was inaugurated by Detective-

Sergeant Oakes himself. They were eating their Christmas dinner on the veranda, for the day had been quiet and hot, when the garden-gate opened to admit a dark figure and a moment later the detective-sergeant entered the radius of lamp-light whose centre was the table.

"Why, it is the dear old Sexton Blake himself!" Monty cried, jumping up and piloting Oakes to a chair.

"I have some news for you," said the detective-sergeant, with absolute vacuity of expression.

"Oh! I hope it is not bad news, Mr. Oakes," Mary murmured, with assumed brightness in her voice, but indicating to him Martin, who was sitting very upright, his face strained with sudden anxiety.

"I am afraid it *is* bad news—for me," replied the detective.

"How so?" demanded the bushman, with a trace of excitement in his drawling voice.

"You'll promise not to rub it in too much after I have told you?"

"Yes! yes! yes!"

"You especially, Mrs. Montrose?"

"I will decide when I have heard the news."

"Well, last night in Flinders Street a man was knocked down by a motor-car."

A disappointed "Oh!" from Mary.

"Not your old pal, Bent Nose?" Monty asked.

"No—not Bent Nose," the detective-sergeant replied with a faint smile. "The man's name is John Travers, and he died at the General Hospital at ten-twenty-four this morning. Before he died he sent for the police and made a confession. Really, you will promise——"

"Go on, man!" Mrs. Montrose almost screamed.

Again the faint smile came into the face of the Sphinx. One could imagine him saying: "Have you a match?" when he brought out his climax:

"The man Travers confessed to the murder of Peterson, the blackmailer!"

CHAPTER IX

A WORM THAT TURNED

THE news was so astounding that no one spoke for fully sixty seconds. Even the old lady was temporarily stunned. And then Monty Sherwood was on his feet with beaming face and pump-handling the faintly-smiling detective with all his might.

"My wonderful, dear old George Gale!" he roared. "I told Mrs. Webster once that I would end up by liking you. Real men and me get on well. I'm glad to know you."

"Give the real man a glass of wine, Monty—he deserves it," commanded Mrs. Montrose. "Set him a place, Mary. I know he came to get something to eat."

"Thank you, but no!" the detective-sergeant said softly. "I am a poor harassed husband and father. My three children would combine with my wife to make things jolly unpleasant if I didn't turn up at their Christmas feed. Not only that, but I am expected to consume an enormous quantity of each course, afterwards become a mettlesome steed, and finally put them to sleep with some of my fiercest detective stories."

"Well, if you won't eat, what about a drink?" inquired the big man.

"Thank you!" said Oakes once more. "A glass of beer, if you have it."

"Too true," agreed the happy Monty.

"Mr. Oakes, tell us about the confession," ordered Mrs. Montrose.

"The document itself is quite long, but the details of the man's story can be put shortly and are absolutely convincing," the visitor obediently drawled. "It appears that Travers also was a victim of the blackmailer, who by the way rented an office in the lower part of Little Burke Street and described himself as a Business Agent. Travers said that he went to this office at two o'clock on the day before the murder with fifty pounds as hush-money, taken from his employer's safe for the purpose.

"The money paid, he left the office at the moment Miss Thorpe was about to enter it, holding open the door to allow her to pass, and closing it as he thought. Happening to glance back, he saw that the door was just ajar, and, creeping to it, overheard the following conversation:

" 'I received your letter, Mr. Peterson,' he heard Miss Thorpe say haughtily. 'What is your demand now?'

" 'I understand by this morning's paper that you are to be married on Wednesday next,' Peterson said. 'As I am financially embarrassed just now, I am prepared, in consideration of your marriage, to hand over to you all the documents relating to your affair on payment of two hundred pounds.'

" '*All* the documents?' asked Miss Thorpe, stressing the first word.

"Peterson nodded, saying:

" 'All of them. I will call on you at the Flinders Hotel to-morrow afternoon at a quarter to four, when our final business will be transacted.'

"With a shrug of her shoulders, Miss Thorpe turned to the door, whereupon John Travers hurried away. He said that he walked about all that afternoon, wondering what action his employer would take when the money was missed from the safe.

"He went on to say that in the middle of the night he decided to call on Miss Thorpe at three-thirty, and by any means obtain a quarter of the money she would then have with her with which to pay the blackmailer. That would give his a chance to replace the money he had stolen before it was missed.

"Which of the chambermaids he was related to we do not know, and he would not say: but, through her connivance, he was let into Miss Thorpe's suite at exactly half-past three. The tenant was not there, neither was her maid, whose absence was known, and John Travers turned burglar. If he could lay his hands on the money before Miss Thorpe returned, all the better.

"But in that he failed. He was in the bedroom when the corridor bell rang. It rang when he was examining Miss Thorpe's revolver, which he had found in a drawer of her dressing-table. Feeling, I suppose, much like a rat in a wire-trap, he crept to the bedroom door, and, when just closing it, heard a key slipped into the lock of the outer door, saw the door open and Peterson enter. Peterson closed the door after him, pocketed the skeleton-key, and walked into the drawing-room. Travers's chance of obtaining any of the hypothetical two hundred sank to zero.

"The man was faced by ruin final and complete, through the efforts of a lifetime being drained away by the bloodsucker in the next room.

"For a long time, so Travers said, he waited, thinking what he should do, as he stood by the partly-opened bedroom door. It was quite upon impulse, which came to him in a flash, that he decided to shoot the blackmailer.

"Opening wide the door, he was preparing to rush into the next room, when another key was thrust into the lock of the hall door which opened to admit Miss Thorpe just as Travers, drawing back, all but closed the bedroom door. When he saw her pass into the drawing-room he stepped into the hall.

"From the drawing-room doorway he saw Peterson standing near the table, just beyond Miss Thorpe, then standing with the left side of her face partly obscuring Travers's view of Peterson. At this stage we were careful to have the confession perfectly clear. Travers saw that Peterson saw him. There was no time to spare then, no time to get Miss Thorpe out of danger. Travers saw the notes thrown on the table, he saw Peterson's hand go out to pick them up, when he fired with the result we know. That is about all."

"No, not quite all," contradicted Mrs. Montrose sharply. "How did he cross the veranda without leaving any foot-prints?"

The detective-sergeant sighed.

"Remember that you promised not to rub it in too much," he said half-mockingly.

"Go on!" ordered the old lady severely.

"Well, he never crossed the veranda at all," came the cool voice.

"Then how did he get out of the room?" Monty demanded.

"He never left the room."

"What!" they chorused.

"He never left the room at all," the detective-sergeant repeated, fully enjoying the effect of his bomb. "He says that he opened the French windows to effect an escape, realized how he would be seen by hundreds of people, probably including a policeman or two, if he climbed the veranda railings and, crossing the strip of lawn, jumped down into the street. No, he did not attempt it. Turning round, he saw Miss Thorpe standing with her back to him. He heard voices in the hall. You remember that a chiffonier stood across one corner of the room, near the French windows: it was behind that he hid."

"And you never looked there?" Mrs. Montrose said accusingly.

"Not until the following morning, when we made a thorough examination of the room. Let me tell you why I believed Miss Thorpe shot Peterson. There were three witnesses who stated that they found Miss Thorpe standing near a shot man, and holding a revolver from which one cartridge had been fired. The man was dead, and the revolver belonged to Miss Thorpe.

"I induced Miss Thorpe, you remember, to occupy the exact place she did when—as she said—a man fired from the doorway killing Peterson. I took up Peterson's position under Miss Thorpe's direction, and, when looking at the door, I saw that any one firing from there would do so only by placing Miss Thorpe in great danger of being hit.

"In the first place, it was not Miss Thorpe but the black-mailer who was the intended victim. In the second place, the shot was fired from a distance of twenty-eight feet, and the bullet must have passed Miss Thorpe's face within three or four inches at most. Thirdly, one man intent on killing another wouldn't run the risk of missing his victim: he would have made more certain by rushing forward, sweeping aside Miss Thorpe, and firing at hardly more than five feet.

"And then, after Miss Thorpe's deliberate statement that the murderer left by the window, on examining the veranda we found no human tracks on the dusty floor, only those of a cat made some time previously: to my mind, and I think to the mind of any reasoning man, there was left no room for doubt that Miss Thorpe herself had fired the fatal shot."

"I do not blame you, Oakes," softly interjected the blind man, who had been a silent but absorbed listener hitherto. "My reason told me that Austiline must have done it; my heart refused to believe her capable of so atrocious an act."

The detective-sergeant sighed again and said:

"It is the most peculiar set of circumstances I ever had to deal with. In our profession one must reason on the law of averages. That Travers was an expert shot we learned only to-day, he having won many prizes for revolver-shooting. He was far above the average gunman, so took the risk without hesitation. If Miss Thorpe had not been so emphatic that the man escaped by the window, if she had stated the nature of the blackmail, if she had been uncertain of the position she occupied when the shot was fired, I would have examined the veranda with a more open mind, and would at least have examined the room at once instead of leaving it till later and giving Travers a chance to walk out of the window after dark.

"Believe me, although I would adopt the same course in a similar case, I sincerely regret that Miss Thorpe should have been played so scurvy a trick by fate. Here is the sum of one hundred and fifty pounds, the amount found on Travers when he entered the hospital. The remaining fifty pounds he evidently put back in place of the amount he stole from his employers. To-morrow I will hand the money to Miss Thorpe's solicitors.

"But here I have something which I am going to ask you, Mr. Martin Sherwood, to hold in trust for Miss Thorpe," the detective-sergeant went on, taking from his pocket a bulky envelope. "When the lady comes out of smoke, which naturally she will do directly Travers's confession is broadcast, give it her with my compliments. On the envelope in Peterson's handwriting are the words: '*Re* A. Thorpe'."

Martin took it, saying:

"What does this mean, Oakes?"

"I found it on the body of Peterson," the detective-sergeant explained. "Without doubt it contains the documents she was to have received in exchange for her two hundred pounds. As she told us that she was being blackmailed by Peterson, I refrained from opening the sealed envelope and learning the nature of the blackmail, for the simple reason that the nature of the blackmail had nothing to do with the fact of blackmail itself. I hope my not having read the envelope's contents and my having returned it intact will help me a little for the inconvenience Miss Thorpe has been caused."

The detective pushed back his chair and rose to his feet, followed by Monty and Mary. He said to Monty:

"Do you know who carried out the gaol-raid?"

"No. I wish I did."

"Why?"

"Because I would divide a thousand pounds among those

who carried it out," the bushman drawled with a smile. "When possible I always encourage good work."

The detective-sergeant's smile was bleak. Mrs. Montrose gurgled.

"Oh, Monty!"

"Why not pay out a portion to Bent Nose?" came the artful question.

"I leave his reward to you," Monty replied, his eyes twinkling. "You owe him compensation for false arrest, you know."

The visitor sighed. Stepping off the low veranda, he said:

"I am as yet not quite sure that Bent Nose was arrested without very good cause. Good night, everyone! When Miss Thorpe comes out of smoke, advise her to live a retired life in the country for a little while. Escaping custody is a crime, in spite of the fact that it is as natural to escape custody—given the chance—as to breathe. Again, good night and a Happy Christmas!"

He left with Monty escorting him to the gate. Mary Webster reseated herself next the blind man, saying to him:

"Austiline will come soon now, Martin. Aren't you happy?"

"I am very happy to know that the law absolves her from that terrible crime," he replied, with strange slowness of speech. "But I shall never forgive myself for half-believing she did it. I don't think she will forgive me either."

"Oh, but Martin, she will!" Mary said earnestly. "She could never blame you for thinking as all of us but Monty thought in face of such evidence. She will certainly come as soon as she reads John Travers's published confession."

.   .   .   .

But the weeks went by and January went out in a grilling heat wave, which prostrated old Mrs. Montrose; but Austiline did not come, nor did they receive any news of her. Sir Victor, through his paper, offered a reward of five hundred pounds for news of her. Oakes and Johns, still on the trail of the gaol-breakers, were unflagging in their energies. But all to no purpose.

CHAPTER X

ONE day in mid-February the big man took Martin to the great eye specialist for the third time, and for the third time the specialist said he could do nothing—only hope. Severe shock or intense excitement might restore activity to the paralysed nerves. In the street again, after the interview, Monty told his brother the result.

"Don't worry, Monty," the blind man said softly on their way to Princes Bridge. "Don't worry. It doesn't really matter. Nothing matters. God! I wish I were dead."

"Stop it, Martin!" the big man commanded, with sternness in his voice and mistiness in his eyes.

And then suddenly the mistiness vanished from two blazing orbs; for across the road, on what is known as Cathedral Corner, he saw Bent Nose—Bent Nose, who on his release from detention as a suspected person had vanished from his usual haunts, and whose whereabouts had become as speculative as Austiline's.

Martin felt the big man's hand tighten upon his arm, felt himself pulled violently to the left, felt his arms forcibly wound round a veranda-post.

"Stay there! Don't move till I come back," he heard Monty snap. Infected by the bushman's excitement, Martin clung to the steel post as a drowning seaman to a boat's gunwale, somewhat bewildered by the roar of the traffic before him, the sound of hurrying feet, and the hum of voices behind him. A passing car splashed him with liquid mud. Every discordant sound he heard distinctly; hundreds of human voices, but never the one voice of the one woman whom he was thrilled with the hope that Monty would bring to him.

As for Monty, he escaped several violent deaths in his wild dash across the road, heedless of the yells of drivers and an indignant policeman on traffic duty. Bent Nose saw him coming, looked about for an avenue of escape, saw none, and met the big man with a crooked smile.

"Bent Nose, for a million!" Monty gasped.

"Yaas, yous right," the man drawled with a Fitzroy accent not unlike a native of East London. "Wot abart it?"

"I've been looking for you for weeks, old son."

"I know that."

"Know it! Then why in hell didn't you let yourself be found?"

"I've 'ad enough barny over Mr. Martin's little affair, wivout wantin' any more."

"Now see here, Bent Nose," Monty said earnestly. "You did my brother and a certain lady a wonderful good turn not so long ago, and my brother feels he owes you something for it."

"No, 'e don't," Bent Nose asserted emphatically. "I owed 'im more'n ever I thought I could pay back. But the chance came, and I took it. 'Im and 'is clinah and me is quits."

"Maybe, but you can still do another good turn, old lad," Monty went on. "Knowing what was going to happen on a certain night before it did happen, you probably can tell me why a certain lady stops in smoke when she can come back without fear. You tell me where she is, and you're on to a cool hundred quidlets. Get me?"

"Yaas, I get you." Bent Nose, gaunt and pale, regarded the big man stubbornly. "But I don't want no 'undred quids, and I ain't selling yous no information. I ain't even giving yous no information at all."

Monty, seeing the look of fixed purpose in the small black eyes glaring at him almost fiercely, changed his tactics.

"Don't say that, Bent Nose," he implored, feeling that he would like to pick up the man and shake him till he yelled out all he knew, which might be nothing or much. "Miss Thorpe means a devil of a lot to my blind brother. She doesn't come to him, so it is up to me to know what's keeping her."

"I'm dead sorry he lorst 'is sight, Mr. Sherwood, straight I am," the man said seriously. "But I durn't say nothing. I've been on the square for a year and a 'arf now. I've got a wife and baby boy to think of. I 'elped to get 'is clinah out of quod for what she and 'im done for me. We're all quits. The blokes on that job don't like me any better for turning honest. If I was to blow the gaff, all of 'em would just love to frame up a job to get me put away for years."

"You needn't fear that," said Monty. "Mr. Oakes, I'm sure, would see that everything was right."

" 'E might and 'e mightn't. Anyway I'm keepin' mum."

Monty looked at him steadily. He played his last card carefully. Holding the man's arm, he turned him round and pointed across the street to Martin, who with his arm encircling the veranda-post was facing the traffic, his white face tilted up in an attitude of listening, his sightless eyes wide and vacant. Said Monty:

"When you were down and out, Bent Nose, that man over there lifted you up to the position of a decent man. He gave you a job which gained for you a home, a wife, and a baby. Bent Nose, I reckon it's your deal."

"S'truth! By Gawd!" the gaunt man whispered as though to himself. Then suddenly he swung round and glared up at Monty. "Yous think I'm forgetting abart me job and me missus and me little boy, don't yous? Well, I'm telling yous that it's 'cos I don't forget 'em that I'm afraid. Yous seem to think that gents in kid gloves pulled orf that raid. Yous think, don't yer, they're all Sunday School teachers? I tell yous where Miss Thorpe is; and wot's going to 'appen to me missus and the kid? Yous don't know. By Gawd, *I* do! I'm going to lie in a bleeding corfin."

"Not you! You're going to live happily ever after."

"I don't think! You promise on yer dying oath to look after me missus and kid for the rest o' their lives, and I'll chance a lump o' lead. Wot abart it?"

Monty saw that Bent Nose was in terrible earnest. Involuntarily he experienced a thrill of admiration when he realized that to do his benefactor yet a further service this gutter-rat, this flotsam of humanity, who had tasted but one year of happiness in all his life, was prepared to suffer violent injury, perhaps death. Yet the big man's voice was quite steady when he said:

"I'm a man of my word, Bent Nose. Your wife and child shall be well provided for, if your late mates get you. And if they do get you, trust me, I'll get them. Now, where is Miss Thorpe?"

"She's within a 'undred miles of Lake Moonba, in South Australia. Now let me go, damn yer!" And, wrenching himself free from the big man, he darted along the Yarra Embankment and dived into an alley near the Majestic Theatre.

Monty gazed after him with a look on his face as near blank

surprise as ever had been there. Lake Moonba in South Australia! Bent Nose might just as well have said the South Pole. It would have been as likely a locality as Lake Moonba in which to find Austiline Thorpe. When he rejoined Martin the blind man almost screamed with excitement:

"Have you found her, Monty?"

A fat man with gimlet eyes, evidently waiting for a tram, edged a little nearer to them.

"Yes, or next to it—I've learned where she is to be found, old son," Monty replied triumphantly.

"Where? For heaven's sake tell me where."

"She's near Lake Moonba in South Australia."

"Where's that?"

"Well up in the Northwest Corner. Come along! I see our tram coming."

Together they crossed the street, the fat man with the gimlet eyes watching them till they boarded a Prahan tram. Then he walked quickly to the nearest telegraph-office, where he wrote on a form which he handed to the clerk:

"B.N. given location of A.T. to M.S. Abe." This was addressed to "Smythe, 14, Wright Street, Adelaide."

There was little opportunity on the tram to converse about the momentous information dragged from a reluctant Bent Nose; and, when eventually they reached the house in the walled-in garden, Mary Webster hurried to meet them. Smiling bewitchingly at the big man, she said softly:

"Tell me, Martin, what did the specialist say?"

She saw his face cloud and hope fled from hers.

"He said he was afraid he could do nothing for me," Martin said quietly. "He thinks that some shock or great excitement might restore my sight."

"Oh, Martin!" Her voice held a little tremble which he detected. He said:

"Don't you grieve, Mary. If my hopes have been smashed in that direction, they have been raised in another. Monty saw and spoke with Hill."

"Bent Nose! Really?"

Her grey eyes flashed to Monty, who was smiling.

"Yes, really," he echoed. "Let us go inside, and then I can tell you and your mother what poor old Bent Nose said. As Dr. Goodhart says, 'Lead on, Mrs. Macduff!'"

"Well, well, well!" was the old lady's reception of the news. "Now, what is to be made of that?"

"Well, it beats me," confessed Monty, stirring his tea and passing Mary the cucumber sandwiches. "I know the country round about Lake Moonba better than the back of my hand, and reckon it's the most God-forsaken part of the whole of South Australia."

"Aren't there any townships there?" Martin asked.

"It is what is called open country—that is, country unoccupied by either squatters or settlers," Monty answered. "I travelled through it about six years ago with a mob of store cattle. There was a sort of house near Lake Moonba, built by a man who tried running cattle in open country. But he had been dead some time, and the house was falling down."

"What is the nearest place to it?" the old lady asked sharply.

"Innaminka township, about sixty miles north."

"It seems a likely place for any one to live at who wanted to escape the law. Is there a police barracks anywhere near?"

"Barracks? Lord, no!" replied Monty, looking keenly at the old lady. "Say, what's on your mind, Mrs. Montrose?"

The invalid, sitting erect in her chair, a lace cap set on her snow-white hair, smiled at him sweetly, her small beady eyes sparkling. Her voice was firm and clear.

"Nearly every day, for ten long years, Monty, I have sat in this chair with nothing to occupy me but reading a little and thinking much. I have had much food for thought these last five months.

"My outlook on life has been moulded to a great extent by my dear husband, and my thoughts have been coloured by his. He was an explorer when he courted me and Chief Commissioner of Police soon after we were married. Even before the Commissionership came to him he was a great student of criminology. He used to say that if he committed a big crime he would not hide in the slums of a city, but in the very heart of the wilds.

"To me it is very evident that the gang which rescued Austiline is an under-world organization directed by very clever men. What their motive was in rescuing her I cannot guess. It might have been on account of her wealth; but I doubt that, because the murderers Earle and Mallowing, and the murderesses Hogan and Jonas—who also have vanished without trace within the last two or three years—were quite poor people. I have a theory—and I have never yet seen it discussed in the papers or heard it mentioned by the wonderfully sagacious Mr. Oakes—that the disappearance of all these takers of human life—with others whose names I cannot recall now—is due to one and the same cause."

"What do you mean, Mrs. Montrose?" Martin asked.

"I mean that I think the one organization has accounted for the disappearance of quite a number of murderers since the war," came the silvery voice. "I am only an old, useless, invalid woman, but I dream my dreams."

The big man gazed at her across the table with parted lips, an expression akin to idolatry on his rugged face. Then, at a thought which flashed into his keen eyes, he smiled slowly. But what he said was not the thought.

"You leave Oakes at the starting-post," he said.

"There is logic in your argument, Mrs. Montrose," Martin said in his quick way. "But after Travers's confession, which was broadcast, why should they keep her, if they don't want her money for the service they rendered?"

"Well, since she is proved not to be a murderess, they have no hold over her now, and probably they daren't let her go, Martin."

"Good God! Do you think she is in danger?" the blind man exclaimed.

"Hardly that," the old lady said calmly. "But I certainly think Monty might go up where Bent Nose said and prospect about a little."

"I'll go with him," Martin said determinedly.

"Martin! you couldn't," Mary put in.

"Better stay with us, Martin. Leave it to Monty," Mrs. Montrose advised. "In spite of our logic and Hill's information, Monty may have a wild-goose chase."

"If Monty goes into that open country to search for my promised wife, I go with him. If he won't take me, I'll hire a couple of black trackers to take the place of my sight, and go without him."

The decision was announced without excitement, but with a determination that made itself felt. The women looked at Monty and he at them. They saw him answer their appeal with a slow shake of the head; and then, his eyes softening marvellously, he laid one hand affectionately on Martin's shoulder, saying:

"We'll both go. We'll leave to-morrow evening by the express for Adelaide, and then by rail to Broken Hill. From there we'll take a car to Turrowangee, where in a good paddock are my camels. With them we'll hike north to Yandama Station, west to Tilsha, and north again to Lake Moonba, where we'll comb that blessed open country so fine that a jew-lizard won't escape us."

Mother and daughter continued trying to dissuade the blind man from an adventure which both realized would be arduous even for a man of Monty's stamina. It surprised them that Monty did not associate himself with their objections.

Yet Monty had reasons, shrewd reasons. Pressed down by the double weight of blindness and the loss of a dear one, Martin Sherwood in those few months of summer had changed a very great deal. Hitherto always quiet and gentle, patient and exceedingly sympathetic, in spite of the crowded years spent in the editorial chair of *The Daily Tribune*, bursts of ungovernable temper, usually directed against his harsh fate, followed by days of morose silence, so changed him that his intimate friends greatly feared for his sanity.

It was with thankfulness that Monty Sherwood welcomed the chance of action. Constant movement, hardship, and hope ever present of reaching a definite goal, would help Martin, he felt sure, to regain his mental balance. Should wise old Mrs. Montrose have guessed the truth concerning Austiline's continued absence, then stirring times might be expected in the near future. And had not the specialist said that excitement might restore Martin's sight?

It was a night for the fairies when he and Mary walked slowly to the gate, while he told her of his hopes and his plans. The moon was full and the shadow cast by the almond tree was inky black. The creepers on the old stone wall held out appealing arms as though to stay them in their flower-scented paradise.

"How long do you think you will be away, Monty?" Mary asked, trying hard to keep her voice steady.

"Dunno, Mary," he said softly. "You see, it will depend on quite a lot of things. It will be all of a fortnight before we strike 'The Corner' of New South Wales. We'll jump off at Minter's selection, where I will dispatch our last letters. After that it will depend on the state of the water-holes, for one thing."

"But you will let us know directly you can what success you've had, won't you? You see, Mother has grown quite attached to Martin, and she will worry ever so."

She was looking up at him while he stood with one hand on the gate-latch, trying hard to smother the ache in her heart and keep from her eyes that tell-tale light. The moon showed her slender yet matured figure clothed in white. It showed the pulse at the base of her throat beating wildly. And then Monty knew, and for the first time in his life trembled.

"And you, I suppose, will not worry?" he asked with assumed carelessness.

"Oh! but I shall, Monty," she whispered.

"For Martin or for me, Mary?"

"For you both."

For a moment he looked steadily into her eyes.

"Which one of us do you love, Mary?" he said.

His voice was very gentle. She saw come into his blue eyes sudden resolution to have a simple question simply answered. She saw, too, that which she had almost given up hope of ever seeing. When she spoke her voice sounded like a sigh of wondrous content. Swaying ever so slightly towards him, she said:

"Can't you guess, Monty?"

And then she was in his mighty arms.

CHAPTER XI

A LOVER OF CATS

THE big man and Martin Sherwood did not leave Melbourne unobserved. Martin escorted his blind brother to a seat in the railway-station, and left him whilst he went after tickets and sleeping-berths. The fat man with the gimlet eyes was behind Monty at the booking-office window, and booked also for Adelaide. It was without surprise that, on returning to Martin, Monty found him in conversation with Detective-Sergeant Oakes, who seemed to have a knack of turning up on any and every occasion, although it was a positive fact that he had stopped the shadowing of Monty. Nodding coolly to Oakes, he said.

"What are you arresting Martin for?"

"I was telling him that his protégé, William Hill, *alias* Bent Nose, was discovered last night in a mean street at Fitzroy suffering from bullet-wounds," Oakes said with his usual blandness. "The doctors found one bullet in his groin, another near his left lung, and yet a third which passed almost through his shoulder. Some one was keen on getting Bent Nose."

"Apparently. Where is he now?"

"In the Melbourne Hospital. He might live. The word 'might' is the doctor's own."

Martin said nothing. Monty was pensive. The detective-sergeant regarded the fat man with the gimlet eyes hurrying to the barrier with the speculative interest of a student of physiognomy, for so far he had not met "Abe" professionally. Also he was wondering why the brothers were going to Adelaide.

"See here, my romantic Nelson Lee," Monty drawled, looking up, "I am going to treat you as a man just now, and not as a human bloodhound. I am taking Martin with me on a prospecting trip away up in South Australia, hoping that the dry heat and constant movement will quicken his progress

86

to complete health. Our arrangements being all made, we cannot now well delay, even if a dozen Bent Noses have been shot up. However, as you are aware, Hill is a kind of ward of Martin's, and his wife was Miss Thorpe's cook at one time. I am going to write you out a cheque for two hundred pounds, and I am going to ask you, my dear old sleuth, to pay Mrs. Bent Nose four pounds every Saturday morning, and to see that no expense is spared in saving Hill's life. I'll keep in touch with you when possible, and you can let me know how things go."

"Your interest in Bent Nose is amazing," murmured Oakes, casually watching the bushman filling in a cheque.

"There you are mistaken, my dear friend-enemy," Monty replied, tearing the cheque out of his book. "You can't expect Martin to write cheques properly, and no one seems to know where Miss Thorpe can be found. So long!"

He rose, holding out his hand.

"Well, well, I'll do my best," Oakes said, rising also with Martin. "I'll do my best for the Hills. Good-bye! It is possible we may all meet again sooner than you expect. Give my regards to Miss Thorpe."

It was absolutely a shot in the dark—and it missed. There was not a trace of any change in Monty's face when he said over his shoulder on his way with Martin to the barrier:

"Righto, old lad! I am sure she will be pleased to know you remember her kindly. When you go out, you mind the steps. You'll be breaking your neck one of these days."

Detective Oakes's chance shot exercised the minds of both Monty and Martin for some considerable time during the journey to Adelaide. They wondered how much or how little the detective-sergeant knew. As for Oakes, he tried to guess the purpose underlying Monty's prospecting trip and the reason of the big man's generous provision for Mrs. Hill. But what were his actual deductions no one ever knew. He did, however, saunter along to the Government Tourist Bureau and dispatch several lengthy telegrams.

Gimlet-eyes, who had acquainted himself with the exact position of the brothers in the train, made sure of being near them when they alighted at the Central Station, Adelaide. He heard the big man direct a porter to put the luggage in the cloak-room and ask the man the time the Broken Hill express was due to leave that night. Apparently that was the information he had travelled to Adelaide to obtain, for from the station he sent a telegram to "Smythe, 14, Wright Street, Adelaide," reading: "Sherwoods leaving Adelaide to-night for Broken Hill. Abe."

He left by the Melbourne express some time before the Broken Hill train pulled out.

At nine the following morning the blind man was guided by Monty out of Sulphide Street Station, Broken Hill, across the road to the Masonic Hotel. And, standing outside the hotel, was the very man Monty had held only a remote hope of meeting.

"Strike me dead, if it ain't ole Monty Sherwood!" roared the huge bearded giant who dashed off the hotel veranda to meet them. "Good ole Monty! How the flamin' hell are yous?"

The big man's eyes twinkled with humour when they regarded the hairy, sun-blackened face and the equally hairy sun-blackened hand held out in greeting. Past experience of shaking hands with Mr. Henry Watkins, otherwise known as Squeezem Harry, warned him how not to accept the bearded man's terrible grip. For a moment the two giants stood with hands clasped, squeezing with tremendous pressure, neither wincing, both grinning broadly.

"Adelaide ain't done no harm to your muscle, Monty," Squeezem Harry said when their hands fell apart.

"Apparently not," Monty agreed. "This is my brother Martin."

"Pleased-ter-meet-cher," welcomed the bearded one.

"Thank you! I, too, am delighted to meet a friend of Monty's. I can't see, but your voice tells me you're honest."

"Honest! Hark at 'im, Monty!" Squeezem roared. "If you seen me and Monty knock over a bullock or two for a feed, you wouldn't say that. What-erbout-er-drink?"

"After breakfast, if you don't mind," Martin decided.

"Yes; give us a chance, Harry," pleaded Monty. "We're heading for a feed just now. And then, after a sleep, we want to talk friendly with you."

"Righto! I'm going down the street to see a bloke about a dog. See you later. Hooroo!"

The big man laughed softly when viewing the towering figure from the rear. Meeting Mr. Henry Watkins was like getting back home after a long absence, for Mr. Henry Watkins had been his partner on many a prospecting expedition; an invaluable partner, too, for what Squeezem Harry had forgotten about geology was the total knowledge possessed by many so-called geologists.

That evening the three men sat on the hotel veranda facing one of the richest lines of lode in the world. The sun had set, but the air was heavy and temperature ran high. The ceaseless roar of the crushers beat upon the ears, but the noise which was irritating to Martin Sherwood was music divine to Squeezem Harry and a "homy" sound to Monty.

"Where you been these last twelve months, Harry?" Monty asked when he had his pipe properly alight.

"I bin dogging round Lake Frome," Squeezem Harry replied, stretching his enormous legs across the concrete flooring. "Yep, an' I didn't do too bad neither. I got two hundred and sixty-odd scalps in nine months, and traded with the blacks for nearly four hundred more. What with them and close on two hundred fox pelts I didn't do so bad. Still, when I've finished this yer jag, I'll be as if I never went dogging in me life."

"Why don't you go in for saving? You'll be getting old in twenty years' time," Martin urged in his gentle way.

"Naw—naw, yous don't!" Harry countered quickly. "Old age don't worry me. Not it. I've always earned good money—more'n good money sometimes; and I've had a danged good time spending of it. What! Save me money for the blasted Government to grab and spend on tours round Europe! Not if I know it. When I throw a seven (die), I won't have a zac about me."

In the deepening dusk Monty smiled happily. Squeezem Harry was the most likable man in the world, a man absolutely free from cares and ties of any sort; the kind of man whose motto appeared to be: "Here's joy to-day, and to hell with to-morrow!"

Which motto is, perhaps, that of ninety-nine bushmen out of every hundred; for the bush is a kind mother, and those who live within her bosom are kind people. In all likelihood Squeezem Harry would stay in Broken Hill, living on credit, long after he had parted with his last note; eventually to roll his swag and walk north again to knock up another cheque. That would be looked upon as quite the correct thing.

"Naw, naw! What yous kicking up such a shine for?" the bearded giant admonished in a soft voice; and Martin, who had never prospected with Squeezem Harry, was surprised to hear a plaintive "miou" at his side. "M'yes; just woke up, 'ave yer?" This to a half-grown white cat that wriggled out of his jacket-pocket. "I suppose youse reckons it's time for another feed, eh?"

"Are you talking to a cat?" Martin asked.

"You bet!" the giant answered seriously. "Let me introdoos yer to Judas Iscariot. He's me wife and kids and aunts and relations all rolled up in a bunch of fur. Picked him up afore Christmas in a dog-trap. Yo'll notice he's only got three hoofs."

"But do you carry it about with you?"

"Yep. 'E rides in me pocket, and when it's too hot to wear a jacket, then in me shirt," Mr. Henry Watkins explained, with more pride than the average newly-made father; adding: "I've 'ad lots of cats in me time. Haven't been without one for years. The pity of it is that they get that danged heavy that I've got to exchange 'em for a little kitten. And when that 'appens I shed more tears than 'ud be in the waterworks 'ere. Yesterday I took Judas to a quack to see if he couldn't squirt some stuff into 'im to stop 'im growing."

"And how did you get on?" asked the interested Martin, whilst Monty chuckled.

"Oh! the quack reckoned he could get some stuff what he called umscumzioidroid gland. Said it would cost thirty quid. I told him to get it quick, and give him 'arf his blood-money. Sooner pay than shed more water. Exhausting thing shedding tears in this dry climate."

The blind man laughed heartily, and Monty felt proud of the humorous imagination of his friend. Martin said:

"I suppose you are serious?"

"Serious! Of course I'm serious. Ain't I, Monty?"

"Yes, Harry, quite. I've never known Harry to be without a cat, Martin," the big man explained. "In fact, I was wondering which pocket the current cat would poke out of. By the way, Harry, what is the country like north of Lake Frome?"

"Dry—danged dry. Same as me. Wot-er-about-er-drink?" pleaded Mr. Henry Watkins.

"Not just yet," Monty evaded. "Any water in the lake?"

"A little in the north end. Mostly mud."

"And the feed?"

"No ground feed at all."

"No buckbush?"

"Buckbush all blown away."

"Humph! What's the feed like between Turrowangee and Tibooburra, Harry?"

"Patchy. There's a bit t'other side o' Fowler's Gap, and it's not bad around Cobham Lake. Thinking of going up that way?"

"Yep. I've got my camels at Turrowangee, and was wondering if it would be better to go up along the Border Fence instead of by the mail route."

"You'd certainly get more scrub. Here, Judas, you come here. Them blasted Afghan camel-drivers 'ave got all the feed eat out along the road. Where you making for, Monty?"

Monty was prepared for that question.

"Was thinking of making up to Innaminka," he said. "You see, my brother here has just recovered from a severe illness and I'm reckoning on a long dry trip doing him good. Say, Harry, do you remember that trip down from the Strzelecki Creek when we came across that house in open country? First time either of us knew it was there. The feller that lived there cut his throat afterwards."

"Yes, I remember," the bearded man said slowly. "Lemme see. Bloke there now called Anchor—William J. Anchor—mad as a fiddler's dog. Living there with a couple o' women and half a dozen blokes looking after pedigree cattle."

"Women, did you say? Describe 'em."

"No, you don't, Monty," admonished Mr. Henry Watkins, poking an iron-hard finger into Monty's ribs. "No—no, you don't, now. I'm surprised at you. At your age, too. Thought you 'ad more sense than go gallivanting around after women."

The big man grinned and his blue eyes softened. His eyes gave him away to the penetrating gaze of the cat-lover. Heaving a stupendous sigh, he said:

"I thought so, Monty. You're in love, sure. Now let me tell you this, Monty: directly a man gets tangled with a woman, it's good-night. He becomes an also-ran, a back-number, a has-been. To his fellow-men he's never more of any account. Instead of hearing: "Hullo, Monty! how the hell are yous?' you'll hear: 'Good day, Mr. Sherwood! and how's the wife and kids?' You take on respectability, but you lose respect, real men's respect. For heaven's sake, Monty, my old mate, get as drunk as Paddy at a wake! Booze is the only thing that'll cure you. Just you think, now. Think of all the glorious busts you've had, all the lovely arguments. Think again of squalling kids, and a wife with 'er hair done up in curling irons, or done off by the barber; of tax-collectors and all the other swindlers wot worry a man into the grave. Would you rather have a yowling woman at yer side in a stinking city, or hear the camel-bells on a quiet night in the bush while yous smoke yer bedtime pipe in peace, perfect peace? Yous think of all that, Monty. I'd sooner see yer take strychnine than a wife. Strychnine's quicker, and less painful."

The brothers seemed to find huge enjoyment in this homily, delivered with all the solemnity of the immortal Mr. Barlow in *The Fairchild Family*. In the gathering darkness Mr. Henry Watkins looked exceedingly perturbed.

"It's no laughing matter, Monty," he reproved. "Marriage is a funny thing. I've known blokes wot used to go on the drunk every year regular, until they got married. Then they changed. They cast their eyes up in the air as though lookin' for galahs in a box-tree, and smile like old Judas did when I found him in the trap, and tell you how wonderful love is. Bosh! Then, after a year at most, they're on the booze again. The year after that they're in the d.t.s., and the next year they are as stiff as a crutch and as cold as a dog's nose."

"Well, well! if you won't tell us of the women, at least describe this William J. Anchor," Monty said, between chuckles. "Is he dinkum mad?"

"Mad! Course he's mad," Squeezem Harry exploded. "They say he's an inventor and went up there to be safe from spies. Flies an aeroplane to Marree for his mail. Mad! Bet-cher-life he's mad. Going to pay 'im a visit?"

"Might do so on our way."

"Hum! Well, you have your squirt handy. Keeps dogs, does William J.—big dogs, biggest dogs I ever seed. They come at me, half a dozen of 'em, as I rode up to the house. William J. went terrible crook when I shot a couple of 'em stone dead. · Said I was the first caller in two years, and reckoned I was one too many. Ordered me orf the place. Would have walloped him one on the kisser, only I seed he had a hand on a gun in his pocket."

"Kind-hearted sort of man!"

"Most! I'll meet him one day in town, and I'll kick his boots up through his neck. Wot-er-about-er-drink?"

CHAPTER XII

THE LAND OF HOPE

TEN days later found the brothers in camp adjacent to the South Australian Border Fence on Quinyambie Station, approximately one hundred and sixty miles north of Broken Hill. In spite of the thoughtful attention lavished on the blind man at all times by his brother, Martin found those ten days a veritable nightmare of prolonged, disjointed fatigue.

The day they left the Silver City the shade temperature rose to 106 degrees at about three in the afternoon. Here, at Quinyambie Station, ten days later and in the last week of February, the mercury rose as high as 118 degrees in what little shade could be found. Dwellers in the Australian cities who fly to iced food and drinks should the weather become a little warm, have no more idea of the heat, the flies and the dust of the Northwest Corner of New South Wales in February than have the Esquimaux.

Politicians and motor-car explorers invariably shun "The Corner" during the summer months. Even the imaginative writers of immigration literature leave well alone and cultivate a blissful ignorance of the heat, dust-storms and pests which make Australia's central districts unfashionable for nine months in the year.

Martin, his muscles flabby and his blood thick and sluggish from many years of city life and a long illness, wondered often if he stood before the very gates of hell itself. The sun blistered red-raw his hands and neck. The cloud of flies which never left his head from dawn till dark, being kept at bay solely by a gauze fly-net, hummed so loudly that hearing was a hardship and speaking a labour. While the dust-storm that raged for eighteen hours, during which it was impossible to eat or smoke, or indeed to sleep, left its mark even on the axe-hewn face of the giant Monty.

Not for Martin's sake only did they travel between sunset

93

and sunrise. Monty knew that to attempt to journey during the heat of the day would be futile, because the camels would find the sandy ground so hot to their rubbery padded feet that they would refuse to move from the shade of a tree. And, if a camel makes up its mind, only a fool argues with it with whip or waddy. Like the elephant, the camel has an exceedingly good memory for its persecutors, with the accompaniment of poisonous teeth lining a vice-like jaw.

Monty saw to it that they travelled in all possible comfort, which is to say comfort as compared with the usual amenities of bush life so far beyond the railway. Their pack-bags bulged with tinned foods and dried vegetables; nevertheless, their bread was powder-bread baked in the hot ashes of a fire, and their meat was canned: for to keep meat fresh beyond a few hours in that heat is an impossibility.

On the tenth night out from Broken Hill they reached Starvation Lake, a large expanse of bone-dry country as flat as sheet-iron. Following the boundary-rider's pad along the New South Wales side of the six-foot wire-netted State Dividing Fence, Monty filled the six five-gallon water-drums and gave the camels a well-earned drink at the tank almost in the centre of the lake.

Towards dawn, having travelled a further ten miles, they came across the boundary-rider of that section of fence, working at night. It was really because of the rider's hearty welcome and pressing invitation to camp with him a day, that Monty decided to give his brother and the animals a longed-for rest.

"Just as well camp for a day or so," the tall, lean, sun-blackened boundary-rider suggested in the inimitable bush drawl. "Your mokes are watered and there is fair-conditioned mulga round here for them. It'll soon be daylight, so I'll boil the billy, and we'll have a feed afore them dratted flies get busy."

And when the flies woke up, which was before it was light enough to see them, the three men were sound asleep within their mosquito-nets which served as fly-nets, lying on canvas stretcher-beds to keep them off the ant-infested ground, with no covering over their pyjamas.

"There are no hot nights in Australia," wrote one famous traveller. Some town-planning expert must have told him that —he was never on the Border Fence in February.

Monty awoke about midday and rose at once to quench his

thirst from a hanging canvas water-bag. Martin and the
boundary-rider, who still slept soundly, missed the sight of
the big man facing southeast by south, the direction of
Melbourne, and smiling gently as though at some sweet memory.
When Martin did awake, Monty was reclining within his fly-
proof net smoking his appalling pipe.

"Want a drink, old lad?"

"Please, Monty. Phew! it *is* hot. Is it daylight?"

"Yes; just gone two o'clock," the big man replied, filling
a pint pannikin from the bag. Carefully raising the net to
exclude the ever-present flies, he passed the pannikin within.

Then, with his arm well shrouded by the net, he searched for
and found the blind man's cigarettes and matches.

For that was a part of Monty's work. Besides the cooking
and the usual camp fatigues, he was obliged to do all the
camel-tailing, or, in other words, hunt for and bring the beasts
back to camp preparatory to the night's march; do all the loading and unloading, and wait upon his afflicted brother even to
cutting up his food and pouring out his drink.

All the responsibility of the expedition fell upon his shoulders,
but, his shoulders being broad, he did not mind. When he
should have been taking his due proportion of rest he was
attending to Martin, which he minded less. It certainly was
a labour, but a labour of love.

Action, hardship, and hope, however, had dispelled the first
phase of Martin's affliction, as Monty had guessed would be
the case. Gone were the impatience, the moroseness, the
really terrible fits of temper. No complaints came from him
now. He was rapidly becoming his old gentle self, sympathetic
to those less fortunate, firm in his opinions, steadfast in his
loyalty. It was the mind rather than the body which had
attracted Austiline to him. It was his strength of mind,
united to a brilliant imagination, rather than his instinct for
business organization, itself no mean thing, which had caused
that canny judge of men, Sir Victor Lawrence, to push him
so rapidly up the ladder of newspaperdom.

Even his brother Monty was viewing him in a new light—a
light, nevertheless, not so new to Austiline or his many friends.
One little trick he brought out now which for long had been in
abeyance, and that was the slight drawing-down of the
extremities of his mouth when he was leading one to final
catastrophe in discussion, or when he was—in vulgar parlance
—pulling one's leg. But the nature of his blindness forbade

that expressive twinkle which he had in common with the big man.

This change in Martin was a source of never-ending gratification to Monty Sherwood. The words of the eye-specialist were constantly in his mind: "Severe shock or intense excitement might restore activity to the paralysed nerves." He lived in secret hope that their goal would provide the necessary shock or excitement. Mrs. Montrose had hinted at difficulties and dangers in the way finding Austiline and bringing her out of "smoke." Squeezem Harry's experience indicated their nature. Even common logic predicted them.

Why should Anchor, if he were only an inventor, settle in the heart of such a wilderness, when equal secrecy could be found within a few miles of a railway which could bring his supplies with economy and dispatch? If Anchor was a master criminal, the head of a great under-world organization for protecting criminals from justice, then Monty knew of no more desirable locality than Lake Moonba. The big man scented excitement as a dingo scents the blood of a beast slain by marauding blacks.

Martin dozed off again after a cigarette, and Monty had taken the smouldering butt from him for fear of fire. Outside the nets the flies kept up a monotonous drone. Sometimes a bell tinkled when one of the camels shook its head, and that occasional sound told Monty that the animals were camped in the shade, waiting patiently for the cool of the evening before they started feeding. Not till five o'clock did the boundary-rider stir, grunt, and roll out of his net to search for the water-bag.

"I bin on this blasted job now for nigh on two years without a spell," he informed Monty when he had drunk at least a gallon of water. "I'm finishing up at the end of next month, when it's me for Sydney with a four-hundred-pound cheque to spend on wine, women and pictures, and then more pictures, more women, and heaps more wine. I bin dreaming about it all for two long, blanky, lonely years."

"Not a bad place, Sydney, for a holiday," Monty agreed.

"Too right. But I'd want fifty quid a week to work there. Couldn't live there under. They tell me the price of booze has gone up something scandalous. Wish that sun would go down and send these flies to bed. I could do with a feed."

Hendry, as the man called himself, was a product of the wilderness. The glare of the sun had screwed his glittering eyes to mere points, the heat had roughened and cracked his skin to the semblance of old parchment. The lack of moisture in the atmosphere had made him lean; and constant labour on the very plainest of food had made him as hard as bloodwood.

Wilderness is a better name than bush for the really appalling country over which runs the Border Fence for nearly two hundred miles in a straight line. The bush country, farther east and south, is kind in its shade, soft in its colours, and homely. Here there was nothing, nothing but sand-hills divided by narrow flats, nothing but stunted dying mulga and needlewood trees, nothing but watercourses filled with blown sand, nothing but the great vermin-proof fence erected to keep back the migratory dingoes, rabbits, and emus from the pastoral country of New South Wales, and in places sometimes buried by the ever-moving sand. The deserts of North Africa are beautiful in placid death: here the wilderness is dreadful with the convulsions of the dying.

They lit a fire towards sunset and sat in its fragrant smoke to cheat the flies, and when it was dark Hendry put the billy on to boil for tea; and Monty, after serving his brother with a meagre ration of water with which to wash, produced tinned delicacies that made Hendry's eyes open wide.

"Say! are yous the Prime Minister?" inquired the boundary-rider.

"Not yet—but I may be lucky. My name's Sherwood, Monty Sherwood."

"*The* Monty! By cripes! I heard tell of yous. Pleased-ter-meet-cher! Where you bound for?"

"Going north for a little dogging."

"So-so. You should do well. There's plenty of dorgs on the South Aus. side of the fence. Prince Charlie brought in a couple 'undred scalps only last week. I'm getting a few along this section."

"Dry time bringing 'em down, I suppose?"

"You bet. They followed the scattered thunderstorms from the Strzelecki Creek and east from Lake Frome, and are having a gay old time on the cattle, which are dying in hundreds."

"Is it as dry as all that?" Martin asked.

"Yep. Had no rain since I bin on the job, bar thunderstorms at Christmas, which came at the wrong time. Up on Melloo Station they shot three thousand head to preserve what little scrub there was left, keeping only a handful of pedigree bulls and cows."

"Feed pretty scarce, eh?"

"Scarce, Monty, ain't the word. There ain't no ground feed at all," Hendry informed them, whilst making little cakes of baking-powder dough and frying them in smoking hot fat. "The country's as bare as the back of me 'and. Course there's mulga and needlewood, but it's almost dead."

The discussion over Hendry's flap-jacks and Monty's tinned beef, tinned asparagus and tinned fruit was mainly about bores and dams, water-holes and soakages, camel-feed and other very necessary information which a wise bushman invariably seeks; for stark tragedy lurks about a dust-dry water-hole when the traveller with empty drums relies for his life on water which has vanished.

The next morning Monty's six camels and the boundary-rider's three came shuffling in their hobbles to stand in the smoke of the camp-fire, like the men, to escape the tormenting flies.

"Dope's getting a bit stale," Hendry remarked, cutting a pipeful of tobacco preparatory to turning in.

"M'yes," the big man agreed. "Better treat them now."

So they nose-lined the beasts and smeared the hair about their eyes with a mixture of fat and kerosene; and, the treatment finished, the sagacious animals rose to their feet, held silent conference with their eyes, and decided to make at once for a patch of shade they preferred.

Camp was broken after sundown that evening, when the mercury was 106 degrees, and the Sherwoods parted with regret from the optimistic boundary-rider, who was going south that night to a sand-hill that needed his attention.

Animals, like humans, follow a path once it has been made, and, like man-made paths, the pads formed by cattle and camels are never straight. Following the pad made by the boundary-rider's camels, which twisted and turned over humped sand-hill and narrow flat, and always within a few yards of the great fence, they pushed northward at a walk all night, making only a midnight halt for "lunch."

Each night, travelling twenty-five to thirty miles, they passed a boundary-rider at work on some part of his twenty-one-mile section. Every day the sand moves. Unceasingly the men have to fight the sand to save the Border Fence from obliteration. It was when the main track from Yandama to

Tilsha Stations was reached that they passed through one of
the few gates into South Australia, reaching the homestead
of Tilsha on the last day of the month.

Here they were received with the universal bush welcome,
being urged to stay a day, or a week, or a month. They
stayed two days, warmly entertained by the news-hungry
community of five persons, who exacted promises that they
would return the same way.

From Tilsha Station they proceeded northward for some
thirty miles to a selector's house set amid serried ranks of
gigantic sand-dunes. Monty had never seen that drought-
stricken country so parched and barren of life. Here there
was no tank water. There was no water whatever between
Tilsha and the selection. When he was tailing the camels the
only tracks he saw were those of scorpions and one or two
jew-lizards. With the exception of crows and eagle-hawks
bird life had vanished. Animal life there was none.

At Minter's Selection they found the man and his wife on
the verge of ruin; but, nevertheless, were received cordially.
Luxuries and many necessities of life the Minters were
entirely without. They were without hope, without ambition,
although the woman pretended to hope. Mentally they were
dying like the stunted, withering scrub-trees.

Minter himself was a little dried-up man of fifty or there-
abouts. His face was a leathery mask, but his black eyes
were lively and keen. Martha, his wife, was tall and painfully
thin, a woman worn to a shadow by hardship and never-
ending labour. Like her hus' ind's, her complexion was burned
black, but behind her light-blue eyes was an expression of
wistfulness which struck Monty as pathetic, a light of both
tragedy and divine trust.

"It was bound to come, this drought," Minter remarked
whilst the guests sat with unaccustomed ease in roughly-
made but comfortable chairs on the tiny veranda of the
corrugated-iron house that evening. "Here's Martha and me
worked all our lives like niggers—to see our savings sink into
the ground as each beast lay down to die. For near twenty
years her and me flogged bullocks from the Hill to Tibooburra
with loading. We been in this back country all our lives. We
were born in it, and we'll die in it, but could we get a living
area of land well into New South Wales? Not on your life.
There's none to get. The squatters, who use about half their
holdings, have got all the land worth having.

"We took a chance here. Martha wanted for years and years a home of her own. And the palaver we had to put up to the South Aus. Government to get this bit of a selection here in country the big men wouldn't take as a gift was amazing. The lying swine tell the English people there is millions of acres of land to be had for development, when they know perfectly well there's none. They don't want 'em on the land; they want 'em working for small farmers at a quid a week, or walking the streets looking for a job, so that when a job does fall vacant the bloke what runs the fastest gets it. Land! Look at it! Nice sort of land, eh?"

The big man cut chips of tobacco off his plug with unwonted energy, and Martin sighed. They were aware, as every bushman is, of the terrible gnawing land-hunger existing in Australia. Martin at least understood the struggle going on between the land barons of the bush and the country farmer near the coast on the one side, and the army of homeless bush people on the other. The former have the land and want immigrated labour because it is cheap; the latter hate the immigrant because he competes in the over-stocked labour market and in the meagre land supply.

Men of vision, men of unsullied patriotic ambition, are crushed between the two; the blind man being but one of a little band with power to speak and gain a hearing. And now blindness had left that little band without a leader. He sighed again. Almost he could hear the woman's plaintive cry, reiterated for years: "I want a home, John. Oh, John! I want a home of my very own."

Minter gazed out moodily over the surrounding desolation. His wife, upright on her chair, her lean roughened hands laid listlessly on her lap, closed her eyes as though with pain.

"I thank God me and Martha was wise enough to have no children," said Minter a little fiercely.

Martin heard a chair pushed back, heard a stifled sob and hurrying footsteps run into the house; and those little sounds so eloquent of many a bush tragedy made him yearn to be able in some way to comfort this heroic woman. Minter swore. Then:

"There, there! I'm always saying something I shouldn't," he said; and Monty, to cover an awkward break, asked him what the country was like farther north.

"About the same as this right away to Birdsville," answered Minter, rousing himself from his lethargic depression. "There is no water in the Strzelecki. Your best route is to travel due north from here for about thirty miles, when you'll come to a creek. I know for sure there's water in a fair-sized hole in a bend beneath a high sand-hill. You can't miss the sand-hill, 'cos it's higher than the others and can be seen for miles. You ought to get some dogs there. Then sixty miles northwest by north from there you'll strike a bore and a house. It ain't but half a mile from Lake Moonba. Feller by the name of Anchor lives there. Sort of inventor, they say, and as mad as Poddy's dorg. You want to go careful of him, though. Appears he don't welcome visitors."

"Are there no other houses between here and Innaminka?" Monty asked.

"Not a one—nor a fence either, when you get through my camel-paddock."

"This man, Anchor: you say he's an inventor. What does he invent?"

"Aeroplanes, I think. Flies one, anyhow."

"Humph! Well, we'll break camp to-morrow," Monty announced. "By those clouds coming up from the west, we're in for a cool change."

"Looks like it. Wind and dust, but no rain. Don't matter much what comes. We're broke."

Later Mrs. Minter appeared, pausing first at the doorway to scan, as had become a habit, the western sky for any indication of the breaking of the drought.

"There's a change coming, John," she said hopefully.

"Looks like it, Martha. Perhaps it'll rain," her husband answered with amazingly assumed cheerfulness.

"Oh, if it only would!"

And, when it did rain, a week or so later, she and her man rushed out of the house and danced like mad people in the torrential downpour.

CHAPTER XIII

THE INVISIBLE TERROR

"CERTAINLY we are now well into the Never-Never country," remarked Monty at the evening meal the day they left Minter's Selection. "We may consider this camp our base of operations, old son."

"Describe it, Monty," requested the blind man, sitting on the soft sand, a pack-saddle for a back-rest. Monty cut up half the contents of a two-pound tin of tongue, added a portion of preserved potatoes, and deposited the enamel plate, together with a slice of damper and a spoon, in his brother's lap. Then, seeing that the pannikin of tea was within Martin's reach, also the salt and pepper—which the blind man easily distinguished by touch of the tin containers—he helped himself, saying in his slow drawl:

"If I were 'A. E. Titchfield' I could do it properly. Being just an ordinary kind of bloke, I can't. Anyway, we are camped on the edge of a bit of a water-hole in a creek described to us by friend Minter. Beyond the creek rises a deep, reddish-coloured sand-hill, smooth and rounded like a whale's back. At the foot of the sand-hill is a solitary box tree."

"Good. In what position am I relatively to the box tree?"

"Facing it. The water in the hole is deep brown in colour and unpleasantly thick. In your pannikin of tea one would easily imagine that cow's milk had been added. Is that enough description, Martin?"

"No, of course not. That, mine eyes, is only half the picture," Martin replied with a smile.

Monty gave a humourous groan.

"All right. Only you will have to excuse my elocution. Descriptive speech doesn't go well with chunks of ox tongue. Well, behind us runs a flat as bare as your elbow, flanked by a sand ridge covered with mulga trees that look as though a fire had swept through them. Still they are not too bad, and

the cracking sound you hear is the branches being broken by
our camels. There is neither grass nor herbage within sight.
How will that do?"

"You are coming on famously, but what colours are there?
A picture is not much without colour."

"Martin, old lad, you'll want flowers on your table next,"
Monty went on with another sepulchral groan. "The sun is
setting behind the purple-looking sand-hill in the far west.
Distance and shadow make it look purple. The foreground
is bathed in gold, with streaks of silver running through it
where the sand-humps beyond cast quarter-mile shadows.
The sky at the zenith is the colour of cadmium, and foretells
wind. Near at hand the putty-coloured forms of our mokes
make light splashes against the almost black mulga trees.
Mahogany-brown is the colour of my beloved pipe; your shirt
makes——"

"Bravo! bravo! That'll do," laughed Martin. "Don't
overload the picture with detail. In time, I think, you will
make a fairly efficient reporter. Let me hear now how you
shape as an organizer. How do you propose to proceed?"

Monty regarded his brother suspiciously, but the tell-tale
droop of the corners of the delicate mouth was not then in
evidence. So he said:

"This Anchor feller attracts me, and his house kind of
draws me like a magnet. I feel as though I am going to enjoy
myself with complete abandon. Certainly we must first visit
Monsoor Anchor. After we have examined him, his dogs, his
inventions, his aeroplane, his people, and all the rooms in his
house, we can decide whether Austiline is with him or not.
If she is, and Anchor doesn't like losing her company, then
we shall have to argue the point; and you told me yourself
that my methods of argument are original and persuasive.
Anyway, I'm tipping that he'll understand my methods.
Should she not be there, then we will cut the whole district
into sections and rake each section so fine that we count every
grain of sand in doing it."

"I cannot help but feeling that Austiline will be at Anchor's
house," Martin said with conviction.

"It will save us a lot of raking if she is. Have some more
damper? Try some dried apples, then, with some condensed
milk?"

"The flies do not seem to be too bad just now?"

"No. They are not such a pest now we're away from the

cattle country. Still, I'll sit beside you and keep 'em off with the dishrag."

So they sat together against the pack-saddle, the one managing his spoon expertly, the other keeping the sleepy flies off the condensed milk with a rag. They had travelled throughout the day on account of the weather change which had brought about cool conditions. The moon, the shape of a steer's horn, hung low in the west, bathed by the ruddy afterglow, and the first of the stars winked through the high-level haze that gave sure warning of wind to come.

Having finished the camp "fatigues," Monty threw more wood on the fire: first, because all men find companionship in a fire even on the hottest of nights; and, secondly, because he wanted the hot ashes for cooking purposes later. Then, after lighting his pipe with a glowing ember, he reseated himself and carried on the interrupted conversation.

"We might be heading for a lot of unpleasantness, old feller-me-lad," he said brightly. "It seems to me that the gang which got Austiline out of gaol will become argumentative when we attempt to get her out of their hands. What do you think?"

"Granted that Mrs. Montrose's theory is correct, I think it more than probable," Martin agreed. "But, no matter what the trouble, no matter what the danger, we have got to get her away. You are not to consider me in the slightest, Monty; think only of the best way to make sure of Austiline. I did not think, when I decided to accompany you, that most likely I would be a drag on you and your actions. For that reason I am now sorry I did come. Anyway, now I'm here, you will have to forget my blindness and carry on just as though I could see as well as you do. The further we go north, the more I feel that we are on the verge of discovering something monstrous, something hellish. Still, we must take what comes."

"You bet. And give a little more than we get."

"Exactly!" Martin agreed, a little grimly. "Before we turn in, you might get me my automatic. I can't see, but I can hear mighty well, and a sound is as good to me as an object to shoot at."

Monty laughed happily. More and more things seemed shaping for his favourite recreation. He scented the coming battle.

"I'll lay out the armament and clean and oil the cannons,"

he said. "To-morrow I must have a little practice. A man soon gets rusty, and when he's rusty he can't shoot straight any more'n a rusty gun-barrel. Shall we camp here for a day, or go on to-morrow?"

"Go on, by all means," Martin urged quickly.

"Right! Then I'll shine up the howitzers now."

The big man thought about that little hardness in an otherwise gentle nature whilst he spread the never-used tent over the ground near the firelight. Martin, like many quiet, lawabiding men, could be and sometimes was deadly in purpose and action when circumstances demanded it.

On the outspread tent Monty first laid his beloved Savage rifle, a weapon of .25 bore which fired a devastating highpowered bullet. Then came a .32 calibre Smith-Wesson revolver, Martin's ugly automatic, a double-barrelled shotgun with full choke, and a .44 Winchester repeating rifle.

During the whole of the half-hour he occupied in carefully cleaning and oiling the weapons, Monty Sherwood whistled blithely the immortal tune to which is set the soldiers' song about a lady of Armentieres. For the big man was intensely happy—happier, if possible, than during those delicious moments when he had held Mary Webster in his arms and felt her lips clinging so lovingly to his own. In many ways Monty had never grown up. The boy's enthusiasm for adventure, the boy's passion for firearms, the boy's insatiable love of excitement had become intensified, if better controlled, in the man. Often had he said: "The only time I really lived was during the hop-overs in Gallipoli and France."

He was still whistling when he rose to his feet and approached Martin with the loaded automatic, but between his reclining brother and the fire he stopped short and ceased the hundredth rendering of the famous tune.

"Say, Martin, old stick-in-the-mud, I've got a brain-wave," he said with comic seriousness.

"Shall I get you some water?" came the musical voice.

"You listen here, and don't chiack about my brain. Remember me telling you how afraid old Bent Nose was that if he divulged the whereabouts of Austiline the under-world would do something rude to him?"

"And apparently his fear was well founded."

"Well, don't it stand to reason that the people he was mixed up with in the gaol stunt knew he had given me her whereabouts?"

"Obviously."

"Then it follows they may well be aware that we are tracking her now."

"Of course."

The corners of Martin's finely moulded mouth drooped slightly, a characteristic which Monty knew meant inward laughter. The big man gave a rueful chuckle.

"I thought I had a brain-wave," he said; "but it seems I've missed the 'bus again."

"I am afraid you have, Monty," the blind man replied. "You see, during this trip, you have had everything to think of in connection with it, while I have had nothing to do but think of Austiline and the problem of her disappearance. With lover's faith I believe that Austiline would have come out of 'smoke,' as the under-world terms it, if she had been a free agent. We guess that her very innocence of the murder of Peterson makes her freedom most undesirable to the very people who rescued her. What their reason was for rescuing her from the law we don't know. They may have been actuated by one of her friends with plenty of money with which to hire them. That, however, I doubt, or she would have been free to come to me. If the people who are holding her in 'smoke' are the same who rescued her from gaol, then we may be sure of meeting with violent opposition. Thinking that, I considered it time to have my automatic handy."

Martin inhaled from his cigarette, faced towards the big man, and smiled softly. He knew that Monty was regarding him blankly. Exhaling the smoke through his delicate nostrils, he went on:

"It might be as well to presume, having been directed to this locality by a man who immediately paid the price for giving you the information, that Anchor's house shelters Austiline, and to proceed with extra caution from now on. The intelligence which directed her escape, and which apparently wants to prevent her return now that her innocence is established, may consider that at all costs we must be prevented from meeting her. It is, I think, improbable that we shall be molested on the way; but more than probable that we shall receive an even less cordial welcome than that given to Mr. Squeezem Harry.

"But we must not count on not meeting with treachery. Our camels might be stolen away one night while we slept; a water-hole in our path might be poisoned. Therefore, Monty, it would be advisable to take all possible precautions."

"I am with you on all points, old son," the giant said, cutting chips from his tobacco plug. "Your idea that our camels may be stolen is a sound one. The loss of the camels would be as fatal as poisoned water or a well-aimed bullet. What say, we start keeping watch to-night?"

"Very well. Let it be four hours on guard and four off— from ten till six, night and night about. You can call me at midnight. I cannot see, but I can hear better than when I saw."

"But that plan is only going to give you four hours' sleep per night," Monty objected.

"What of it? I can sleep before ten o'clock, or even in the saddle."

"Righto, capting! And the next?"

Martin laughed. "No, no, Monty. I'm finished. It's your turn."

"Very well," the big man said. "I'm going to make up your bunk. It's eight o'clock. You'll get four hours before twelve o'clock, and two more after four."

"Oh! Kiss me good night, general!" Martin mocked, saluting and lighting yet another cigarette.

It took the giant nearly half an hour to set out the bed-stretcher with a couple of blankets, and rig above it the box-shaped mosquito net, then help to undress and get his blind brother into the bunk. Martin, on this night, was particular to have his watch beneath his pillow.

"Now, you mind, Monty! You'll call me at twelve o'clock sharp," he pleaded. "I can tell the time by removing the glass and feeling the hands, remember."

"All right. I'll play fair. Good night, old son!"

"Good night, Monty—and thank you!"

"Thank me! Oh hell, Martin! A man couldn't do less. Cut out the rough stuff."

Only those who dwell in the wild places of the earth can imagine how helpless is a blind person, especially one to whom blindness is yet new: how dependent he or she is upon sighted assistance. Those in the dark cannot move a step without guidance, for in the open they have no kerbstones to direct them along a well-paved street; nor about a camp are there furnishings and fixtures to feel one's location by, as in a familiar room.

Martin Sherwood had survived the first terror of perpetual darkness only to be beset with a fresh terror, one which grew daily from the moment he came to rely solely upon his brother for guidance, for life itself. If anything should happen to Monty while they were in the bush, he himself would be as good as dead, because the problem of finding either his way back to civilization, or to water to sustain him on the way, was beyond solution. He remembered how, in his young days, an outlaw horse had thrown him when miles from his father's house, and he had suffered a hundred deaths before he was found on the very verge of actual death from thirst.

But to his credit it must be said that he realized the inevitable coming of the second terror when he made up his mind to accompany his brother in search of the woman he loved. The sole purpose of this journey was, first, to set Austiline free from the bondage which seemed so probable; and, secondly, to relieve his mind as to her personal safety as quickly as possible. Inactivity, suspense, a crescendo of horrible imaginings, would have sent him crazy in spite of the affection and care of Mrs. Montrose and Mary, had he remained in the house with the walled-in garden.

The big man put in his turn of duty sitting by the fire and indolently watching the little pile of ashes crack as the damper buried in the depths rose under the gentle heat. The unknown factor of the immediate future was the manner of Anchor's welcome. He realized that the man might be an eccentric inventor, he might be antagonistic to visitors in case they took too much interest in his secrets. In such case they would have to move carefully and use diplomacy in making sure Austiline Thorpe was not there.

A man's house is his castle, even in the wilds. One could not force an entry and search. Even the police could not do that without a warrant. What exercised his mind during those quiet hours was how to proceed if Anchor flatly declined to admit them to his house. He knew, of course, that Anchor could not refuse them water; was very doubtful if the man could order them off the bore-drain, should they make camp beside it for any indefinite period.

Force—or argument, as he called it—he could meet with laughing ease; but quiet refusal would require tact, and, if it actually came to this latter supposition, the big man decided to hand the leadership of the expedition over to his brother.

Knowing that Martin would be really hurt if he delayed

calling him for his watch, the big man awakened him exactly at midnight, and, turning in himself, reminded the blind man that four o'clock was the next change. "I can tell time in the dark just as well as you can, remember," he said.

"All right, Monty; I'll play fair," was the laughing response.

The moon was little more than three fingers above the horizon when Monty dropped off to sleep immediately he lay down on his stretcher-bed. Martin, after a search about his pillow, found his cigarettes and matches. It was with great care that, by feeling the exact position of the surrounding netting, he avoided setting fire to the bedding when he struck a match. And when he had smoked the cigarette, and, also with great care, dropped the butt beyond his bed, he lay thinking of the probable climax of this possibly somewhat desperate adventure.

Across the flat on the opposite sand-hill the four bells, slung round four sinuous and graceful necks, told him that the camels were finished feeding and that they were resting and sleeping. A camel-bell tells a tale to those who can understand. A good bell can be heard for several miles on a night as quiet as this was; and the listener, from long familiarity with its varied sound, is informed if the animal, to whose neck it is attached, is galloping, cantering, walking, feeding, or sleeping. A sharp clatter, a pause, another clatter, an ordinary tinkle, indicate without possible error that a camel has laid itself down.

Monty had heard that peculiar tune, and had informed his brother that the camels were resting. The occasional tinkle of one bell told Martin that its carrier was biting at some parasite lodged on its skin; another tinkle informed him that a camel had stretched out its long neck over the ground and was sleeping or preparing to doze. Other than the bells there was not a sound. The silence pressed in upon the blind watcher as something tangible, a substance to be felt. The silence of the grave could not be more profound.

When, later, Martin opened the face of his watch, he found the time to be a quarter after two. It was not long after that that the terror came upon him which was, because of his blindness, far worse than any nightmare.

It started with a sound like the far-away escape of steam, a sound so unfamiliar that Martin paused in the very act of applying a match to the box. The sudden clatter of three of the bells told him that three of the camels at least had been awakened by that sound and, like himself, were listening intently.

The following silence was as unbroken as that which preceded the peculiar sound. The very stillness of the bells took to itself an atmosphere sinister and threatening. Very slowly Martin sat up with the automatic in his hand, the safety-catch drawn back and his forefinger barely touching its trigger. On his ear-drums the silence was intensely oppressive, even as utter darkness is oppressive to the eyes of a seeing man.

For what seemed to him an eternity he waited as still as an image of Buddha, his nerves as taut as violin strings. He was undecided whether he did or did not hear a soft, very soft, sound, like the regular falling of leaves from a fig tree. Having heard the leaves fall from the trees in Mrs. Montrose's garden, he was inclined to think his imagination was over-excited.

And then, quite suddenly, he heard soft and regular breathing. Someone was close, very close, to him. A chilly sensation ran up his back and splayed out over his scalp. For he could not define the exact place whence the sound proceeded. In spite or possibly because of the utter silence of the night, that menacing sound seemed to surround him, to fill the world.

To shoot would be foolish without any sense of the direction in which to shoot. Behind him, of course, he dared not fire, because in that direction lay his sleeping brother. The bells remained silent. He could almost swear that six pairs of black eyes were watching a drama being enacted by the muddy water-hole—a drama which contained himself and something which was regarding him from beyond the flimsy net. If he could only see, if only sight were granted to him for a fraction of time! But darkness, as of a dungeon in the bowels of the earth, rendered him helpless.

Again that sinister sound of falling leaves, that sound of death and decay. The breathing ceased for a while and then returned, whilst the leaves continued their regular fall.

Something knocked against his bed at the foot, yet the sound was so fleeting that he had no time to point his weapon. The breathing became louder, now almost a panting sob. The bed rocked beneath a blow, the netting was ripped asunder and a waft of cool air fanned his face. He knew now where the terror was. It was close up on his left side. But, before he could swing round his weapon, the silence was split by a rifle shot as a black sky is rent by lightning.

CHAPTER XIV

A VISITOR

"**D**ON'T move, Martin, old son," Monty Sherwood called, immediately after having fired. "Everything is jake, but just wait while I light this lamp."

The effect of the rather musical drawl was to release the blind man from his nightmare chains; for, like the age-long nightmare which is found to have lasted in reality but a fraction of a second, the space of time between the report and the sound of Monty's voice was to Martin a measure of many hours. The sudden mental relief caused his previous excitement to subside into a peace which by contrast was lethargy.

"Jumping nannygoats! what's this?" he heard his brother exclaim close beside him. Monty, by aid of a hurricane lamp, was looking down at the inert body of a huge dog that had been killed with a bullet from the rifle still in his great hand. "It's a dog, Martin."

"A dog! Only a dog?"

"M'yes. But a kind of dog that would make four fair-sized cattle dogs. Were you asleep?"

"Certainly not, Monty," came the indignant response. The blind man, sitting up again and swinging his legs out through the rent mosquito net, sat on the edge of the stretcher and related his ordeal.

"A bit rotten, old son," Monty replied sympathetically. "We'll read his tracks in the morning. From what you say, he must have slithered down yonder sand-hill, when the falling sand would make a noise like escaping steam. What you took for falling fig leaves was the sound of his paws when he walked about over the sandy ground. No doubt he first paid you a visit and then made a tour of inspection. What awoke me I don't know, but it was to see what I thought was a man crouched by your bed, a much bigger man than you, or I would never have fired. This looks like a wolf-hound, like one of those Russian wolf-hounds our O.C. bought in Egypt from a Greek."

"They're not man-eaters, Monty. Perhaps this one was quite friendly and only wanted me to make a fuss of him."

"Well, his luck was dead out, no matter what his intentions were," the giant remarked with that steely tone in his voice which made it on occasions very grim. "Little wuppy-wups should be kept on a chain at night time. I wonder now if Herr Anchor owns or owned him. Perhaps he'll be rather annoyed. Let's hope so. Now—what in hell!"

Out of the darkness, from some point along the flat, came a long hallo. The camel-bells clanged and jangled, betokening that the beasts on the sand-ridge had jumped simultaneously to their feet. Again came the shout. Monty, cupping his hands, replied. The voice adjured him to keep his crimson rifle pointed downward, since the owner of the voice wished to visit the camp.

"Perhaps it's Senyor Anchor himself," chortled Monty. "I'll put some wood on the fire to make a cheerful blaze. I do hope he's in an argumentative mood."

A couple of armfuls of tinder-dry wood, set alight by the heap of hot ashes, routed the shadows cast by the lamp; but extinguishing the lamp, Monty stepped unhurriedly into the shadow cast by Martin's torn mosquito net, offering thereby no target for a possible enemy.

"Pull up, you crimson bitch!" they heard the voice command, followed instantly by a camel's complaining grunts at being forced to kneel. Half a minute later a man stepped into the circle of light.

With a swift appraising glance Monty took stock of the visitor. He was of medium height, big-boned but lean. He wore elastic-sided riding boots, high-heeled and spurred, white moleskin trousers, a black cotton shirt, and a felt hat with a brim of at least six inches. Strapped to his thigh was a revolver lying in its leathern pouch. In age Monty decided he was not yet twenty, in spite of his sun-darkened complexion. And it was a face which Monty did not like, for in it was the cunning look of the rat and the relentless ferocity of the tiger-snake.

"Who the devil are you shooting at?" demanded this strange being, planting himself in the middle of the temporary camp and gazing boldly about him. When Monty stepped into the light he held his Savage against his hip, with the barrel pointing directly between the night rider's eyes.

"Good evening!" he greeting lightly.

"Evening be damned! It's getting near morning. Can't you point that blasted rifle away from me optics? What are you shootin' at?"

The small coal-black eyes, set very close together beneath overhanging eyebrows of yellow, looked impudently into the cold blue eyes of the giant for an instant, wavered, gained strength, and finally turned away.

"You will oblige me by not moving an eyelash," the big man said silkily. When he approached the other, much like a stalking cat, Monty saw that he could not hold the youth's eyes with any continuity. They watched him, to be sure, watched him, and yet appeared to look anywhere but at him. But not even when the rifle barrel was within an inch of the bridge of his nose did his eyes blink. They moved ceaselessly, but never shut. With a swift movement Monty secured the revolver, and, stepping back, said:

"I am afraid your education has been sadly neglected. It is not considered quite the thing to enter a camp at this time of night and to snarl at people. We are pleased to see you, nevertheless. You will find a drink of tea in the billy by the fire."

The youth managed to look Monty in the eye, with his lips slightly drawn back, revealing white, small and pointed teeth. When he removed his hat he revealed what Monty considered the smallest forehead he had ever seen on a human being.

"You're very clever, ain't you?" came the soft snarling voice. "I like clever people. I'm clever myself. I'm generally the last to be clever."

"How interesting!" mocked Monty. "You know, I feel quite sure that presently I shall begin to love you. You have such charming manners, such a prepossessing personality."

"Glad you think so," the youth retorted, with a look that was positively murderous. "Bah!" And, turning sharply, he made his way to the billy can.

Monty yawned openly and sat himself on a pack-saddle, where he filled his pipe with his usual care, having laid aside the rifle and passed the purloined revolver to Martin.

Carrying a pannikin of tea, the stranger left the fire, and, coming close, sat on his high-heeled boots in a manner which proclaimed long habit. After sipping the jet black fluid for nearly a minute, during which he thoroughly examined the brothers, he said:

"Is your name Sherwood?"

Monty nodded.

"You lookin' for a clinah named Austiline Thorpe?"

Not a muscle on the broad features of the giant moved. It was Martin who replied, the blind man suddenly aroused from curiosity to excitement.

"Yes, we are," he answered sharply. "Whereabouts is she?"

"Don't you fall over yer feet, mister."

That was advice which appeared to call for no comment. Martin sensed that the youth would not be hurried, might indeed be difficult to manage if the attempt were made. Wisely he henceforth left the matter in Monty's capable hands.

Presently the youth said slowly:

"I got a letter for Mr. Monty Sherwood."

"Pass it along then," the big man said.

But the youth calmly finished drinking his tea before he produced a soiled envelope from a pocket in his skin-tight trousers. With it, the rifle in the crook of his arm, the big man walked backward to the light of the fire, and, keeping —figuratively—one eye on the youth, broke the seal and read the message. It ran:

"DEAR MONTY,

"I am informed that Martin and you are on your way to visit me, and in ordinary circumstances I should have been eager to welcome you. However, the special circumstances compel me to ask you to return to Melbourne. The friends who rescued me from prison have been delightfully kind and considerate, and I feel that I owe my host here a debt and some respect for his natural desire for privacy. He is an inventor and, like most inventors, is very jealous of his secrets. You will, I know, understand the situation. At present I am gaining very valuable information for a new book; and, when I think I have sufficient material, I shall call upon you at Melbourne.

"Trusting you are both well, and with kind regards to your poor brother, believe me,

"Sincerely yours,
"AUSTILINE THORPE."

There was neither address nor date. He was at first bewildered, then astounded, at the calmness, the coldness, of that letter, and especially at the almost slighting reference to Martin with which it concluded. Putting it in his pocket, he rejoined the others, and then, standing over the still squatting youth, he said:

"Go to the tucker-box and get yourself a feed."

"Don't want one."

"So!" The big man stooped swiftly and caught hold of the front of the youth's shirt. Twisting it for a hold, he lifted the lad's ten stone without effort, lifted him till his feet were clear of the ground. "You are an uncivil lout," he said quietly. "I'll give you a chance to walk to the tucker-box near the fire. If you don't take it, I'll throw you into the fire from here. Get along!"

With a push he sent the young blackguard staggering away, almost falling. The youth spun round on gaining his feet, and from his mouth poured such a flood of verbal sewage that even Monty Sherwood was appalled. For fully a minute the most horrible language was screamed at them. Foam gathered about the slavering lips; fire gleamed dully in the black eyes. Then, quite suddenly, the torrent ceased, to be succeeded by a low, diabolical laugh—a laugh which, in spite of its softness, appeared to be thrown back at them by the sand-hills with added deviltry.

"The fellow must be mad," Martin whispered. "What does Austiline say?"

By the light of the lamp Monty read the letter. Both were silent then, and the blind man's face greyed a little. Monty laid an encouraging hand on the younger man's arm.

"It's a stall—a put-off, old feller-me-lad," he said softly.

"It may not be. Austiline may not want a blind man."

"Well, we'll go on and have it from her lips," the giant answered firmly.

"Yes, certainly we'll go on, Monty. Somehow that letter is unconvincing. Forget what I said about her and my blindness, brother mine. I was a cad. That letter is not Austiline's style, I'm sure. She wrote that under pressure."

"M'yes. I'm glad you think so," Monty said, smiling. "If yonder is a sample of the considerate people who surround Austiline, I am sure she would be better off in the kinder atmosphere of a slaughter-house. I'll call our guest and pump him. Hi, you! Come over here!"

"Go to hell, you——!" came the snarling answer.

"I'll go to you in two ups and jump you about the scenery so much that you'll flatten it, if you don't do as you're told."

The youth hesitated, finally obeying and taking up his former position on his heels.

"What do they call you—Tom, Dick, or Harry?"

The black, deep-set eyes, fringed with yellow lashes, looked up at the seated giant from behind a veil of cunning.

"Let it be Jack," he replied, with less of a snarl in his voice. "Do you want to read me birth certificate, or me marriage lines?"

"I'm not that interested in you, my lad. Where is Miss Thorpe at present?"

"You'd like to know, wouldn't you?"

"I want to know." The words were quietly uttered, but in them was a command.

"There's lots of things we want and can't get," responded the youth with a sneaking kind of grin.

" 'Tain't often I don't get what I want, son. Just as well be frank now, as wait till you're tied down on an ant bed."

"Think you're putting the wind up me, 'cos you've collared me gun, don't you?" The words were spoken calmly enough, but the eyes became more shifty and the corners of the lips drooped slightly. "I got me orders."

"And what are they?"

"To keep me mouth shut if you goes south, and to steer you if you goes north."

"Well, we've decided to go north, or rather north-west."

"Oh! have yer? Well, you'll be going ter your own funeral, let me tell you," the youth informed them with unmistakable joy—joy so dreadfully sinister with pre-knowledge of future events that Martin could not repress a shudder.

"You appear to like funerals."

"You bet! Yours will be extra special. You leave it to me."

Monty tried a random shot.

"Mr. Anchor's house is about sixty miles from here, isn't it?"

"About."

"You might ride on at daybreak. Give Mr. Anchor my compliments, and tell him we will be calling upon Miss Thorpe in a day or two."

"Righto! 'Ere, how did you know Austiline is with old man Anchor? I didn't tell you."

"No, that's right. It was a little dicky-bird, something far more intelligent than you."

Once more the lips drew back, revealing the even, pointed teeth.

"What's your favourite depth for a grave, six or only one foot?"

"Time enough to discuss graves when you've both your feet in one, my lad. I'm thinking that that time is not far off. And in future you will say Miss Thorpe, not Austiline."

"I'll say what I——well like."

"You'll say what *I* like, which is a different thing. Do you own that dog over there?"

"What dog?" ejaculated the youth, bounding to his feet.

Monty casually lit the lamp and led the way round Martin's stretcher-bed to the carcass of the great hound. Swiftly the youth bent forward and scanned the inert heap.

"Shot—by hell!" he said almost in a whisper. "Poor old Carlo! Shot!"

When he turned, Monty was shocked by the awful, livid glare of hatred which blazed from the black eyes. The rat's face was convulsed by the tempest of fury which surged through his warped brain, the teeth literally gnashing in a terrific effort to aid the tongue to formulate the string of oaths and horrible profanity which poured from the narrow lips. With a cry as of a tormented devil the youth ducked under Monty's outflung arm and disappeared in the darkness, still screaming profanity.

They heard his camel roar out on being kicked viciously to his feet, heard the youth's screams of uncontrollable madness growing fainter and more faint, whilst the animal bore him swiftly from the camp.

"Phew! I'm sort of glad Jack Blank decided to leave us," drawled Monty.

"A madman, if ever there was one," pronounced Martin.

"Absolutely. I'll drag away this corpse, and then we'll make a billy of tea. I can see the dawn in the east."

CHAPTER XV

THE morning of the second day north of the water-hole where Martin had experienced the terror preceding the visit of the youthful lunatic, found the brothers camped on a flat that Monty estimated to be about fifteen miles south-east of Lake Moonba.

Here the country was worse even than that of Minter's Selection, the sand-hills higher and more numerous, the scrub trees far more sparse and much more stunted. The big man had been compelled to make advance by the snake-like track of least resistance, surmounting the ridges at their lowest point, skirting the higher bluffs, but always bearing north-west by north. The fear of circling or taking gigantic curves never worried him, who by sheer instinct born of long years of training could keep to any given direction without mental effort.

Martin Sherwood had been improving visibly in health with the passage of every day. The rawness of face and hands caused by the fierce sunlight had healed and hardened into a deep tan. Gone were the tired lines about his eyes and the listlessness of his actions. There had stolen over him a certain quality of alert grimness, a masculine hardness, which years of city life had held in abeyance, and this grimness accentuated his good looks, adding physical strength to his existing mental strength. He was becoming a smaller edition of his brother·Monty.

Wearing a khaki shirt, opened wide at the neck and the sleeves rolled up above his elbows, a leathern strap about his waist supporting dark blue twill trousers, and his feet encased in elastic-sided riding boots, no one, Monty was sure, would recognize in this outfit the formerly delicate-looking and well-groomed editor of *The Daily Tribune*.

The packing done, Monty brought in the camels, "hoosh-ing" each of them down between the saddle and the load it

was to carry.   Habitually he began this operation at the
rear end of the string, leaving his riding beast to the last.
This animal, a bad-tempered, obstinate brute, generally provided
trouble of some kind.   It was a finely built bull, a magnificent
racer, worth at least a hundred guineas: otherwise the big man
would have discarded it long since.

With firm and patient persuasion he had got it down on
its fore knees, when the stillness of the day was broken by a
sound like a carpet being struck by a stick.   The camel sagged
forward a little for an instant, a rich red stream spurting
from its throat; then pitched to the ground in a lifeless heap.

Monty was dumbfounded for the space of about two seconds;
but when, over the flat, came the dull crack of a rifle, he broke
into a whirl of action.

The sudden end of the riding camel, followed by Monty's
rush to get Martin under cover, was more than sufficient to
stampede the train.   Realizing that in the difficult conditions
the stampede was the best thing possible, the bushman made
no effort to stop the thoroughly frightened beasts from
careening wildly in all directions, with roars of protest.   The
rifle cracked twice before Monty, handling the saddles and
gear much like a porter emptying a luggage van, surrounded
the blind man and himself with a temporary wall.

The horrible impact of a bullet against the flesh of a camel
which, having galloped away by itself, had paused to see
whither its mates had gone, came to the crouching men at the
same instant as the report.   Monty gritted his teeth when one
of his best pack-animals screamed with agony and floundered
helplessly with a broken hind leg.

"What   is   causing   the   excitement,   Monty?"   Martin
inquired, casually lighting a cigarette while he lay full length
on the sand.

"A gun," came the grim reply.   "Some Johnny is shooting
from a sand-hill down the flat.   Old Bulldog's dead, and Emma
is roaring her heart out with a broken leg."

"Better finish her," said Martin compassionately.

"Will have to in a minute.   Trying now to locate the
pirate's possie before I open up.   You lie still."

This last injunction when a bullet screamed but a few
inches above the encircling saddles.   The bushman's keen
eyes searched the sand-hill hiding the rifleman, and discovered
a wisp of blue vapour hovering about the butt of a dead
sandal-wood some three hundred yards distant; and, the

sights of his beloved Savage requiring no adjustment for that distance, he brought them at once to bear on the butt, waiting then for the next shot.

Thirty seconds later it came. Monty saw the almost invisible burst of vapour and replied with a devastating high-powered bullet, which an observer would have sworn struck the spot whence the vapour issued, and that before the vapour cleared.

"Did you get him?"

"I don't think so," Monty replied slowly, ejecting the empty shell and pumping a full one from magazine to breach. "The gentleman knows how to take cover. I haven't seen him yet, but I'll part his hair when I do."

"Well, for heaven's sake, kill that camel. Her roars get on my nerves."

The big man's rifle again cracked, and the noise ceased suddenly, accentuating the stillness of the day. Of the other animals there was now no sign. A bullet struck and splintered a side-stick of the saddle behind which the bushman lay peering through a crevice and over his rifle-barrel, and this time there was no film of vapour at the foot of the sandal-wood. But Monty discovered it at a point about one hundred yards along the summit of the sand-hill and some fifty yards nearer.

"Artful! Artful!" he remarked softly. "Going to shift his position after each shot. I must have got mighty close to him at the sandal-wood. It is ten to one now that he'll move along the ridge a bit for his next shot. Like a lady, I'll wait for him at that cotton-bush with becoming modesty."

"Must be Anchor's brand of hospitality," Martin opined.

"More likely that black-eyed youth on his own."

"Probably. He's mad enough."

"I'll turn his yellow eyebrows into rainbows if I can get on to his smoke quick enough. That's one advantage about this damned climate. The atmosphere is clear enough to spot him by that. Oh hell!"

A metallic "plonk" plainly indicated that the enemy had put a bullet through one of the water-drums; and, again too late, Monty saw the vapour of the exploded cartridge hover at the base of the sandal-wood.

"He's gone back to his old possie," he announced. "Or there may be two of them. Deliberately aimed at the water can, because it is all of ten yards beyond our 'fort.' He's using a .44 Winchester, too, in a way which raises my admiration. Practice makes perfect, as he would have found out before this had I been ten years younger."

"Doesn't he show?"

"Nary a bit of him," Monty sighed. "Fact of the matter is I'm getting old and slow. Soon be sitting on the veranda wearing slippers and recalling the good old days when 'men was men and byes was byes, me pimply-faced young shaver —h'rumph!'"

"He'll get careless presently."

"Maybe. Still, he's 'cute."

That the enemy was "'cute" could not be gainsaid. He possessed every advantage in that maze of sand-hills, which could cover the operations of an army corps from any observer on a flat. The brothers, being on a flat some hundred odd yards in width, could not move from their flimsy fort to reach any kind of cover, but the enemy could circle them entirely with the greatest ease and safety from behind his walls of sand.

"I think it must be our late visitor," Martin observed, after another water-drum had been holed, wasting its precious contents.

"Why?"

"Because, if dear Brutus had any sense, he would have waited till we were on the move. The camels would have bolted just the same, and one or both of us would have been bucked off and left on the flat without any gear to protect us. Our caller did not sound to me as if he were overstocked with intelligence."

"M'yes, that may be so, old lad," Monty agreed, slipping more of the flat soft-pointed cartridges into the magazine. "Still, we'll be in Queer Street all the same if he punctures all our water-drums. And he seems to have intelligence enough for that. If only I—ah!"

The Savage cracked, and for a fleeting instant Monty saw a wide-brimmed hat rise a little above the ridge—almost at right-angles to the sandalwood. If he had not bored his man, at least he had shot his hat off—a good shot indeed, because the blue vapour had appeared almost over his rifle-sights and he had dispatched a bullet before the enemy's bullet let the water out of the third drum.

"How now, my brother?"

"I think I spoiled his hat," the big man replied, chuckling. "But I never hurt the little dear. I couldn't, you know. My! What glorious practice the chap is giving us! Reminds me of dear old Gallipoli."

His blue eyes aglow with the joy of battle, Monty felt no inconvenience from the humming flies which persisted in drowning themselves in his eyes. The conditions for rifle-shooting were ideal. There was absolutely no wind. There was no shimmer of hot air just above the ground, and the atmosphere was so clear that objects one hundred yards distant appeared but one hundred feet. He was sublimely unaware even of the fierce sunlight pouring down upon their open fort; and it was only when Martin, like himself on fire with excitement, searched aimlessly for shade, that he remembered the uncomfortable and dreadfully tedious part the blind man was forced to play.

"Hold on, old stick-in-the-mud," he said, laying aside the rifle. "I'll fix the pack-bags on the saddles there, and rig a little shade with the tent."

This operation all but cost him his life, for a bullet snatched a shred of material off his shirt at the shoulder, a bullet that came from the opposite direction to the last. But by then the job was practically finished, and, throwing up his arms, Monty very realistically slumped down over the saddle wall, thence slowly to slide off and down behind the cover.

"What are you doing now?" Martin demanded, knowing by the uninterrupted whine of the bullet that the big man was unharmed. Monty laughed softly.

"I'm supposed to be wanting a grave," was his answer. "Our undertaker friend aimed at me, and was very pleased to see me throw up my arms as I threw a seven. Believing me to be a lovely corpse, and knowing you to be a non-combatant, he will probably be game enough to show himself. Then it will be 'Good-bye, Dolly Grey!'"

"Wing him, Monty! Only wing him!" urged Martin.

"You bet! I'll give him a lovely pair of wings, which shortly afterwards will be much singed."

For nearly an hour the enemy kept up a desultory fire, perforating all the drums, but leaving intact a canvas water-bag hanging in front of a riding-saddle outside the "fort." Monty decided that the gunman could not see the drab-coloured bag from his distance, and rejoiced.

Both the besieged were by this time suffering from thirst, made worse possibly by the knowledge that about a gallon of cool water was just beyond their reach till darkness fell and made it reasonably safe to leave the shelter. Bullets "flunked" into the straw-stuffed pack-saddles, others entered the joints between them, and yet others screamed just above their heads.

Another torturing hour passed before the constantly moving marksman showed himself for the fraction of a second. That was the first sight of him, for which Monty had been waiting with absolute certainty. He knew that it was merely a matter of time when the attacker would persuade himself that he had actually killed the brother who enjoyed his sight.

Monty had not fired a shot since he was supposed to have been mortally hit. It was a waiting game that he disliked intensely, but it was the only one to play when the greater enemy, thirst, joined forces with the unseen rifleman.

The man who eventually wins in such circumstances is he who possesses the greatest patience, and patience is a test of a strong character. A weak intellect can rarely be patient, because it cannot for long follow a predetermined course, being beset by doubts and ungoverned imaginings.

Below his casual surface manner, Monty Sherwood was a thinker and a student of men. Once decided that it was their night visitor who besieged them, he realized that the waiting game was the only one that he could play with any hope of success. At any moment a searching bullet might find one of them through a chink between two saddles, and the longer he replied to the firing the longer would the attacker keep in his impenetrable cover, waiting merely for heat and thirst to madden them and drive them into the open to become an easy prey. Both sides, therefore, were playing the waiting game in differing ways. It was low, vicious cunning opposed to cold, calculating cunning.

It was about three o'clock in the afternoon when the enemy peered over the stem of a fallen needlewood tree lying in a cleft between two ridges. All that Monty could see of him was his rat-like face with the glittering snake-like eyes. Cautiousness still ruled the killer's brain, but no longer could Monty delay action. Delay meant madness and death for Martin and him if their tongue-blistering thirst was much further prolonged. Already the heat and the awful dryness of his skin caused lights to dance before his eyes.

The queer lights danced beyond the foresight of his rifle, coming between it and that hateful, peering face. He prayed that the lights would flicker out before the face drew back.

Then the lights vanished, and he pressed firmly upon the trigger.

CHAPTER XVI

WILLIAM J. ANCHOR AND FRIEND

THE big man, rising, laid aside his rifle and at once secured the water-bag from the front of the riding-saddle. Into a pannikin he poured but a little more than a medium wine-glass measure of the precious liquid, which he gave to Martin, managing to speak the one word: "Slowly!"

Even less did he give himself. Taking one sip, he allowed it to soak into the crevices of his tongue; another loosened the sticky saliva clogging the muscles of tongue and lips; a third and a fourth sip he allowed to trickle down his throat with much more than the appreciation a connoisseur of wine bestows on a famous vintage.

Another half-hour, and the waiting game as played by the besieged would have had to be abandoned. For some time Monty had been estimating his chances of rushing out of their improvised fort and returning unharmed with the water. The absolute dependence of the blind Martin upon him was the only reason why he did not attempt it. The odds were in favour of his securing the water without injury, yet if a bullet *had* found him Martin's plight would have been hopeless.

His ration of water taken, the big man seated himself in the small tent-made shade and, proceeding to cut tobacco, said quietly:

"Well, that's that."

"You got him?"

"I did."

"Did you merely wound him?"

"I gave the blighter wings. There was nothing else for it. He asked for all he got."

"There was only the one?" pressed the blind man.

"Only the madman who visited us the other night. Apparently he returned to engage in a private war. I think I'll fill the billy before I go after the camels. They'll have gone miles by this time."

"I say, Monty!" called Martin, while the big man gathered sticks for a fire. "Are you sure the enemy is dead and not wounded?"

"Positive. Why?"

"Only, if he is wounded, I think you ought to attend him."

"Don't you worry," the bushman assured him grimly. "All I had to aim at at three-fifty yards was his face above a dead log. The face is still there. A soft-pointed high-powered bullet does extraordinary things, old son."

"All right," Martin said gently, sipping the last of his issue of water. Although he knew Monty's brutality of speech to be an acquired habit and in direct contrast to his kindly nature, yet it hurt him to hear so shocking a death spoken of in that way. No matter the crime committed, the death of a criminal was as solemn as that of a bishop.

The big man estimated that there were but three quarts of water remaining in the bag; a small enough quantity in that heat, when he first had to bring in the camels and then get his brother fifteen miles—the journey itself a matter of five hours at least—to Anchor's homestead, where there was a certain water supply. The drums were so badly holed by the youth's accurate shooting that he saved barely sufficient to fill the half-gallon billy he placed over the fire.

An hour later he set off for the camels, leaving Martin smoking a cigarette in the shade of the "fort," and carrying with him half a dozen spare nose-lines, as well as several nose-plugs to replace those which might have been torn out when the animals stepped on their lines in their mad rush. When Martin removed his watch-glass he ascertained the time to be a little after four.

Monty, more as a duty than to assure himself, first examined the dead youth, and then circled the sand-hills till he cut his camels' tracks, which he followed till he found them placidly chewing their cud in the shade of a clump of belar. They were four miles from camp, and at the end of an hour Martin began to worry at his long absence. For an hour is a long time to be without water in that terrific temperature, probably 114 degrees in the shade.

Quite soon after the blind man took the time, he first heard the far-off drone of a powerful motor which, increasing rapidly in loudness, betrayed itself as the power unit of an aeroplane. With sensitive ears he followed its course, first flying high overhead and then shutting off its engine to swoop earthward, its pilot, so Martin surmised, having observed the apparently deserted camp.

When next the engine crackled into its fierce song, it told the blind man that the 'plane was flying low over and about the flat on which he lay.

Monty and the camels were uppermost in his mind then. Should the bushman be approaching camp with the four remaining beasts, that 'plane would stampede them again. Monty, or a dozen Montys, would be unable to manage them unless he were provided with rope. And Monty had nothing like that with him.

Finally, the aeroplane engine was shut off and a peculiar whistling indicated that it was coming to earth, which it did on a flat beyond the sand-ridge on which lay the dead youth. But for his blindness, Martin would have seen two men, attired in faultless white duck and pith helmets, descend from the cockpit.

The first to reach the ground was a thin man, of medium height, whose age might have been anything between fifty and sixty years. The small military moustache matched perfectly the fine silvery hair crowning a really magnificent head. The expression of benevolent placidity was discounted heavily by the slaty agate colour of the eyes, which were peculiarly brilliant when, beneath straight brows, they peered up at the body of the dead youth.

"It is confoundedly hot here on the ground," he said to his companion.

"Hot! It's a damned oven," his fellow flier agreed, producing and lighting a cigarette. "Now to investigate this affair."

The second man was almost ten inches taller than the other, but quite as thin—too thin for his height. His eyes were effectually hidden by the tinted glasses of his spectacles. Clean shaven, his black hair just shading white, he appeared to be under fifty years of age. A rubicund complexion suggested the imbiber of spirits. The peculiarly toned voice placed him on the lower levels of England's upper classes.

Together they walked to the body. It lay in the exact position taken when the youth peered over the dead log at the "fort" below. The expanding bullet had removed the rear part of the head. Stooping, the tall man turned the body over, and, calmly surveying the face, still bestial in death, said:

"It is Gilling all right. The hangman cheated once more, Anchor. Must have been a high-powered bullet that did that. I am sorry to have lost such a promising subject."

"Well, your experiments could have made him no worse than he is just now," remarked Anchor with the ghost of a smile. "Even the Malay was better off after you had done with him and before I attended him."

The tall man grunted—it was nothing else. He said, indicating the "fort":

"Sherwood must indeed be a good shot. Assuming that they took cover among those saddles, and by their formation it is evident that they did, the distance must be at least four hundred yards."

"M'yes. And, as the Sherwoods don't show, it appears that young Gilling has saved us some trouble. Gilling, you know, was a good shot, too."

"I hope he missed the Sherwoods," his companion said quickly. "I am quite looking forward to their help in some experiments I have in view."

The man addressed as Anchor looked at him sharply.

"You will wait, Moore, until I give you leave," he said coolly. "I have a little chess game to play with Miss Thorpe, using these Sherwoods as pawns. If you take away my pawns before the game is finished, I shall be most annoyed. When I announce 'mate,' we shall decide what to do with the pawns."

The tall man laughed unpleasantly, and was about to speak when he changed his mind, threw away the butt of his cigarette, and picked up the youth's Winchester rifle. Then, without haste, they descended to the flat, and, strolling to the little mound of saddles and gear, halted just beyond them.

"Is any one at home?" called Anchor with sarcastic politeness.

"Most certainly!" came Martin's voice, now firm and as hard as ironstone. "You will find the front door open. Be pleased to enter."

The airmen glanced significantly at each other. Then, smiling faintly, Anchor moved softly round the "fort," with his right hand in his jacket pocket. Moore at his heels, he came to where Monty had pushed aside a saddle and, within the enclosure, saw Martin sitting bolt upright with his automatic trained upon him. For a moment the silver-haired man thought the blind man could see him.

"It is very warm this afternoon," he said with undiminished politeness.

"Warm, but bracing," Martin replied. "Being a windless day, my hearing is quite good. Believe me, only yesterday I shot a galah on a tree-branch, aiming merely by its screech. Even the rustle of your clothes is quite distinct."

"These details interest me exceedingly," Anchor said, but making no slightest movement.

"I am glad of that," Martin assured him grimly. "Whom have I the pleasure of addressing?"

"William J. Anchor," was the blandly spoken reply. "I am accompanied by my friend, Dr. James Moore."

"Ah! My brother and I were intending to call on you this evening. Unfortunately, we have been delayed by a lunatic taking pot-shots at us. He, my brother tells me, is now dead."

"As Queen Anne," Anchor confirmed. "I am indeed upset by his extraordinary behaviour, and must accept part responsibility for it. Indeed, I am most pained by this tragic affair. No wonder you are suspicious of strangers! Gilling, the lad who so madly attacked you, was under my care, and it was only after his absence with one of my guns had been noticed that Dr. Moore and I surmised he had unfriendly intentions towards you. Our surmise, so unfortunately correct, is the real cause of our coming to meet you. Please accept my sincere regrets."

The blind man smiled and placed the automatic in his pocket. Rising to his feet, he fearlessly held out his hand, which Anchor, stepping forward, took in a warm grasp; an action repeated by the tall man, who bent upon the bronzed face a piercing look.

"You must be Mr. Martin Sherwood," he said, in a well-bred drawl. "May I offer you my sympathies?"

"Thank you! My affliction places me to a certain extent in your hands, as my brother is absent hunting the camels. However, your voices assure me you are gentlemen, and gentlemen never take unfair advantages, even in war."

"War, Mr. Sherwood!" came Anchor's horrified tones.

"That was the word I used," Martin said quietly, adding with a smile: "Now, my brother, you know, unlike ourselves, regards war as the finest sport in the world. He simply loved that shooting duel with Gilling, saying it reminded him of dear old Gallipoli."

The airmen laughed. Anchor's laugh was a genuine chuckle, the doctor's less genuine—a fact the blind man's sharp ears did not fail to detect. He continued:

"I am sorry I cannot offer you a drink. You see, your late ward shot our water-drums to pieces, and we have but half a gallon of water left."

"Indeed! That is most awkward for you," Anchor said seriously. "However, we can replace Gilling's waste to a certain extent. Dr. Moore always carries a four-gallon water-bag on the 'plane. We must leave it with Mr. Sherwood, Moore."

"Certainly. I'll get it."

"How far is it to your house, Mr. Anchor?" Martin inquired when the tall man had departed.

"Some fourteen miles, I think," Anchor replied, seating himself on a saddle and mopping the perspiration from his face with a silk handkerchief. "But the bore-drain runs this way, and you should reach its farthest point at not more than ten miles from here."

"That is good. We are sadly in need of a bath and clean linen."

"All of which you may obtain at my house, Mr. Sherwood. Everything it contains is at your disposal, I assure you."

"Thank you very much! But, really, we must make ourselves a little more presentable," Martin countered, doubtful of Monty's plans.

"Well, well! Come as soon as you can. I am anxious to obliterate this afternoon's unpleasantness by any service possible in this desert region. You will be made welcome. That's right, Moore! Place the bag here, within Mr. Sherwood's reach. With your permission, Mr. Sherwood, we will return home. I would have offered you a lift in the 'plane had there been room."

"Thanks! But we shall now be quite all right, with your most acceptable gift of water."

"Well, then, good-bye for the present! Oh! by the way, perhaps Mr. Montague Sherwood would be good enough to bring Gilling's camel along. We saw it tied to a tree beyond a dead sandalwood tree east of here, tell him."

"We will bring it with pleasure."

"Thanks! Ah well, good day, then! We shall expect you not later than to-morrow."

Martin heard them moving away. Not a word about

jealously guarded inventions, not a word of Austiline! Nothing but regret at Gilling's hostility, and a warm welcome. What did all that mean? Welcome, when they expected a harsh rebuff!

It was a problem that fully occupied his mind. He heard the aeroplane engine roar with life, heard it "zoom" in its swift upleap into the air, heard the noise fade slowly into silence. He was still pondering the baffling behaviour of William J. Anchor and Dr. James Moore when Monty's cheerful voice and the tinkling of camel-bells came to him from across the flat.

CHAPTER XVII

THE moon, three-quarters full, idealized the devastating ugliness of the dying bush, changing it so that one thought it was the beautiful spirit risen from the decaying body. A many-curved bar of brilliant silver marked the course of the bore-drain where it found its natural level between the humped sand-hills.

It was the night following the rifle duel between the youth, Gilling, and Monty Sherwood. To be precise, it was midnight, and the brothers were newly encamped beside the drain at a point the bushman estimated to be two miles from the bore-head.

They had been discussing Austiline Thorpe's apparent lack of warmth at the possibility of receiving them, Martin voicing a growing impression that perhaps Austiline found it impossible to continue loving a blind man. Strangely enough, it was the big, casual man and not the lover who championed her.

"Women, old son, are all difficult to understand for the simple reason that we men do not seriously try to understand 'em," he said, when his pipe was properly alight. "The difference between the sexes is simple enough. A man's body is governed by his mind; a woman's mind is governed by her body. You take a real man, the sort of man 'A. E. Titchfield' writes about. Old clothes, even rags and tatters, don't affect his mind; but is there a woman who can be pacified and content when her body is arrayed in old rags? I mention clothes, but there are other things which govern woman's mind.

"When the little boy put the cracker underneath the cat, he didn't know which way the cat would jump, least of all did he expect it to jump on him. Now, to my mind, every woman can be placed in one of three classes, and if they belong to either of the first two you know perfectly well what they are going to do when the cracker explodes. Interested?"

"I most certainly am. Go on, please."

"There is a very small class of woman which I have named T.T., or the True Type," Monty expounded. "They are those women exemplified by the scriptural Ruth, who are prepared to suffer hardship, a broken heart, even death, rather than be parted from those they love. Another class, more numerous maybe, comprise those women who shrink from adversity. This class may be labelled R.T., or Rat Type. Like the rats which leave a sinking ship they will desert husband, children, parents, or lover if there comes a cloud on the horizon, especially a financial cloud.

"I know several women, and I expect you do also, who can be placed in this latter class. Old Mrs. Montrose and Mary and Mrs. Minter, you and me can fully agree to put in the classed called True Type, and of those I have named Mrs. Minter is the most splendid example.

"The great majority of women, old lad, can be put in my third class, which can be ticketed simply by the letter X, meaning unknown quantity. Until adversity proves them with its fire we cannot tell with any degree of certainty how they will act in given circumstances, although we can often shrewdly guess.

"No, I'm a pretty good guesser, Martin, old lad, and as far as we know Austiline is still in the X class. But I am guessing she will hop right into the T.T. class when the time comes. I like the way Austiline looks at a man. There is no veil before her eyes. There is no veil in front of the eyes of Mrs. Minter, and I'll stake my life against your cigarette-butt that if old Minter went blind she wouldn't turn him down. There are times, Martin, when you make me feel inclined to jump on you with both feet."

"Why don't you?" Martin said seriously. "Do you know, old man, there are times when I wish you would. I envy you your cleanness of mind and abhor the thoughts which sometimes come to me, thoughts engendered by the daily reading of the sins of humanity. I am saturated with the details of murder, rape, and arson, trickery, unfaithfulness, and debauch. Because Austiline didn't send me a love letter by Gilling and a love message by Anchor, I unconsciously almost persuade myself that she will make my affliction an excuse to break our engagement. I know Austiline. I ought to have more faith in her. I am ashamed."

"I agree with you," said Monty, his eyes soft, his voice

blunt. "Let Austiline prove herself before we decide which class to put her in. That's only fair. It's my belief that there is something sinister behind the letter she wrote me. It's my belief, too, that she didn't know of Anchor's visit to us to-day. It's my belief in the third place that we're due for a gay old time."

An hour later Monty was squatting over a fire with the blind man asleep beside him. The big man likened his brother to a thoroughbred racehorse, alert, fine in aspect, but nervous of the crowd, quite expecting to be frightened by and therefore quite ready to shy at any unfamiliar object. That Martin was worried was obvious; that he should look at the underside of every black cloud was probably natural in a lover, and in a blinded lover more than natural.

As for Monty, he felt that he was faced by a dark wall which effectually hid events that might be either harmless or sinister, but which could not be gauged or met by forethought.

Anchor, indeed, might be nothing worse than a secretive inventor; on the other hand, why did he harbour a suspected murderess and a degenerate like Gilling? Supposing Austiline Thorpe was detained against her will, or kept in ignorance of Travers's confession? Would not her word of honour have been sufficient to protect her gaol-breakers from the consequences of that episode? What other motive could Anchor have for keeping her virtually a prisoner?

They had discussed the position before Martin turned in, agreeing that Anchor's welcome was somewhat similar to the invitation so cordially extended by the spider to the fly. That Anchor was aware of their journey and its object was, of course, evident. But his attitude to them had none of the hostility he had evinced when a wandering dogger had ventured to call for water and rations. Why?

The most likely reason, Monty decided after long cogitation, was that Anchor was sure of the fulfilment of some plan he had conceived. Perhaps, being unable to prevent their calling on him, he had decided to remove them "without trace" at a favourable opportunity—an action that would be simplicity itself on account of the remoteness of his house from civilization.

Possibly once in a year a police-trooper might pay him a duty call, and, since such visitors are invariably the guests of the squatters, Anchor probably would be notified of the approximate date of the trooper's arrival, if nothing was suspected against him by the law.

Assuming that Anchor was villain enough and clever enough to remove them "without trace," and the inevitable search for them instigated by Mary Webster and Sir Victor Lawrence were made, the search party would be obliged to accept Anchor's word that the Sherwoods called and went on in some direction. He would have plenty of time to prepare for the search party, even to the extent of forming a camp with their gear beside some dried-up water-hole—a sure enough indication that the brothers had perished in the search for water. The tale would read that they had separated at the water-hole, or that Monty first and then Martin had wandered aimlessly from the camp to be swallowed up by the ever-moving sand-hills.

Feeling that Anchor held all the trump cards as well as any quantity of spare aces, Monty had advocated a bold, ruthless offensive against the supposed inventor, assuming him black guilty until he proved himself white innocent. Martin, however, had urged diplomacy and caution until Anchor showed his hand. It took much persuasion to win Monty's consent to this latter course—he argued that Anchor would probably play his hand without showing it; but, having once accepted this diplomatic policy, the big man was thorough in prosecuting it.

The moon becoming obscured by a thick, high-level haze which gave it two great rings, Monty buried a quantity of tinned foods, and a small iron box filled with flour and other rations, at the foot of a blue-bush growing on the flat, and but a few yards from the naturally formed bore-drain. In another cache he put the Winchester rifle and Gilling's revolver, together with cartridges fitting those weapons. The time might well arrive when they would wish to be independent of Anchor's hospitality, or when they might, whilst Anchor's "guests," find themselves without most necessary weapons.

When Martin had wakened to take his turn at watch duty, the big man acquainted him with what he had done, and urged him to think of "any further measures of precaution" whilst he, Monty, took his sleep as arranged for that night.

Not till nearly eleven o'clock the next day did they leave camp for the inventor's house, which came into view in less than an hour; when, rounding a bluff and still following the bore-drain, they moved slowly towards it; Monty, for one, wondering how many aces the waiting Anchor held.

It was a large, rambling structure encircled by wide, fly-netted verandas, the whole painted a light brown shade, excepting the corrugated iron roof. There was an absence of the plants and creepers with which most homesteads are surrounded; the reason for this lack of plant life being the scarcity of rain-water, since the flow from the bore was too heavily charged with minerals.

Clustered about the main dwelling were numerous out-houses, from one of which came the "chug-chug" of a petrol engine.

Circling the entire homestead was a six-foot, partly netted fence, the posts squared and painted white. Outside this fence were the stockyards and kennels, and at these Monty observed three great hounds regarding them with bristling manes and greeting them with savage bays.

The artesian bore, also outside the fence, gave a constant supply of water, the iron casing conducting it to the service being bent at the top so that the flow gushed steaming hot into a concrete basin, from which it flowed away along its self-made drain for several miles before it wasted into the ground. Here, along the edges of the drain, the ground was snow-white with crystals from the sun-evaporated water; but within a few yards of the basin, as well as on the floor of the basin itself, there grew and thrived a fungus of brilliant green, slimy to the touch, and looking much like the first growths adhering to ships' bottoms.

Beside the bore-head stood a cane-grass shed protecting the distillery plant. Another shed erected near the basin was obviously a laundry, for when they drew near a young woman issued thence with a basket of clothes which she dumped into the concrete basin, from which clouds of steam arose. It was labourless laundering, for so loaded with minerals was the water that all she had to do was to fish them out at the end of five minutes, allow to cool, and rinse in a tub of blue.

"Good day-ee, Miss," Monty drawled, now walking and leading his string of beasts. "It looks as though we're in for a wind-storm."

"And a cool change after, I hope," she said pleasantly. "Do you want Mr. Anchor?"

She was a pretty woman, about twenty-five years old; but

in her large dark eyes was a hunted look, quite out of keeping with the peace of her surroundings. Rather over medium height, but well proportioned and graceful in movement, an air of tragedy appeared to weigh upon her. She smiled as though smiling were an effort when the big man smiled at her.

He was still arrayed in the garments of a bushman: elastic-sided brown boots, spotless khaki drill trousers, and white shirt open at the neck and rolled up above the elbows; but Martin, having failed to induce his brother to don city clothes, had himself accepted the white duck, the white canvas shoes, and the white pith helmet so necessary to a gentleman, even in a shade temperature of 120 degrees.

The younger man bestrode his riding-camel, and it was the significantly aimless stare of his sightless eyes that caused the woman's mouth to droop commiseratingly. From him her eyes wandered along the train; pausing at the unsheathed Savage rifle so attached to the saddle that it could be snatched and used at a moment's notice, and finally to rest on the magnificent figure of the giant. Monty observed her study of him, and when their eyes met she blushed a little.

"I didn't mean to be rude," she said in a cultured voice; "but visitors are so rare that I forgot."

"It's quite excusable," Monty said laughing. "A great, hulking brute of a man always creates interest, like a lion escaped from a circus. Yes, I think Mr. Anchor is expecting us."

"Good morning, gentlemen!" greeted a masculine voice, and, turning about, Monty saw a little tubby man, round-faced, clean-shaven, pink-complexioned, looking at them alternatively with twinkling blue eyes. His collar and tie, tweed trousers, and dancing pumps decided Monty that he was the bookkeeper. Irrepressible joyousness radiated from him.

"Good day-ee!"

"Mr. Anchor asked me to introduce myself and to convey his regrets that he cannot personally welcome you. As a matter of fact, he is just now engaged upon a very delicate experiment which chains him to his laboratory until its completion. If you will accompany me, I will show you where to store your gear and paddock your camels."

"Righto!" agreed Monty, and, raising his felt to the laundress, walked beside the little man to the wide iron gates giving entrance to the compound.

"By the way, you must be Mr. Montague Sherwood,"
chirped the guide, speaking then over his shoulder. "We
are to have another dust-storm by appearance, Mr. Martin
Sherwood. However, the house provides adequate protection, and we will soon have you comfortable." Then, as
though to both of them: "My name is Mallowing—George
Mallowing—and let me add my personal welcome to that of
Mr. Anchor. I am delighted you have come: visitors are,
indeed, a luxury to us."

Martin heard Monty say something in reply, and then the
three vertical lines between his brows deepened. He was
searching his memory. Where had he seen the name of
George Mallowing? He was sure that the name at some time
had been given publicity. His camel came to a halt, and he
heard the man chirp:

"Mr. Anchor has placed this hut at your disposal, Mr.
Sherwood. Not for your persons, of course, but for your gear.
Here is Earle. He will entertain Mr. Martin whilst we un-
load."

Earle bowed to the big man with old-fashioned courtesy.
He was stoop-shouldered, spectacled, and dreadfully thin.
His cheeks were two patches of bright red in a face of alabaster.
Grey-haired and clean shaven, he looked like the proverbial
university professor.

"Good morning!" he said in a gentle, refined voice.

"Good day-ee!" Monty drawled—a puzzled Monty, for this
man was dressed in a neat blue city suit, and appeared never
to have done any manual work in his life.

"Hooshing" down the beasts, the big man assisted Martin
to alight, and led him to the short shade of the hut Mallowing
had indicated for their use. Then, with the dexterity of long
practice, he removed the loads and saddles, which Mallowing
helped him to carry within.

"Now, Mr. Sherwood, I will show you the best of our two
horse paddocks, where your camels will find fair feed and
water. Earle, we leave Mr. Martin Sherwood in your care."

"This is really terrible weather," remarked Earle, when the
other two had moved away with the camels. "Heat, dust,
and flies. I no longer wonder at people refusing to live in the
bush."

"Nor I," Martin agreed, an expression of well-subdued
surprise on his face. "Excuse me, your name is Earle, is it
not?"

"Yes. Percival Earle, one time of Bathurst," came the answer, in a slightly hardened voice.

"Surely you were prominently featured in the newspapers about twelve months ago?"

"Yes, I believe I did receive some attention from that quarter. But may we not discuss a subject less personal?"

Martin's eyes were wide, but astonishment showed plainly on his face. This human being, who moved outside his world of darkness, took shape in the eyes of his mind as something monstrous. Only with effort did he calm his voice.

"What kind of a place is this?" he asked quietly—a simple question which brought a simple answer.

"It is a house of refuge for poor harassed souls, Mr. Sherwood. Here we find peace and rest, and security from the world, and try to find peace and rest and security from our thoughts. We can shut out the world, but it is hard to shut out memory."

"I wish I could see," Martin said almost absently.

"I wish you could, too."

The tone of the words rather than their bare meaning seemed to emphasize their significance. They were spoken as though Earle devoutly wished that Martin could see him as he was, and not as he imagined. It was Earle who spoke next.

"Mr. Anchor is now coming to us," he said softly. "You will find him quite a gentleman, but be guarded in your acts and speech."

A moment later Anchor's well-modulated voice reached the blind man.

"Kindly accept my regrets, Mr. Sherwood, that I could not receive you in person. I requested Mallowing to explain my dilemma."

Martin, recovering his composure, played for time.

"We understand perfectly," he said. "Through Mr. Mallowing, you most kindly provided for our arrival at an unfixed and unfixable hour. The reading must be high to-day, surely."

"When I crossed the veranda just now I noticed the mercury touching 121 degrees," came the suave voice. "By the sky we shall have a cool change, probably to-night. Let us heartily hope that this is the last heat-wave of this summer."

They chatted about the weather until Monty and the little man returned, when Anchor, having been introduced to the bushman, himself guided Martin and led the others to the wide, darkened veranda, where the sun-glare was kept out by green bead blinds. And, when his guests were comfortably seated in low wicker chairs, he rang a tiny bell, saying:

"It is a relief to get away from the flies. Lunch will be ready in half an hour; but, before I show you to your apartments, what can I offer you in the way of refreshment—liquid refreshment?"

Martin somewhat hesitatingly suggested a sherry and bitters. Beer out of a bottle was Monty's preference.

"I believe in cultivating a little comfort," Anchor remarked when he had made known their wants to a maid who answered the bell. "Comfort makes for longevity; good food and good liquor assure it. I boast an ancestor who, it is recorded, served as cabin-boy on the *Mayflower*. Every day, for one hundred years, he consumed four gallons of beer stiffened with rum. So, you see, I have authority."

This appeal to "authority" brought a delighted chuckle from Monty and low laughter from his brother.

"Pardon me," the blind man said. "But beer and rum do not seem to mix with the *Mayflower*."

"Ah! but the records don't state that the beverage was consumed whilst at sea," came the silken voice. "By the way, I have to say that Miss Thorpe is resting now, but will meet you at dinner this evening."

"Then she is expecting us?"

Anchor looked steadily at Monty, who asked the question. His mouth smiled, but his eyes did not.

"But certainly," he said. "We have been expecting you throughout the last week."

"You mystify me."

"Quite simple, as I will explain later. Forgive me for hurrying you, but I must explain now that, although you are to consider this house and ourselves entirely at your disposal, there is one hardship we all suffer from, and that is punctuality at meals. Our *chef,* you will soon know, is really an artist, both in cooking and in English of the Billingsgate flavour. He is a gentleman of peculiar temperament who, when annoyed, becomes alarmingly violent with the plates and things if any of us are late at meals."

"All cooks are bad tempered," Monty asserted from experience of bush cooks.

"My *chef* is horribly so," said Anchor, rising and leading them along the veranda to the hall. "Yet we cannot possibly do without him. Once we were without a *chef,* and Mallowing practised on us with the result that we were all bad tempered."

Monty was astonished by the hall furnishings, which were in a manner quite unfamiliar to him. A visitor to the average squatter's home would have been no less surprised by the taste displayed in the perfect Jacobean hall, complete with carved black oak chest-seats, high-backed narrow chairs and small round tables bearing knick-knacks of the period. The polished armour of a Crusader stood in one corner beside a large illuminated tapestry entirely covering the further wall.

Anchor led them across the polished black oak floor to a corridor from which opened many rooms, led them to the end of it, without a glance at the Hogarths decorating the walls, to a large and lofty bedroom lit by two pairs of French windows which opened outwardly on the veranda.

"The luncheon bell will ring in five minutes," the host warned them. "Here I think you will find everything necessary for a hasty toilet. I will show you the bathrooms later. Now, please do not linger. I myself will come for you when the gong sounds. I am afraid of but one human being in the world, and that is the tyrant of our kitchen. Au revoir!"

When the door closed behind him the big man stepped to Martin's side and whispered:

"Friend Anchor would be a nice, kind sort of bloke if it wasn't for his eyes, old son."

"There is something about his voice which I do not like," Martin said as softly. "Monty, I have made two discoveries."

"You have! Pass 'em over."

"First describe Mallowing and the man Earle."

The big man did so in surprisingly few words.

"It fits, brother mine," Martin went on. "Mallowing is George Mallowing, wanted by the Victorian police for the murder of his wife. As for Percival Earle, you will remember that this time last year he killed his three children at Bathurst."

A low, long whistle broke from Monty.

"I think, Monty, we are within a hornets' nest."

"Then you watch me stir 'em up," the bushman drawled, his eyes alight, his face wreathed in a broad smile of genuine happiness. "Somebody has brought our suit-cases here, old son, so we will get along with our toilet, from which we must not omit attention to the cannons. How's yours?"

"Loaded—and in my hip pocket."

"Good! I'll sling mine under my arm. I know, absolutely know, for a sure fact, that there's going to be lots of doings in the very near future."

But, if Monty temporarily had forgotten the existence of Austiline Thorpe, the blind man had not. He felt sick with apprehension.

CHAPTER XVIII

DISTINGUISHED COMPANY

THAT remarkable man, William J. Anchor, tapped on the door almost immediately after the silvery-toned gong was struck.

"I trust you are quite ready for lunch," he said on being invited to enter, and for the life of him Monty could not decide whether their amiable host was really anxious not to arouse the wrath of his cook or was enjoying some subtle joke invented for his own delectation.

With Martin's hand resting on Monty's fully-sleeved arm—for after much pleading he had imprisoned his neck in a collar and donned a light jacket—Anchor led them through the corridor, across the hall, and into a spacious room cooled by electric fans.

This room, like the hall, was furnished in the Jacobean style and was tastefully if not elaborately decorated. Three French windows extending from floor to ceiling, and now wide open, gave free access to the veranda. Beyond the fly-gauze could be seen the gushing bore, and the surrounding expanse of stunted bush growing on sand-hill and flat, now without the usual dazzling glare and inky-black shade, owing to the high-level haze having totally obscured the sun.

Near the central pair of windows was the tall, lank form of Dr. Moore, in conversation with the tubby Mallowing, who, turning at their entry, smiled broadly at the bushman. Monty nodded at him, then began to examine the doctor-aviator with the calm, casual gaze of a horse buyer. Moore as coolly returned the stare, inwardly admiring the splendid physique and lithe carriage of probably the most magnificent specimen of the race he had ever seen. Silently, for some three or four seconds, they regarded each other.

Then, with the grace of a courtier, Anchor placed the tips of his fingers behind the big man's left arm and escorted them to the doctor for introduction. The act, simple though it was, had its significance, because Monty knew that the light fingers had discovered where he carried his gun, and that the action had been performed for that purpose.

"You face Dr. James Moore, Mr. Sherwood," came the bland voice of the owner of this strange house. "Moore, be pleased to meet Mr. Montague Sherwood. You have already met Mr. Martin Sherwood."

"Not an unexpected pleasure, Mr. Sherwood," the doctor said in his slightly high-pitched drawl. "You were away hunting your camels when we called at your camp yesterday."

"How do?" responded the big man in that purring voice of his which was so musical when he chose to make it so. "I must apologize for my absence on the occasion of your visit; in consequence of which I fear my brother's welcome was somewhat lacking in warmth."

"It was quite warm enough, Mr. Sherwood," chuckled Anchor. "It gave me a shock to find myself covered expertly by an automatic. Come! luncheon is served. Let Mr. Martin sit here, and you here, next to me."

On turning round, Monty discovered several persons standing about the long table laid for twelve diners. Their host chose the end of the table farthest from the door, placing Monty on his right and Martin next him along the board. Opposite Monty sat the doctor, with Earle next him and Mallowing beside Earle. Seated at Martin's right was a huge, vicious-looking mountain of flesh, having the body of a whale and the face of a gorilla.

At the door end of the table sat a plump and good-looking woman of perhaps forty years of age, still handsome in spite of her years and the climate. On her right was the laundress girl, and on her left the pretty maid who had brought them their drinks on the veranda.

Between the laundress and Earl lounged the most remarkable looking member of the company. He was perfectly bald, and his eyebrows contained no more than some half a dozen hairs. Standing, he measured less than five feet; sitting his head did not reach the top rail of his chair. At first glance one received the impression that he was a very old man, but on further and more careful examination one was startled by the obvious fact that he was quite a youth. He appeared to be a rejuvenated octogenarian; in point of fact, he was an incredibly aged infant.

He is the last to be described because on account of his situation he was the last to be examined by Monty's keenly alert eyes. The big man had already decided that both Anchor and Moore might be dangerous, but he was convinced that this degenerate could be most dangerous. As for the gross personage beside Martin, he could be regarded with contempt in any scene where quickness of action was of paramount importance. His strength and vitality had been sapped by gluttony. The bushman was introduced to them all by name, and over the table decorations nodded and bowed with a happy smile. Some there were who thought him a fool, but his name did not hold for them the significance it held for the real dwellers in Central Australia.

"You will observe, Mr. Sherwood, that we are a democratic little crowd. The only exception is our famous *chef*: not for want of invitation, but because he too often prefers solitude, and we have found it prudent to indulge his preferences," Anchor remarked whilst expertly carving a cold roast of beef. "Mrs. Jonas, at the other end, attends to the tea-urn —provided to conform to Australia's tea-drinking habit—and between us we manage to feed the multitude."

"After all, the distinction between squatter and man is absurdly overdrawn," Monty returned, looking across at Dr. Moore. "It is the last surviving relic of serfdom among the enlightened and free people of the bush."

"Well, you know, as an American I am in agreement with you; but the doctor, being an Englishman, pins himself to feudalism," Anchor said, glancing slyly at the dark-spectacled medico. "What really baffles my friend is that I, an honoured descendant of the cabin-boy on the *Mayflower,* and therefore of aristocratic and four-bottle lineage, should be so unworthy of that lineage as to wallow in the mongrelly doctrines of Karl Marx. Really, my dear Moore, you of all men should appreciate that we are all made of the same muck, and all give forth the identical effluvium when we have been dead a month."

The doctor grunted unintelligibly, and attacked his meat with not a little show of temper. Obviously Anchor was touching a raw spot. Mallowing smiled, and unashamedly winked at Monty. The aged infant smirked, whilst the laundress smiled faintly at the maid. But Mrs. Jonas continued to gaze sternly at the tea-urn.

"Well, somehow I seem to enjoy eating a little more than

when Master Gilling graced the board," observed Mallowing with twinkling eyes.

"Tut, tut, Mallowing! I am surprised at you," Anchor said to him, his bland features certainly indicating no surprise. "Poor Gilling was badly born, badly reared, had everything against him from the start. Under our influence and discipline he had the first real chance, I think, in his life. Let us deplore the loss of this opportunity to show brotherly love."

For a while the conversation became general, Martin entering the lists with Anchor on the deplorable tendency of modern fiction to clothe sex immorality in the garments of virtue, wherein he was very ably seconded by Mrs. Jonas. Between them they routed Anchor, who effected masterly retreat with colours flying. It was towards the end of the meal that their host again asserted command of the table.

"You find yourselves, gentlemen, in distinguished company," he said in dulcet tones, addressing the Sherwoods. "Not only are we democratic, we are also perfectly frank with one another and with our few visitors. In the hope that you will get to know us intimately, and therefore feel more at your ease, I will venture to outline part of the history of each of our present members, and the reason we are joined in such domestic amenity."

"Is that really necessary, Anchor?" interposed Dr. Moore sharply.

"Permit me, my dear Moore, to emphasize my great age and mellow experience," replied the host, smiling gently with his face, but a hard glitter flashing into his agate eyes.

The words were innocent and spoken calmly enough, but the visitors detected the ring of ruthless authority in the voice, a will that would brook no interference. That trait has the drawback that sooner or later it leads to downfall.

"Pray excuse me," requested Mrs. Jonas, rising abruptly.

"Certainly," Anchor acquiesced, still smiling blandly when, Mallowing having opened the door, she sailed from the room, disapproval plainly visible in the angle of her head. She was followed, a little more submissively, by the laundress.

"You will remember," Anchor continued when the tubby man had regained his seat, "that some few years ago the third wife of an American millionaire died rather suddenly while staying, accompanied by her husband, at a hunting lodge in the Adirondacks. A young and clever medico, also a guest, attended her with the keenness to be expected in a quondam lover. Not being satisfied with the—er—symptoms of the lady's illness, he insisted on an autopsy which revealed rather an extravagant quantity of arsenic in her body.

"The husband was so affected that he disappeared, and not long after that the inquisitive doctor was the immediate cause of the unfortunate millionaire's two former wives being exhumed from their peaceful graves and subjected to analysis. It was then ascertained that the three bodies contained sufficient arsenic among them to inconvenience an army."

"You are referring to the rubber king, William J. Hook?" Martin asked.

"I am, Mr. Sherwood. Believe me, William J. Hook found a speedy and painless death most necessary. His next incarnation was in the person of William J. Anchor."

This amazing confession nearly brought the blind man to his feet; but, feeling Monty's cautioning hand on his arm, he restrained himself. They were regarded curiously by the remainder of the diners as though it had been usual in the past, when such a confession was made, for the hearers to be stunned or galvanized into horrified action.

Across the corner of the table Monty gazed steadily at their urbane host, who returned his look with a faint smile through hard, unwinking eyes. That this mild-looking, smooth-spoken, elderly man, who would have adorned any bank parlour in the world, was the most infamous murderer of this century, was to the Sherwoods a veritable bombshell. But not for an instant did the startling nature of the communication affect the big man's expression. He was smiling with much of the air of a generous man listening to the first romance of his only son.

"My sympathies are entirely with. you in your domestic troubles," he said slowly. "Arsenic, most certainly, is the stuff to give 'em."

For the merest fraction of a second Anchor's eyelids lifted before he continued, with a deep sigh:

"Imagine a domesticated man, like me, unable to win women's genuine love because of my money. My first wife said she loved me, and, being then unsophisticated, I believed her. Imagine the anguish, the humiliation, of my disillusionment. She lied, as I suppose she had been brought up to lie. She loved my money, or the luxuries my money bought her. She sold her charms to me for money. If I had divorced her, she would have been wealthy for life on my alimony. One morning, in her dressing-room, she told me with brutal frankness that she had married me to be divorced. So I divorced her—in a quiet and economic fashion of my own—with arsenic."

"Well, it was what she asked for, wasn't it?" murmured Monty.

"My second wife's assurances of devotion I accepted with more reserve," Anchor went on. "Even so, it was a painful shock to me, and ultimately a fatal shock to her, when she allowed hatred to blaze in her eyes when I showed husbandly affection. As for my last wife, poor thing! she was considered the loveliest woman in America. She swore she loved me; but, after my previous experiences, I could not believe her. My experiences had taught me the impossibility of my gaining—at least as a millionaire—a woman's real love; so I forced myself to be content with what poor substitute for love I was able to command. What did annoy me considerably was the fact that she gave my love-money to the doctor I have mentioned. I was paying for the satisfaction he received when he held her in his arms; and that, I think, I was entitled even legally to resent. However, she passed away quite peacefully; it was the doctor who raised objections."

The blind man shrank as under a succession of blows. The speech of the man was deliberate; he picked his words; the thoughts he expressed were perfectly coherent: yet he discoursed on murder and his own terrible actions with an evenness of voice and absence of emotion absolutely astounding in a human being. So gentle were the inflections of his voice that the blind man could almost imagine that now and then it held a sob. He could not visualize what Monty saw, the slaty agate eyes, empty of ordinary human softness, tenderness, compassion. Anchor was human, possessing a human brain, human sanity; but instead of human nature he had the nature of a tiger. Mentally he was monstrous; as much so as in physical constitution was the little bald-headed aged youth.

"Perhaps the fact is that I started to pursue domestic happiness somewhat late in life," Anchor drawled. "Perhaps had I started earlier—and poorer—I might have attained it. We all seek for something in life, but seldom does one of us obtain just what is sought for. Dr. Moore, for instance, chased after fame, and would have obtained a lasting hold upon it had it not been for the scurvy interference of Fate.

"With a colleague he, in London, spent several years in painstaking endeavour to discover the cause or causes of cancer. With Dr. Talmadge he was prosecuting a series of experiments on plants, when his partner startled him by announcing that he had won another of Nature's secrets, partly by chance; not the cause of cancer, but the sure means of destroying the bacillus of consumption.

"Most unnaturally, Dr. Talmadge declined to share his certain renown with Dr. Moore, an attitude betraying ingratitude, for my friend here was financing the experiments. In the circumstances it was, perhaps, excusable for Dr. Moore to remove his colleague by the cave-man's method of hitting him behind the ear with a stone-headed implement used for pulverizing crystals in a mortar. I emphasize the neolithic method advisedly, my dear Moore. It always astounds me that a man in the front rank of modern medical science should have used so crude a means. I know, of course, that all doctors resort to primitive measures in emergency, and perhaps this was such a case.

"However, my friend found Talmadge's memorandum of the discovery, and, leaving the body in the laboratory, retired to his bed in the room above. You will doubtless remember how Fate fired the house, and how a policeman, seeing smoke issuing from the laboratory window, rushed in and rescued the body. Dr. Moore was compelled to leave hurriedly on a visit to friends, while through some inadvertence the priceless memorandum was consumed together with the house."

"Then you must be Dr. Walling?" Martin interrupted in horrified tones. Moore made no reply.

"Let us not probe into the past too deeply," suavely advised Anchor. "We come next to Earle, who, a little more than twelve months ago, was a prosperous business man of Bathurst.

"Earle had not long been left a widower, burdened with the responsibility of bringing up three young children. Passionately fond of them, as he was, he became greatly alarmed at their probable future on learning from his medico that he had but six months longer, at most, to live. Having no relations, either his own or his late wife's, his fears became a nightmare that his sweet mites would be at the mercy of harsh and unsympathetic strangers."

Only Martin's training as a journalist, only the instinct of the news-getter, kept him a silent listener in his seat. The pleasant, gentle voice flowed on.

"Possibly Percival Earle may be excused for thinking that, when he was dead, no matter what provision he made for them, his children would be dragged up, unsheltered by a father's love from the evils besetting young men and maids in this wicked world. So, conceiving the idea that heaven—to my mind a problematic sphere of existence—would be preferable for his innocent children to earth, he—er—lulled them painlessly into eternal sleep."

Silence fell after that last word. The aged infant and the fat man went on eating unconcernedly. The maid poured herself another cup of tea. As for Earle, he sat slumped down in his chair, his eyes closed, but from them falling large tears. His face was white as milk, the red cheek blotches absent, and his hands lay on the table before him, excessively thin, blue-veined, and long fingered. Monty, at heart no less horrified than Martin, looked at Earle with wonder. The man's behaviour was rational, yet he believed it impossible for him to be sane.

"We come now to the interesting personality of Mallowing," Anchor continued. "His case is, as far as I know, unique, because he has got what for many years he sought in vain. Picture him tied to a shrew of a woman for fifteen years. Imagine him as a sensitive, cultured man, his personality swamped by that of the virago, fearful of her temper, subservient to her lightest whim, living a joy-blasted life for a decade, his naturally sunny nature subdued to the acid mentality of his terrible partner.

"They lived in a house near the railway station at Charlton, way down in Victoria, where he was earning a good living as manager of a wide estate business. To satisfy his exacting wife, it became his habit to leave his office punctually at five o'clock, and as punctually enter his house a quarter of an hour later.

"But one afternoon, when leaving his office, a motor-car knocked down a man; and, temporarily forgetting his too affectionate spouse, he spent several priceless minutes in rendering first aid. Consequently it was six o'clock before he reached his home, forty-five minutes later than the time fixed by his wife.

"He dreaded the explosive greeting, the cross-examination,

the suspicious questions, the crowning insult of sniffing at his breath. It was when he saw his wife grimly awaiting him in the hall—waiting to demand fiercely the reason of his being forty-five minutes late, and to give him forty-five minutes' hell for it—that, almost or quite subconsciously, his long-suppressed manhood asserted itself, and he freed himself in a moment from his hideous bondage by merely raising—and dropping—his reversed walking-stick.

"The simplest of action, yet it meant a recreated life. Behold Mallowing to-day. A happy, care-free man able to laugh again, able to remember that he has human instincts and a personality of his own, joyous with the joy of freedom from intolerable oppression."

The rotund figure sat up squarely in his chair, and, gazing across the table at the bushman, picked up and drank his tea as though responding to a toast. There was nothing sinister, no trace of insanity, not even an indication of ordinary masculine temper in that chubby, friendly face. When Monty regarded him, the big man doubted for the first time the truth of Anchor's revelations, in this case, at any rate. Mallowing looked the sort of man who would turn away from the swatting of a fly with horror.

"Then there is Smith," went on William J. Anchor, nodding towards the little bald youth. " 'The Cat' they call him in Sydney, on account of his astonishing ability to climb walls and stroll about house-tops. You would be surprised at the difficulty I have in restraining him from viewing the scenery from the roof above us. Constant attendance at the moving-picture shows imbued him with the ambition to be—ah!—'quick on the draw,' I think they call it. I do think the cinema has a detrimental effect on the character of our youth today ; any way, Smith neatly holed a policeman who apparently was anxious to inquire the time, and that wretched policeman gave his colleagues a most excellent description of 'The Cat' before he departed this life.

"To observe Lane, next to Mr. Martin, one would hardly credit the fact that only two years ago he was passionately fond of a lady at Brisbane. Nevertheless, I assure you, such was the case."

The fat man raised his huge unkempt head, and for a fleeting second his piggy eyes glared at the ex-rubber king. But only for a second. He continued eating his enormous meal long after the others had finished.

"Lane feared to be displaced in the affections of his lady, and, to minimize the danger, strangled a rival. The feat being performed with an utter absence of artistry, Lane would certainly have come to an untimely end had we not made him welcome here. I think, Lane, they would have given you only a five-foot drop."

Again the huge man raised his head, but this time the expression in his small eyes was softened to a dog-like devotion. Monty chuckled.

"You seem well up in the hanging process," he said.

"I have given the matter some attention, I admit," Anchor replied coolly, sipping the last of his tea. "But to proceed. A case of human interest is that of Mrs. Jonas. Our house-keeper is an exceedingly respectable and—er—an excessively religious woman. She is strong on sex morality, and rules us with a rod of iron. A little more than three years ago she lived with her husband, a pillar of the church, as, indeed, was she, at Port Augusta. Imagine, gentlemen, her horror and disgust when she discovered that her husband was keeping a separate establishment. I do not wonder that she infringed medical and legal etiquette by prescribing and administering to her husband and his paramour a remedy containing strychnine, which in such cases as a rule is effectual.

"Madeline Fox, who remains with us, has a temper which will, I much fear, get her into serious trouble one of these days. Forgive me, Madeline, we all have our faults, I know; but between our *chef's* temper and yours I am sure poor Mrs. Jonas is sorely tried. Nevertheless, gentlemen, Madeline has had numerous lovers, which I admit is not surprising."

The girl, hardly turned twenty, smiled boldly at Anchor and as boldly at Monty. Anchor did not smile in return, but Monty did. He smiled at her again when Anchor went on to explain how she had murdered a faithless lover by stabbing him to the heart with a hat-pin.

"As for Mabel Hogan, her romance also was flavoured with strychnine, when the father of her child, instead of marrying her as promised, was blackguardly enough to taunt her with their sin.

"Gilling, whose unfortunate absence we all deplore," with a steady look at Mallowing, "killed a little girl of ten years with an iron bar because he coveted the sum of two shillings and one penny which she was conveying to the grocer to pay her mother's bill. And last, gentlemen, but by no means least, is *the* most important member of our family, comrade Johnston, our wonderful *chef*. I admire Johnston, his nerve is superb. He most artistically carved into small pieces his lifelong friend because the said friend made some paltry objection when he, Johnston, relieved him of his bank account. We have all learned to respect Johnston.

"That, I think, completes the outline of the histories of all who at present compose our happy community. Several have left us to take up again their worldly burdens: we hope to have with us in the future friends equally as dear. Shall we adjourn to the veranda for a smoke?"

The question was asked with the polish of an ambassador. The recital might have been that of an interesting sea voyage, so passionless and deliberate was its delivery. Martin felt that he was surrounded by a ring of beasts, human beasts, waiting crouched to spring upon Monty and him. Without sight he could not visualize the pathetic Earle, the cheerful Mallowing, or the prim, good-looking Mrs. Jonas. Even the big man was surprised and found it difficult to credit that all these ordinary, very human-looking people, were takers of life. He wondered what Mallowing's face looked like when he struck that fatal blow.

Horror was writ plainly on Martin's face, but if either Anchor or Moore expected Monty to blanch they must have been disappointed, for he beamed on the company with twinkling eyes, even while his arm cuddled the revolver.

"Well, well, well!" he warbled genially. "I am indeed pleased to find myself in such congenial company. Having started quite a promising graveyard of my own—the latest addition being young Gilling, who wanted me to adorn his— I feel already at home among you."

Pushing back his chair, he helped Martin to rise, taking then an arm preparatory to leading him to the veranda. Looking steadily into the agate eyes of his host, he added:

"To me excitement is the breath of life, Mr. Anchor, and, so far, the dank clamminess of death to the other fellow."

CHAPTER XIX

THE HOUSE OF CAIN

AS Martin well knew, Monty Sherwood was by no means of the callous disposition which, by way of accommodating himself to his company, he had put on. The fact was, he regarded evil in other men much as a governess regards naughtiness in her charges—a naughtiness grown to evil in the adult. When he met with evil and was able to punish it his methods were original and drastic. In punching a card-sharp into insensibility, his object was not the mere infliction of pain, but to apply such corporeal chastisement as at least might induce the sinner to consider "safety first" in its moral aspect. Seldom does a teacher feel satisfaction in the act of caning a scholar, but he does feel satisfaction if the act produces, even temporarily, better behaviour.

The big man regarded evil in men and women as a childish trait which they had never grown out of. Criminals he looked on as people whose minds had not kept pace with the growth of the body. He believed that the ancient idea of casting out devils by inflicting pain on the body they inhabited was preferable to inflicting pain on the mind. He had told Martin once that "a good wallop on the nose will cure a thief of itching fingers when ten years of imprisonment will fail. A bleeding, broken nose will not jar his mind so much as gaol, and heaven knows that the man's mind is jarred and warped enough as it is. A criminal is like a little child: shutting the child in a dark room doesn't do it any good. A good spanking does."

Whereas Martin had come to regard Anchor and his friends as a company of fiends, Monty felt like a master who, having left the classroom for a moment, returns to find his scholars engaged in a general fight. Here were people who had never grown up! As infants they probably had delighted in murdering insects and birds; their infantile taste for killing remained a part of them. Thus he was able to regard them with benevolent amusement until such time as their desire to kill recurred, in which case he would inflict chastisement. It could not be helped if the chastisement had to be inflicted by the impact of a bullet instead of a cane. The punishment must grow in severity with the growth of the body.

Many will disagree with Monty Sherwood's opinions here expressed; nevertheless, it is an actual fact that card-sharps did not practise their depravity in Monty's presence oftener than once.

So it was that the big man smiled on the company as a doting father smiles on his wayward children. They regarded him as a simpleton, a child-like giant, and William J. Anchor smiled in return and accompanied them to the veranda with a chuckling: "I think we shall appreciate your visit, Mr. Sherwood."

"Not more than I shall do," Monty said, first introducing Martin to a chair and then seating himself.

"I sincerely hope you will enjoy your stay," their host observed when, reclining in a deep lounge, he regarded them while biting at a long, thin cheroot. "We are a queer community, but a peaceful one. War and strife we leave to the outer world."

"Not a bad idea," agreed the bushman, lighting his pipe.

"We did not come here with any intention to disturb your peace," Martin put in. "If you are what you say you are, we could not possibly be anything but friends after the great service you have rendered my promised wife, Miss Austiline Thorpe. I am unaware if you are the direct instigator of her rescue from gaol, and consequently from a shameful death; yet, on account of your protection of her, I for one shall forget my duty as a citizen. It is therefore, with no thought of strife that I speak to you now."

"I am delighted to find that you accept in such a spirit what must be a most disturbing situation," Anchor murmured.

"I think we now understand one another," Martin said, exhaling cigarette smoke. "What does puzzle me, however, is why Miss Thorpe has not appeared. She must realize how anxious I am on her behalf, and she cannot have forgotten that at least we were lovers."

"My dear sir, never be surprised at a woman's whims," Anchor replied softly. "Long ago I decided that trying to understand a woman was a waste of precious brainstuff. I used to worry myself ill trying to please women; now I most emphatically decline to be worried by any woman."

"Nevertheless, her non-appearance surprises me."

"I have not known Miss Thorpe so long as you have, Mr. Sherwood, but I should not expect to understand her if I had known her all her life. It takes a woman to understand a woman. Last evening I informed her that you had disregarded her request to bother no further about her, and that you would visit us to-day. My gossip appeared to bore her. This morning, when I went to her apartment to tell her of your arrival, she said that, feeling unwell, she would defer meeting you until dinner this evening. Believe me, I understand your anxiety. Follow a woman if you like, but never attempt to lead one."

Even Monty was bluffed, and Anchor, elated by his success, diverted them from the dangerous subject by asking:

"What is your opinion of my great humanitarian scheme?"

"What do you mean?" inquired the blind man.

"Why, my Home!—and I used the word in its proper sense —my Home for those bearing the brand of Cain. I see I had better explain it from the beginning.

"Even when I was debating the future of my first wife I realized that some inconvenience might follow, should the general public become acquainted with the precise method adopted," went on this extraordinary man, who appeared to regard murder as one of the homely details of existence. "And so, some time before her decease, I transferred considerable sums—in ways known to financiers—to the safekeeping of a gentleman named William John Anchor, of Baltimore. That forethought saved me much trouble when the fool doctor, my later wife's lover, began to stir up the waters of the past.

"But, although I successfully created the personality of William J. Anchor, I could not enjoy in his name the measure of business activity which I had done as William J. Hook. Therefore, I realized the necessity of opening some fresh channel for my energies. I was in Paris, whither I had drifted for pleasure, when I found myself gazing at a picture in the Louvre in company with a stranger whom afterwards I came to known as Dr. Moore, and later still as Dr. Walling.

"Now, we were both takers of life, both wanted by the law which wanted to take our lives. Neither of us cared much about the overrated pleasures of Paris. In each life had occurred a cataclysm which had rooted us up and placed us on unfamiliar soil, and as a consequence of this coincidence we became great friends.

"It was really the cramped and fettered conditions of my new life which made me feel the want of a home for murderers of both sexes, much as I should imagine the poor of gentle birth are made to feel the want of a genteel refuge of some sort in which to hide and die. Recognizing the want and being able to finance some adequately framed effort to meet it, I suggested the idea to Dr. Moore, who agreed at once to assist me.

"We searched the world for a suitable locality, and found the world to be a very small place. Of necessity the Home must be at a safe distance from civilization, yet not beyond touch of it. My own country was far too closely settled to provide a suitable site; South America also was too crowded, if not with white folk, then with black. Africa was the same. India was out of the question, whilst the Pacific Islands were too much within the orbit of trade. Here, in this vast semi-desert, within reasonable flying distance of a railway, we found what I wanted. There are not even black people to gossip and invent romantic stories about my Home. For explorers there is no attraction—no gold, no publicity—to induce them to visit this desert region. I know of only two localities in the world less inhabited, and they are the Poles.

"Finding this house and bore for sale was indeed a God-send," went on the drawling voice, its owner lying back with half-closed eyes, his cheroot burned out, his hands clasped behind his head. "To mask my scheme, to make the place habitable, and to maintain a certain amount of seclusion, I gave it out that I was engaged (as indeed I am) upon an important invention, and that I would resent any intrusion.

"The Home brought into existence, it then became necessary to make it known to those for whom it was intended. Moore and I got into touch with the Australian under-world, and formed an organization in every city to spirit away to this house those unfortunates whose lives were threatened by the law. The expenses in connections with the transfer here of each such case averages two thousand pounds, and in that of Miss Thorpe, with its spectacular features, came as high as six thousand pounds."

"But surely you are not a philanthropist to that extent?" Martin interjected, his journalistic soul thrilled to the core by this string of amazing revelations.

"It is a fact," was the blandly spoken reply. "The thirty thousand which this scheme costs me every year is but a tithe of my income, which continues to mount in an embarrassing manner. It is essential to open up fresh avenues of expenditure to absorb the interest accruing from my investments. Such a project as a Murderers' Home you will agree is at least original. It amuses me to study the various types sent here by my organization: it enables me to replace my lost interest in high finance by a fresh one which requires keen organization, incessant watchfulness, and iron leadership. I am one of those persons who must always be doing something; and you will readily understand that my unfortunate adventures in matrimony have narrowed my field of activity to a very serious extent. Sometimes I am tempted to wonder if it would not have paid me better to have obtained divorces in the ordinary way; but I am one of those who greatly dislike to be outwitted or 'done' by any one.

"I have plenty to do, I assure you, outside the direction of this establishment. Miss Thorpe's terrible position in the Melbourne gaol gave my brain pleasurable exercise in working out a solution, and I will outline her rescue by way of giving you a general idea of our methods. Another cigarette, Mr. Sherwood?"

"Thank you, but with your permission I will smoke one of my own," Martin returned, producing his case. Observing the brand, Anchor said:

"Ah! I see you favour 'Three Circle' cigarettes, Mr. Sherwood. They are a little too strong, as a cigarette, for my palate, but an excellent smoke nevertheless. Yes, in the first instance the chief of my Melbourne organization wirelessed me in code the facts governing Miss Thorpe's arrest on the charge of murder. Had she been accused of murder before her arrest was possible, he would have acted without further instructions; but, as Miss Thorpe was behind prison bars, he felt bound to learn my views.

"Feeling that the life of a brave woman was too much to pay for that of a mean blackmailer, I decided in Miss Thorpe's favour. I ordered my agent to get her out and dispatch her here at once. Every hour I learned how the plans were maturing. I knew that Hill, *alias* Bent Nose, a thief turned honest, was the best man to do the inside work, as ten years previously he, with other convicts, had been engaged in structural alterations to the women's wing. At first I was surprised when Bent Nose refused payment for his very valuable work, but later learned that he owed Miss Thorpe a debt of gratitude.

"He it was who, after the wardresses on night duty had been dealt with, roused Miss Thorpe and commanded her to dress. The whole scheme was carried on by stop-watches, tested and compared beforehand. Bent Nose was given ten minutes to locate Miss Thorpe's cell. She was allowed twenty minutes to dress. Bent Nose was given another five minutes to get her to the landing window, the bars of which he had melted asunder with oxy-acetylene whilst she dressed, and thence lower her to the ground. Five seconds were allowed him to follow her. And so perfect was the timing that on the instant that his feet touched the ground the fuse fired the explosive which tore down a portion of the outer wall, and a confederate had his arms round the neck of the sentinel in the watch-tower.

"Even while portions of brick were in the air Bent Nose and Miss Thorpe left the wall of the building for the breach, even before the thunder of the explosion had died away in echoes the driver of a powerful car at the corner of the street let out the clutch and stepped on the gas. The car slowed down at the hole in the wall precisely as Miss Thorpe and her escort emerged to jump into it.

"Yes, it was very neatly done, and the pleasure of the achievement was well worth my six thousand pounds. The car brought Miss Thorpe to a lonely farm near Sunshine, where she was transferred to an aeroplane which flew her to Gawler, north of Adelaide. Coming then under the protection of our South Australian organization, she was motored to Port Augusta, where she caught the train to Marree. At Marree she was met by Dr. Moore, who flew her on the last stage of the journey to safety.

"It is all those little details, those wheels within wheels, which make this game to me no less interesting than high finance. Its originality attracts me. I can direct it in the seclusion and comfort of this my Home, the aeroplane and the wireless being valuable aids. It banishes boredom, which otherwise would swamp me; it provides me with amusement and scope for the study of human nature, which has been a lifelong hobby.

"Of course, I have to take the rough with the smooth. I have decided that takers of human life are of two classes.

Most of us kill upon impulse only, the impulse brought about by circumstances both rare and complex. It is Dr. Moore's theory, and so far I am in agreement with him, that, under circumstances sufficiently complex and compelling, any human being will attempt to kill—soldiers, for instance. Where he forges ahead and I lag behind is in his advanced theory that there is a portion of the human brain, equally as useless as the appendix, the removal of which would prevent the subject from killing when the complex circumstances which arouse murderous emotion are present. We must get him to expatiate on the subject. It is a favourite one with him, and he makes it interesting.

"Of course, we get people here like Gilling, whose sanity I doubted from the first, and Lane, who is little removed from the brute. In 'The Cat' we have a lurid example of heredity. Dr. Moore's removal of a part of his brain would not make a sound man of him any more than it would Lane; or, rather I should say, the operation, in my opinion, would not have prevented the temporary lapse. They are killers by instinct and from birth.

"So you see I am content to exercise my brain with the operation and studies I have outlined, and my friend, Dr. Moore, is content also to carry on his experiments in searching out the causes of cancer. He is keen to experiment on humans, too; but I am loath to allow that after what happened to a half-caste Malay. On two other occasions, however, I was obliged to consent, in order to preserve our domestic harmony."

"Experiments on humans!" Martin exclaimed.

"Yes; to remove that part of the brain which creates the impulse to kill."

"Oh! I see. And was he successful?"

"I think it can be said that he was not," Anchor murmured, looking dreamily at Monty. "This is not an experimental laboratory, but a home for those poor souls who sinned less than they were sinned against, so that as a community we do not suffer from Moore's non-success."

CHAPTER XX

"YOU are very frank, Mr. Anchor," remarked the blind man after a pause. "Why are you so frank?"

The silver-haired, distinguished looking founder and superintendent of surely the most original "Home" in the world opened his eyes and gazed with well-assumed perplexity at his guests. He sat up in his chair, relighting his cheroot before replying.

"Really, I have nothing to hide," he asserted. "Moreover, I think I may be excused from taking a little pride in my efforts on behalf of suffering humanity; precisely the same pride that a Carnegie must take in his libraries or a Rhodes in his scholarships."

"Yet, surely, you cannot expect the world to regard your Home or its inmates with like complacency. Surely you understand that were it discovered you all would be hanged, or shot if you resisted arrest?"

"That elementary consideration has not been overlooked."

"Then allow me again to put my recent question. Why are you so frank with us?"

"Dear, dear! How persistent you are!"

"I am sorry if I appear too much so," came Martin's quiet voice. "We are not here to pry into the secrets of your Home, but to interview Miss Thorpe and induce her, if possible, to return to civilization."

"You know, I really do dislike difficult and to my mind needless explanations on these hot afternoons," Anchor said, and Monty for the first time saw amusement in the slate-coloured eyes. "Still, if you insist——! When recently it was reported to me that a member of my Victorian organization, otherwise Bent Nose, had given you the locality of Miss Thorpe's temporary refuge, I naturally felt upset; for, you see, I already knew all about you two, and was certain that you, Mr. Montague, would pay me a friendly call.

160

"By the way, you may not have heard that Hill paid dearly for his lapse. That, however, was not with my sanction, and when I heard that he had been severely shot I ordered that, should he live, he was not to be molested again. Since then I am given to understand that the man is rapidly recovering."

"Why is he not to be molested again?"

"For the simple reason that, as a healthy man, he would not have informed the authorities for the same reason you recently stated you did not desire to war upon us. But Hill, very near death, might do so in a spirit of revenge. To return to your case. My Melbourne agent was obliged to accompany you to Adelaide before he ascertained which route you intended taking: via Port Augusta and Marree, of via Broken Hill and Turrowangee.

"We knew when you left Broken Hill, also the date of your departure from Turrowangee. We guessed the probable time you would reach the water-hole at the foot of the giant sand-hill, which was why Gilling arrived there but a few hours after you did. He was to camp there and wait for you."

"Can you tell me why Miss Thorpe requested us to return?" was Martin's next question.

"Really I do not know, unless it was that she thought as I did."

"Does she know of Travers's confession, which exonerates her from the crime of murder?" Monty asked bluntly.

"Certainly. The newspaper report of it was sent us immediately."

"What, then, is her object in remaining here?" the big man persisted, watching with admiration Anchor's deep inhalation of the none-too-mild cheroot.

"Ask me something easier," William J. drawled softly. "I suspect she is writing a novel of the bush, and intends leaving us when she has obtained sufficient local colour. That may not be the reason, however. A woman is an enigma which no man can solve."

"She is not prevented from leaving the house, then?"

"Well, her departure would certainly place us in very grave danger," Anchor murmured.

"If so, our departure also will place you in grave danger?"

"I am afraid that is so."

"I think I begin to understand your frankness," Martin put in.

"I am glad to hear it. I am glad to know you appreciate

the difficulties in which Miss Thorpe's affair and your interest in it have involved us. You see, I could not well treat you with our usual hostility to strangers, knowing that you would never be satisfied until you had found Miss Thorpe. When you had narrowed the field of your activities this house would have had your exclusive attention. Pardon my mentioning the fact; but, although I hate doing so, I must remind you that I did not wish nor did I invite you to come here from Melbourne. However, since your stay with us must be indefinitely prolonged, I hope it will prove as enjoyable to you as certainly it will be to us. Frankness is a virtue for people living under one roof."

"In other words, you have deliberately made us more dangerous to you?"

"And intend keeping us here?" Monty inquired mildly.

"Much as we all regret it, gentlemen, that is, I think, the situation," was the bland reply, containing not even the hint of a threat.

The big man smiled broadly. Circumstances were developing the sort of complexity he liked. Here was the kind of adversary whom he never yet had met—astute, calm, confident, ruthless—a foeman indeed worthy of his steel. He realized that the coming upheaval would be a contest demanding the keenest brainwork, as well as iron-hard fists and quick shooting. Well, so be it! Martin could supply the brains and he the rest.

He beamed upon Mr. William J. Anchor, his eyes twinkling and his strong, even teeth revealed by parted lips. The ex-rubber king got the impression that the bushman's intelligence had not yet grasped the full import of the situation as outlined by him. Monty's antecedents, sent him by the leader of his Melbourne organization, gave him no reason to doubt the strength of character of the genial man; therefore, the smile could not be engendered by sympathy with him and his fellow criminals.

"I am delighted that you accept the position in such a friendly spirit," their host drawled. "Make this house your own. There are plenty of books in the library if you like reading; and Dr. Moore, I think, will be most pleased to have you accompany him on some of his flights."

Still Monty smiled with genuine amusement. When he spoke, which was not until he had seen a fleeting flash of uneasiness in the agate eyes, his voice was very low.

"Personally I don't like novels, and crashing in aeroplanes does not appeal to me," he said. "But, if you've no objection, I will spend a few days trapping crows. When released from traps, you know, they make excellent target practice for revolver shooting."

In spite of the sinister meaning underlying Monty's last words, William J. Anchor broke into a hearty chuckle. Rising to his feet, he held out his thin, well-shaped hand, saying:

"For at least one reason I am glad you came."

The big man, on his feet, took the proffered hand, refraining with difficulty from giving it a Squeezem Harry grip.

"You're no less glad than I am for every reason," he said with sudden seriousness. "I believe I am going to enjoy myself even better than I did at the Great War."

"Well, well, we can do with a little stirring up; but allow me first, I pray you, a few days of peace. I have an experiment to complete, and would simply hate to leave it—ah—unfinished. I suggest a siesta now, but before we part for a little while allow me to warn you that my hounds are vicious brutes. They cannot come within the surrounding fence, but if you pass without do not hold me responsible. You know, I hate to cage birds and chain dogs. I am such a lover of freedom myself."

"Ah, yes, the wuppy-wups!" Monty murmured, even more beamingly. "Sorry I was obliged to shoot the one Gilling brought. I thought it was a man, and I like shooting men. They jump higher than rabbits."

Anchor's eyes clouded.

"It was unfortunate," he admitted. "Carlo was the finest but the most docile of the pack, of which but three remain. Now, au revoir till six. I advise a bed and pyjamas. Be ready for the gong at six. Already, I am told by Mrs. Jonas, we are becoming perilously short of china. During lunch to-day Johnston threw a glass jug at a cat which invaded his sanctum with a kitten in its mouth."

Nodding, he passed through the French windows to the dining-room, and a moment later was followed by the brothers, who unhurriedly walked to the hall, where they were met by Mrs. Jonas. As previously stated, Mrs. Jonas was good-looking, the face being well coloured, the expression thoroughly maternal. Yet her eyes, when she smiled, hinted at the tragedy which had sent her life under a cloud. Meeting her gentle smile, Monty found it hard to credit the story of her atrocious crime; looking into her large hazel eyes, he recognized the truth that a murderer is not necessarily a criminal.

"I think we shall have a wind-storm presently," she said in a clear, precise voice, fanning herself with a lace handkerchief. "I got Mabel to bring in the beds from the veranda, and if there is anything we can do for your comfort, be sure to let me know."

"You are most kind, Mrs. Jonas," replied Monty, bestowing on the outcast woman his wonderfully attractive smile. "We hope we shall not be too much trouble to you."

"Yes; we should not like to think we were making extra work, Mrs. Jonas," the blind man put in.

Her eyes softened at sight of the afflicted man. Monty felt a sudden great pity for this refined and gentle female Cain, on noticing her gaze diverted to himself in a searching, appealing look of the naked soul that is totally without hope. When she spoke again her voice was hardly audible.

"I ought not to speak to you," she said, "but you are the first human beings without God's terrible brand that I have seen for three years. No man could smile as you do and be unclean of soul, and meeting you is a little balm to my own." Drawing a little closer and laying one hand on the big man's sleeve, she added, in a tremulous whisper: "I wish you hadn't come. Indeed I do. You must be very careful."

With a slight bow she turned and walked to a passage opposite that which led to their room; and the big man, with a wistful expression, led his brother from the hall without speaking. When the door of their room was shut Martin observed:

"I am very sorry for that woman, Monty."

"You! Sorry for a murderess! A newspaper editor sympathizing with a murderess!" came the big man's mock reproof.

"I fear that what Anchor said about some killers sinning less than they were sinned against has some truth in it. The fact of her husband being a double liver of the worst kind certainly does not lessen the enormity of her crime; nevertheless, it put her to one of the most terrible tests known to human nature, and causes me to hope that God's judgment will be more merciful than man's."

"Too right," Monty agreed, helping Martin to doff his clothes for pyjamas. "There's many a murderer's victim I'd have liked to have murdered myself. I reckon, though, that

His Highness, My Lord William J., and that ruffian with the tinted spectacles, are not the sinned-against type of killers, and that they'll bear watching. With that type murder becomes a habit, like smoking. Well, here is your bunk. Do a think, old lad. I leave the declaration of war to you. If you decide—— Jumping nannygoats!"

CHAPTER XXI

A USTILINE THORPE'S rapid spiriting away from Melbourne to the far-away wilds of South Australia had allowed her little opportunity to think. One vivid impression had followed another with the bewildering swiftness of film drama. Her arrival at Anchor's house was succeeded by prostrating reaction, and only by degrees did the horror of gaol and the nightmare of a terrible death give way to more normal impressions.

Mrs. Jonas found in Austiline scope for her instinct to serve, an instinct that the untimely death of her husband had deprived of its main outlet. Under the care, and what developed into affection of the housekeeper, Austiline rapidly regained her usual balance. Anchor exuded sympathy, Moore was ever courteous and interesting, Mabel Hogan had a personality that drew from her all her wonderful understanding.

By gentle degrees only did she learn the history of her fellow guests; and, though shocked at first, daily familiarity brought about the easy intercourse usual in every well-ordered household. There was nothing about the life of the house which could suggest offence to the moral code even of a Quaker, Anchor proving himself both friend and, when necessary, master to all.

Lane, Gilling, and "The Cat," as well as the two younger women, all belonging to the worker class, and, consequently, having no financial standing, were expected to work at various tasks, for which they received handsome wages, plus a generous bonus; so that, when the time came for them to return to civilization without undue danger of being recognized, they each would possess a small nest-egg with which to start life afresh. The guests of higher degree were not expected to do menial work. Mallowing kept a set of books and looked after the stores; Earle supervised "The Cat" and Gilling, who tended the few cattle remaining from a substantial herd. Lane occasionally did blacksmithing and plumbing, while Mrs. Jonas served as housekeeper and general supervisor of decorum. Inmates of this latter class also found themselves possessed of ample means when they once more entered ordinary society.

It was really because Austiline Thorpe knew herself to be free from the blood-brand that she decided she could not live at the expense of a murderer; insisting upon paying a monthly sum for residence and board, and intending eventually to refund the costs of her rescue from gaol. Anchor at first demurred, but on her showing firmness gave way, arranging to draw the money when she should return to the world. Certain difficulties he foresaw in connection with this arrangement caused him amusement, but he refrained from enlightening her.

Morally, as has been indicated, Anchor's household left nothing to be desired. Those guests whose moral code was not of the strictest dared not misbehave. While they respected Anchor's suave firmness, they all appeared to regard Dr. Moore with not a little fear, a fear that on the surface seemed peculiar. Had it not been for his general fear of a man who was openly subordinate to the millionaire, Austiline would have considered her host's model sanctuary almost as peaceful and harmless as a monastery. But the fear of Moore was a disquieting element. At first she was puzzled. It seemed so utterly baseless; for, if a little morose, Moore was an exceedingly well-read man of advanced and interesting opinions.

Then had occurred the affair of Mainwright, just after Christmas; which revealed the doctor in a new light, and in a measure accounted for the fear he inspired. Mainwright was a quarter-caste Malay pearl-diver of Broome, and had been spirited away from that place the day following the discovery of the bodies of two full-blooded Malays who had lodged at the same house as himself.

The man showed little trace of the black blood running in his veins. His physique was magnificent. He had reached the very prime of life. It was his black, flashing eyes, set in a care-free face, which proclaimed the animal; it was the dark strain in his blood which gave him overbearing assurance. He was a human volcano.

Immediately on his advent at the Home, the alluring smiles

and inviting eye-play of Madeline Fox had captured his fancy. Mrs. Jonas at first frowned and then scolded; but the scolding came too late, for by that time the girl realized that she had focused on herself the desire of a lustful devil who would not rest until he had consumed her. During their Christmas dinner the ex-pearl-diver had bluntly asked Anchor to marry them.

"Only a clergyman or minister can do that, and there is not one here," Anchor had replied as bluntly, becoming aware of the prologue to a drama.

"Then we'll do without marriage," came the passionate voice, low and menacing as the distant approach of a typhoon. At which Madeline had risen to her feet and laughed him to scorn.

That the girl was a natural courtesan was evident. But, having made a conquest, her fear of Moore had checked her adventurous spirit, and her laughter proclaimed that she stood on the side of morality.

A scene, probably of violence, had been averted only by Anchor's deadly coolness: when, with his hand on the butt of an automatic in the pocket of his white drill coat, he had politely requested the quarter-caste to retire to his room. Mainwright, regardful of the bulge at Anchor's hip, had obeyed with flashing eyes and proud carriage.

Afterwards the millionaire had interviewed both the girl and the Malay; and, on discovering the situation created by the she-vampire, sent her running to her room with chalk-white face, and the man out into the fierce glare of the sun like a hunted beast.

For several days tranquillity had resumed its sway, the man temporarily cowed, the girl visibly afraid of him, but much more so of Anchor. Then came the night when, at two o'clock in the morning, Madeline's screams had aroused the household, whose members, rushing in a body to her room, witnessed a struggle which undoubtedly would have ended in tragedy.

Whilst Mainwright held the girl, one hand over her mouth, in an effort to stifle her screams, oblivious to the entry of Moore, Anchor, and Mabel Hogan, the doctor had deftly administered a hypodermic injection which in less than half a minute had reduced the ravenous tiger to a whipped cur. Like a man stupefied, the quarter-caste had followed Moore to his laboratory, in which he remained for several days.

On his reappearance he was an absolute madman, a gibbering idiot. Austiline, with Anchor and his henchman, was sitting on the veranda when, somehow, the man escaped from the laboratory and walked out of the French windows. His head was bandaged, but the terrible contortions of his face caused Austiline to scream. Seeing her, the madman sidled toward her, being stopped almost as he came within reach by a bullet from Anchor's automatic.

"Not quite a success, Moore, I am afraid," Anchor had drawled when, with unruffled politeness, he led Austiline from the scene of horror.

Until the arrival of the brothers she had enjoyed full freedom. It was only a week before their coming that she had been made acquainted with Travers's confession. But her new-found joy had been short-lived.

In his suave tones Anchor had congratulated her, and then had gone on without the slightest trace of emotion to propose marriage. That Austiline was both surprised and shocked may have been due to the fact that, shortly after her arrival, she had informed him of her engagement to Martin, for whom she handed Anchor a letter which she begged him to dispatch to assure Martin that she was well and safe.

Naturally she had rebuffed Anchor's approach. Yet her cool demeanour was assumed, since by that time she realized Anchor's cynical heartlessness and Moore's utter ruthlessness in his quest for knowledge. When she regained her apartment she became very much afraid.

The next day, when Anchor joined her in the library, she implored him to send her even to Marree, promising to repay him all the money he had expended upon her, with the addition of any interest he might fix; but, smiling, he had regretted his inability to comply with her requests, and again had proposed marriage as calmly as if it meant as little as a stroll in the cool of the evening.

But, though his smile was gentle, his eyes glared into hers with the fixed stare of a cobra; and she, realizing her terrible position, shrank from him in horror. His words had appeared to come to her from a far distance.

"I regret, Austiline, that you see fit to refuse my suit," he had said. "You have the honour to be the first woman ever to refuse me. That, of course, raises you greatly in my estimation. I love you intensely and offer you marriage; but, after all is said and done, the mere ceremony is not all-important."

Before she could recover sufficiently to reply to this veiled threat, he had proceeded:

"I am informed, my dear Austiline, that the two Sherwoods are on their way to this part of the country in search of you. We cannot, of course, have them here; and, because I love you, you cannot go to them. Even if I were indifferent to your womanly charms, your liberty would now be a menace to ours."

"But you would accept my word of honour, surely?" she had cried, starting up in terror when the appalling implications of this speech penetrated her mind.

This appeal, however, had drawn from him only a low, cynical laugh and an intimation that honour had perished with the Crusaders; after which he suggested that she might like to write to Monty Sherwood, since Martin was blind.

"You see, Austiline, you must inform them that you desire to be left in peace. At all cost to your natural feelings—and mine, for I am by nature hospitable—they must be turned back. If they persist in coming, our difficulties will be increased and their persons will be in danger of violence."

Deceived by his face, always disguised by a mask of laughing cynicism, she had failed at first to grasp his hidden meaning, but this he proceeded to make unmistakably clear by adding:

"You understand—of course you must understand—that their presence here, as is your own, will be a serious menace to every legitimate guest in my Home. Such being unfortunately the case, in order to maintain peace and security, it would be necessary to—ah—remove them without trace. A simple illustration of the first law of nature—self-preservation—you know.

"Your best course, Austiline, is to drop them a line or two, ordering them back to Melbourne, and allaying their anxiety on your behalf. Your success in that direction would best serve Mr. Martin Sherwood, believe me. And to revert to my love for you. Remember that had it not been for my brains, my money, to-day you would have been but a tragic memory. You owe me your life. I want but a husband's share in it."

He was still smiling gently, humour and kindliness in his expression, but the relentlessness of Satan in his eyes, when, starting to her feet, she had fled.

And late that night she had concocted the message Monty received, hoping that its very brutality would arouse in him opposition to her expressed wishes. For she, having seen and spoken to the bushman, felt that he would prove extremely difficult to "remove without trace"; that, once he understood the awful position in which she was placed, Anchor and his company would experience at least a time of trouble and unpleasantness.

William J. had smiled sardonically over her letter, purposely left unsealed for his inspection. He, too, read the hidden desire to provoke Monty Sherwood into continuing his search of her, but had sent Gilling off with it early the next morning. Austiline had unwittingly strengthened his hold over her.

Then had come the morning of the brothers' arrival, when Anchor presented himself at the door of her sitting-room and requested audience.

"I have to inform you," he said, "that the Sherwoods have arrived, thereby creating difficulties, to overcome which your co-operation is necessary."

She stood regarding him with an expression of haughty disdain alternating with dread, her bronze-coloured eyes blazing into his slaty orbs regarding her with unveiled admiration and determination to possess.

"Moore and I have discussed the difficulties," he went on. "I am for quietly dispatching them, but Moore wants them as experimental subjects. I only object on account of the effect of his experiments, as shown by Mainwright, the quarter-caste Malay, whom you may perhaps remember.

"Being friends of yours, my objection will hold. You must send them away, Austiline. You must give Martin his *congé*, and then I will accept their words to keep our existence a profound secret."

"Oh, Mr. Anchor! surely, surely you cannot be so heartless," she cried, her voice breaking. "Let me go with them; please, let me go! I can never love you, as you must know. Let us go; and, far from informing on you, we shall always think of your kindness with gratitude."

"Austiline, Austiline!" he murmured, as though her name were music to him. "Always have I got what I wanted, excepting women's love. But I'll make you love me for the happiness I and my wealth can give you. Even if you break your wings against the bars, I'll have you." And then, suddenly drawing near, he caught her in his arms, crushed her to him, and, forcing back her head, kissed her on the lips once, twice, a dozen times, she coldly impassive in his embrace until the storm subsided and he let her go.

Triumphantly he smiled at her, thinking he had conquered. Without hate in her eyes, without passion of any sort, she deliberately wiped her lips with a handkerchief. The flimsy wisp of cambric she regarded as if she expected to see dirt on it from her lips. Again she wiped them. Then, with the essence of all womanly scorn and loathing in her eyes and voice, she whispered the four words:

"Lower than a dog!"

It may not have been the words; probably it was the loathing in her eyes and the contempt playing about her mouth that stung him, that stripped him of his cynical armour, tore aside the outer semblance of a gentleman, of a decent man even. For a moment he saw himself as she saw him, stripped, a thing exciting unutterable disgust. He saw that she judged his handling of her a crime far worse than murder. He read her mind with ease. A dog would kill another dog, but never attack a bitch.

Yet the pose of cynical humour, the habit of a lifetime, was easy to regain. When he spoke his voice was gentle, suave, belying the terrible import of his words.

"After dinner to-night I will bring the Sherwoods here, Austiline," he said. "When they arrive, Dr. Moore and 'The Cat' will be concealed behind those wall-hangings. You will be given the opportunity of sending them away satisfied that no longer do you love Martin Sherwood, satisfied that you freely desire to remain. If you fail in that, if you cry for their help, my friends will shoot down Montague, and afterwards Dr. Moore will experiment on Martin. For by then I shall have no objection. If I remember rightly, Mainwright did not look nice. Good morning!"

A woman of stone, she saw him go, heard the door close behind him. For several moments she stood there, unable to move for the terror which chained her limbs. Then came a moan of anguish. With tottering steps she gained the inner room which was her bedroom, and, falling beside the bed, burst into a passion of weeping.

At that time William J. Anchor was warmly greeting the blind Martin. The scene with Austiline was the "very delicate experiment" which had prevented his being the first to welcome the brothers.

CHAPTER XXII

THE OMEN

"JUMPING nannygoats!" repeated an astonished Monty, gazing towards his bed.

"What is the matter?" Martin demanded.

"An infant."

"A what?"

"There is a sleeping baby on my bed," Monty replied in a hushed whisper. "The loveliest baby you could imagine, old son. Must be between three and four years old, but I'm beaten badly in deciding whether it's a boy or a girl. Anyway, sex don't matter—it's a miniature angel, Martin, the most beautiful kid you ever saw."

Knowing his brother to be a lover of children, Martin was not surprised at the other's raptures. He said:

"Describe it, mine eyes."

"It'll be hard, but I'll do my best. It has a round chubby face unlike the full, fat, balloon kind of kisser of most kids of that age. The colouring of the face is a marvel of beauty, equalled by the colour of the long, curly, pale gold hair. I'll bet you a fiver that when those eyes are open they'll be dark blue, and big. My! I wouldn't mind owning it."

"This is a peculiar house in which to find a child," Martin said softly.

"M'yes. A little angel kept prisoner in hell. It's a damned shame."

"'And a little child shall lead them'," quoted the blind man.

"That infant could lead me all right," Monty assented, now in his pyjamas. "Well, I'm for a snore off."

"I doubt that I shall sleep," Martin opined, lying full length on the most luxurious of beds. "My mind is too much excited by Anchor's revelations. I wish—oh, I wish I could see them all! To me they are so unreal, so inhuman."

"Reckon they are human enough," said Monty sleepily.

173

"This child, though, is extra human. It's like finding a diamond in a muck-heap. If it had belonged to Mrs. Minter . . . she wouldn't . . . have run . . . into the house like . . ."

The big man slept. The infant slept at his side, a mother's dream come true, God's hope so patent in two pure faces. Martin, however, as he foretold, found sleep difficult to woo, even though the scant periods of slumber during the past few days engendered an intense mental weariness.

With the eyes of his mind—and it was wonderful how he could now often escape his black prison and journey in the light—he pictured newspaper contents bills, with deep, thick headlines and startling phrases. Subconsciously he was aware of the stillness of the world about him, the only sounds drifting through the open windows being caused by the small petrol engine, evidently driving a dynamo, the occasional caw-caw of a sleepy crow, and once the far-off bellow of a cow.

A hundred questions clamoured to be answered, the most momentous of them all being why Austiline Thorpe held back from meeting him. He pictured her as she always had been : understanding, loyal, a warm-hearted loving woman beneath her proud, beautiful exterior. The only possible explanation of her attitude was his terrible affliction, cried insistently that small voice of doubt which he vainly tried to drown. It was a lover's doubt, and he was ashamed of it, but it persisted. Yet, according to cool reason, it was more probable that she was a prisoner, unable to follow the dictates of her heart ; and, hugging this consoling thought and determined to advise drastic action on the morrow if their interview with her was delayed beyond that day, sleep captured him before he knew of its approach.

Almost together the brothers were awakened by the slamming of several doors and windows. Martin, who awoke with a start, listened uneasily to the sound of hurrying feet on the bare veranda floor and along the corridor ; but Monty, who awoke, as was usual with him, without other sign than the quiet opening of his eyes, heard a low, far-off roar in the short pauses in the human commotion. That sinister sound he recognized as an approaching sand-storm, and guessed that the occupants of the house were closing every opening to shut out the besieging sand. Some one tapped on their door.

"Hullo !" the big man called.

"Will you please close your windows?" he heard Mrs. Jonas say. "There is a violent dust-storm approaching from the south."

"Very well, Mrs. Jonas," the big man replied, proceeding immediately to close the two pairs of French windows, reaching from floor to ceiling. When he turned he found the child sitting up, regarding him solemnly with great, glorious eyes of sapphire blue.

"Cheerio, Bubbles!" he said. "How do?"

"Is the mite awake?" Martin inquired, fumbling at his cigarette-case.

"He is. Hear him!" Martin heard in a child's singing voice the sounds: "Ooo-oo! Ooo-oo! Ooo-oo!" uttered while the little body was executing a sort of war-dance on the bed. "He's going to be a musician, is Master Bubbles," concluded Monty.

"Anything like the picture?"

"Dead image."

"You have decided, then, the question of sex?"

"Yep! I'll bet on it," replied the big man, sitting on the edge of his bed and lighting his pipe. When he withdrew the match from the pipe bowl, he discovered the child beside him on all-fours, ready and eager to blow out the flame.

That accomplished, to the intense satisfaction of the child, the blue eyes stared with what to the average person would be uncompromising directness. Then Monty smiled broadly, and great was his amazement when, with a delighted gurgle, the mite leapt forward into his arms.

"You mine daddy—you mine daddy come back?"

"Let's say I'm your play-daddy," Monty returned swiftly. "What's your name?"

"Daddy! Mine daddy! Mine daddy come back!"

With his tiny arms round Monty's great neck, the child pressed moist, warm lips against the big man's mouth with joyous abandonment.

"Daddy been far 'way. Now daddy come back. Ooo— mine daddy!"

"Well then, who is your mummy?" Monty managed to say.

"Mummy! Go tell mine mummy."

With surprising agility the baby slid out of the big man's arms, and in a practised manner kicked his legs over the edge of the bed and lowered himself to the floor; whereupon he ran to the locked door and, just managing to reach the handle, half-turned it, crying:

"Opey! Opey door! Go tell mummy! Mine mummy!"

With some misgiving the big man opened the door. The child scampered along the carpeted corridor, shouting for "Mummy" at the top of his voice. Wearing only pyjamas, Monty dared not follow, but was relieved when a door opened further along the passage, and the laundress girl, appearing, swept the child up into her arms.

"Mummy! Mummy! Daddy come back!" he heard the excited infant shout, and, with only his head thrust outside the room, saw Mabel Hogan give him a grateful look before she drew back. When he closed the door his eyes were wonderfully bright. To Martin he said in a voice which held a song:

"Bubbles apparently belongs to the laundress. She lives a little way down the street, and dived out to meet the youngster who escaped me."

"You seem quite enthusiastic about the boy," Martin observed, with his whimsical droop of the mouth.

"I think you would be, too, if you could see him. What particular brand of murder is Mabel Hogan addicted to, do you remember?"

"Anchor said, I think, that she gave her betrayer strychnine."

"Ugh!" Monty shuddered. "I'll bet she never understood just how strychnine acts, or she would have used a gun instead. Never saw a human die of it, but it gives a dog ten minutes of hell."

"It must indeed be a frightful death. To me the surprising thing is the carelessness of the average bushman who handles it."

" 'Tis amazin'. But familiarity, you know——" Monty chuckled, and from that chuckle Martin knew something was coming. "Knew a bloke once who used to empty a bottle of strych. into a waistcoat pocket and carry it around over his trap-line in case a beast died handy and could be baited. Used to eat his tucker with the waistcoat flapping against him and grains of poison flying all over the country. And yet he was dogging and foxing for fifteen years before he eventually poisoned himself, a grain of it falling on his meat one dinner time. I'll bet he was surprised."

Martin had to laugh at Monty's quaint surmise.

"You should tell that at the dinner-table—it would set

them in a roar," he said. "Like our friend Anchor, you can show us even tragedy in a comic light. Naturally, after fifteen years' immunity, the poor man *would* be surprised."

"Naturally! That's why I said it. Here comes the wind."

With startling swiftness the daylight vanished. Beneath the ever-increasing roar came the baying of the huge hounds —cries quickly swamped when the storm swept over the house, rocking it with its tremendous pressure. Through every crack and crevice the wind forced long streams of fine sand into the spotless interior. In five minutes every article was covered with a red-brown film.

In the light of the electric bulbs the room appeared as though filled with red-hued smoke. Outside, the world, seen in the dim twilight, which was not of fading day, was being swept up in thousands of tons and thrown to high heaven as by the explosion of a million mines. For two long hours the roaring wind beat furiously on the rambling wood and iron bungalow. Then the storm ceased as suddenly as it had arisen.

The ensuing calm was as stupendous as the storm. By Monty's watch it was five minutes past seven. The light began to return, to filter through the high-flung sand particles which slowly fell like rain. Then gradually the light took on an orange glow, and with the passage of minutes grew steadily in power, the tint changing gradually to pink, then to red, and finally to the colour of fresh blood.

When Monty opened the windows and stepped out on the sand-covered veranda he was faced by one of the rarest and most beautiful of Central Australia's natural phenomena. The sun, setting behind the blanket of sand moving at cloud height and, in cloud fashion, letting fall a rain of sand, caused the whole world to appear as on fire. The buildings opposite the house, the bore vomiting blood, and the sand-hills beyond, appeared exactly as though viewed through crimson-tinted glasses.

Above the house the moving canopy whirled in and out upon itself, bellying downward in bright crimson masses of fire, criss-crossed by masses of deeper red. Such a sky it must have been in that dreadful hour that witnessed the destruction of Sodom and Gomorrah.

When Monty struck a match to light his pipe the flame appeared blue-white by comparison, but his hands looked as if he had washed them in gore. He saw Earle emerge from one of the outbuildings, and, holding his hands before his face, look at them with wide, dreadfully staring eyes. A raindrop fell on the corrugated iron roof as a hammer striking an anvil. Thunder rumbled far away and, racing towards the house with a series of crackling strides, halted over it with a single sharp report. Earle, turning about, dashed back into the outhouse and crashed the door behind him.

"Does it look like rain?" asked the dweller in darkness.

"It looks exactly like hell," Monty replied, re-entering the room. "Only once in my life have I seen the bush bathed in blood. That was New Year's Day, 1912. This makes the second time. I wish you, too, could see it, old lad. It is very beautiful and very terrible, I should think, to the superstitious."

"Perhaps it is the end of the world," Martin said softly.

"It will be the beginning of a new one if it rains. It's trying hard enough."

But not more than a dozen drops of rain fell. The glow slowly faded with the dipping of the sun below the invisible horizon. Martin was helped to wash and dress, after which Monty attended to his own toilet. Not till eight o'clock did the dinner-gong sound, and, on opening the door, a waft of cool air, made fragrantly earthy even by the few drops of rain that had fallen, met them coming from the south, cooling the sun-heated house, sweeping away the clamminess of both body and brain. Such was the sighed-for, prayer-for, cool change: so important, so desirable, in and to the lives of those who year by year live in Central Australia.

Moving along the passage, they heard a child's plaintive cry.

"I want mine daddy! I want mine daddy!"

"Hush, darling! See daddy to-morrow. Come now, bye-bye now," they heard the mother say; and Martin, while they moved towards the hall, felt the big man's hand tighten on his sleeve.

"That kid's arms get around a man's heart as easily as they slide around a man's neck," Monty said slowly.

"It is a shame for it to grow up in such a——" A firmer pressure on his arm cut short the sentence and started him off on another. "However, one is thankful for this cool change."

"It is certainly much appreciated here, Mr. Sherwood," he heard Mrs. Jonas say. "It really has been a terrible afternoon, and I am so sorry dinner had to be postponed to such a late hour. I hope I did right not to disturb you with afternoon tea at four?"

"Quite right, Mrs. Jonas, thank you," Monty assured her. "We both enjoyed a sound sleep. Who would not sleep soundly in such beds?"

The woman smiled up at him wistfully, and, drawing nearer, commandeered the blind man's arm. Monty found himself joined in the hall by the rotund Mallowing, who chirped:

"What an extraordinary evening, Mr. Sherwood! Never before have I seen the atmosphere turned to such a vivid colour. One might almost take it as an omen."

"Of what?" inquired Monty smiling.

"Oh! of blood and war; of the end of the world; some might say of the Day of Judgment."

"The Day of Judgment will probably prove disastrous to a lot of people," pointed out the big man, still smiling broadly. He meant his own day of judgment.

"Ah! I see you believe in a hereafter," the rotund little fellow said quietly. "Now, my philosophy will admit of this life only."

"You must find, then, your philosophy to be a comforting one."

"Sir, I am glad to say that I do! Philosophy is made for man, not man for philosophy; and I believe in each man being his own philosopher. My philosophy is one of happiness. To be happy is to live; to be fearful and wretched is to be better dead. But come! Johnston is in an evil humour. As practical philosophers, let us not be late for dinner."

CHAPTER XXIII

THE SKELETON AT THE FEAST

"WHERE is Earle?" Anchor inquired when every one was seated and he was carving the roast.

"I think he is unwell," Mrs. Jonas informed them. "The storm has upset him and he is keeping to his room."

"Poor fellow! I feel his days are numbered. How many do you give him, Moore?"

"Give him! I don't give him a minute. He should be dead by this. His Bathurst doctor was right in his diagnosis, but life is a wonderful thing in that it will cling to decayed or diseased bodies like a plant tenaciously growing in a hot, dry crevice of a sun-scorched rock." The doctor accepted his portion with a nod, adding: "The will to live. or to die has never been given its due."

"Why, or rather how, is that, may I ask?" questioned their host with his customary politeness. The doctor glanced round at the company, and, observing that in general every one was interested, he said:

"A person who, for any length of time, has lived among primitive people, like those of the Pacific, is soon convinced beyond question of the fact that if a nigger makes up his mind he is going to die he will assuredly do so. His body may be free from disease, and from any foreign substance of a disruptive nature; but, if you get him to believe he is marked for death, that belief will kill him more surely than poison.

"Among the natives of Northern Australia the witch-doctors practise what is known as bone-pointing. The victim is unaware at the time, usually at night, that the specially contrived apparatus is being pointed at him, and continues to live with the utmost cheerfulness until he is told that the bone has been pointed at him and he is a doomed man.

"Physically there is absolutely nothing the matter with the poor wretch. In the majority of cases the witch-doctor does not even trouble to administer poison. Knowing that to poison without necessity is waste, he carries on as usual, merely speculating on the precise hour when he will hear the wailing howls of the victim's gins."

"Quite a casual sort of bloke," remarked Monty.

"Exactly," Moore agreed, with a dour frown at the big man's irrepressible flippancy. "On the reverse side we have the man who, like Earle, continues living when by every law of pathology he should be dead. When I enjoyed an extensive practice in London I had experience of several similar cases. To instance two. A man was brought back from the river of death when already he was wading into it by his wife repeatedly imploring him to return to her. Not only did he come back; he regained complete health. In the other case a woman, obviously at the edge of the river, stayed herself from wading in, being kept back merely by her will to live until her son arrived from America. That will failed her immediately he did arrive, and the river claimed her. It is my belief she would have lived a further three weeks at least, had her son been delayed so long."

"It must be very trying for a doctor to ease the passing of so many fated souls," ventured Martin. "I am afraid that the death of a person I was trying hard to save would upset me greatly."

"Most medical students feel like that at first, Mr. Sherwood," the doctor replied; "but nearly all become hardened —fortunately so for all concerned, and for the progress of medical science. In an official capacity I have observed several executions, both by electricity and the rope. I witnessed hundreds of deaths in the hospitals during the Great War. To a doctor, in general, death, like birth, is a mere incident."

"I read a book once wherein a South American State adopted the electric chair," the big man put in, a broad smile playing over his mahogany-tinted features, the philosophy of happiness in his twinkling eyes. "The prison officials decided to go one better than Uncle Sam and supply twenty thousand volts as a curative treatment to gentlemen who fell from grace. Having taken a lot of trouble and spent heaps of money over the stunt, it was only natural that a very important personage should—er—open the bazaar, as it were. Therefore, the President himself, in spite of some natural diffidence, was persuaded to be seated. He took the twenty thousand volts like a lamb, and when they unstrapped him after half an hour with the current full on, he bounced up like a young man, declaring that electricity was the finest thing on earth for lumbago. The switch operator he made a General of Transport; the second-choice President got a mere two thousand volts and busted."

Dr. Moore smiled darkly and the fat man next Martin guffawed. Smith, the aged infant, showed two very yellow teeth in an astoundingly evil leer; but Mrs. Jonas, sitting very straight, looked bleakly at Mabel Hogan, who had just come from putting her child to sleep.

"Ah yes, I am told that too much electricity does not bring about the officially desired result," Moore responded. "Most nations nowadays boast of the quickness of their executions; but, with the exception of the guillotine of France and the axe of mediæval England, both of which remove the head, not one of the modern methods is instantaneous."

"Dear me! is that really so?" inquired Anchor with perceptibly raised brows. He was regarded steadily by his friend.

"Unfortunately, yes," Moore said with finality. "Perhaps, seeing we are at dinner, I had better not go into this unpleasant subject."

"Oh! but do, Dr. Moore. I am *so* interested."

Monty raised his eyes with a startled expression. He could conceive no subject to be more rigorously barred from conversation among confessed takers of human life than the death penalty; yet here were these people calmly discussing its details, and one of them, a woman, urging a continuance of the subject because she was "*so* interested"! To Martin it was incredible that human nature could become so callous as to favour, for dinner-table conversation, one of the most horrible problems known to civilized society.

"Very well, Madeline! As you are interested and no one else raises any objection, I will give you my conclusions," came the high-pitched drawl. "I was remarking that other than by removing a person's head the law's method of killing is not instantaneous. The law in respect to homicides is revengeful, inasmuch as the man or woman awaiting execution suffers a thousand deaths in imagination before the physical event takes place.

"Let us take my case as an instance, and from other cases add a bare description from what would have been my fate under the usual legal procedure. When I killed Dr. Talmadge he had no pre-knowledge of his end, which was entirely physical. He suffered neither pain nor mental torture. Being the living instrument of his death, I am tried and condemned to die. My death affords no compensation to Dr. Talmadge for being killed. When I die he doesn't return to life. Neither will it prevent any other Moore killing any other Talmadge when the same irresistible urge arises.

"We regard the tortures practised upon homicides in the Middle Ages with horror, because our imagination is so coarse that it can easily picture burning flesh and breaking bones. Yet the rack, the thumbscrew, boiling water, and red-hot iron are mild forms of torment to the law's modern torture of the mind. Our imagination is not yet fine enough to appreciate the mental torture of waiting, waiting, waiting, during three interminable weeks, for an unnatural death.

"Try to realize the mind of the person awaiting death. The hour and the day are written in letters of blood on every square foot of his cell walls. Those letters are burned into his brain. The hour, the minute, takes on life, the aspect of some terrible Thing that creeps to him ever nearer. As in a nightmare, he is bound by chains which hold him motionless and powerless to evade or fight the oncoming Thing.

"Day by day his personality ebbs. He comes to regard himself as inhuman, to look on his few visitors and the warders as automata beyond his ken. Nothing can free him from his chains, nor conquer the Thing ever drawing nearer.

"He knows that they know how many pounds he weighs. He knows that already it is decided how many inches he will be dropped from the trap. Daylight goes and the darkness is peopled by awful faces till daylight comes again. Another day nearer to the terrible Thing.

"Collapse comes when on the fatal morning the hangman enters with his shackles. The victim is a man no longer. He is a screaming, writhing imbecile. The public read how he walked with firm steps to the scaffold. Lies! all lies! He is urged forward. But he will not go, will not follow the surpliced figure, the representative of Christ. Still screaming, foam upon his lips, he is carried along the corridor, into the yard, stationed on the trap.

"The law says he must be hanged by the neck until he is dead. Banish from your minds the brave man standing to attention on the trap. Picture him, limp with fear, held up, supported by the hangman's assistants standing safely outside the trap, who signal its release and spring away when the wretch drops. They hang not a man, but something that used to be a man. The law is satisfied. It has had its revenge. But the victim of the murderer is no less dead."

"Your point of view is most interesting," observed Martin quietly. "But surely something must be done to takers of life. Granted that the punishment of murderers might and should be much less crude than clumsily killing them, yet an example must be made, and the awful death penalty is probably a deterrent where life imprisonment would not be."

"Your line of argument would be sound if applied to ordinary crime," Moore continued. "As a deterrent the death penalty would, I think, lessen to a great extent crimes like embezzlement, forgery, and swindling. But the death penalty will never lessen murder, because murder is the result of a temporary mental derangement, a derangement over which the sufferer has no control. Ninety-nine murders in every hundred are committed upon impulse, the impulse being the effect of excitement, which in turn is the effect of a complication of circumstances. But let us keep to our subject."

"By all means, my dear Moore," murmured William J. Anchor, helping himself to a very fine Stilton.

"Yes, one subject at a time," agreed Monty. "You were saying that the law's present method of murdering murderers is a bit slow."

"That is so, Mr. Sherwood. When the unfortunate is on the scaffold the noose is tied so that the knot passes under the side of his chin. When he drops, the medulla oblongata is jagged and broken, for that is the extension of the brain which receives the blow from the rope. It contains the respiratory centre which, when shocked, causes paralysis of breathing; the consequence being that the victim dies of suffocation.

"No doctor can say, truthfully, that the hanged man dies instantaneously; neither can that statement be made in regard to the electric chair. Of the two, I should very much prefer the rope. Imagine being strapped into an ordinary high-backed chair, your head fixed by a clamp, your shaven poll kissed by an electrode, another being applied to the calf of one leg where the trousers have been slashed to ribbons by a warder.

"For five seconds you are given full voltage, then two

hundred volts; up the scale to two thousand five hundred;
an interval; two hundred volts again; and so on, till your
face becomes livid, partly cooked. The method does not take
quite so long as the antique rack; but it is anything but
instantaneous.

"Here, again, death comes from paralysis of respiration—
shock to the medulla. The current is turned on the victim
when the lungs are empty of air, and at least one minute and
a half elapses before he is dead. I have attended five such
executions, and I know. So you see that the boasted
instantaneous death is somewhat a prolonged affair. We kill
animals more humanely than we kill murderers, and therein we
show not justice but revenge. The veterinary surgeon's
pistol, used to dispatch horses, is placed against the centre
of the upper frontal bone, and instantaneously smashes the
brain. That is the way I should like to die."

"Indeed! I should much rather die in bed at a ripe old
age, surrounded by my children and grandchildren," declared
the millionaire mildly. At this Monty chuckled, and Madeline
laughed outright.

"Tosh!" the doctor exploded. "Why make death a
screen picture? There ought to be established in every city
and town a suicide chamber, to which anyone might resort
when life became a problem. No fuss, no gloating relatives
greedy for legacies, no doctor mourning your coming absence
from his ledger, no howling women thinking how nice they'll
look in black."

"Your suicide chamber idea is great!" chortled Monty.
"In it there should be an automatic arrangement to pass the
body into an incinerator, so that even the undertaker would
make nothing out of your mortal remains. Screen picture!
Your way, my dear doctor, would make death a regular
Charlie Chaplin affair."

Again the mountain of flesh guffawed, and "The Cat"
showed his two yellow teeth.

"A dustman would still be required to take away the ashes,"
said William J. Anchor gently.

"There always is a fly in the ointment," chirped
Mallowing.

Then came the clear-toned, disapproving voice of Mrs.
Jonas.

"I really think that you should treat death with less levity.
Death is a very momentous, a very solemn change to the

immortal soul. It is as tremendous as will be the day of Universal Resurrection, and should be regarded with awe."

"I am perfectly in agreement with you, Mrs. Jonas," Anchor said, now with a serious mouth, but with eyes that laughed. The big man noted that peculiarity, and marvelled at the oddity of a man so seldom smiling with both mouth and eyes at the same time. "Death is a serious matter, especially when it concerns us."

The very slight emphasis on the last word escaped Mrs. Jonas, who gave him a gratified look and rose from the table; whereupon "The Cat," exhibiting extraordinary good manners sprang to the door and, holding it wide to allow the ladies to pass out, bowed with exaggerated politeness.

For a moment Anchor regarded him sternly. When he spoke it was to the chubby Mallowing.

"To-morrow Dr. Moore is flying to Marree," he said, helping himself from a thin-necked bottle of Rudesheimer. "When I informed Madeline that arrangements had been made for her journey to Canada, in which dominion she would be able to live again a normal life, she amazed me by confessing that she would rather remain here. It does seem a pity that the expense of the arrangements should be wasted. Would you care to take the opportunity of leaving us?"

"Is that a command, sir?"

"Not at all. You may please yourself entirely."

"Then, in that case, I would much prefer to remain."

"Very well, my dear fellow; remain, by all means. We should miss you, I feel sure. What about you, Smith?"

The old young man leered and shook his bald head. When he used his fingers to make known his views Monty realized, with a sense of shock, that he was dumb. Their host said, with a short laugh, genuine pleasure and gratification on his face:

"There, Moore, you see our friends will not leave us. You will have to go alone."

"It appears so," the doctor drawled, in a voice perilously like a grunt. "I trust that to-morrow will give me better visibility than this afternoon. If you will excuse me——"

Moore had risen to his feet when, with startling suddenness, the door was flung wide open and into the large room stalked the skeleton at the feast of the man-killers in the person of the ghastly, emaciated Earle. The doctor and those sitting round the table gazed on the apparition with a sudden fear clutching at their hearts.

Like the Egyptians reminded of common mortality by the customary bringing in of the skeleton, the company saw in this tall, swaying lath of a man the inevitability of their own decay; and what remained in every mind from a mother's teaching—no matter the cynicism, no matter the atheistic pose—that after death would come judgment, a judgment which neither lying nor evasion could avoid, or prevent from being just.

For a full, long, portentous minute Earle, his eyes blazing, saliva trickling from the corners of his drawn and sunken mouth, glared at the diners; and they, as turned into images of stone, mutely reflected his stare. When Earle did speak it was at first in a low tone, but as he proceeded his voice rose up the scale into a scream.

"You sit here and eat," he said, his head thrust forward over his sunken chest. "You smoke and talk and make merry while God's fire hangs over this house, red fire descending upon the world, fire like blood, fire the colour of the brand of Cain which marks us all.

"In that descending fire I saw my three children. They came down to me from heaven and at me pointed their tiny fingers. There was no happy smile on their sweet faces, just terrible regret that they were dead, and at me they pointed with accusing fingers.

"What use," his voice rose in cadence, "what use for me to tell them, to implore them to believe, that I sent them to heaven because I feared that without my loving guidance their souls would perish? What use to tell them that I knew when I slew them that in saving their souls I was dooming myself to eternal hell? Ah, no! No use! No use!

"They want earth-life, my children. They cry for the lost chance of becoming worthy of heaven on this earth. They say they can never grow up because I—*I* stopped them from growing up. There was no hate of me in their faces"—the man's voice rose into a scream of horrible agony—"but neither was there any love—no love for me who adored them —me, who, for their sakes, forwent my birthright for the certainty of hell. They cry always and always for life. And I destroyed life."

The man was swaying like a reed. Never had Monty seen human eyes so big and brilliant; never had Martin heard a human voice so full of terror, so laden with unutterable remorse. The thin, sagging shoulders shook violently with a suffocating fit of coughing. And then with heightened fury Earle went on, his voice almost a shriek:

"Cursed—cursed am I! You, too, are damned, forever damned. Prepare yourselves for everlasting torment, ye killers of men and women. Be ready for the Breath that shall raise your souls from the dust of your bodies. For then Cain's bugle shall sound his 'fall in,' and he shall lead his army down, down into the fiery pit. You fools—you fools that are damned! Neither your screams nor your pleadings will avail you. As you withheld mercy, so mercy shall be withheld from you."

The animal Lane pushed back his chair and slid to the floor, gurgling with a terror that helped to unnerve the others. "The Cat's" face was ashen and he trembled as a mass of jelly. Mallowing's forehead glistened with beads of sweat. The doctor—the doctor was smiling. During the pause when Earle was again seized with coughing, Madeline Fox giggled. It was the laugh of the Devil triumphant.

Anchor, rising from his seat, approached Percival Earle with the evident intention of pacifying him, but halted when Earle flung up his hand and, crouching back with fear-convulsed face, screamed:

"He comes! I knew it. I knew he would come in the end. There stands our father in blood, the leader of our army, the blazer of the track we murderers must follow, follow down the steep path into the depths. There stands Cain! Cain, who in the beginning slew Abel—Cain, whose fate it is to marshal the killers of men and lead them to eternal damnation.

"I see the ruddy glow way down that road. It will burn, burn, burn. Oh Christ! I cannot go. I will not go, I tell you. I cannot. I cannot stand pain, the bite and sear of flame. I tell you I cannot bear it, I will not."

With a last piercing shriek, Earle turned and rushed from the room. They saw him cross the hall, heard his feet on the veranda boards beyond, heard his screams grow faint, and more faint, until they were lost in the distance among the sand-hills.

Came then the baying of hounds, followed by hurrying feet, and in the doorway stood Mrs. Jonas, her face like paper, her hands pressed over her breasts.

"My God! whatever is the matter?" she panted. In the

silence greeting her question they heard a child crying, the opening and slamming of a door. Then came Anchor's soft, drawling voice:

"It is only Earle rehearsing the lead in Macbeth, Mrs. Jonas," he said.

CHAPTER XXIV

THE LIE

ANCHOR'S reassurance was followed by a silence so profound as to cause Martin to think its callous jocularity, succeeding so closely a scene that had touched the heights of human tragedy, had temporarily stunned the company. Though the majority had committed murder, and two were evidently degenerate, ordinary human sympathy held the upper hand.

"You are incorrigible, Anchor," Moore accused his friend, a little irritably. Then, turning to "The Cat," he said: "Come along, Smith. I want you to help me with an experiment."

The aged infant, now himself again, rose obediently and preceded the doctor to the door. They heard Monty say to Anchor that again they had been disappointed at the non-appearance of Austiline Thorpe, and heard his reply to the effect that he was to take them to her at nine. Just before he closed the door Anchor drawled:

"It is now five minutes to the hour. We will wait for the precise minute. Let me offer you smokes. And this Rudesheimer is really excellent."

When in the hall Moore laid a hand on "The Cat's" shoulder and talked to him in a low voice. The mute signified that he understood; and, being satisfied, the doctor led the way to the great tapestry, one side of which he pulled back, revealing a black oak panel. Low down, near the floor, he pushed to the right a part of the panel frame, when the panel itself opened inwards like a door. Beyond was a landing paved with cork, from which descended a flight of cork-paved steps.

Electric bulbs showed the way. The panel clicked behind them and they descended the steps, which ended in a wide and lofty cork-paved passage leading off at right angles. This passage they traversed at a leisurely pace and without sound, ignoring several doors on each side, till eventually they stood before one at the extreme end, on which Moore knocked.

Here, twenty feet underground, were the quarters of the élite of Anchor's guests. Here the temperature was maintained at about the comfortable level of 70 degrees. The millionaire murderer's system of ventilation was admirable, while the dryness of climate and soil ensured the absence of damp.

When Moore requested permission for his satellite and himself to enter, Austiline Thorpe was reclining on a Louis XV sofa set at the opposite end of the room near the door leading to her bedroom. She was very pale, a paleness accentuated by her bronze-flecked eyes and deep auburn hair. Agitated she was, undoubtedly, for her breast rose and fell under the stress of powerful emotion. With wide, fascinated eyes she watched the two men stride the length of the room, when, bowing low with a hint of the sardonic, Dr. Moore said softly:

"Good evening, Miss Thorpe! Mr. Anchor has deputed Smith and myself to ensure that his rotten drama is well and truly played."

Rising suddenly, she looked at him with a face of appeal.

"Oh! *Must* I go on with it?" she cried, clutching at the straw of his sympathy. "Won't you help me, Dr. Moore? Won't you try to persuade Mr. Anchor to let us all go in peace?"

"I am afraid, Miss Thorpe, that Mr. Anchor is not a man to be persuaded from any course he has resolved on," he said, with a shrug of his narrow shoulders. "Believe me, I urged him to accept your word and send you to the railway immediately we learned of your innocence. I pointed out to him the fact that some one, if not the Sherwoods, would search for you when you did not return to civilization. He would not listen to me, nor would he do so when we knew that the Sherwoods had been given our locality and were coming in this direction. In many ways my friend, Mr. Anchor, is a very fine man, but mulish obstinacy is one of his weaknesses."

"You know what he expects me to do?"

Nodding, he said:

"I am aware, too, of his infatuation for you, Miss Thorpe. Of that I heartily disapprove. Society may regard me as an outcast, yet at least I am still a gentleman."

"But you could compel Mr. Anchor to let us go, could you not?" she pleaded, her voice breaking. "You could accept our promises not to reveal any secrets. Surely you could not stand calmly by whilst a woman was ruined and an innocent man crushed by a terrible lie?"

Dr. Moore sighed deeply. Doubtless he had verbally disapproved of Anchor's infatuation and his plans to gratify it. It is possible that his instincts as a gentleman revolted at his friend's ruthless desires; but the sympathy he displayed that evening was partly spurious, for he was looking forward to use both Monty and his brother as subjects for experiment.

"I can do nothing," he said in a tone of finality. "This house belongs to Mr. Anchor. It is his money which runs it and provides sanctuary to me and the others. I cannot bite the hand that feeds me. Self-preservation must come first. Therefore, it is impossible for me to side with you openly against my friend.

"Try to understand my position. Circumstances which you can well imagine compel me to conform in everything to Mr. Anchor's wishes. I am utterly in his power, just as you are. Be advised by me, Miss Thorpe. Summon strength and courage. Be absolutely cruel to your lover, so that there will be no question of him and his brother leaving us without further trouble. If you fail, if you allow either of them to glimpse the actual truth, I and 'The Cat' here are instructed to shoot down Montague from behind the wall hangings, when Martin will be placed under my care. You understand the probable result affecting your lover, do you not?"

Her face was deathly pale, her eyes fixed and brilliant with horror.

"I—oh!" she moaned.

Moore was not wholly lost to humanity. A glimmer of genuine pity flashed for a second into his eyes. But the look was hidden by his tinted spectacles. From a pocket of his white drill jacket he produced a small phial. Offering it to her, he said:

"There remains but one thing to do. This is a means of escape. It is prussic acid, and would mean an almost immediate and quite painless death. It is your only way out. Believe me, I shall not be thanked for giving it you."

For a moment she looked at the frail glass container, without shrinking, without fear. It was the file that would cut the bars of her cage. Her voice was hardly above a whisper.

"If—if I use it, will you swear that you will get the Sherwoods away unharmed?"

There must also have been some chivalry left in Moore, for he replied immediately and candidly:

"That I cannot do," were his emphatic words. "Indeed, it would be an impossibility when Mr. Anchor discovered the object of his passion to be beyond his reach. The means of escape is for you alone."

The woman's glance rose to Moore's face. Slowly she shook her head, then sank down on the sofa and covered her face with her hands. When she looked up again she was strangely altered. Gone was her pleading femininity, gone like a cast-off cloak. The lank doctor was astounded at the change. She was as unemotional as a statue. Her eyes were hard and bright, and her mouth had lost its gentleness.

"I thank you, doctor, for your offer," she said, her voice cool and passionless. "I am not cowardly enough to accept it when by my so doing my *fiancé* and his brother would suffer. Will you please give me your cigarettes and matches?"

Austiline Thorpe had made her decision. To save Martin from Moore's horrible experiments, to save him from the quarter-caste Malay's fate, she realized that she must strike him herself, even if her blows broke his heart. The huge Monty, with the smiling boyish face and wistful mouth, she did not think of much during that dreadful moment. It was Martin, only Martin, who filled her mind.

And to help her in her task she called to her aid a mental trick by which, under the name of "A. E. Titchfield," she had made her books famous. From early girlhood, when she wrote her first story, she had acted the characters her brain had created. It was a trick which practice made easy to perform, so that it came to require little mental effort to submerge her personality and take on that of the character she had created. That was the secret of her success. It caused the critics to wonder, to say that her characters were portraits of living people, and to warn the youthful author against the pitfalls of libel.

There came a knock on the passage door. The two men darted to the silk wall hangings, disappearing behind their voluminous folds. With quick fingers Austiline produced and lit a cigarette, lying then at a reclining angle along the sofa. She was Eva Tilling, the wicked vampire in her most famous book, *The Heart of John Strong*. Eva's voice was low and vibrant when she called out permission to enter. Eva controlled also the facial muscles, even the expression of the eyes of Austiline Thorpe.

The door was opened and quietly closed. That portion of the room was in semi-darkness, the only light coming from two electric bulbs attached to the ceiling beyond the sofa. She saw two figures advancing slowly towards her, one guiding the other, one a giant of a man, the other appearing a mere boy beside him.

Even as Eva Tilling drew daintily from one of Moore's cigarettes the heart of Austiline Thorpe almost ceased to beat. For a moment her real personality all but triumphed. She wanted to run to that slowly approaching figure and lay her lips against the up-cast sightless eyes. But an inflexible will kept Eva Tilling in command.

Her attitude, the expression on her face, caused the big man instant anxiety. He felt that here for the first time was his character-reading utterly at fault. Martin's instinct had been right. He knew her better than did Monty. So, after all, Austiline had classed herself as belonging to Monty's "Rat Type." He was shocked. His faith in feminine goodness and loyalty was shaken.

The silence which greeted their approach at first indicated to the blind man that he was not yet in the presence of his adored. Realization came slowly. The scent of verbena intermingled with that of Virginia tobacco: the former filling his mind with memories of one woman whose presence was betrayed by it; the latter appearing to indicate that she was not alone, for Austiline, he knew, was not given to smoking.

But Monty saw, and held his breath. He saw Eva Tilling expel a cloud of smoke from between carmine lips. He saw a woman dressed in a low-cut green gown reclining on a blue and gold sofa, one hand holding a novel and the other a cigarette, her head thrown back, her face in full light. One silk-stockinged leg lay along the couch, shoeless and uncovered to the knee, the other dangled over the edge and softly tapped the head of the magnificent dragon sprawled over the immense yellow and white Chinese carpet.

The two men stood before her, a sudden grimness in the face of Monty, eager wistfulness in that of the younger brother. It seemed to Austiline that months and years dragged slowly past in those four or five seconds. Her body ached. Almost she screamed, with the agony of the chained desire to spring up and clasp Martin tightly in an embrace of divine affection, both passionate and maternal. But it was Eva Tilling, the rampant harlot, the virago, that governed her. The stranger, using her voice, laughed.

"So you *would* intrude on my privacy?" she said, half mockingly. "How dull is the masculine creature, to be sure! Quite unable to resist running your heads against brick walls, are you not? I advised you not to come. Can I do anything for you?"

The blind man blanched at her words, at the tone of her voice, the voice he knew so well, loved so dearly. Voice and words struck him as the crest of an ice-cold wave, chilling him, depriving him of the glow and spring of life. He tried to speak, but was restrained by the pressure of Monty's fingers on his arm. As though beyond a thick curtain he heard Monty drawl, with unruffled calmness:

"I think you can, Austiline," emphasizing the last word. "The average man likes butting his head into a brick wall for the fun of seeing the wall collapse. Perhaps you will have no objection to explaining that short, sharp note of yours and, forgive me, this somewhat theatrical reception. Permit me first to adjust a couple of chairs."

Leaving Martin for a moment, Monty whisked two chairs into position in front of the sofa and gently guided the blind man into one. Then, taking a lapel of Martin's jacket, he abstracted from an inner pocket the cigarette-case, with deft fingers opened it and from it took two "Three Circle" cigarettes. One he placed against the blind man's lips, which parted to receive it, when Monty struck a match, saying:

"Light up, old feller-me-lad. We'll all have a smoke to show there's no ill feeling."

To Martin the situation became like a dream. It seemed preposterous that Austiline should be smoking, and unreal that Monty should be so ill-mannered as not first to request permission. He had yet to learn that Monty's behaviour in society was always entirely guided by circumstances—that in the presence of a gentleman he acted like one, and in the presence of a cad he also was a cad; until the time for action arrived, when he became merely Monty Sherwood.

"Tell us first, are you quite well?" Monty inquired, his face one broad smile, his grey-blue eyes emitting sparks.

"Yes, I am quite well, thank you," she replied mockingly. "How are you?"

"Right on top gear, thanks. By the way, you would enjoy your cigarettes more if you were to inhale the smoke—like this. I see that you are yet a novice. I suppose you have read or heard of Travers's confession, which absolves you entirely from the murder of Peterson?"

"Oh yes!"

"You have! When?"

"About a week ago," Austiline replied; but, realizing her slip, she added quickly: "A week, a month, or even a year. It matters little, anyway."

"I agree. The time doesn't matter much. Let's call it a week. Congenial surroundings here, apparently. I suppose you feel you cannot tear yourself away and return with us to civilization?"

"Your supposition is probably correct. Believe me, I can and will return to civilization just when it pleases me to do so. It is possible that I shall remain here for some time. You see, I am going to marry Mr. Anchor."

"Austiline!"

The name was wrenched from a tortured man, a man struggling in the fetters of nightmare, a man whose very soul was being cut to pieces by the light mockery in her voice and words. The smile vanished from Monty's features; his mouth hardened and became grim.

Eva Tilling regarded the writhing face of Austiline's lover and had the temerity to smile. Monty would have spoken; instead, seeing that she aimlessly held the extinguished cigarette butt, he emptied the matches from his box, which he proffered her by way of an ash-tray. He was meditating a further reference to her being a novice at smoking, when she said:

"Well, really, Mr. Sherwood, you could never expect me, or, for that matter, any woman to marry a blind man."

It was Eva Tilling's first flash of hostility: the stranger in command up in arms at the bare idea of such an alliance, her true self quivering with each added wound. And around her was the ever-present menace of the hidden murderers filling all that room.

"No . . . no, possibly not," Martin whispered with effort. "I came quite prepared to release you, Austiline. In fact, for many months I have been steeling myself to do so. But— but, I never expected it. Even now I find it difficult to believe when memories of happier days are so vivid."

There was quiet dignity in the words, an underlying bravery which aroused Monty's admiration.

"I knew you would accept the situation like that," Eva Tilling drawled while with lowered eyelids she abstracted another cigarette. Then she partly returned it to Moore's case, and, glancing coyly at the big man, went on: "You should really congratulate me, you know. Mr. Anchor is a polished man of great wealth, and will, I am sure, make me a good husband."

"A most excellent husband of the popular he-man type," Monty observed dryly. "Let me see, now; you will be the fourth to die of arsenical poisoning, or will it be the fifth? They tell me that arsenic is superior to morphia in its rejuvenating effects, and not quite so energetic as strychnine."

"You are pleased to joke," Eva Tilling said severely, whilst Austiline felt the breath of failure.

"Joke! Of course I am joking. You cannot scold me when you joke yourself."

"Surely, Austiline, you must be joking," Martin put in earnestly.

She flashed the blind man a look when the stranger was momentarily off guard. The big man saw the very faintest shadow of a tremble about her lips: he noticed, too, that hardly ever did she look at Martin. Was that because she was ashamed of her despicable conduct, or because she was afraid to? If the latter, of what was she afraid? Her emotions?

"M'yes," he drawled. "Quit your joking, and name the hour you will be prepared to leave this murderers' nest."

"You must be peculiarly lacking in common sense if you fail to understand that I am perfectly serious," was Eva's assurance.

She found her eyes caught and held by the giant's blazing orbs whilst he leaned forward in his chair. For a moment she was fascinated by their penetrative power and sought to escape them, only to find her eyes held by his as by a magnet, and slowly her lids lowered so that she gazed at him mockingly between fine lashes. Deliberately she stretched herself, yawning like a great cat. Her face expressed the acme of boredom. For the second time she took the cigarette from Moore's silver case, and—found Monty beside her with a lighted match.

"Thank you!" came her mocking voice. "But you have

not Mr. Anchor's grace. Excusable, perhaps, when one remembers that you are but a common bushman—bush whacker is the technical name, is it not?"

"Your mastery of Australian slang is perfect. Contact with low-class murderers, I presume," was his countercheck. "Pardon my insistence, but are you seriously engaged to marry Bluebeard?"

"Mr. Anchor! Of course I am serious."

Again Austiline yawned with studied rudeness.

"You appear to be very tired," Monty remarked calmly.

That brought her sharply to a sitting posture, her ruddy brown eyes wide and flashing. Now she was openly spiteful.

"Tired! Indeed, I am," she said shrilly. "You bore me to distraction, you with your *gaucherie,* and your brother with his pathetic, martyrly airs. Why cannot you see that you bore me to distraction? Why leave it to me to request you to go? Please—oh, please—go!"

"With pleasure," Monty assured her politely, at once rising, and placing a hand beneath Martin's arm. "Come, Martin, the lady desires to be alone to dream of her Landru." Turning to her, he said with no trace of anger: "Good-bye! I promise to send along a set of silver coffin handles to your prospective husband as a wedding present."

"Stop!"

The command came from the blind man, who, shaking clear of Monty's guiding hand, swung about, facing the woman he still loved. She was standing now, her face white as chalk, her eyes wide and horror-filled.

"I do not think, Austiline—you really can have no objection to my still calling you that—that I have done anything to deserve your scorn, or your gibes at my affliction," Martin said in a strangely steady voice, his face tilted upward, his vacant eyes fixed unwinkingly on the dazzling lights. "Neither has my brother earned your insults. We have come to this desolate place at no little inconvenience and expense, both gladly incurred in what we thought was your service. Even now I don't regret having loved you, but I do profoundly regret that my brother, whose respect I value, should have come to know that I loved—and love—such a woman as you now show yourself to be. Monty, please take me away."

But the stranger possessing the body of Austiline Thorpe saw her chance to administer the *coup de grace,* to make

certain that neither would desire to remain another day in
that house. Standing erect, she threw back her head and
laughed, the laugh of the wanton taxed with her sins.

"Pathetic to the end!" she mocked. "But really I have
no use whatever for an imitation man." And then her voice
rose to a scream and, turning her back to them, she cried:
"Go! Go away! I never want to see you again. I hate the
sight of affliction. Please go—at once!"

"We are going; even now we are on the move," replied
the big man, he and Martin half way to the door. At the
door itself he turned, to see her still with her back to them,
a figure flooded by soft light, a figure whose shoulders shook
and whose hands at the side clenched and unclenched
spasmodically.

Then it was he thought he understood. And, understanding, a flash of inspiration came to him. If she had been
acting a part it was possible some one beside themselves was
watching the play. Before he closed the door, he said lightly:

"Good-bye, little butterfly! I will not forget the coffin-
handles, but they will be of gold."

A minute of utter silence passed before Dr. Moore and his
companion emerged from their hiding-places, the lank man
smiling sardonically, "The Cat" showing his yellow teeth in
a leer of balked desire.

"Certainly you are to be congratulated on your histrionic
talent, Miss Thorpe. I have never enjoyed a performance so
much." For a moment he waited for her to speak. Then:
"Good evening!"

An eternity elapsed before she heard the door close for the
second time. Then the statue came to life, raised its hands
above the auburn head, and laughed and shrieked alternately.
Flinging herself on the sofa, she pressed a cushion to her
mouth and tore the satin covering with her teeth; then, leaping
to her feet again, her hair fell in a cloud about her writhing
shoulders, and her fingers clutched at and tore her dress to
ribbons in a paroxysm of terror and mental agony.

Then the door was flung open and Mrs. Jonas, in a dressing-
gown, ran to her with outstretched arms.

CHAPTER XXV

CIGARETTE SMOKE

THE door closed behind them, Monty led his brother slowly along the underground passage, and, without speaking, guided him up the cork-paved steps to the movable panel giving outlet to the hall. The mechanism of this door was very simple. This panel was not meant to be a mystery to any of the inmates; the intention being merely to conceal the existence of the basement rooms from casual or unwanted visitors.

On the inside a wooden knob operated the fastening, and, moving this, the brothers gained the hall. Meeting no one there, they walked to their bedroom. Once within, with the door shut, Martin groped his way to his bed, on which he flung himself with despairing abandon.

In silence the big man removed his jacket and collar, and, seating himself near the open windows, produced pipe and tobacco. He felt that his ideas of women were inadequate to cover the situation; at the same time he was by no means clear what the situation really was. That Austiline had been acting he was certain. What baffled him was whether she had acted to serve her own end or ambition, or at the compelling behest of some one else, probably Anchor. In this latter case, he felt sure that the millionaire would want to know their personal opinion about it all, and would even go so far as to hide a dictaphone in their room to get it pure. That move he thought he could counter. He said:

"Have a cigarette, Martin. It will steady you."

"Damn cigarettes!" the younger man said slowly, adding, with sudden access of rage: "What I want is sight, eyesight. Oh God! Why am I alive?"

"Now, now! Don't get into a paddy," Monty exhorted. "It only serves you right for chasing after women. Perhaps now you'll leave 'em alone."

"Monty!" There was both surprise and pain in Martin's voice.

"I mean it," asserted the big man sternly. "Directly a man gets tangled with a bit of skirt he starts stumbling on jagged rocks. Women are all right as playthings. They amuse a man in his spare time, and it's only a fool who allows them to be amused at him. For every Ruth there are ten thousand Rats. A man has got a better chance of winning the Melbourne Cup Sweep than he has of winning a Ruth. Forget her, Martin, old lad. Racehorses are better sport."

Although not understanding the reason for this remarkable and most un-Monty-like speech, the blind man instinctively guessed that Monty would render an excellent one in due course. Still, the pain of the wounds inflicted by Austiline was in no way alleviated; for, sightless as he was, only her voice was his guide, whereas her actions had aroused Monty's suspicions.

"I am going to carry the beds out to the veranda," Monty announced after an interval of silence. "Then I'm going to sleep. I allow no woman to interfere with my sleep. If you do, you're an ass. To-morrow I'll repair the water-drums, and the day after we'll poke off back."

The part of the veranda immediately beyond this room was partitioned off from the remainder by fine-meshed fly-gauze, which shut in the whole. This formed another room, an ideal sleeping-place in summer, when the nights are almost as hot as the days. He had observed that a door gave exit to the compound beyond, on the further side of which were arranged the several small outhouses, one of which contained their gear.

Martin, too sick at heart to talk, allowed himself to be undressed, and to be conducted, with a reassuring pressure on his arm, to his bed outside. Five minutes later Monty lay on his own, smoking his asthmatic pipe.

The night was exceedingly dark despite the full moon, for as yet the high-level sand-cloud had not passed away. The soft southerly wind coming through the fly-gauze was appreciated, nevertheless the house still radiated its sun-stored heat.

For half an hour the big man lay still, listening. The reflection of a light in a room farther along the veranda vanished suddenly. Twice he heard doors closed; never once did he hear footsteps. A dingo barked from a great distance. The only continuous sound was the fall of water from the bore-mouth. It was a quarter to eleven when—emulating Martin—he removed his watch-glass and felt the position of the hands.

A riddle to Monty Sherwood was a most objectionable form of mental exercise, yet he was engaged in solving one whilst lying on his luxurious bed, his hands clasped beneath his head. There appeared to be no possible answer to the riddle, the riddle of Austiline Thorpe. Instead of answers, came other riddles.

Why, in the first place, did she take upon herself the unpleasant task of telling them personally of her transferred affections, and in so insulting a manner? Why did she smoke cigarettes when it was so evident she was unused to smoking? Again, what was behind her possession of Moore's case and match-box?

Had she been acting a part? If she had, then she was a wonderful, a superb actress, a trained actress, and that he knew she was not. He recalled the tremble of her mouth when she looked at Martin. Again he saw her standing with her back to them, her shoulders twitching, her hands clenching and unclenching; and once again believed, perhaps almost was convinced, that she had played a part.

Granted that she had, what was the reason? To use her own metaphor, that was where his head met a brick wall, and, in spite of what he had said, this wall refused to collapse under the impact. If she had been compelled to act, who had compelled her? If Anchor, why? He had intimated that he and his associates would obstruct their departure, so that he could not have compelled her to act, under dire penalties should she refuse, just to get rid of them.

It was no light riddle for any one to solve; it was a dark enigma. Whatever might be the solution, he felt sure they would not be allowed to leave without a fight. Another thing he was sure of was that, when they did leave, Austiline Thorpe would leave with them, even if he had to carry her off.

Having thus decided, he slid off his bed with an entire absence of sound, and on hands and knees crept to that occupied by his brother. Martin, still awake, started violently when he felt Monty's fingers on his face, and was relieved to hear the big man's breathed reassurance. Then, with his mouth right against the blind man's ear, Monty whispered:

"Some one might have been listening, or some patent eaves-dropping machine might have been fixed up," he said, "That's why I gave that little sermon on women a while ago, and moved our beds here. I had no wish to sting you, old son, but I figured that Anchor would be keen to know our views of Austiline as quickly as possible. Can you hear me?"

Martin moved his head in assent. The big man continued:

"I don't want to raise any false hopes, but I suspect that your girl was playing a part—a kind of part she didn't like playing in the least. If she acted, her acting was mighty good, and she is wasting her talents writing books.

"You try and answer me these questions in the morning. One, what was Austiline doing with Moore's cigarette-case, for that was what she took her smokes from? Two, why was she smoking at all, for you have told me that is not one of her habits, and I could see she has not got the trick of it yet? Three, why did her lips tremble when she looked at you, which was about twice, and why was she trying to stop her sobs when we were leaving the room, turning her back to us to hide the effort? If she was genuinely stuck on Monsoor Anchor, why the sobs, why the melodramatic interview when a letter would have done, why the cigarettes, why—oh, a hell of whys!"

"Can't you make a guess, Monty?"

"Nope, Lazarus, I can't. I'm no good at all on the thought stakes. As for Austiline, I'm half convinced that she was speaking lines written by some one not herself. She seemed just a little too narked with us, just a little too anxious that we should leave in a hurry. Our best policy is to wait a day or two and see what the sun brings up out of this stinking ground. Bye-bye!"

The big man stole back to his bed, happy to have dressed the wound in Martin's heart. From his mind he put the enigma of Austiline's strange behaviour, and began to plan his future actions. That war was inevitable with Anchor was evident. The question which was less difficult to answer was: should he wait for Anchor to declare war on him, or should he throw down the gage on the morrow? Had Martin not been blind, or had he remained in Melbourne, Monty knew that without hesitation he would have opened hostilities that night.

He had decided that his best policy was to gather his camels early the next night or the night after, endeavour to remove at least one pack and one riding-saddle, with rations, from the store opposite, and get Martin away to a camp established at some distance. Then to return and remove Austiline, using force if necessary. By forced night marches he was confident he could reach Minter's Selection.

Just then one of the great hounds barked in a half-hearted manner, and, raising his head to listen, he discerned a light in one of the outhouses. The time then was twenty minutes past one.

It is quite probable that had his mind been free from sinister suspicion the bushman would not have felt sufficient interest in that light to investigate it; but, his brain demanding relief from complex thinking, and his rested body action, he quietly changed into dark trousers and shirt—for his night attire was white—and soundlessly left the veranda.

Knowing that an upright figure would be seen too easily by any watcher at the house, he bent almost double and made rapidly to the line of outbuildings. He moved with the noiselessness of a shadow over the deep, fine-grained sand covering the compound.

And then that happened which made him pause but two yards from the building containing his gear. The light proceeded from a weather-board and iron hut at the end of the row. At several places cracks between the sun-warped boards were visible, and at the house side a small square of light showed where there was a window. And at this window, looking in with his face low down in one corner, Monty recognized Dr. Moore.

Dr. Moore was greatly interested in something going on inside; he also displayed caution in not allowing himself to be seen by any one within. The big man decided that what interested the lank medico would assuredly interest him.

Slowly he gained the rear of his store-hut, and along that side of the row crept to the end building, at the rear of which he crouched with his eyes on a level with a chink between two of the wall-boards.

Monty found himself surveying a chamber of horrors.

To his left stood an instrument which he had often read about, but never seen. Between shortened uprights gleamed the heavy and polished blade of a guillotine, set deep into the half-circular cut of the neck-rest. Before this weapon of a nation's insane wrath, now considered the most humane instrument of human execution in current use, stood the emaciated Earle, his hair dank and ruffled, his face besmirched with semi-grimed sweat-marks, his white duck suit dilapidated and dirty.

Without any show of haste Earle seized a cord which ran through several small pulley-blocks and raised the massive blade to the full height of the supports, where it came to rest with a slight click. For a moment he regarded the glittering blade with a faint smile playing about his sunken mouth. Then, taking another dangling cord, a red cord with a bulb at the end like that which releases a camera shutter, he pressed the bulb and witnessed the blade flash downwards with a resounding thud.

For a while the man stood slightly swaying on his feet, gazing down at the deep broad blade. Five, ten, thirty seconds he remained thus, a whimsical smile on his chalk-white face, his head moving slowly sideways like that of a clockwork bear.

Monty heard him sigh deeply, saw him turn to a small table. There he took up a shining lancet and laid it gently against the main artery of his left wrist. Putting that back, he examined closely several small bottles, reading the written matter on the labels.

A garrotting chair next interested him. It was set in the corner to the right of the window, and for the time Dr. Moore's face vanished. By the side of the chair was a lever which Earle pulled forward, whereupon the steel arms winging the neck-rest opened wide. A red cord he suddenly jerked sharply, when the steel arms snapped shut and from the neck-rest protruded a shining steel spike. Earle shuddered visibly, and, passing the window, paused at a second table, upon which lay a box of cigarettes and a match-holder. When Monty looked at the window opposite it was again to see Moore watching with strangely glittering, unspectacled eyes.

When the big man's gaze reverted to Earle, the latter was selecting one of the cigarettes, which were of unusual length. Having applied a match, he inhaled deeply, a feat which astonished the bushman, remembering as he did Earle's racking cough during his appearance before the diners that evening.

Beside the cigarette box lay a dainty, ivory-handled five-chambered revolver, which Earle picked up and examined. With a start, Monty saw him reverse it in one hand and pick up a mirror with the other. The watcher held his breath. Earle placed the muzzle of the gun against his forehead and held the mirror before his eyes.

It was an intense moment. Monty drew in his breath sharply, preparatory to giving vent to a distracting yell; but he made no sound and exhaled his breath normally when

Earle laid down revolver and mirror and shook his head slowly for the second time.

Had it not been for the proximity of Dr. Moore, Monty probably would have entered the chamber of lethal instruments and sought to know what Percival Earle was doing there at that hour. Beginning to feel satisfied that the consumptive had no design against himself, the big man decided to remain inactive and learn what lay behind Moore's secret interest.

Like a visitor to a museum, Earle passed round the hut till he stood before a weighing machine such as may be seen on any railway station. Above the dial was a paper with two rows of figures undistinguishable by the entranced watchers. And from a stout beam dangled a rope with a noose at the end lying on the floor immediately behind Earle.

For almost a full minute he gazed at the weighing machine; then, turning, at the rope. When he turned again to the weighing machine his attitude was one of deep cogitation. The face beyond the solitary window had become glued to it.

When Earle again moved it was to stand on the weighing machine. His weight noted, he ran his finger down the left-hand column of figures, pausing a little way down, when it moved to the right and rested beneath the corresponding figures.

It came quite suddenly to Monty that the right-hand figures indicated the drop required for the execution of a man who weighed the figures given in the left-hand column. Beyond realizing this the big man's thoughts did not travel. His brain was too busy with what he saw.

He saw the skeleton of a man pick up the sinuous rope and examine the noose, before climbing a chair and altering its length at the overhead beam. Although Monty was quite aware of Earle's actions, he was honestly unaware of his intentions.

The bushman was experiencing a growing wonder at the almost spiritual light emanating from the ascetic face. It seemed as if a look of supreme happiness shone from the hazel depths of his large and brilliant eyes; the gentle smile transformed his face, giving it an ethereal beauty that the big man never forgot. Then Earle nodded vigorously, as though agreeing to some plan or request, and, stooping, picked up the rope and slid the noose over his head.

The watchers saw him tighten the noose against a staying

knot beneath his left ear. Once he glanced down at the floor and moved a little forward. Now, with his face thrown a little upward, the cigarette still between his lips, he appeared to be listening—listening for what?

The rapt look of wondrous happiness still played about his features, giving it dignity as well as beauty, as though before his fixed eyes some scene of heavenly glory was unfolding. Again he nodded vigorously, blinking now from the cigarette smoke curling upward from the butt. He was still gazing at that wonderful picture when he stretched out his hand and caught a dangling red cord with a camera shutter release.

The next moment he had vanished.

Monty, who wanted to yell and could not, saw the taut rope twitching in the yawning trap which the red cord had released. Beside it a thin spiral of cigarette smoke was still mounting; and in that smoke, cutting it as moths dancing in a sunbeam in a darkened room, he fancied he saw shapes, baby shapes, floating down to the thing at the end of the rope.

CHAPTER XXVI

MABEL HOGAN

THERE are moments in human life when Time stops or is left far in the rear by the racing mind. We read a phrase such as "an Eternity passed" perhaps without taking in its meaning, because we never have experienced that timeless, measureless period. While Monty gazed with fascinated horror at the twitching rope such a period elapsed, a period of which he was more sensible afterwards than at the precise moment.

The unnerving, wailing howls of the three great hounds seated on their haunches beyond the compound fence galvanized him into life just when Dr. Moore burst into the hut. The lank man literally jumped to a trap-door at the far end of the chamber of horrors, and, flinging it back, almost slid down what proved to be a ladder.

Monty did not wait for the doctor to disappear. He darted round the building and in through the door. The rope, he now saw, was limp and swaying. Lightly stepping to the trap, he dropped on hands and knees and peered into its depths.

Directly below him was Dr. Moore kneeling beside the prostrate Earle, electric torch in one hand, stop-watch in the other.

Earle's face, framed in a circle of brilliant light, was not pleasant to behold. The still tableau lasted but a few seconds, when Moore laid down the torch on the earthern floor in position to light up both the prostrate man and himself. The group suggested to Monty an obscene vulture gloating over a new-found feast.

"Ah!" he heard Moore grunt.

At that moment Earle's horribly staring eyes moved, and the lips, twitching, let fall the cigarette butt which had remained between them. The big man is almost certain that at the moment Earle died he said faintly:

"My darlings . . . come nearer!"

208

He is quite sure, however, that Dr. Moore's subsequent statement, that Earle died some time after he, the doctor, cut him down, was correct. He watched Moore spring to his feet and press down a wall-switch that flooded the underground chamber with light. He saw him jot into a notebook the time by his watch, with some further memoranda.

What occurred then was so sudden that his swift actions were instinctive rather than determined. The voice of Anchor was suddenly audible, shouting from the veranda to the wailing dogs. A door shut, and he guessed the disturbed millionaire had left the veranda and was coming to investigate the illuminated hut. Just then Dr. Moore began to mount the ladder.

Even during the time it took Moore to raise a foot from one rung to the next Monty decided against clubbing him when his head came within reach and then attending to Anchor and locking them both in that dreadful pit. Had he been alone he would have grasped this as a heaven-sent opportunity; but Martin's safety came first. Martin must be moved out of harm's way; therefore it was not yet time to open fire.

With the silent agility of a panther the big man reached the guillotine, behind the blade of which he flung himself into hiding. Had not Dr. Moore's mind been so full of what had just happened he doubtless would have heard the boards creak under Monty's rapid movements. As it was, he was almost at the top of the ladder when he thought of something he had omitted to observe, and redescended.

A quick step announced the arrival of William J. Anchor, who, as Monty saw from around one of the solid teak uprights, was in his pyjamas and carrying an automatic. From below Moore called out: "Who's there?" but received no reply until Anchor stood above the trap looking down.

"Why this excitement, Moore?" he inquired softly. "Have you hanged Earle?"

"Certainly not; he has hanged himself," replied Moore emphatically. "I say, Anchor, come down at once!"

"I am glad he hanged himself and was not hanged, my dear Moore. I liked Earle."

The latter sentence held a world of meaning. It was uttered in the millionaire's usual bland manner, but the edge of the tones boded no good to the doctor if it had transpired that Earle had been subjected to one of Moore's experiments.

Anchor disappeared down the ladder, and Monty again was tempted to deal summarily with the two most formidable inmates of the House of Cain. Quietly, however, he left the hut and gained his veranda-room and his bed unobserved.

Half an hour later the light within the chamber of horrors was extinguished. The hounds had hushed their eerie clamour. The night was quiet and dark. And Montague Sherwood slept the sleep of a tired child.

He awoke when the moon hung above the western horizon and all but the largest stars were invisible. The outbuildings and the sand-hills beyond were coming out of the night before the rushing dawn.

A glance at Martin showed him still sleeping, and as a matter of habit rather than desire the big man sat on the edge of his bed and cut tobacco-chips for his pipe. In all his adventurous career he never had met with so weird an episode as had occurred within the few past hours. From it stood out boldly the utter callousness or the scientific enthusiasm of Dr. Moore. His actions could be viewed from either angle. Came next the telling demonstration of the truth of Moore's theory that modern execution by hanging is not instantaneous. The judicial formula, "hanged by the neck *until you are dead,*" had now for Monty very real meaning. In the baby-shapes floating down to Earle through his cigarette smoke and in Earle's dying words the big man was not disposed to believe. He will tell you that it was the only time in his life that he was made aware that he possessed what people call an imagination.

William J. Anchor, presiding as usual at the breakfast table, startled the company, with the exception of Moore and Monty, with the news of Earle's suicide. Mrs. Jonas dropped her knife and fork and almost gaped at him. The others, excepting Lane, who preferred to go on eating, looked at the host and guardian with varying expressions of astonishment.

"Yes, poor Earle has seen fit to end his life in a manner both unnecessary and tragic," Anchor murmured.

"You don't say!" exclaimed Monty.

"I do! I do, indeed. I don't think I have yet told you that we have a Suicide Chamber fitted with a dozen—ah—remedies for life's fitful fever. I conceived the idea after a guest shot himself most clumsily in the drawing-room and spoiled a priceless snow-white Persian carpet. Moore had occasion to visit the Suicide Chamber late last evening, and came upon Earle standing on a trap, a noose about his neck and the trap-release cord in his fingers. On seeing the doctor the foolish man released the trap beneath his feet. Horrified, the doctor rushed to the underground—er—receiving-room and at once cut Earle down, but Earle died precisely eighty-three seconds after launching himself through the trap."

"Good God!" ejaculated Martin sharply.

Monty refrained from commenting on Dr. Moore's evident readiness with a stop-watch and diplomatic sub-editing of detail. Anchor continued:

"The news has quite unnerved me." Whatever substitute for nerves he used was evidently an efficient one. "I am greatly grieved. I liked Earle. I think we all did. He was a great gentleman. In my opinion, he was the bravest man who ever lived."

"Was he at the war?" asked the big man calmly.

"No. He was much too old, even had he volunteered. When I stated that he was a very courageous man, I meant really that he was braver than any soldier; more heroic, in my opinion, than any martyr. To appreciate Earle one must study his mentality, especially at the time he killed his children. The public in their ignorance said, and they were led to say it by what their newspapers printed, that Percival Earle was a monster, far worse than Deeming, or the unfortunate Frenchman, Landru, or myself. If not a monster, he was insane.

"You have known the man, and I think will agree with me that he was neither a monster nor a lunatic. What the newspapers, the public, and what a judge and jury failed and always would have failed to understand, was Earle's marvellous self-sacrificing love for his three children.

"No doubt that sounds paradoxical, when we remember that he killed them with veronal. Yet the fact remains that he was passionately devoted to them. His life was unblemished. He was a successful business man. But his wife was dead, and there were no near relatives to whom he could entrust them when the germs of tuberculosis sapped his physical defences.

"Earle was of Scotch descent. He was a staunch upholder of the Kirk during his youth and early manhood. His belief in heaven, full of angels playing orchestral instruments, and in hell, containing devils misusing implements of agriculture, was real and sincere. He believed, before he killed his children, that the act would condemn him to everlasting torment by the said devils. He deliberately condemned himself to hell in order that his children would never run the risk of hell when growing up without his love and guidance in the care of unsympathetic strangers. To him, sacrificing his life on the scaffold was a mere trifle to sacrificing his immortal soul. Have I made myself plain?"

"Quite," assented Martin. "Yet what remains obscure to me is the fact that Earle escaped to this place. Apparently he was very careful of his life till it became unbearably filled with remorse."

"Like Miss Thorpe, Earle had no option in the matter."

"Ah! the fog clears," said the blind man thoughtfully. "In that case—and I have never heard of anything like it—Earle was indeed a courageous man."

At that point the doctor rose, intimating that he must be off to the hangar erected on the edge of Lake Moonba, whose dry bed made a perfect landing ground.

"Is there anything I can bring you from Marree?" he asked, looking at Monty.

"There is," replied the big man. "It would be a real good turn if you brought me a hundred rounds of thirty-two Winchesters. And your cigarette supply is getting low, isn't it, Martin?"

"Yes. If you would be so kind, do you think you would have room for five hundred 'Three Circle' cigarettes?"

"I will bring the tubes of comfort and the messengers of death with pleasure," Moore agreed gravely. "With luck, I will be back about nine. Don't let them forget to have the flares going, Anchor."

"They shall be lit. *Bon voyage!*" farewelled the millionaire gaily.

"The Cat" had a horse harnessed to a gig awaiting the airman, who drove off immediately afterwards. Monty learned from their host that Marree lay some hundred and sixty miles southwest of the Home. Later in the day he mounted to the roof of the house with Anchor, who showed him the encircling box timber of the lake about two miles north, with the faint dark line of the trees marking the course of the Strzelecki Creek on the horizon beyond.

Breakfast over, the big man made Martin comfortable on the veranda and sought out the cheerful Mallowing, whom he found in the office, or the tiny room that served as one.

"Say, my dear old Friar Tuck!" he said cheerfully, "can you put me on to a soldering outfit? I want to mend the water-drums that your bright young friend so expertly holed."

"Certainly, Mr. Sherwood," came the hearty assent. "Come with me, and I will show you the tool-house."

They were walking across the compound when, espying the hounds chained to their kennels beyond the fence, the big man remarked:

"I wondered last night why those poodle-dogs were howling. It seems strange that dogs know of a human death, or are you a disbeliever in the theory?"

"By no means. I, too, heard them, and they must have started their commotion just when Earle died. Come and see them closer. They are always chained between sunrise and sunset."

"Mr. Anchor, I think, said there used to be a pack?"

"That is so," Mallowing stated expansively. "Mr. Anchor imported them from, I think, Bokhara. The number then was eleven. In spite of natural increase, these three are all that remain. Five were poisoned at various times. A visiting dogger shot two, since when the rule of chaining them in daytime was made. One died in a fight and the other had to be shot whilst you accounted for Carlo, Gilling's favourite."

"Um! They're massive brutes."

Through the netted fence the big man regarded the dogs with admiration; they glared at him with snarling malevolence. Their shaggy grey coats added to their apparent size. They stood not less than four feet high.

"It seems strange that Gilling, who was low and vicious, passionately loved those dogs," the little man said. "They were the only things he did love. They seemed to understand that, for they would fawn and play about him like pups. They were his especial care."

"Ah! And whose especial care are they now?"

"You would never guess. I wouldn't dare approach them. Nor would Lane or 'The Cat.' The keeper of the dogs is Madeline Fox."

"The fair girl?"

"Yes, she. She can do what she likes with those three brutes. Whatever you do, never venture outside the compound when they are loose. They would kill a man in three seconds."

"If the man didn't kill 'em in less," Monty murmured.

"Precisely. This is our tool shop. Within you will find anything, from a lathe to a tin-tack."

The happy man who had regained his freedom left Monty and returned to his office, and, while the big man selected irons and started a blow-lamp, he thought of those three huge dogs and wondered how he would best them when he attempted to get his camels and Martin clear. Shooting would then be prohibited. Also he was without strychnine, generally included in his bush kit. He thought of the assorted poisons on the small table in the Suicide Chamber, and wondered if they included anything as reliable as strychnine, if not that identical drug.

Above the roar of the blow-lamp came now and then the sharp creak of the iron roof expanding in the sun's rays. The wind was blowing from the north, and was hot. It had cleared the air of sand, but foreboded another storm within a few days. Not far away, sounds of a hammer smiting iron on an anvil made the big man wonder if Lane was at work, and a picture of the huge accumulation of flesh and fat working in that heat made him chuckle softly.

"Ooo-h!"

For a moment he was startled, when the tot he had found on his bed the previous afternoon jumped through the doorway. Realistically, Monty dropped a sheet of tin and the cutters, falling back on a sawing-bench with pretended fright. The child let loose a whoop of joy, and, dashing towards him, clung to his knees and looked up at him with dancing eyes and a laughter-lit face of astonishing purity.

"I flighten you," announced the mite with a gurgle.

"You did that," Monty gasped. "Where did you spring from?"

"I runned away from mummy," the youngster confided. Looking round at this place forbidden him, he saw the tin-cutters on the floor, for which the big man raced him, only just winning. The child stood looking up at the bushman with a suddenly drooping mouth, which sight made Monty feel an out-size in beasts. As a sop, he offered two shining sticks of solder, and was happy to see the threatened tears vanish and the sun come out once more.

"What's your name, Bubbles?" he inquired, whilst busy with the lamp.

"Me Fleddie," came the solemnly-spoken reply; and, seeing Monty's big leather pack-bags—for he had brought them there to repair when he had finished the drums—"Fleddie" went on a voyage of discovery.

"So you're Freddie, are you, Master Bubbles? Well, well! You go easy with those tucker-bags."

Monty went on with his work, whilst the curious child produced from the leather bags several small calico bags containing tea, sugar, salt, and a butt of flour, which he dragged out only by exerting all his strength. The first bag to be opened and emptied on the floor was that containing tea; and, this not suiting his taste, he examined next the salt which, proving of little interest, joined the tea. Of the sugar, however, he did manage to save a handful before it was added to the pile. The flour came last, and proved the star attraction.

When a woman's voice called "Freddie!" from one of the veranda doors at the house, the big man, turning from his work, gasped at the sight. Bubbles was wildly happy, absorbed in scooping up from the floor a glorious mixture of the contents of the tucker-bags and throwing it up over his golden crowned head. Flour whitened the delicate pink of his cheeks and filled the air with whirling particles, while the salt and tea gave his hair a piebald appearance.

"Jumping nannygoats!" Monty breathed, adding with raised voice: "Look out! Here comes your mother."

Bubbles regarded him with rapturous eyes. He had not heard his mother's first call. He did when she called again. Dropping handfuls of his wonderful mixture, he darted to Monty's side, crying:

"Mummy come! Mummy come! Me hide! Me hide from mummy!"

When the child slipped round his great figure, Monty saw Mabel Hogan crossing to the hut. Bubbles was clutching at his trousers and stamping his sandal-shod feet with excitement; and, with a smile of joy, the bushman picked up the mite and set him down behind the sawing bench, on which he seated himself.

"Hush! Mummy come!" he whispered tensely.

"Mummy come!" whispered back the thrilled child. "Look out!"

A shadow fell across the threshold, and, glancing up, Monty encountered the dark eyes of Mabel Hogan regarding him curiously.

"Good morning!" he said.

"Good morning!" she replied pleasantly. "Have you seen my baby? I cannot find him anywhere."

Monty did not speak at once, but studied with interest the woman who had murdered her betrayer. Hers was a likable face, possessing a rare beauty seldom found among Saxon women, but more often seen in Western Ireland and Northern Spain. It was a beauty enhanced by the expression of sorrow and tragedy which marked it with vivid lines. He was wondering where Bubbles had obtained his Saxon eyes and hair when her slightly almond-shaped eyes lit suddenly with understanding on noticing the indescribable mess of foodstuffs covering the floor.

"I think that Freddie cannot be far away. He must be hiding somewhere," she said.

"Maybe," Monty agreed. "Probably a habit of his."

"I wonder where he can be."

Not till she had called his name twice did the babe find the suspense insupportable, when, with a shriek of delight, he dashed out of his hiding-place and flew to his mother's out-flung arms.

"What *have* you been doing?" she demanded, holding him from her and noting the grains of sugar adhering to his Cupid mouth, and the flour and tea covering the rest of him.

"Ooo. I hide from mummy!" Bubbles gurgled, and then, pointing at the wreckage, struggled for freedom and cried: "Sweetie! Sweetie! I want sweetie!"

"You can't want any more, surely. What you really do want is a bath."

"Better let him down," suggested Monty, smiling at her and the fighting Freddie. "He's a broth of a boy."

Mabel Hogan saw in the bushman's smile what she had not seen for many a day—honesty, fearlessness, and cleanness. The woman was an idealist, and in a fraction of time she realized that here was her ideal man, a man whose feet were not of clay like that other whom she had loved. She smiled at him in return; and, if Monty thought her face lovely then, the child must have considered her an utter stranger, because, ceasing his struggles, he regarded his mother solemnly. Monty sensed that she had not smiled like that for years.

"Did he make all that mess?" she asked, putting Bubbles down. Monty's grey-blue eyes danced.

" 'Fraid he did," he admitted. "He enjoyed doing it, and

besides it took his mind off these cutters that he wanted badly to keep. How old is he?"

"Three years and seven months."

"So! Well, he's a bonzer kid. I'd like to have a boy like that. We'd get along good."

"I've no doubt whatever about that, after what you've allowed him to do," she said with a sigh. "You may have him, if you like."

"Eh!" Monty spoke sharply, for he saw that she was strangely earnest. While she regarded him her eyes became moist. Then, very softly:

"He is all I have," she said. "Yet I must not keep him here with me. You look a good, fine man. I believe you are. Your brother, too, is wonderfully gentle and patient, despite his blindness. Oh! if only you would take him with you when you go: take him to your home, and let him grow to a splendid man in an atmosphere clean and wholesome. Would you?"

For a moment he studied her face.

"But you wouldn't care to be parted from such a treasure, would you?" he asked doubtfully.

"I! I'm not to be considered whatever, not a little tiny bit, where his future is concerned. I've forfeited all right to the slightest consideration. *You* know what I am, something terrible, something you should shudder to look at. What chance in life will he ever get here amongst us? In a few years it will be too late, and his innocence destroyed. As the son of such a mother, what will become of him? If you take him with you he will forget me, he will grow up perhaps loving some other woman as his mother, and admiring and respecting such a man as you, if not as his father, then as his guardian. Will you at least think about it?"

She stood before him, her hands clasped, her voice low and pleading, with a hint of sobs in it.

"I have neither a wife nor a home," he said. "Nor is my mother alive, who would have set Bubbles on a pedestal and worshipped him. Mr. Anchor tells me that my brother and I will not be permitted to leave here, but regarding that I have other views. We leave when we wish to leave. However, I know a woman who has been denied the love of children, and who is hungry for a child's love. She and her husband are hard-working people. They would give the boy affection. I could attend to his education, which would be the best

Australia can offer, and I would give him a start in life. Would you like that?"

"Oh, I would! I would!"

"Then I won't think about it. I'll take him with me. You are very right and very brave to part with him, rather than let him grow up here. A woman who can love like you could not have an unworthy son."

Her breath caught, and her hand flew to her mouth. Tears streamed down her face and blurred her eyes while for half a second she looked at him. Then suddenly she snatched up a protesting Bubbles and fled back to the house, leaving a very thoughtful man repairing water-drums, work which up to that time had not greatly advanced.

When a hand-bell was rung half an hour later, calling all for morning tea, Monty, while not regretting his promise to Mabel Hogan, wondered how he was going to get Martin, Austiline, and the child one night secretly away.

"Reckon I'm going to be terrible busy," he remarked to the blow-lamp, the flame of which died out when he unscrewed the cock.

CHAPTER XXVII

THE following morning found two groups of talkers on the broad veranda of the House of Cain.

Dr. Moore had returned from Marree late the evening before, bringing with him as passenger a new guest named Anthony Cotton. Neither of the Sherwoods had met the new arrival, who had retired to his room immediately after his reception by Anchor. He had not yet made an appearance, but was expected any moment.

Breakfast had been disposed of with the usual unconventional conversation, and now Martin sat with Mrs. Jonas at one end of the veranda, whilst Dr. Moore and his friend and protector occupied the other.

The lady and the blind man discussed the pros and cons of spiritualism, the theory and practice of which Mrs. Jonas emphatically disapproved. Of the regular inmates she was the most enigmatic in character. Her earnestness and honesty, together with her so evident disapproval of the callous nature of the table-talk, were so startlingly inconsistent with what must have been a solitary manifestation of her under-nature, that Monty found it difficult to believe she was a murderess.

Martin, however, learned from that veranda talk a great deal about Mrs. Jonas. She gave him several glimpses of her naked soul, and ever afterwards Martin regarded murderers less with inward shudderings and more with pity as unhappy sufferers from a lesion of the brain. It was the quiet, earnest voice of Mrs. Jonas, seeking neither pity nor censure, but sympathetic understanding, which converted Martin from the view that a destroyer of human life should suffer summary execution.

The subject debated by the two leading spirits in their corner, if not a deep question of human ethics, was in another way as grave. While watching indolently the huge figure of Montague Sherwood engaged in boiling out his repaired water-drums with a solution of caustic soda to cleanse them, with Bubbles busily gathering chips from odd corners for the fire, William J. Anchor imparted to his friend a disquieting news item.

"I received a message from our Wirra-wirra wireless station, outside Port Augusta, last night, just before you got back," he was saying. "I was listening-in to Adelaide and enjoying a really good concert, when friend Smythe, the announcer, signalled me, by the usual method of coughing during an announcement, to alter the wave-length to Wirra-wirra."

"Ah!" the doctor murmured. "That sounds serious."

"Exactly. It was with not a little trepidation that I got in touch with Mason, of Wirra-wirra, for you know that he has instructions to communicate with us only in exceptional circumstances."

It may be explained here that Anchor's wireless communication with the outside world was necessarily somewhat intricate. The leaders of his organization reported important news by code telegram to a man in Adelaide named Smythe. He was the announcer at the Adelaide Symphony Broadcasting Company's studio. By means of a special code of punctuating his announcements by various coughs, long and short, occurring before, during, and after his announcements, he passed to Anchor every night, at nine o'clock, any simply expressed items of news.

News messages of greater length or difficulty were telegraphed to Mount Barker, in the Adelaide Hills, where an experimental wireless expert reported direct to Anchor at nine o'clock precisely. Urgent information demanding instant dispatch in the evening was telegraphed to a man named Mason, who owned a small transmitting set at a selection on the outskirts of Port Augusta. Since this latter sending station was illegal, and the authorities were already hunting for it, only information of supreme urgency was sent by it.

A man who loved to play with his audience, the millionaire dawled in imparting to his companion the kernel of the news he had received from Port Augusta. Anchor would have made a great actor. Straw after straw he added to the fire of Moore's impatience, until at last the irritable doctor burst out:

"Well, and what the devil did Mason say?"

Having elicited the outburst for which he had been angling,

Anchor replied with his usual suaveness, unruffled and deadly cool:

"To-day is Friday," he said. "On Sunday the police from Innaminka will pay us a call."

"Well, they have done that before."

"Precisely. But then they were not ordered to do so by Headquarters at Adelaide."

"The devil!"

"It is, I agree, the devil. When I deciphered Mason's code, the message ran: 'Innaminka police instructed by Central Office investigate you. H.Q.'s motive unknown, so far. Believed not serious, but caution advised."

In silence the two men pensively watched Monty at work outside the tool-house. They were quite used to police visits, as is every outback squatter. In the remoter regions of South Australia a police-trooper's beat extends for many hundreds of miles. His duties are various. He takes the census, issues summonses against defaulting or reluctant income-tax payers, checks the electoral rolls. Invariably he sends word before him of the date of his arrival at a station homestead, an act of courtesy which ensures hospitality for himself and his horse. In common with other station-holders, Anchor always knew when to expect one of these duty visits, during which the most conspicuous members of his household lived in the secret underground rooms. Being himself a Justice of the Peace, the millionaire thoroughly enjoyed his temporary and official guests' conversation, and treated them as comrades and friends.

But this coming police visit was a cat of another colour. It was a perturbing thought that official circles in Adelaide had suddenly conceived suspicions of him.

"Can Hill be at the bottom of it, do you think?" asked Moore.

"No. Hill is passionately fond of his wife and baby. Melbourne organization sent Hill a visitor to his bedside at the hospital. Hill admitted to the visitor that it was to Monty Sherwood only that he had given information, and that only because he was under a great debt to Miss Thorpe and the blind man. The visitor told Hill that, should he be so inconsiderate as to give to any second person the same information, 'Mrs. Hill and baby would be found very dead.' No, it is not Hill."

"Then possibly Monty Sherwood left instructions behind."

"That may be so. He may have instructed some person to act, failing news of his whereabouts after the lapse of a certain time. But, so far, the two have not been here long enough to cause anxiety at home. The bushman would have estimated the number of days required to get here and back, to say nothing of several days' grace.

"Remember, Hill told him only that Miss Thorpe was within a hundred miles of Lake Moonba. He told nothing about us. If Sherwood did leave instructions, they could only provide for a search in this direction should he fail to report after a certain time."

"Humph!"

Anchor lit a cigarette. His eyes were dreamy.

"To-day is Friday. The Sherwoods must leave to-morrow at the latest. So far, Austiline is amenable to my will. From the Sherwoods' conversation immediately after they left her, which I collected per dictaphone, I am sure she has convinced them that she desires to remain here. I understand from you that she declared she is to become my wife. Doubtless she will be known here as Mrs. Anchor, but I think no record will ever be made in a register. I do not suffer insults gladly.

"However, I am obliged to humour her to a certain extent. She declines most emphatically to become Mrs. Anchor until forty-eight hours have elapsed from the time she herself, from this veranda, watches them leave. So leave they must."

"Anchor, you're a fool."

Moore's voice was low and tinged with passion.

"Probably, my dear Moore, you are right," came the drawled assent. "But, as all poets agree, it is divine foolishness."

The doctor leaned forward in his chair and almost glared at the unconscionable millionaire. He said:

"If you allow the Sherwoods to get away, I am quite sure it will be the end of all things for us. Certainly, never again shall we feel secure from the illogical fate which this Home has helped us so far to evade. You had better give me a free hand. Let me take care of them in my laboratory, since you decline to allow Miss Thorpe to accompany them. You could have depended upon the honour of the three of them; but you mistake the big Sherwood if you think he will be satisfied to let such an affair be tamely forgotten."

"Tut, tut!"

"It is not 'tut, tut,' Anchor, believe me. You have made

up your mind to conquer the woman, which is one foolishness. For heaven's sake, don't commit the second and fatal foolishness of allowing those men to depart. Give them to me! Let Lane and 'The Cat' plant their gear in the bush, and, when the police have gone, stage a deserted camp somewhere fifty or sixty miles distant."

"My dear Moore, what you don't grasp is the fact that there are real gentlemen in this world outside of England," Anchor said blandly. "Even I, the descendant of the *Mayflower* cabin-boy, hold to my given word of honour. One need not necessarily be related to a duke to be a gentleman. The Sherwoods are gentlemen. I like Montague's strength of character and Martin's firm but gentle nature. If they promise utter silence about us, you may depend on their keeping their promise. I intend depending upon that. Besides, it will please Austiline. And really I must please her during, at least, the period of our—er—engagement."

"Have your own way, and damn us all! I can say no more."

"Gently, my dear friend—gently, I implore you." The doctor found himself looking into the blazing slate-coloured eyes of his patron, yet Anchor's voice was in no way altered. "Understand, Moore," he added, "I have wanted Austiline for some considerable time. The conditions she lays down for her surrender shall be complied with. You will not, I trust, interfere with my little romance."

"Hell!" muttered the tall man; and, rising suddenly, he passed along the veranda to the hall.

The millionaire remained smoking as though without a care in the world. Five minutes passed in their drowsy way. Then Mabel Hogan, who had been hiding among the dining-room window curtains, quietly stepped across the room and made her way to her bedroom. She was glad and sorry that Monty and Martin would be leaving the next day. Bubbles would go with them. She cried silently while packing his tiny garments in a suit-case.

In the Australian bush it is the custom to drink morning and afternoon tea, at ten and three respectively. This light refreshment is in addition to the three usual meals, and one becomes so used to a cup of tea and scones or cake at ten in the morning and three in the afternoon that to miss the tea makes something like a gap in the day.

Monty had just finished cleaning up after his work when

the bell for morning tea was rung. With Bubbles clinging to his hand he walked over to the house, where Mabel Hogan took charge of her baby and the big man repaired to the bathroom to wash his hands. When he regained the veranda, where morning tea was invariably served, it was to find gathered there all the inmates of the house excepting Austiline and the unsociable *chef*.

The fair-haired girl, Madeline Fox, brought in the tray, and a moment later the new guest appeared, in company with Dr. Moore. The scene reminded the bushman of a Sunday gathering of a family of farmers, a common enough sight, when sons and daughters with their partners and children congregate at the old folks' farm in a kind of weekly reunion.

Although tall, Mr. Cotton's frame was slight, and his shoulders indicated the student. He was immaculately dressed in a grey flannel suit, soft collar, and white canvas shoes. He wore a light brown beard trimmed to a point. His large hazel eyes peered about through pince-nez. He seemed nervous and ill at ease.

At his appearance Anchor hurried to his side, and, taking his arm, led him with friendly assurance towards the waiting group. To each of them he introduced Mr. Cotton with old-fashioned courtesy, reciting in his interesting style the reason and the details of the crime committed by the person figuring in the introduction. When they came to the mightily amused Monty, the millionaire said with his habitual silkiness:

"This, Mr. Cotton, is Mr. Montague Sherwood. So far he is but an honorary member of our little community. However, he is not entirely without claim upon us, for at extremely long range he deprived us of one of our guests in a rifle duel. You will observe that the result of the duel nowise affects our mutual regard."

Monty found himself looking into a pair of partly veiled eyes observing him quizzically. The brown, curly beard he noticed was of recent growth. Holding out his hand, he drawled:

"Happy to know you, Mr. Cotton. What is your favourite brand of murder?"

The new guest seemed hardly prepared for this somewhat unconventional opening, but was spared the embarrassment of reply by their host tugging at his sleeve and urging him forward to the seated Martin.

"This is Mr. Martin Sherwood, who is paying us a brief

visit in company with his brother. Mr. Martin Sherwood is editor-in-chief of the Melbourne *Tribune*. Unfortunately, a recent severe illness has affected his sight, let us but hope temporarily."

"In happier circumstances I should have appreciated more keenly the honour of meeting so distinguished a journalist," Mr. Cotton remarked in a soft voice.

"And I no less, to meet so distinguished a writer," Martin responded gently, without, however, offering his hand. That he could not bring himself to do, at least not yet, to a murderer.

The company became seated. Mrs. Jonas presided at the teapot and Madeline Fox was an attentive waitress. It was plain that the new guest was the centre of keen interest and that all the others were longing to hear his story. The millionaire beamed over his teacup at the nervous Mr. Cotton, and said:

"A rule we practise here, my dear Mr. Cotton, is frankness. I have read your books—who has not?—and I admire your work because of your candour in treating the relations of the sexes. If you will but treat the affair which led to your being here among us with equal candour, you will interest us all and benefit your own mind. Monsieur Coué I consider to be one of humanity's greatest benefactors.

"You will have observed that we are a people who make a strong point of discussing our little affairs without reserve, and the object of that is to prevent brooding and—er—bad dreams. The more we discuss a thing, especially our cupboard skeleton—the more often we drag the skeleton out into the light of day, count its bones as it were, examine it calmly and at leisure from all points of view, the less able does the skeleton become to disturb our sleep. The skeleton held up to public view loses all its terrors, becomes almost comic."

The bearded man shuddered slightly. He consumed a scone, but made no attempt to speak.

"There is a type of person," Anchor continued, "who has no control over his or her imagination. Mrs. Jonas will not agree that imagination is acute consciousness, but to my mind the two are one. Your books, Mr. Cotton, prove that you are strongly imaginative. It follows that you are highly temperamental. As for that, we are all more highly strung than the ordinary person.

"Unfortunately, imaginative people who experience regret

—or remorse, to give it a conventional name—suffer in that the act regretted assumes enormous and ridiculous importance. We have here a Suicide Chamber, which I will presently take you to see. Should you at any time be so unfortunate as to find yourself unable to control your imagination, and desire to enter that state of blessed vacuity called death, I trust that you will make use of one of the dozen or so proved methods of self-annihilation which that chamber contains. My house is full of antique furniture and objects of art. I take special pride in my unmatched rugs and carpets. When a guest shot himself in the drawing-room last year, he ruined a priceless Persian rug. To avoid such losses I inaugurated the Suicide Chamber."

Again Mr. Cotton shivered.

"I think it unlikely that ever I shall be courageous enough to destroy myself," he said.

"I am glad to hear you say that," returned Anchor. "Thank you, Madeline!"—this in accepting a second cup of tea. "Believe me, Mr. Cotton, there is no truer saying than 'Confession is good for the soul'. As I have just indicated examine your skeleton at all hours of the day, and the familiarity thus assured will prevent the skeleton from examining you at night. Tell us now, I pray you, the history of your great adventure."

CHAPTER XXVIII

MARTIN SHERWOOD admits that he received Cotton's recital with a calmness which later he could not understand. That his inherent sense of justice had lost some of its keenness he attributes in part to Anchor's practice of making an open and everyday matter of the cupboard skeleton. In a way, too, it was the result of mixing on easy and familiar terms with this astonishing group. Continued contact with these persons would in the end, he doubted not, have brought him into real sympathy with them, a sympathy not in general to be justified. At the same time he realized, as a permanent impression, that in some cases, as that of Mrs. Jonas, his sympathy was not misplaced.

When Cotton spoke, the blind man at once was perplexed by his voice. He had read some of Cotton's books with mingled admiration for their eloquence and dislike for their lurid sex realism. Indeed, on the latter ground, he had criticized them severely in the *Tribune*. Although he could not remember having met the author before, he did consider it probable that he had heard his voice at some social gathering. That he had heard the voice long before his arrival at the House of Cain, he was positive. At first haltingly, then with accumulating confidence, Cotton told his story.

"I will confide my trouble, although it will pain me severely," Cotton said. "If only I could forget it!"

"Exactly," agreed Anchor. "Yet we can forget a thing by making it too familiar and commonplace to remember. The more we bully ourselves to forget it, the more unforgettable it will become."

"Well, well, I will make confession," came the soft, tired voice. "I am, ladies and gentleman, a writer. I originate from Durban and came to this country twelve months ago, after living many years in London. I settled at Mount Barker, in the Adelaide Hills.

227

"One of my near neighbours was a doctor with whose daughter I fell in love. I proposed and was accepted. Then followed a period of incessant work which so engrossed me that, I must admit, I neglected her shamefully. Pardonably furious with me, she fell like a ripe apple into the arms of a bounder named Ross. He poached on my preserves with success.

"Naturally I was much upset, and was in an ill frame of mind when, five evenings ago, I met my love cooing into the ear of this Ross fellow. The meeting occurred not far from my home, at a lonely place on a by-track. We broke into heated words. My former sweetheart fled. I struck the blackguard and felled him. His head must have hit against a stone, because when I examined him he was dead."

"Quite a Sunday School kind of murder," Monty murmured; but, if Cotton heard, he made no remark. Continuing his story with his head sunk between his hands, and his voice hardly audible, he said:

"With the blood of my enemy on my hands I rushed home, and, hurriedly packing a few things, drove myself to Adelaide, left the car outside the Post Office, and took a room at the Bull's Hoof Hotel under an assumed name.

"The afternoon papers of the following day were full of my dreadful deed. I read the account of it in the bar of the hotel. I remember seeing a lounger regarding me keenly. I knew he guessed who I was. When he left hurriedly, I thought he had gone for the police. Somehow I cared but little.

"I was trying to drown my thoughts in whisky, and was astonished by the fact that, though the spirit affected my legs, my brain remained clear and my thoughts like crystal. A gentleman approached me and asked me to accompany him. He did not look like a detective, but I believed he was. I felt glad. I hoped they would hang me quickly. On the pavement he said:

"'Are you Mr. Cotton?'

"I said I was, and without another word he led me to a waiting car and took me to a house in Glenelg. At Glenelg, late that night, I was put aboard a small hell-fast motor-boat which finally deposited me at Port Augusta. The rest you know."

When the big man glanced at the company at the close of this haltingly given recital, a replica of millions of similar

crimes dating back to that first slaying in the dawn of time,
he found each one raptly attentive. Mabel Hogan appeared
tragically sad; Mrs. Jonas gazed steadily at the teapot; Moore
appeared about to doze; Anchor was smiling gently; Mallowing
and "The Cat" were merely interested; Lane's eyes glittered
with strange intensity; whilst Madeline Fox regarded Mr.
Cotton with undisguised approval.

Madeline Fox was almost as enigmatic as Mrs. Jonas. She
was fair and pretty. Her smile, however, was studied. It
never varied in expression. Her blue eyes were big and she
used them at the slightest opportunity. She had given up
the idea of enslaving Monty, for the bushman no longer
responded to her smiles and coquettish glances, she being
one of the few women he distrusted and disliked. At all times
did she display her feminine arts and graces, no matter who the
man. With her, to make herself desirable or desired was a
mania.

From Madeline Fox, who returned his stare with a grimace,
Monty's gaze reverted to the new guest. It was the enormous
Lane who broke the silence with the accents of Wapping.

"You got me sympathy, Mr. Cotton," he said in a wheezing
voice. "This wouldn't be a bad sort o' world if a bloke got
a free go with a clinah, and other blokes didn't butt in. No
bloke butts into my little playground and enjoys 'isself long."

Anchor tapped the distraught Cotton on the shoulder.

"Cheer up, my dear Mr. Cotton," he said gently. "You
will find that after a few days the little cloud hanging over
your mind will vanish. Talk about your little incident on every
occasion, bring it out of the cupboard at every opportunity,
and you will come to regard it as of no importance whatever.
After all, it is not really of any importance, you know, unless
to rid the world of one cad is important." Rising, he urged
Mr. Cotton to his feet, saying: "By way of agreeable
diversion, allow me to show you our Suicide Chamber, our
private graveyard, and the other amenities of our monastic
estate."

It was the signal for general dispersal, and a minute later
only the brothers remained on the veranda. Monty hitched
his chair closer.

"Martin, old feller-me-lad, I've made a plan to get going
to-night," he said softly. "I have finished the water-drums,
and have only a little work to do on the pack-bags. Now,
when it gets dark to-night, I'm going to quiet the wuppy-

wups. I hate doing it, but needs must when Anchor drives. The dogs put to sleep, I'll slip out for the camels and camp 'em on the other side of yonder sand-hill.

"By the look of the sky to westward we're in for a dark night, which is why I have decided to hasten matters. Once I have the camels in camp, I'll carry our gear, or what I can of it, to them and load up. Then I'll come back for you. Then I'll come back for Bubbles."

"Bubbles!" exclaimed Martin.

"Certainly. Bubbles is my adopted son. Mabel Hogan gave him to me. When I have given Bubbles into your charge —probably fast asleep—I'll come back for Austiline."

"But she may not want to come," objected the blind man.

"I think she will. Anyhow, she's coming. I'll interview her about midnight, and, should she threaten to kick up a row, I shall pacify her with chloroform. She is coming, willingly or not, as far as Broken Hill. If then she wishes to return, I will extend her every assistance."

"But the poison and the chloroform, where will you get them?"

"From the well-furnished Suicide Chamber."

"Ah! Well, proceed."

"We should be able to leave our temporary camp not later than one o'clock. We shall get at least six hours' start. After that, our greatest danger is from the aeroplane. But, unless Anchor has bombs or a machine-gun mounted on it, we can give almost as good as we get—with luck, better."

"Your plan can be slightly improved, Monty."

"Improve away, general."

"If you were to remove Dr. Moore before we left, the aeroplane would be out of commission. He is the only pilot. Anchor admitted to me as much."

"You would have me corpse him?"

"Well, yes, if he resists," Martin said with, for him, unnatural hardness. "The risks of our escape will be increased, but once away we shall run no danger of being overtaken and shot down from the 'plane. Pack-saddle forts will be no protection against the sky."

For a little while Monty regarded his brother with wonder. That Martin should advocate killing was indeed a new side to his character. Monty's silence was read correctly by the blind man.

"Remember, mine eyes, that we are dealing with ruthless

men. Remember, too, that you have in your charge a child, a woman, and a blind man. You will find the child more useful than I can be. Austiline is of the most importance. If we are right in our suspicions that she is the centre of some intrigue, or if we are wrong and she actually wishes to marry Anchor, it makes no difference to the fact that she must be got away from here. I agree with you there. If anyone objects to that, they must be dealt with drastically. I myself will shoot to kill without compunction. My hearing, at least, is good."

"Good old gladiator!" murmured the surprised Monty. "Here comes Bluebeard himself, so I will leave you and go to finish my repair work. We were just talking about friend Cotton, Mr. Anchor. Martin says that no matter the provocation Cotton was not justified in handing a wallop to Ross, or whatever his name was. You try to convince him of the contrary. I have further work to do."

"I will do my best to put the matter in a reasonable light," Anchor drawled, taking Monty's vacated seat.

This time without the help and general supervision of the delightful Bubbles, the big man plied needles and waxed cotton to restore his leather gear within the confines of the tool-house. And he had not been there a quarter of an hour when Mabel Hogan stepped inside, her eyes, both eager and wistful.

"Are you still decided to take little Freddie with you?" she asked without preamble.

"I certainly am," replied the big man, smiling at her. "And you had better come as well."

Sighing, she said: "I would like to, but I daren't. No, I must remain."

Monty had been sitting with his work on his knees. He now put down his pack-bag and, rising, drew near to her. Then, hardly above a whisper, he said:

"It is going to be a dark night, Miss Hogan. My brother and I intend taking advantage of it. Could you have little Bubbles dressed and ready for me about midnight?"

"But why midnight? Miss Thorpe insists upon herself seeing you and Mr. Martin depart sometime to-morrow. I overheard Mr. Anchor telling Dr. Moore."

"Ah! Anchor must have changed his mind."

"All he will require from you is your word of honour not to betray us to the police. You wouldn't do that, would you?"

"In the circumstances, no," he said. "My brother, as well as Miss Thorpe, owes a great deal to him. I am going to owe you a great deal for Bubbles. Do you know Miss Thorpe very well?"

"We've had long talks."

"She tells us that she is going to marry Anchor. Do you think she is in love with him?"

Mabel saw the grey-blue eyes boring into hers. There was no evading them.

"I know that she is not," she whispered.

"Thank you, Miss Hogan."

"What do you intend doing?"

For a moment he regarded her steadily. Then:

"In spite of your being here, I believe that you are a good woman——"

"I am a murderess. I poisoned a man because he called me a street woman when I implored him to marry me to save my honour and give my child a name."

"You did right," he told her grimly. "It doesn't affect my belief in your general goodness. That's why I'm going to trust you. I am not leaving this place to-night, to-morrow, or at any time, without Miss Thorpe. Do you think you could get to her and tell her that—tell her to hold herself in readiness for instant departure? Probably about midnight to-night?"

He saw her face blanch, her hands rise to a suddenly heaving chest.

"Would you, if—if things went wrong, protect Freddie with your life? Would you see to him—first?"

"Naturally, he would take first place. I am beginning to wonder why I didn't marry years ago, and have a baby like Bubbles."

"Then I will tell Miss Thorpe what you say. But, if Mr. Anchor ever knows, he will give me over to Dr. Moore for his terrible experiments."

"Then you had better come with me. As for experiments, I have thought of a few to entertain Dr. Moore with, when circumstances permit."

She wavered. He saw her jaw harden. She shook her head.

"No, Mr. Sherwood. Even if I were given a free pardon for the crime I committed, I mustn't keep Freddie. Don't you see what it might lead to? In after years some one might tell him of me. In any case, nothing can undo the fact that

I am a murderess. My nearness to him would harm him. I am unclean. He would be contaminated."

"I think you are looking at it from the wrong angle," he told her. "But I appreciate your nobleness and capacity for sacrifice. Think it over, and let me know some time this evening."

"I shall not change my mind. I know—oh, I know!— that I can trust you with my baby. But I must go now. They are watching and will suspect."

"One more question. Why does Miss Thorpe say she is to marry Anchor when she does not love him?"

"He—Mr. Anchor—is a beast," she said with sudden fierceness. "She is to be his reward for allowing your brother and you to go without hindrance."

"Ah!" Monty saw the light at once; and, after looking at his changed face for a second, Mabel Hogan turned and vanished through the doorway.

Monty never could smoke while he worked; he never could think without smoking. Whilst he loaded his cracked pipe he was filled with self-pride at having judged Austiline's character correctly.

Up till then, he admitted to himself, he had looked upon Anchor and Moore with easy-going tolerance. He recognized that Austiline owed them a debt; in fact, she owed Anchor her life. His tolerance, therefore, was on that account. His mind flew back to the dreadful scene in Austiline's room, and the lines about his mouth deepened when he finally grasped the significance of her wonderful acting and understood the reason To save Martin she was prepared to sacrifice herself.

More than thankful was he to see daylight at last. He rejoiced for Martin's sake that the uncertainty was at an end—the uncertainty about Austiline, which after all had not been so very great. Now there was clear going! He knew now precisely what to do. Austiline, his brother and Bubbles must be got away that night. Moore must be put out of action, and for that he would have to ascertain the location of the doctor's room.

Later, when he had got his charges safely to Broken Hill, or even Melbourne, and under police protection in case of under-world activities, he would return alone and discuss, with Anchor, the millionaire's unspeakable conduct towards Austiline. The discussion, he promised himself, should be conducted according to the established Monty Sherwood rules, which usually left the subject a safer if not a better man to live with.

During the afternoon he took occasion to report to Martin his conversation with Mabel Hogan, and reiterated his intention of carrying out his plan to get away that night.

"If I had a mate who was a good bushman, I'd bale up this crowd at breakfast to-morrow and keep 'em fixed for several hours while he got you all well away," he said. "As things are, I have to superintend the get-away, and therefore we cannot afford to risk much opposition. If anything goes wrong and the crowd gets lively, then it's shoot first, shoot quick, and keep on shooting. Diplomacy, my lad, is our cue."

"If only I could see!" was Martin's lament.

"If you could, we'd take charge of the lot of 'em and march them off to gaol. Now I'm for a snore off. You had better indulge, too. There will be little sleep for either of us for a week or so."

Monty was awakened about five o'clock by the roar of a low-flying aeroplane engine, and, slipping to the veranda door, was in time to recognize the doctor's 'plane speeding southward. At the time he thought that Dr. Moore and "The Cat," whom he had seen in the rear seat, were out on a practice flight. The 'plane did not return till a little after eight, and it must have been to allow the fliers time to return from their aerodrome that the dinner-gong did not sound until eighty-thirty.

That night both Anchor and Dr. Moore were late. Monty was engaged in conversation with Mallowing when they came in, the host apologizing profusely, the doctor visibly elated, an unusual smile, suggestive of triumph, lighting his ruddy face. The smile "intrigued" the big man. It continued to do so even after Anchor exploded his bombshell.

Of this, however, the time-fuse was delayed until the close of the meal. Then Anchor said:

"When you put your camels in the horse-paddock upon your arrival, did you hobble them, Mr. Sherwood?"

"Mr. Mallowing assured me that once the paddock was reserved only for your bulls. He told me this when I asked him why the horse-paddock fence was five-foot-six high, with a barbed wire top. I was assured, too, that the fence all round was good. Accordingly, I did not hobble my camels. Why do you ask?" inquired the big man calmly, but secretly perturbed.

"Because your camels, with three of my own, have escaped the paddock. Your camels are leading mine straight to that natural water-hole where you were visited by Gilling."

Monty wanted badly to swear. Even while he saw his plans for that night destroyed he wondered why Anchor was so much annoyed by what would only mean a delay of perhaps a day or two, at most. With his usual philosophic calm he said:

"How did they get out?"

"The last sand-storm shifted a sand-hill on a part of the fence and buried it. The camels walked over the sand-hill. Dr. Moore, who has been out with 'The Cat' in search of them, discovered them some twenty-seven miles away, walking in the direction of the water-hole."

"The water-hole is sixty miles from here, is it not?"

"Yes, about sixty."

"Humph! As they are making for that surface-water they will camp there for a while. I know they did not relish the bore-water here. Too much soda for their taste. It's both unfortunate and annoying. You will have to give me permission to fetch them back. Dr. Moore perhaps would fly me to the water-hole."

"And when would you arrive back?"

"Sometime Sunday afternoon, if the doctor and I left early to-morrow morning. It will depend on how far the beasts have got when we overtake them."

That was what Dr. Moore had said, and what Anchor knew. It was impossible for the aviator to leave the Home before daybreak the next morning, impossible for him to land in the uncharted bush in the dark. And the police from Innaminka would pay their ominous visit on Sunday. Of that also Anchor was sure. He knew the daily stages the police would make.

The millionaire rose suddenly and strode to a chiffonier, from a cupboard of which he took a bottle of wine. His back was towards the diners. No one saw him take from his pocket a phial of colourless liquid, withdraw the cork with finger and thumb, place the tip of his little finger against the uncorked mouth, and then run his moistened finger round the inside of two of the four glasses he placed on a salver. The expression of annoyance was still on his face when he returned to the table.

"Fate has served us a scurvy trick, Mr. Sherwood," he said

with his usual silkiness. "I was looking forward to giving you good news, instead of which the news I gave was anything but good. Because of that I am going to open this Amontillado which was bottled the year of the Battle of Waterloo. Let me fill your glasses before I tell you what my good news was to have been."

"I often wish I had been at the Battle of Waterloo," drawled Monty, watching the golden tide rise in glass after glass. "In those days war must have been good sport, a stand-up affair between man and man. Somehow I always did like to feel a feller when I corpsed him."

"I agree with you that modern warfare lacks the personal touch," came Anchor's voice, accompanied by a dry chuckle. He himself offered the wine. Monty accepted the two glasses nearest him, placing one in Martin's hand. Moore took the third and Anchor the last glass. Evidently the wine was too precious for ordinary occasions. The others had burgundy within reach. Martin sipped his, and Monty also tasted once, twice.

"They certainly *could* make wine in those days," was Martin's tribute.

"The wine-grower's cunning is equalled by Father Time," the millionaire drawled. "I am glad you appreciate the result of their collaboration. Let it be a peace-offering for my being unable to comply with Miss Thorpe's wishes, which in a way affect you. This afternoon she informed me she would not leave her apartments for fear of meeting you. For some reason or other she has conceived a strange antipathy towards you both. When I pointed out to her that for our safety you would be obliged to remain with us indefinitely, she was both surprised and angry."

He was watching Monty, and wondering what the big man was smiling at. Continuing, he said softly:

"You know what women are, and how they twist a man round their dainty fingers. How could a prospective groom ignore his bride's pleading? And such a bride! I consented to allow you to depart from us after giving your words of honour to keep our secrets."

The blind man rose suddenly to his feet. His face was very pale. Monty waited for denunciation; but Martin, throwing up his arms, fell forward over the table with a crash of glass and china.

The other diners were very quiet, excepting Mabel Hogan,

who gasped audibly. The big man was surprised at what he thought to be Martin's faint. Never had he known his brother to faint. He was about to gather him up in his arms and take him out to the veranda when Anchor's quiet voice intervened:

"One moment, Mr. Sherwood."

The big man turned his head. He looked straight down the barrel of Anchor's automatic pistol.

Then he understood. Martin was drugged or poisoned. It was he who should have drunk the doctored wine. Slowly his grey-blue eyes extended, cold glittering light in their depths. Above the pistol-barrel he saw Anchor's eyes, the lids narrowed but unwinking, the eyes steady as those of a snake.

Monty realized that, until the automatic wavered or Anchor blinked, it would be simply suicidal to move his right hand a fraction of an inch towards his gun.

For seconds the two men remained thus, like marble effigies in a Grecian tableau. Then the electric lights appeared to wane, and for an instant Monty thought they would go out and give him his chance.

"Just one moment more, Mr. Sherwood," pleaded Anchor.

Dim and dimmer became the lights. They flickered. They flared into a brilliant yellow flame and went out. Monty dropped across the table beside Martin.

CHAPTER XXIX

DR. MOORE'S AMBITION

MONTY SHERWOOD was back in London on leave from the Army. He heard Big Ben strike eleven. He was in hospital somewhere, though he could not remember how he got there. The top of his head felt as if it were being pressed in by some mighty force.

For a while he dozed, then on opening his eyes he thought at first he was gazing at the black vault of heaven, the stars hidden by an unbroken canopy of cloud. His head ached atrociously and he again closed his eyes. Gradually the pressure at the top of his head relaxed, and when next he opened his eyes and wished to rub them he learned that he was bound hand and foot—very securely bound. Came then remembrance.

So the wine had been drugged, or that portion of it destined for Martin and himself. For the first time in his life he felt, to use the hackneyed but expressive term, "cheap." He considered that he had been tricked with the ease one tricks an innocent child. It was one of the very few occasions he allowed anger to disturb him, and this anger he vented on the binding cords without in any way loosening them.

He found himself lying on his back on an uncomfortably hard bench or table. A deeper darkness passed across the ceiling, and, turning his head, he made out the form of Dr. Moore seated at a large table writing beneath the solitary electric bulb that rendered the room less dark.

It was a very large room, and the shadows exaggerated its dimensions to the vastness of a cavern. The table at which Dr. Moore wrote was situated almost centrally—to Monty's left and a little to his rear. The operating-table on which Monty lay was set some six feet from the wall on his right. Beyond Moore's table was the door, whilst from the door to the left-hand corner fronting Monty and along the wall to a point directly opposite his feet ran a broad bench littered with scientific apparatus, the metal and glass of which glinted in the subdued light. He wondered where Martin was, being unable to catch sight of his blind brother who, similarly bound, lay on a second operating-table immediately behind him.

Dr. Moore laid down his pen and rose, pushing his chair back with his straightening legs in doing so, and after several adjustments studied a slide through a large microscope set at the end of his table. What he examined must have been of unusual interest, for he seized a notebook and wrote in it several times during his observations. When Monty spoke his throat felt lime-kiln dry.

"We appear to be a happy family, my dear old doctor murderer," he said.

"I am glad you think so," came Moore's affected voice.

"You know, dear Brutus, you remind me of the traditional student burning his last candle. Why this economy?"

Moore reseated himself, took up his pen and said:

"I will attend to you presently; please do not speak just now."

"It's a habit of mine," Monty confessed. "Only don't tell any one."

Moore went on writing at an accelerated pace. Said the big man mockingly:

"'And the villain seized her round the waist, and, lifting her high above his head, heaved her over the cliff.' Have you decided on a title yet, doctor?"

Without speaking, Moore again applied his eye to the microscope. Monty went on gaily:

"'Standing upon the very edge of the abyss, the villain watched her slowly drown. "Ah! ah!" he cried. "At last your millions are within my grasp . . . So—so!" he hissed as our brave hero dived from the cliff to the rescue.'"

To continue the study of Dubini's disease, or the rare bacillus which causes it, with Monty interrupting in that disgusting fashion, was a sheer impossibility, even to a man who prided himself on his powers of concentration. Dr. Moore viciously slammed down his pen, and, rising abruptly, stalked to the electric switches beside the door and flooded the room with light from an arc-lamp suspended over the operating tables. With a grin of amusement, the big man saw Moore produce two rolls of bandages and pick up a Spanish stiletto from the table on his way to Monty's side.

The expression on the doctor's face was one of speechless

rage. For a moment the big man thought he would plunge the dagger into his heart. Instead, Moore literally snarled:

"Open your mouth—quick! Or I'll prise it open with this hatpin."

Seeing that resistance would bring unnecessary pain, the big man obeyed, and half a minute later was effectually gagged. And when the doctor stood looking down at him with a faintly exultant smile, Monty closed one eye in an impudent wink.

"I admit that the situation contains no little humour—to me," Moore said in his affected drawl. "Perhaps the real humour of it will dawn on you later."

Again Dr. Moore smiled, and again Monty winked.

With an imprecation the doctor turned back to his table, leaving Monty to speculate uneasily as to what was coming. Long before this he had convinced himself of the impossibility of freeing himself from bonds that kept him as stiff as a board. There was no possibility of rescue, little hope of intervention, none whatever of mercy.

Lying there in the semi-darkness, for Moore had switched off the arc-lamp, he tried to puzzle out the reason for the drugged wine when Anchor had stated that they would be allowed to depart. Mabel Hogan's confession that she had overheard Anchor inform Moore of that decision was convincing evidence that Anchor had meant to fulfill his promise.

Had she repeated to him the entire discussion he would have understood precisely how and why the escape of his camels had affected Anchor's decision; but Mabel Hogan's first thought was for her child, and her last for herself and her protectors. She foresaw that if Monty learned of the impending police visit it was probable that he would either refuse to leave, or would return when the police had arrived.

He gave up the problem after a while, and fell to surveying the apartment. The temperature decided him that it was one of the underground rooms. From contemplating his surroundings his mind began to recall the hints he had picked up of Dr. Moore's experiments. Mabel Hogan had evinced great fear of them; and, after witnessing Moore's callousness at the death of Earle, Monty realized that the doctor was quite capable of the most diabolical vivisection of humanity. Was he lying on that operating-table for that dreadful purpose?

A clock on Moore's table chimed twelve. The silvery notes recalled the dream of Big Ben striking eleven. He wondered if it were noon or midnight. Moore went on industriously with his writing and microscopic observation, which entailed the handling of many slides. Some time later he heard a sigh and the voice of Martin:

"Where am I? Why am I tied down? Monty!"

The giant tried hard to thrust out the gag, but only succeeded in making a gurgling sound, alarming his brother still further.

"Monty! Are you there, Monty?" No reply coming, he called again: "Hullo! Is any one there?"

Moore put down a glass tube and came over to the blind man.

"I am here," he murmured dryly.

"Ah! Is that you, Moore? Will you please explain this peculiar treatment?"

"Now that you have recovered from dining unwisely and too well, I will define the situation with all Mr. Anchor's candour," assented the doctor, drawing up a chair so that he faced both the bound men.

"I would have you both understand," he went on, "that I have been in favour of allowing Miss Thorpe to return south ever since we learned of Travers's confession. Her word to divulge nothing about us would have sufficed to secure our safety. However, Mr. Anchor took a fancy to Miss Thorpe and held other views. He was right when he said he had agreed to allow you to go to-morrow, or rather to-day, for midnight has passed; but, being now unable, as your camels have strayed, he was compelled to alter his decision because on Sunday, to-morrow, we are to have a police visit.

"You will appreciate that from our point of view it was not advisable to have you running about to-morrow, so that Mr. Anchor showed a glimmer of his former acumen and consented to my taking charge of you."

"Well, you are not going to keep us tied down till the police have left, are you?" inquired Martin.

"The police will in no way affect your future. Your future is now my sole concern. Mr. Anchor tells me he has described to you an experiment I once performed on a cat-killing gorilla. In spite of his scepticism, that experiment was entirely successful.

"It proved my theory that a portion of the skull with a slight inward curvature is responsible for a human being committing murder; because, when that part of the brute's skull was raised, it no longer killed cats, but regarded them with friendly tolerance. So that we arrive at the conclusion that murder is not a reasoned and deliberate crime, but an impulsive or reflex action due to a congenital defect of the human brain.

"This is but one of several such subjects which I study as opportunity serves. In this case my aim is to discover by simple examination those persons suffering from the defect causing the murder impulse, and by an equally simple operation to remove it, thus freeing them from the very possibility of committing a murder on impulse.

"I admit the experiment failed in the case of a quarter-caste Malay, who, having offended the morality of this place, was put into my hands. The operation I performed on him produced an effect the very opposite of what was intended; but he had escaped my custody prematurely, and the failure probably was due to some accidental cause."

"Whilst you slept, I took occasion to examine your heads, concluding that you both are free from that inward curvature of the skull which under the force of great excitation produces the homicidal madness. You are free from the secondary personality immortalized under the name of Mr. Hyde."

"We are to be congratulated," Martin murmured sarcastically.

"You are, believe me," replied Moore. "It is my intention, however, to implant that secondary personality within you. It is my intention, by operation, to form the inward curvature in that particular part of your skulls; to observe, I hope, the homicidal tendency so pronounced that there can be no mistake; and, all being well, to operate again to remove the defect and restore you to your natural mental equilibrium.

"Should I succeed, you will have the pleasure of knowing that, through your experience, which will be broadcast throughout the world, murder will become almost extinct. On the other hand, should I fail, I am reluctantly obliged to conclude that you will at best be homicidal maniacs. I will, however, promise faithfully to kill you both in the event of failure."

"I must say, Moore, that though your conceptions are quite brilliant in a way, you are an inhuman beast," Martin said quietly. "Even though your experiments are successful, how will you benefit by them?"

The doctor replied without hesitation.

"If I can prove to the medical world that murder is not a

crime, but the result of an uncontrollable impulse due to physical defect, the murder laws will be amended. When the law is satisfied to have a murderer placed in the care of competent surgeons, who will perform the operation that will eradicate the impulse to kill, then I can declare myself, claim my reward, and suffer myself to be operated upon. After that, I can return to the world in which I was making name and fortune."

"I think I understand you, Moore. But the world is not converted by one or two experiments. To my mind, too, your theory is based on illusion, and your ambition is a dream that will never come true."

"It is a dream that can be made to come true," Moore asserted confidently. He rose to his feet and, with his hands in his trousers pockets, regarded them alternately.

"The nature of my studies prevents me from indulging the human failing of feelings or nerves," he drawled. "At the other end of the room there is a hutch containing rabbits. They are for purposes of experimentation with the Dubini germ. You are here for experimentation also, and, therefore, so far as I am concerned, of equal importance, no more, with the rabbits.

"I am studying Dubini's germ just now, and have reached a stage which demands all my attention. If you talk, I shall gag you as I have gagged your brother. I am taking several hours' sleep by and by. About nine o'clock I shall be ready for you. Be advised by me and try to sleep. Calmness in the subject goes far to assure success."

Moore went back to his table. Martin shivered. He thought it strange that Moore should be so dispassionate, so utterly callous. He spoke with conviction about his mad theory, but not with so much conviction regarding success. Suddenly a horrible fear of going mad fastened on him, and he groaned.

As for Monty, he recognized that they were in a very evil plight. Little hope remained to him of escape, but his natural buoyancy refused to admit defeat or succumb to despair. Hours upon hours seemed to pass. He thought of Bubbles, now condemned to grow up among these frankly-confessed takers of human life. He thought of Mary Webster, cool of brain and warm of heart, a woman compact of goodness, sympathy, and feminine charm—a wonderful woman who then must be anxiously awaiting news of him.

The doctor continued his work on the Dubini germ, his

scientific ardour wiping from his mind all thought of the two hapless men he had condemned to a horrible vivisection. So absorbed was he that it was quite evident that he had not libelled himself in claiming to have no interest in his human victims beyond their use as subjects for experiment—no more interest in them than if they had been rabbits.

He worked with his back to the door, at which Monty suddenly stared. The big man at first doubted his sight, considering that what he saw must be an optical illusion. For the door was slowly, very slowly, being pushed open. The light hung so low over the table that Moore's head and shoulders shadowed the moving door. But the black ribbon between the door edge and its frame widened imperceptibly.

The small clock chimed once, but Monty had no ears for the sound. He saw eventually the pale blotch of some one's face set in that ribbon of black made by the dark room or passage beyond. The door opened a third of its extent, soundlessly, as though the blotch belonged to a spirit from beyond the vale. Now it was half open, and a figure glided into the room. Then slowly and without sound the door was closed behind it. The figure was that of a woman, a lighter shadow than the oaken door.

For almost a minute she stood motionless, the black pupils of her wide eyes scrutinizing everything in the room. Then slowly, foot by foot, she edged along the wall to that end of the bench nearest her. And, when her face drew out of the shadow, Monty recognized Mabel Hogan.

The thick carpet, stretching from wall to wall, made possible her movements to be unattended by the slightest sound. So carefully did she steal to the bench that not even a rustle of her dress betrayed her. Real, almost paralysing, terror glared from her staring eyes and drew back the corners of her mouth. One hand was pressed tightly against her heart as though to still the wild beating which must have pounded in her ears like the crashing of some gigantic hammer.

To Monty a thousand years rolled by before she reached the end of the bench. And there she stopped and shrank back against the paraphernalia, for suddenly Dr. Moore rose from the table. It was only to delve into a side drawer for a sheaf of papers, however, and after he had resumed his seat for some three minutes Mabel Hogan moved again along the bench to the corner where it made a right angle.

Right at the corner she made a noise, her hand bringing into slight collision a Bunsen burner and a metal bowl. Moore suddenly turned his head in that direction. Mabel Hogan stiffened to a woman of stone, her hands pressed to her mouth to smother a threatened scream. A cold sweat broke out on the bushman.

But, either the electric light by which he was working partially blinded the doctor when he gazed into the semi-darkness, or else he was acting the part of a cat; for he again went on with his interrupted study. Thenceforth the big man alternately watched both Moore and the woman. He saw her leave the corner and follow the bench to its farthest end, which was directly beyond his feet. When he again looked for her she had disappeared.

From his elevated position he could not see Mabel Hogan creeping towards him on her hands and knees, and he was next made aware of her presence by the feel of her fingers against the back of his right hand. Thrilling triumph at the prospect of freedom surged through him at her touch. Unbounded admiration of her bravery in such terrible circumstances filled him with amaze. And then came breath-catching dismay when Dr. Moore got up suddenly from the table and walked over to him. Monty could have groaned.

Was not the alluring prospect of freedom one of the exquisite tortures of the Inquisition? The big man felt sure now that Moore was acting the cat with Mabel Hogan as mouse, playing the part of the Inquisitor who greets the wretched captive on the threshold of freedom with a sinister smile and a polite invitation to prolong his visit. Moore came close and gazed down at him through his spectacles.

When Monty glared up in return he saw that not for a fraction of a second did the eyes leave his face and look beyond to where Mabel Hogan must be crouching. By no possible chance could he miss seeing the woman, thought Monty, not knowing that she then was hidden beneath the operating-table. The torturer coolly put a forefinger on the pulse at the base of Monty's neck, timing it by his illuminated watch, his long head nodding slowly with satisfaction.

He did not speak. He acted as though Monty was a rabbit. Then he passed beyond the bound man's head, out of his range of vision, to where he guessed Martin lay. Even then he was not sure that Moore was ignorant of the woman's presence. He could have yelled with joy, with stupendous relief, when the doctor returned to the table, and, seating himself in the chair, resumed his work.

Frantically he waved his right hand from the wrist, where it was secured to his legs. The movement caused him intense pain, but he continued in spite of it, with the object of attracting or reassuring the woman. Momentarily expecting to be freed, he became uneasy at first, then alarmed, when Mabel Hogan remained invisible and inactive.

Mabel Hogan was ill. The intense excitement overtaxed her, caught her breathing, and she was stifling her gasps with a handkerchief. Minutes fled, and Monty's heart sank with disappointment and despair. He thought she had fainted, and waited with the small hope that Moore would finish his work for that night and leave the room before the woman recovered. For he was positive that when she did come to she would betray her presence by a moan or a deep-drawn sigh.

And then suddenly the pressure of the cords about his ankles was relieved. His right arm suddenly fell down over the side of the table. It was benumbed, as dead as wood. He knew it hung down towards the floor by the slight feeling of heaviness at his shoulder. He saw white arms hovering over him. The gag was plucked out of his mouth. His other arm was free. . . .

He was a free man, but as helpless as a log. The blood was loth to circulate again through his cramped limbs. A sensation of warmth crept up his arm, and he found that the woman was rubbing it. Pain, agonizing, torturing, began to move down his legs and the other arm, such pain that the sweat broke into beads on his forehead.

The clock ticked innumerable seconds whilst he fought an overwhelming desire to move his legs and arms. He fought it because of the need to wait until the numbness should disappear and he again had command of his limbs, so that they would respond with wonted alacrity to his will.

Presently he raised his head. He saw Mabel Hogan crouched on her heels, looking at him with wide, staring, black eyes. After a pause he gently drew up one leg, then the other, and then raised his arms alternately, the while watching the absorbed doctor. Gently he swung himself to a sitting posture. Slowly he slewed sideways so that his feet touched the carpet and he sat on the edge of the table.

Not for nothing was Monty Sherwood acclaimed the

greatest kangaroo hunter in Central Australia. More wonderful even than his soundless movements had been the actions of the woman encumbered by her dress. Monty followed her course in reverse, knowing that by following the bench he would take the widest detour from the central table.

Soundlessly as a stalking tiger-cat he reached the bench angle, his gaze centred always on Moore, ready to spring forward should he inadvertently make a sound or arouse the doctor's suspicions. He was without a revolver. If he had to spring, he must do so before Moore could bring out a weapon and fire.

Towards the door he moved step by step. He reached that end of the bench. Six seconds later he was at the door and directly behind the scientist.

Now he smiled. It was a smile both of childish delight and terrible grimness. No matter what happened now, Moore was at his mercy. He decreased the distance between them. He drew to within a foot of the doctor's bent back whilst he wrote. He could have flung out his great hands and gripped his absorbed, unsuspecting enemy. He saw over a sloping shoulder the tiny clock, a small, gold-mounted gem of unique beauty and value.

The clock chimed twice. Moore sighed as though well satisfied with his work for that night. He laid down the pen and leaned back in his swivel chair.

Monty brought his lips close to Dr. Moore's right ear and blew into it.

CHAPTER XXX

A PYRAMID OF MATCHES

THE effect of that blast of air in the doctor's ear was not precisely what the giant expected: which was that Moore would spring to his feet, face about, and begin fighting for his life.

Actually Moore froze into a marble block. The shock of the unknown presence behind him paralysed his nerves, making him as helpless as was the benumbed Monty a little time before. Almost his heart stopped beating for ten or fifteen deathlike seconds. Then the blood rushed to his head with revivifying warmth. Slowly he rose to his feet, his hands pressed on the table for support. Slowly he turned whilst rising, Monty drawing to the left: so that, when finally the two men faced each other, the light cast neither into shadow.

The colour drained away from the doctor's face. He hardly breathed. With one hand still gripping the table-edge, he glared at the broad, grim countenance of the man he had believed to be securely bound to an operating-table. Fear, numbing and terrible—fear that pricked at the roots of his thin, grey-black hair—fear which played about the corners of his mouth and violently oscillated the nerves beneath his cheekbones, gave Monty a moment of compunction. Yet, while the thin lips drew up disclosing the clenched teeth, the lid of Monty's right eye slowly fell in a ponderous but terribly significant wink.

The eyes of each bored deeply into those of the other. The strain became terrific. As a snake's head drawing back an inch at a time to strike, so the doctor's right hand moved to his jacket pocket. And when it touched the cloth the big man's left fist struck him full on the throat.

The blow sounded as ordinary as a wet bag hit by a stick. In effect it was not nearly so spectacular as it would have been had the huge iron-hard fist smashed against the point of the long, lean jaw. It was not delivered with any spectacular purpose.

It lifted the doctor off his feet and sent him sprawling on his back over the table, there to lie with hands clutching at nothing, while his lungs fought for air. Monty, seeking and finding the automatic pistol, was nauseated at sight of the ruffian's blackened face. Gradually Moore's motions ceased and he lay inert, grotesque as a huge spider, his head lolling over the further edge of the table, his feet dangling from the near edge.

Movement behind him caused the big man to turn in a flash. It was Mabel Hogan, both hands pressed fiercely to her breast, her face hueless as snow, her lips purple blue, her eyes wide, extraordinarily large and bright. Terror lay in their dark depths.

"I—I'm so ill . . . my heart . . . oh, my heart!"

She swayed forward and Monty caught her in his arms. For a moment her head rested on his shoulder and her loosened black hair swept his face. When she lifted her head her eyes searched his with strained appeal, and from her blue lips issued a whisper:

"My baby! I am dying! Love my baby for me! You promised!"

Monty smiled reassuringly, his wonderful magnetic smile. He saw her answering look of confidence. Tender joy settled upon her drawn features. He felt her shudder, saw the light in her eyes fade, go out. And so it was that a woman wronged by man, execrated by the society which had cynically declined to protect her, sacrificed her life that her baby might live uncontaminated by her crime. The fearful strain of the last half-hour had been too much for her weakened heart.

The big man could not see very clearly while laying her gently on the operating-table to which he had been bound. All his fine, generous nature went out to the outcast who had paid, he sincerely hoped, the final price. He closed the eyes and covered the now beautifully serene face with a handkerchief.

It was then he acted quickly. Darting to the door, he opened it and stared into the darkness beyond. The electric lamp behind him revealed another room. Closing the door, he locked it. He pressed down the switches, and at once the room was ablaze with light. In two leaps he was beside Martin, cutting the binding cords.

Martin was almost insane with the excitement caused by strange noises and the hiss of Mabel Hogan's last words. Monty, expecting countless questions, commanded him to move his arm, while he himself set to work to put into circulation the blood-of Martin's legs. The blind man groaned, and with swift effortless energy Monty lifted him down to the floor, then darted to the table bearing the body of Dr. Moore.

The bushman ripped off the doctor's collar and tore open the fine silken shirt. Feeling for his heart, he discovered it to be beating still, but feebly. Beneath Moore he slid his great arms, and, carrying him to the operating-table vacated by his brother, stretched him thereon, bound him with the remains of the cut cords and several straps, and gagged him with his own gag.

Once again he went to the door, listened for a full minute, opened it wide and stepped into the next room. The increased light in the laboratory dimly revealed a bedroom and a second door beyond. Reaching that, he again listened. He saw in a rack an electric torch, which he pocketed. Then soundlessly he opened the door a few inches and saw the unlit cork-paved underground passage beyond. Drawing back, he locked the door with the key that was in the lock.

"How's things?" he drawled, when he returned quietly to Martin, now sitting up.

"My arms are better, but my legs hurt like the devil," the blind man gasped. "But tell me—for heaven's sake, tell me— what has happened."

Monty cut chips of tobacco for a smoke, whilst he told of Mabel Hogan's heroic action and sacrifice.

"I am convinced, old son, that but for her it would have been U. P. with us," he said. "We owe our lives to that girl. I could have sworn that Moore was wise to her intentions, and I had a sickening time for half an hour or so. She was superb. I'm no end knocked that she's thrown a seven. I'd have given her a real good start, and to hell with the law, which cheerfully hangs women, but hasn't the equity to protect 'em. Anyway, Bubbles is my adopted son. I'm going to be terrible proud of Bubbles."

"Give me a hand, Monty; I'm feeling better." Then, when he was on his feet searching for his cigarette-case, Martin added: "We're still in a dickens of a hole, aren't we?"

"M'yes. But it's the Better 'Ole," growled the big man.

"We have all the advantages but numbers. I've got your gun, which Moore pinched. The element of surprise is with us, and I have a kind of knack of fancy shooting.

"It seems to me, my bonny old digger, that we're about to enter the shoot first, shoot straight, and keep on shooting stage. We're hemmed in by the most original crowd of ruffians off the picture stage. None of 'em will show us any powerful affection, and I'm thinking that love and kindness will be wasted on 'em. It's shoot first and shoot good. Now——"

When Monty's voice trailed into silence, the blind man thought that the next act was to be played then.

"I got a brain-wave!" exclaimed Monty. "I'll not expose it to criticism just yet. You stay just where you are; you'll be quite all right. Now, don't argue—Spink's sausages are the best. I'll not be gone two minutes."

The problem of Martin's immediate disposal was solved. That had been a very tough problem, where to place Martin in safety whilst he, Monty, went into battle. Leaving the laboratory, he crossed Moore's bedroom, and, unlocking the corridor door, listened for a while before stepping out, closing and locking the door after him. His swiftly moving light assured him that the passage was empty; it showed him, too, Austiline's door at the farther end. With no more noise than a feather he reached it, and, turning the handle, found the door to be unlocked.

Passing within, he closed that door and locked it. The brilliant circle of light from the torch moved steadily about that luxurious apartment, resting finally on a second door which Monty guessed led into Austiline's bedroom. On this door he tapped gently.

No answer came. He changed the tapping to soft, insistent knocking, continued till he heard her voice demanding to know who knocked.

"Monty Sherwood," he whispered through the keyhole.

Rustling sounds indicated movement. When she spoke again it also was through the keyhole.

"Who is it?" still suspicious that it was not the big man. Recognizing his voice when he repeated his name, she opened the door about an inch, allowing the light from her room to fall on the dishevelled head of the visitor. With a whimsical look in his grey-blue eyes Monty drawled:

"I thought you would like to know that Martin and me are

having stirring times. Anyway, I want your help rather bad. Don't be nervous—I won't bite."

A tremulous smile played about her naturally sweet mouth when, opening the door wider, she came out fearlessly to Monty, and, pressing down a switch, lighted their end of the room. A pale blue wrapper covered her night attire, her naked feet were thrust into velvet slippers, and her glorious hair fell over her shoulders, twin ropes of glinting auburn. Far more was she the eternal woman than when last he had seen her.

"At the present moment," he explained, "Martin and me are like a couple of dog-chased iguanas—well up a tall tree. Friend Moore and your prospective husband are the dogs. I've bitten Moore so hard that he's pretty helpless, and I'm looking for sanctuary for Martin while I go biting the rest of 'em. This morning I got Mabel to tell me you didn't love Bluebeard and that you sent us away under compulsion. At the time I didn't think you admired Anchor good enough to erect a statue to him."

"I hate him," she said fiercely. "Mabel told me to be ready to escape with you to-night. Then she came again to say that your camels had wandered away. But tell me what has happened."

In a few words he detailed the events leading up to his knocking on her door. He saw the flame of indignation light up her face. When she spoke her voice trembled with passion.

"The traitorous hounds!" she said. "Mr. Anchor made a bargain with me, a bargain which I would have kept."

"I know," he responded grimly. "I'm going to remember that bargain when I get my gun-sights on him. Now, listen! I can't carry on till I've found a place of security for Martin. You see, his blindness makes him so helpless. I thought, if you didn't mind, I'd bring him here."

"Mind!" she echoed with shining eyes. "Of course I don't mind! I'll look after him while—while—oh Monty! Be careful! If anything happens to you we would be lost. I—I had given up all hope. It would be awful if anything happened to you now."

Patting her gently on the arm, he smiled at her, and his smile renewed her courage and utter belief in his indestructibility. He looked what he was, a superman, huge in size, tremendous in mental and physical force, his limbs as flexible as a cat's, his vision keen as an eagle-hawk's. Seeing the automatic he still held in his hand, she shuddered faintly, saying:

"Go now and bring him."

When he returned with Martin he found her where he had left her, the electric radiance falling on as fair a vision of womanhood as ever man beheld. With shining eyes and parted lips she came to meet them, her bare arms held out to the lesser of the brothers, whose face was suffused by an indescribable light of joy.

"Austiline!" he breathed. "Austiline, where are you?"

"Here!" she whispered. "Oh, my dear! my dear!" she sighed, her arms slipping round his neck and drawing him closely to her.

For a moment the giant looked down on them, smiling happily, more with the eyes than the face. A soft, joyous laugh broke from him, and, turning abruptly, he walked to the door and passed out on as perilous an adventure as ever had appealed to a brave man.

His most precious need was shells fitting the automatic, and two boxes of fifty apiece he knew were in a pack-bag then among his gear. In all probability, he thought, there would be quite a lot of cartridges fired before breakfast.

The torch guided him along the passage to the steps. Here he removed his canvas shoes to relieve his mind from the strain of remembering to move silently. At the panel door he paused in thought, before sliding to the right the simple opening catch.

"It is good soldiering to split the enemy in two," he murmured, and then strained to listen.

From beyond the door came a dull, muffled roar.

Somehow that sound reminded him of the borrowed blow-lamp. He thought of burglars attacking a safe. When he slid back the catch and drew the door open, he understood.

It was raining. A steady, torrential downpour, indicating, without doubt, that the flaring, burning drought was broken. He thought of the Minters, and smiled. The rain roared on the iron roof above, and gurgled and rilled over the ground beyond the veranda. He was thankful now that the camels had strayed, thankful he had not essayed their escape that night, for camels would be unable to proceed far over ground now slippery and deep in bog.

Other than the sound of the rain on the roof there was tomb-like silence; but the roar on the roof, although effectually blanketing any chance sound he might make, would as effectually mask any movement caused by a prowling enemy. With his torch extinguished, he slipped like a crow's shadow into the hall.

The patch of lighter darkness showed him the position of the glass door leading to the veranda. He found it unlocked and was not surprised, for few doors are locked in Central Australia. A veranda board creaked when he crossed it, but the rain muffled the sound. It hissed down through motionless air in streams as from a stupendous watering cart. When he reached his store-hut he was drenched to the skin.

A few seconds later he emerged with his pockets weighted with shells, and slipped into the tool-house, where after a little hunting he found a box of four-inch screws, of which he took two. Another hunt brought forth a gimlet and a screwdriver.

Crossing the compound to the hall door, Monty felt a mighty impulse to sing. Joy of living, joy of action, bubbled up and sought escape through his lips: a happiness so wonderful that, had it not been for Austiline and his blind brother's dependence upon him, he doubtless would have aroused the enemy by a yell to come out and fight.

As it was, he regained the hall without sound, without sound crossed to the panel-door, and noiselessly with gimlet and driver screwed it to floor and frame. The screwdriver he pocketed, and made then a trip to his bedroom, where he borrowed four broad ribbon curtain sashes and a set of lace dressing-table mats.

The big man's plan was simple to understand, but less so to carry out. At that time he knew what rooms were occupied by Mallowing and "The Cat," also the position of Mabel Hogan's room, where he felt sure Bubbles was. His plan was silently to overpower Mallowing and from him learn the whereabouts of the other inmates, then to secure Lane and "The Cat." He anticipated little trouble from Cotton, and none from Madeline Fox. Johnston, an unknown quantity, and Anchor, doubtless would provide excitement.

Thirty seconds were devoted to noiselessly turning the handle of Mallowing's door. When the little man awoke, it was to be dazzled by the glare of an electric torch in his eyes, and, revealed by it, the ominous muzzle of an automatic pistol within two inches of his forehead. A soft voice hissed:

"Silence!"

Mallowing was silent. Not a sound did he utter, whilst a huge, vague, but substantial shadow bound his ankles together and his hands to the bed-rail above his head. When next the nightmare spoke, he recognized Monty's voice, and felt better.

"I like you, Mallowing," the big man whispered. "And, because I like you, I'd simply hate to pump lead into your body. You, my dear old freed galley-slave, of course know that Anchor has declared war on me. Like the Irishman, I'm agin the government, and it follows naturally that I'm agin Anchor's government. You're for his government; which is where we begin to argue. Don't yell, now, or you will compel me—much against my wishes—to bash you. Where does Anchor sleep?"

"I am afraid I can't tell you," Mallowing said, for the first time in his post-murder years without his jovial, care-free expression.

"Or won't. Which?"

"Won't."

Sadly Monty shook his head, and, opening his metal box of wax matches, built a pyramid with them on the bridge of the little man's nose.

"When I fire these matches, loveliest, you'll see comets by the million before the fall of eternal darkness. My brother doesn't recommend eternal darkness, you know."

"You'd torture me!"

"With tears in my eyes, I would," Monty assured him, but with an absence of tears in his voice. "I am at one with our dear enemies in the late war, in that I believe the side which is deficient in man and brain power may kick hard below the belt on any and every occasion."

Monty struck a match. "Where did you say Anchor sleeps?" he asked blandly.

"Down in the basement," Mallowing whispered with a groan.

"What room?" came the remorseless voice.

"Next to Dr. Moore's rooms, where you were taken."

"Who else is below, bar Miss Thorpe and them?"

"Mrs. Jonas."

"Where does she sleep?"

"Opposite Mr. Anchor."

"What's in the other rooms?"

"Some are empty, some contain stores and art treasures."

" 'The Cat' sleeps next door, doesn't he?"

"Yes."

"Where's Lane?"

"In the room on the left."

"We are getting on. What about Cotton?"

"He occupies the bedroom opposite your own," replied the little man, now more freely.

"And the sweet-tempered Johnston?"

"In a room off the kitchen."

"Humph! There's the girl Fox. Where's she?"

"Opposite this room."

"Which reminds me I haven't heard the hounds. Where are they?"

"They'll be loose outside the compound. They rarely bark when they're loose."

"Well, I think we have 'em all catalogued now. Where is your cannon?"

Mallowing blinked when a slight tremor sent the match pyramid tumbling into his eyes. The big man carefully rebuilt it.

"Your gun—where is it?" came the insistent voice.

"In the left drawer of the chest."

"Thank you!" Monty returned politely. "As I have said, Mallowing, my lad, I like you. I would spare you a lot of discomfort if it wasn't for our private war. As we used to say in France, 'permitty-mwar, monsoor,'" whereupon Monty expertly gagged his second prisoner.

CHAPTER XXXI

MONTY'S "PRIVATE BATTLE"

ONCE more in the corridor with Mallowing's door shut, Monty listened intently, but heard nothing other than the roar of the rain on the roof. He had decided that his services should be rendered next to "The Cat"; but, finding "The Cat's" door locked, stole back to the room occupied by Lane. Lane's door was not locked.

Despite his utmost care in turning the door handle, it made an uncomfortably loud click. For nearly a minute he stood motionless, then gently pushed the door inward. From somewhere near the window Lane snored loudly. Now with the door behind him, Monty gently closed it, slowly releasing the inside handle. It, too, clicked with what seemed a great noise.

For another minute he listened to the monotonous snoring, and then, deciding that the noise made so far had aroused nobody, he turned on his torch, when a pencil of light stabbed the inky blackness and revealed a circle of ordinary carpet at his feet. The revealing circle slid across the floor, paused at the washstand, moved away at an angle, and finally rested on the foot of a single bed showing Lane's naked feet and pyjama-clad legs.

To the fat man's brutish nature, or perhaps more likely to his gluttonous habit of consuming vast quantities of food, the soundness of his sleep was due. His snores never varied while Monty crossed the room to stand by his bed. They came with the unbroken regularity of a clock during the operation of lashing the shapeless ankles together with one of the curtain sashes, and the wrists with a second. A third sash lashed the wrists to the right thigh.

To carry out this operation the big man had propped the torch against a spare pillow so that its light was reflected from the papered wall. The automatic he held between his teeth. But a final phase of Lane's complete subjugation remained, that of gagging him; and to stop the fat man's oral protests would mean speedy and ruthless action.

The fourth sash he laid in a convenient position and began rolling a lace mat into a ball for the gag, when the door-handle clicked precisely as it had done when he himself had turned it twice. At once his light was out.

There was no time now to gag Lane; no need, in fact, to prevent his shouts, for one of the other sleepers on the ground floor was outside the door. In the Stygian darkness it was impossible to distinguish the door, to see it slowly open. A red pencil of flame darted venomously from it, then came a thunderous report. Monty sensed the passage of a bullet so close to his head that the hair of his crown was raised by its passing. Unaware that the door was open, he was hardly prepared to shoot at the red pencil in turn. He dropped on all four instead.

Pandemonium broke loose from the bed, a vast bellow of rage proceeding from Lane, who now struggled fiercely to free himself from his light but strong and well-knotted bonds.

When the mountain in labour paused suddenly for breath, the succeeding silence was accentuated, not diminished, by the ever-present sound of falling water. Monty waited. When Lane resumed his bellowing, the big man crept doorwards like a huge, grotesque cat.

When he butted into a chair, there came instantly a second darting pencil of flame, which gave fleeting glimpse of the door wide open and a short, crouching figure of a man within its oblong frame. The bullet crashed into the basin on the washstand and certainly would have found Monty had he been standing.

Lane's description of the shooter, his ancestors, and his future offspring, if lacking literary finish was decidedly picturesque. It brought a grin of amusement to Monty's face, and, under cover of the hullabaloo, he pushed aside the fallen chair and moved yet closer to the door.

Lane's objurgations apparently made the enemy more cautious, for he did not again fire when Monty, coming across a boot, hurled it into the opposite corner, making there a deceptive thud.

What puzzled the bushman was why the enemy did not switch on a light, how it was he suspected anyone to be in the room but Lane, why he did not call to Lane demanding the reason for so much noise and so little movement.

Inch by inch he slid to the door, the automatic in one hand raised before him, his finger barely touching the trigger. Presently he found the edge of the open door, and there lay on his chest listening. A door somewhere else was thrown open with a crash against the wall, and Monty realized that enemy reinforcements were on the march. Again he moved forward, and again paused when he was in the passage.

Every sense was on the stretch. Somewhere in the impenetrable blackness, within a few feet of him, was a human being ready and lusting to kill. A second door, this time plainly in the hall, was flung open. Heavy thudding footsteps crossed to the passage, paused, shuffled, stopped. Then suddenly the passage was abaze with light.

The first object thus revealed to Monty was "The Cat" crouched against the opposite end of the passage, his lined face not more than twenty inches from Monty's pistol pointing straight at him. "The Cat's" revolver was held against his knees, but before his brain had time to command his hand holding the weapon he was a dead man.

Footsteps thudded along the corridor. Monty was on his knees sitting back on his heels. He saw a raw-boned, white-faced, lobster-eyed, black-moustached man rushing towards him. Even while he raised his pistol a tomahawk whizzed through the air, skimmed along his rising arm, and struck him full on the chest with a blow that knocked all the breath out of his body.

Luckily the implement, used by bush cooks to cut down carcasses, hit him flatwise. As it was, the impact paralyzed his chest muscles. Deprived of breath though he was, he fired. The bullet hit Johnston, for it was the *chef,* but merely grazed his neck. The man leapt to clear "The Cat's" body; and, even during the half-second allowed him for recovery, even whilst Johnston hovered at the apex of his leap, Monty fired again twice, and it was not a living man that crashed down upon him with the weight of twelve stone, hurling him sideways, his legs pinioned beneath the *chef's* body.

Agonizing pain tore through the big man's chest, and for half a long minute he fought to regain his breath. With a final mighty effort he filled his bursting lungs with air; when, even though his great chest felt like a mass of splintered bone, he could not resist a croaking laugh. Just then he felt supremely happy; for he, who loved fighting, was fighting the battle of his life in a good cause.

The excitement of the grim conflict affected his bruised and bloody chest as a local anæsthetic. No longer was he conscious of pain: he was like a pugilist consumed with fury and oblivious of the blows battering him into defeat. When he dragged his legs from under Johnston, he was obliged to claw his way up the wall to regain his footing.

Uppermost in his mind then was the coming encounter with the next on his list, Cotton; and he was not a little surprised when he saw no sign of the new guest: but he did see, between the slightly open door opposite and the jamb, the blanched face and wide china-blue eyes of Madeline Fox, glaring at him with remorseless, insensate hatred.

His vision of her was a fleeting one. Her door was slammed shut, and he heard her running across her room and the veranda door flung open. Then vertigo seized him, and, slipping sideways, he almost fell, would have fallen had he not clutched at Lane's doorpost. The light was flickering in an alarming manner. He felt sick.

Came a single crack of thunder from within Lane's room, and a stabbing, red-hot pain across Monty's left side. To the astonishing fact that the fat man was free and firing at him, as well as to the shock of the bullet itself, the big man reacted as possibly no other man would have done. He laughed again, a richer, louder laugh. The light suddenly steadied, the nausea vanished. A step took him along the wall, out of Lane's vision.

Followed then another period of comparative silence. Monty wondered how Mallowing would act if the fat man released him. He wondered again where Cotton was, and if the new guest was the only coward of them all. The fact that homicidal mania is not allied to cowardice occupied his mind for a while, and the act of slipping out the cartridge clip, refilling it with shells from his pocket, and replacing it in the butt of his pistol, was absolutely automatic.

He thought he heard Madeline Fox's shrill scream from somewhere outside the house, and remembrance of her brought back the danger from Lane. Exhaustion was creeping on him. His mind now was not so clear. He did not see his shadow cast by the electric light across the threshold of Lane's door. But he did see a long-barrelled Colt revolver slide round the door-post, followed by a fat, red, hairy hand which held it. With a wry smile he sent a bullet through the wrist.

A yell of anguish followed. The sudden jerk backward of the

smashed hand sent the revolver thudding on the carpet inside the room; which was unfortunate, for had it dropped at the doorway Monty might well have secured it. Lane screamed oaths and threats at him from the dark interior of his room, and, when he paused for breath or fresh inspiration, the big man called to him:

"Better come out, Lane, and get corpsed. It's your turn. Come on, now—I'm getting dry. I promise you it won't hurt, and I pass my word of honour to close your little eyes and cross your lily hands over your gentle breast. Come on, please, Lane. You'll look a lovely corpse—just lovely!"

The fat man declined to enter into discussion regarding his probable appearance as a corpse, nor did he jump at the opportunity to become one. Monty heard him bathing his wrist in the water-ewer, and moaning with the pain. Since the man wouldn't come out, he decided to go into the darkened room after him, trusting to Lane's inability to shoot straight with his left hand.

But first he must go to the hall end of the passage and switch off the light. To attempt to enter a darkened room from an illuminated corridor would be suicidal.

On moving his left foot the sock felt sticky against the sole, and on looking downward he found himself to be standing in a small pool of blood. Blood oozed through the left trouser leg. He had forgotten the wound caused by Lane's bullet; and, realizing the significance of his forgetfulness, decided that the matter of first importance was to stanch that wasting stream of blood. Lane must wait.

Placing the pistol between his teeth, he was in the act of removing his jacket, when suddenly the main glass door of the hall was thrown open, and the corridor resounded with the deep-throated, savage bayings of the monstrous dogs. He heard Madeline Fox's voice, shrilled to a scream:

"Sick 'em, Boy! Here, Prince, sick 'em! Fly! Fly! Here, Fly! Sick 'em, old girl! Fool 'em! Sick 'em!"

Dimly in the hall's half-light he saw the girl in the centre of a whirl of huge, grey, long-haired beasts, almost as tall as herself. When each of them came directly into the light from the passage he saw, too, the flash of ivories in crimson, slavering jowls.

Now with his coat off, he stepped rapidly past Lane's door, so that the fat man could not shoot him from behind whilst he did battle with the brutes urged forward by an insane woman. He saw one dog enter the passage, its half-pricked ears raised high above the great head, its black eyes regarding him balefully. The others came up behind it. Behind them, wildly gesticulating, stood Madeline Fox.

Lane's door suddenly crashed shut, a sound eloquent of the fat man's opinion of the animals. The sound appeared to give them their direction, for with a fresh outburst of baying they flew along the passage towards Monty.

The fog that dimmed his brain cleared. He thrust aside the temptation to slip into one of the rooms and follow Lane's example in shutting the door against them. To do this, he realized, would put him in the position of the besieged, giving the enemy time to link forces and recover from their surprise. His decision was based on the principle that his best strategy was to deal with each enemy in the order of appearance.

His automatic cracked twice so quickly that the reports blended. The leading brute dropped with a guttural howl. Again the pistol spoke, and one of the remaining beasts charging abreast dropped dead across the body of Johnston. But the third, bounding upon him like a huge projectile, hurled the big man back to the floor.

Gnashing jaws barely missed his throat. He saw the flash of the long white teeth before they sank in his right shoulder. He heard the crunch of bone and wondered curiously if it was his shoulder-bone that made the noise.

Man and beast rolled over and over along the passage. Yelping, worrying snarls came from the dog: grim silence from the man, fighting for his life with but a quarter of his strength remaining to him.

With his right arm thrust up round his neck Monty protected his throat; but the beast, having obtained a hold, tenaciously clung to it. So rapid was it in its body movements, and so close to him, that Monty found it extraordinarily difficult to use his weapon without endangering himself. He fired once, but the bullet merely cut off a strip of flesh and hair from the animal's back, which it did not seem to notice.

The hound's forepaws tore Monty's shirt to ribbons with their needle-sharp claws. Again the automatic cracked, and the bullet, striking the ceiling, brought down on them chunks of plaster and filled the air with white, choking dust. Above the horrible snarling he heard the girl's shrill scream, urging on the dog. Then he heard a man's voice, steely and dispassionate, commanding her to back along the passage.

But Monty saw neither woman nor man. His chance, his prayed-for chance, had come. With canine sagacity, the brute began to mill with his hind legs whilst still retaining the grip with his jaws. It was the action of an experienced fighting dog, an action which eventually would have enabled it to wrench out flesh and bone in a corkscrew pull. But the milling brought the brute's body round and free from Monty's right arm, and when the automatic once more exploded the hound suddenly let go its rat-trap grip to snap at its side. Again the big man fired. There came a plantive yelp which was the end.

A tattered, half-naked man scrambled to his knees, and lurched forward on his blood-smeared face. At a second attempt, he clung to a near door-handle and by it clawed his way to his feet, whereon he swayed to and fro drunkenly.

His shirt and trousers hung from him in strips, his bare right shoulder was a mass of bleeding flesh. Blood-matted hair fell wildly over his broad forehead to meet grey-blue eyes still emitting a steady light. His Gorgon face was the more terrible by reason of the broad grin of genuine happiness baring his white teeth. Human he was, made of flesh to be torn and bone to be broken; but unconquerable, even as Austiline had deemed him, in courage, in purpose, in determination.

He was above that state where the brain registers pain of the body. The only thing he realized, realized with boundless joy, was that he was still alive, still able to carry on the battle, his own "private battle," to use his own words.

Beyond the three dead beasts and the bodies of Johnston and "The Cat" he saw Madeline Fox standing with her back to the wall, her eyes regarding a pair of shining handcuffs encircling her wrists. On her face was a look of incredulous wonder. He saw, too, the new guest, Cotton, surveying her grimly—Cotton, with water streaming from his white duck suit, and from his neat brown beard and his hair.

From Monty came a roar of laughter. It was all so funny, so stupid. It was purest farce—one murderer baling up a murderess with handcuffs. In a cracked voice he said:

"Thanks, Cotton, old boy! But you just drop your little pop-gun *toot sweet,* or I'll drop you."

"Steady, Monty, I'm an ally," replied Cotton, his voice soft in drawling intonations—intonations which Monty had heard in the voice of one man only. The giant's underjaw sagged for a moment beneath the tremendous surprise. The automatic fell to his side. Very slowly his feet slid across the passage, and his back slid down the wall, till finally he reached a sitting posture on the floor.

"Jumping nannygoats!" he exclaimed.

Cotton opened the door of Madeline's room, and turned on the light within. With his hand on her arm he led her to her bed, where, releasing one cuff, he snapped it on the bed rail, making her an absolute prisoner. In the passage once more he paused in amazed admiration. He saw Monty calmly reloading his automatic pistol with shells taken from his jacket. He saw, too, the big man sitting in a pool of blood.

"How is it now, Monty?" he asked gently.

"Goodo!" replied Monty, looking up with twinkling eyes. Holding out his free hand he added: "Put it there, my dear old Sexton Blake. Somehow, Oakes, you have the bad habit of popping up like a jack-in-the-box. But I'm pleased to see you, nevertheless. What do you think of my private battle?"

CHAPTER XXXII

WILLIAM J. ANCHOR lay on his magnificent Queen
Anne bedstead. He had awakened suddenly, but was
unaware of any disturbing cause.

Lying in the darkness of his sumptuously furnished underground bedroom, sleep banished for the time, his thoughts
turned idly to the Sherwoods, whom cimcumstances had made
necessary to remove from active life. For them he had no
dislike. In fact he admitted often that he admired Monty;
and, although regarding Martin with jealousy as the accepted
lover of Austiline Thorpe, the blind man on some few occasions
aroused in the millionaire a sense of pity. Anchor possessed
imagination; also he had a horror of blindness.

A revolver shot, muffled by several walls, made him start
and listen. Half inclined to doubt his hearing, he raised
himself on the bed, his eyes staring into the utter blackness,
his brows knit into a straight line, his breathing suspended.
Then, with a quick gesture, he caught at the dangling cord
operating the switch and turned on the light. The tiny clock
on the bed-table told him it was twenty minutes past three.

He recognized the sound of the shot for what it was. He
had heard revolver firing too often to mistake the sound for
a clap of thunder, the explosion of gelignite, or even the report
of a shotgun.

Quite calmly he donned a dressing-gown and slipped into
one of the pockets an automatic pistol of smaller calibre than
that possessed by Monty. His bedroom opened into a larger
room wherein was installed his wireless and his experimental
paraphernalia, including a large, strange-looking model, the
purpose and nature of which was a secret that died with him.

He crossed this larger room to the passage door, where
from a hook he took down an electric torch similar to that
which the big man had taken from Moore's door. He paused,
listening, with the passage door open.

His torch showed him the cork-paved corridor. He walked to the steps, climbed them to the panel-door, stooped to the catch.

It was immovable.

That fixed panel, making him a prisoner unless he chose to batter the wood to pieces, caused him his first qualm. He heard the *chef's* bedroom door flung open, and recognized Johnston's heavy, lumbering footsteps entering the hall. Then he heard more distinctly a pistol crack, followed by a slight pause, when it cracked again twice in rapid succession.

Anchor was completely mystified by the shooting and by the fastened panel-door. He was inclined to credit the police with a much earlier visit than he had believed possible, especially in view of the rain. Was it they who were in conflict with "The Cat" and the others on the ground floor?

Deciding to seek the help and advice of his doctor friend, the millionaire retraced his steps to Moore's room. Entering the bedroom, he switched on the light and saw at once that the doctor was not on his bed. Hastening to the laboratory door, he flung it open, to be faced by the blinding glare of the arc-lamp over the operating-tables.

First he noticed the central table, with its unusual disorder of papers and upturned microscope. His gaze passed thence around the long room, resting finally on the figure of a woman lying on one of the operating-tables.

He almost ran across the room. Snatching the handkerchief off Mabel Hogan's face, he stepped back with an expression of mingled surprise and fear. His features went suddenly ghastly white. The handkerchief dropped from his nerveless fingers. He recognized that she was dead.

Feverishly he sprang to the second operating-table; and, on seeing his friend bound and gagged, realization came to him, together with the stunning shock that Dr. Moore also was dead.

The mask of benevolent cynicism had fallen momentarily from his face. His slaty agate eyes were wide and his lips parted, frozen by fear. He was a devil horribly afraid of being cast into his own furnace. But the cultivated self-control of many years came to his aid, and this astonishing man pulled himself together and smiled with his usual blandness, although his eyes shone with unveiled ferocity.

Now he knew who was firing, or causing to be fired, the

revolver shots on the floor above. He was less in fear of Monty than of the police. When he had dealt with Monty Sherwood and his brother, he would be finished with them; but, as for policemen, no matter how many he "put away" there were innumerable others to follow.

Having decided to reinforce his friends above, Anchor, his face fixed in a slight grin, left Moore's suite and re-entered his room, where from among his tools he selected a heavy hammer. Again in the corridor, he heard another revolver shot, and at that precise moment Mrs. Jonas opened the door and came out, dressed in a black silk wrapper.

"Whatever is going on?" she demanded, her face ashen grey, her handsome large eyes wide with apprehension.

Anchor's grin became a smile; he set down the hammer at his feet, and produced a cigar-case.

"A little midnight shooting practice, my dear Mrs. Jonas," he said softly. The case flashed open and snapped shut. A match was struck, and calmly he lit one of his favourite black cheroots. He proceeded: "Apparently the Sherwoods have escaped and are creating a little diversion for Lane and 'The Cat.' I suspect strongly that others also are being amused, and I hope presently to join in the fun myself. Have no fear, dear lady. The Sherwoods soon will be unpleasantly cold."

"Is it necessary to bring murder into this house of sanctuary?" she asked wildly. "Cannot we leave killing behind us for ever? I begged you not to harm them—to let them go as well as Miss Thorpe; but no words of mine could recall you to sanity or turn the doctor from his devilish inventions. Where is he?"

"Dead," he replied laconically.

For a moment she stared at him; then said very calmly:

"I am glad."

"I am not, Mrs. Jonas," he told her; "I am greatly upset," he added, though no one would have thought so from his tone or look.

Came to them then, as if a thick curtain had been suddenly withdrawn, the hideous baying of hounds and the mitigated echoes of Madeline Fox's screams. Anchor regarded Mrs. Jonas with calm significance. A revolver shot followed a few seconds later, then two rapidly together.

"The dogs are taking a hand, and Madeline with them," Anchor murmured.

Bangings on the floor overhead, and the snarling of a dog,

told of Monty's terrific struggle. Then came several more shots, followed by blank silence. At that sudden cessation of all sound uneasiness flashed into Anchor's eyes. He realized for the first time that the Sherwoods might now become, if they were not so already, masters of that upper floor. Mrs. Jonas saw and understood his expression.

"You may well be afraid, Mr. Anchor," she whispered. "It is the end of us and of this house. It is the inevitable triumph of good over evil. Had you and Moore repented of your past misdeeds and tried to live out your redemption in meekness and humility, God, I am sure, would have permitted us to continue in peace and safety. The fire awaits you, Mr. Anchor, as it awaits me."

He would have made some sarcastic if politely spoken rejoinder, had not she abruptly withdrawn into her room and locked the door. To him the silence was ominous, especially that of the dogs. A passage floor-board above him creaked, betraying the movement of some one walking quietly.

The sound of Mrs. Jonas dragging something heavy across the floor of her room reached him, but when it ceased he forgot her; for, darting off at a tangent, his thoughts fastened on Martin Sherwood. He, too, recognized the impossibility of the blind man taking any active part in the struggle. And then, suddenly, his thin lips drew back in a bestial snarl. A jealous suspicion had entered his mind; and, instead of making for the stairs, he picked up his hammer and walked rapidly to Austiline's door.

Finding the door locked, he unhesitatingly placed an ear against the keyhole. Distinguishing no sound, and no reply being made to his knocking, he knocked again loudly and repeatedly.

Half a minute passed. Came to him then the swish of a woman's clothes, followed by Austiline's voice asking who was there.

"Anchor," was the one word he spoke.

"But what do you want? Surely you know the time."

"It is about a quarter to four or a little later. Let me in, please. I have news for you."

With wide eyes and heaving bosom, Austiline clung to the door, the fear engendered in her by the dull reports of firearms now trebled by the faint note of menace in the voice beyond the door.

"If you will kindly open the door, you will save me the trouble of breaking it down with the hammer I have with me," the millionaire said silkily.

"Please wait a moment till I throw on a gown," she gasped; and, without waiting further, flew back to Martin Sherwood, who sat on the sofa with a lighted cigarette between his fingers.

"It's Anchor, Martin," she whispered agitatedly. "He wants to come in to tell me some news. He mustn't find you here, sweetheart. Come, let me hide you."

She took the half-consumed cigarette from him, putting it between her own lips; and, when he rose, almost a madman from his inability to see, she gently but firmly guided him to her bedroom and pushed him behind a curtain concealing a row of clothes pegs.

"If you want help, call me," he commanded fiercely. "If only I could see! Oh God! If only I could see!"

"Hush! It will be all right, dear. I'll get rid of him quickly," she replied bravely; and, catching his head between her hands, kissed him passionately and left him.

Closing the bedroom door, she passed through along the sitting-room, replacing the cigarette in her mouth before unlocking the outer door. Anchor strolled in, the cheroot clenched between his teeth, a smile of indescribable evil hovering about his thin lips.

"Good morning!" he said coolly, closing the door behind him. "Really I must apologize for intruding at such an hour; but our quiet life has suddenly boiled up into melodrama, so acceptable to the 'gods' and faintly applauded by the critical stalls. Have you heard the shooting?"

"Yes. What does it mean?"

She stood, a beautiful and gracious woman, in her becoming dressing-gown, which accentuated the soft curves of her figure and cried her femininity at him. Over each shoulder hung a rope of hair, glinting as antique copper in the light. Through narrowed eyelids Anchor regarded her. Had his spotted soul not already belonged to Satan, he would willingly have sold it for love of such a woman. Yet his voice was steady when he replied in his most casual drawl:

"It would seem that the Sherwoods have grossly abused our hospitality. I gather from the commotion that Brother Montague is engaged in shooting my guests, if they in their righteous wrath have not already shot him. As Brother Martin would be worse than useless in such a situation, I was beginning to wonder, Austiline, if he had sought refuge here and you in your goodness of heart had taken him in."

"Here!" she echoed.

Removing the cheroot from his mouth, he bowed sardonically. Then, with sinister pleasantness, he said:

"Forgive me my thoughts, I pray you. However, I must express surprise at your newly acquired habit of cigarette-smoking. And indulgence so early in the morning, too! I observe that you smoke 'Three Circles' cigarettes. The marks are so distinctive. If I recollect aright, Martin Sherwood also favours that particular brand. Where did you say you had concealed him?"

"He—he is not here," she faltered, the baleful glitter of his eyes breaking down her coolness, her courage.

"Permit me to compliment you on your poor lying," he said softly. "I hate a brazen liar. When I reflect that you are my promised bride, my lovely Austiline, I feel that my honour is gravely affected by finding a man in your apartments at this time of the morning." Then, in a flash, his suave smile vanished. His dulcet voice became a snarl. "Where is this blind fool? Tell me—quick!"

"He—he—no, you shall not!" she cried unsteadily, when he tried to pass her. She backing, he followed her, his agate eyes boring into hers, the fury of the baffled animal gathering into and distorting his fine face. Thus she brought up against her bedroom door, unconsciously betraying Martin's whereabouts, her staring, horror-filled eyes like those of a woman whose baby is threatened by the emissaries of Herod.

"Move aside!" he ordered.

"Never!"

"So! Then you must be taught to obey."

A steely hand gripped her bare arm. He pulled her forcibly towards him, and she, in a last despairing effort to protect the blind man, struck him on the mouth with all her strength. The blow sent him backward a pace, and she was dragged after him. Again she struck, and then screamed at the demoniac look blazing from his eyes.

Martin Sherwood heard distinctly every word spoken beyond the shut door. Consternation and fear for Austiline gripped him with icy fingers. The sound of Austiline's blow fell on his straining ears as a douche of cold water, and, unable any longer to remain inactive, he stepped from the curtain on hearing her second blow.

With his arms outstretched, his fingers working as though searching for Anchor's throat, he stumbled over a chair that sent him crashing to the floor. Yet, unconscious of any hurt, he scrambled to his feet and set off on a wild, hopeless search for the door, his sense of hearing now blunted by a terrible fear for the safety of his beloved. His knees meeting the edge of the bed, he sprawled into it with pathetic comicality. Off that he rolled to run full tilt into a glass panelled wardrobe, his hands missing it, his face coming violently against the plate-glass.

The impenetrable darkness of his world was filled with invisible objects barring his every step. The bed, the dressing-table, the octagonal book-rack, the chairs and other furniture, assumed life, taking on the malevolent spite of mocking enemies leagued together to frustrate him.

Austiline's scream halted him at the head of the bed. For the first time since he had left the curtain he realized the absurdity of the over-eagerness which stunned his hearing, the all-important sense of his remaining four.

His hands met a small occasional table, and, tipping this up, he grasped it by one spidery leg. He knew now the position of the door, from which came sounds of a man's fierce breathing and a woman's sharp, panting sobs. Cautiously now, all his will-power urgently directed to steady him, Martin slowly crossed the room and found the door-handle.

A jerk and he had flung wide the door, and he, a blind man, whose only weapon was a frail occasional table, set out to battle with a man armed with an automatic pistol, enjoying perfect vision, and as ruthless as the combined inmates of all hell.

At his appearance, his clothes torn, his face bleeding from the collision with the wardrobe, Austiline, clinging like a limpet to the maddened millionaire, shrieked and screamed out:

"Monty! Monty! Come quickly, Monty!"

"Monty, you vixen! Monty's shot to pieces!" Anchor gasped triumphantly.

Her gown was torn to ribbons. Anchor's face streamed blood where it had been lacerated by her finger-nails. Gone was Austiline the beautiful, the joyous, the tender. Here instead was woman as she has been throughout the ages, as first she was when she fought against the beasts who would consume her, and against man who would club her into submissiveness. Martin, the blind and helpless Martin, was her child, whom the primordial woman in her fought to protect.

And towards this swaying, struggling pair lurched Martin Sherwood—gentle, sympathetic, lovable Martin—a new creation and yet the same. The quiet, dignified editor of *The Daily Tribune* was no more. From him civilization was shed. The blackness before his eyes was ribbed by red streaks. He was possessed with an awful, overpowering desire to kill the man who defiled his woman by his touch. The complications of circumstances had evoked even in him the terrible impulse that makes the murderer.

And then suddenly he paused. Like nausea realization came, remembrance of his utter, pitiable helplessness. For to strike haphazard with his table would be madness indeed, since it was an even chance that he would hit his beloved. His mouth sagged and tears sprang into his sightless eyes.

Helpless! What a word!

"Sight! Sight! Please, please God, give me sight!" he wailed.

His cry was followed by another scream from Austiline on being flung back by Anchor, who, having torn himself from her weakening hands, ran to the blind man. Primitive hate, primitive lust was so overpowering that the millionaire forgot the weapon provided by lethal science with which to kill with ease. He was mad to strike, to kill with his naked hands. Deliberately he measured the distance, and then struck at the defenceless man with all the power of his shoulder-muscles, backed by all his weight.

The blow caught Martin exactly between the eyes, sent him flying backwards like a ninepin. Dazed by the terrific impact, the blind man lay stretched on his back, still as death, with the ex-rubber king standing over him, laughing with maniacal shrillness. His hand dived into a pocket, gripped the butt of the automatic pistol, drew it out.

And then, with the strength of ten men, Austiline threw herself upon his arm.

Still laughing, he turned on her, and tried to wrench himself free. For an instant they faced each other, her fair skin smeared and fouled by the blood from his face, her hair a flaming cloud. Swiftly she bent and sank her teeth into the hand holding the weapon. His laughter changed to a howl of agony. The pistol fell to the floor. With his left fist he struck her a cruel blow beneath the ear; but the distance was too short, his aim too uncertain for the blow to be effective.

Neither of them saw Martin stir. Neither did they see his eyes open, and then close with visible pain. The blind man sat up with a hand covering his eyes and the purple bruise between them. Although red-hot irons were gouging into his brain, Martin cried out, a great vibrating cry of overwhelming joy.

Lignt! He could see the light—soft, glowing, radiant light. Through his fingers, partially obscured by what appeared to be a maze of whirling light particles, he witnessed the struggle taking place, but a few yards from him, with a sudden surge of conscious power.

"Hold on, Austiline!" he shouted. Slowly he attempted to rise. The effort brought on giddiness which almost made him vomit. The second attempt succeeded. Rolling over on his side he flung out his arm to assist his rising, when his hand touched Anchor's pistol. Slowly and painfully he got up on his feet, his legs trembling violently, the floor and the combatants seeming to him to rise and fall as the deck of a ship at sea. Then came a calm. The floor became steady. The mist dulling his brain vanished. Looking through his fingers still, for the light—the glorious new-found light— burned his eyes, he stumbled up to Anchor then bending Austiline over in a back-breaking grip. Viciously he jammed the muzzle of the weapon against Anchor's neck.

"Throw up your hands, you cowardly swine!"

At the touch of metal, at the sound of Martin's voice, as cold and as hard as the pistol, the millionaire's hands lifted. Very slowly he stood up; slowly, too, he turned and gazed with deadened, lack-lustre eyes down the barrel of his own weapon. He was like a man whose limbs are doomed to move but a fraction of an inch at a time.

In Martin's eyes he saw reflected vision. He did not wonder how Martin had come to see. He knew only that he could see.

Suddenly the door was flung open from without.

"Monty! Oh Monty! Come quick!" cried Austiline from the floor.

CHAPTER XXXIII

DETECTIVE-SERGEANT OAKES, of the Victorian
Police, should he ever write his memoirs, doubtless will
have many gruesome sights to record; yet, up to that time,
the scene of that passage was of all he had encountered the
most terrible.

He said afterwards that it was not the vision of two dead
men and three huge hounds forming a rampart from wall to
wall which filled the picture; but the great figure of one man,
who appeared as if he had passed through a sausage machine,
sitting in a pool of his own blood, and calmly reloading an
automatic pistol.

And then the quietly asked question, asked with that irrepressible twinkle of the grey-blue eyes: "What do you think of my
private battle?"

"Ye Gods!" the detective-sergeant whispered. "A private
battle!"

"M'yes. Would have been a lively affair had it been a
public one, wouldn't it?"

"It would, if the public consisted of Monty Sherwoods,"
Oakes agreed. "Are you wounded badly?"

"A few scratches," the big man admitted slowly, his eyes
now lacked lustre, his head nodding. "You might tear up a
few sheets and things. I'm leaking a lot of juice, and friend
Anchor is still in particular need of my services."

"Lane and Mallowing—where are they?"

"Mallowing sleeps, I hope, on his little bed. I tied him down
on it. Lane is comforting a smashed wrist."

"Humph! Keep an eye open for Lane. I'll not be a
moment."

The detective-sergeant disappeared within Madeline Fox's
room, to dart out almost instantly laden with bed-sheets and
pillow-slips. Tearing these into strips, he said in his old-time
drawl:

"Who, do you think, is moving about in Mabel Hogan's room?"

With an effort Monty rallied his senses.

"It can't be Lane," he said. "Ah! I know. That, probably, will be my son."

"Your son?"

"My adopted son, to be precise. Mabel Hogan gave him to me."

"Oh!" Oakes said, understanding not at all what Monty was talking about. "Let's have your shirt off, or what's left of it. Send Lane a messenger if he appears."

They heard a chair being dragged to Mabel's door. The sounds of the dead woman's child clambering upon it diverted their minds from themselves. Monty felt an unwonted lassitude; the detective felt as in a dream. Oakes marvelled that a man with Monty's wounds could live, let alone joke. His ministrations were quite primitive: a surgeon would have shuddered to see Oakes "plugging"—it is the only word—the long, deep, open furrow across Monty's side with wads of unsterilized sheeting, wads kept in place by swathe upon swathe of rough bandages.

Into the passage stumbled little Bubbles, his great blue eyes blinking in the light, his yellow hair in sore need of brushing. For a moment he surveyed the massive bulk of Monty lying on his chest, one hand still gripping the pistol, with Oakes working over him surrounded by yards of ribboned sheets.

The big man groaned. Should Lane open fire now, well might he hit the child.

And then the boy ran to him, sat down to be more on a level with his face, and cooed:

"Mine daddy! 'Tis mine daddy!"

Monty was kissed, and the moist wonderful kiss drove back the strange darkness below his eyes and vanquished the giddiness.

"You come a little beside me, Bubbles," he said coaxingly. "I want to see up the passage, in case Mr. Lane comes to look for us."

"Lane! Mis'r Lane!" echoed Bubbles uncomprehendingly.

"Yep. Monsoor Lane, if you like. Now, don't touch the cannon. It's hot."

Oakes had just secured the bandages round Monty's torso with safety-pins he had snatched from a tray on Madeline's dressing-table, when Monty's pistol cracked with nerve-shatter-ing suddenness.

"Carry on," Monty drawled. "It's only Lane. Can't you hear his gentle whispers? He's got to the hall now."

"Did you drop him?"

"No; I walloped him in the left arm. He's out of action now." And then, as an after-thought: "Didn't want to kill him, anyhow. I'm rather curious to know how far the hang-man will drop a man of his weight. Never mind the shoulder. Just shove my shirt on again. We're losing too much time."

"It's in a hell of a mess, Monty," the detective-sergeant said doubtfully.

"No matter. As Lane is now harmless, slip along to the dining-room and get me a drink, will you? Look out for Anchor."

Ignoring the moans coming from the fat man lying in the dark hall, the detective brought a decanter of whisky and a glass. It was a tumbler glass.

"Say when!" he commanded.

Monty shut his eyes. When he took the glass it was full.

"Bottled beer is more in my line," he spluttered, when he had drained the glass. "Never did like reptile preservative." Clinging to Oakes he managed to gain his feet, adding grimly: "Now for the beloved Anchor!"

"Here! wait a minute. Where are you going?"

"Down among the dead men," mocked the giant.

The thin, keen face of the detective had lost entirely its bland mask of vacuity. The terrible realities of the situation were too strong for facial make-believe.

"Stop your foolery, Monty," he said. "I'm serious."

"Aren't you aware of the underground rooms?" the big man demanded, the wall supporting him, his free hand now holding the screwdriver which had been in his jacket pocket. Seeing the puzzled look in the other's eyes, he blamed himself for thinking that the detective-sergeant was over-cautious. He saw understanding dawning upon Oakes.

"So that was where they took you two fellows, was it?" he exclaimed. "Anchor kept me talking at the dinner-table, so I did not see what they did with you. I've been hunting for you outside for two solid hours in the damned rain. How do you get to these underground rooms?"

Monty smiled. He felt only a little stronger from the stimu-lant, yet he smiled.

"No, you don't," he said reprovingly. "Don't forget I'm rather good at bluff-poker. Anchor is my meat. You go a-hunting Lane."

Just then the fat man roared from the hall.

"Hey! Sherwood!" he called.

"Well?"

"I chuck in the sponge. I'm bleedin' like a stuck pig."

"Come and see the glorious white flag flying," Monty told him; and, while Lane staggered along the passage towards them, he said to Oakes: "Now, don't you go butting into my private affairs. You look after Lane and my son."

He passed the fat man holding out his broken limbs. He made the length of the passage with the wall for support. At the end he turned to see Oakes engaged in bandaging Lane. He called back:

"Don't let Bubbles follow me yet. When you've fixed Lane, come along quick. You'll find the door to below behind the tapestry here in the hall."

Monty heard Bubbles crying frantically to be allowed to accompany him; heard, too, the detective-sergeant swear vividly and almost snarl about having to double the parts of hospital nurse and mother's help.

Whilst he had the passage wall for support the giant was able to keep his feet; but, as soon as he left it to cross the hall to the tapestry, the recurrent giddiness engendered by the weakness that had come over him forced him to his hands and knees. To his iron will alone was his progress due. With pistol in mouth, the torch in one pocket, and the screwdriver clenched in one hand, the big man at last gained the panel-door.

Anxious not to allow Oakes to catch him up before he dealt with Anchor, Monty worked feverishly at withdrawing the screws. When he had them out and the panel-door slid back, his hands and the floor, now lighted by the electric-bulb over the steps, appeared as though they were deep in a sea of ink.

Looking down the steps, vertigo seized him. The steps heaved and swayed in an alarming manner. Like Bubbles getting off a bed, Monty slid down legs first.

He was thankful that the millionaire did not meet him just then. He could imagine his pleasant greeting, accompanied by a ruthless shot. At the foot of the steps he tried hard to stand, but failed. During this effort he heard Austiline screaming for him to come quickly, and knew then exactly where Anchor was.

Wasting no further time in vain attempts to rise, he set off along the passage on his hands and knees, rolling from side to side like a grotesquely drunken dog. Agonized groans reached him from Mrs. Jonas' room in passing, but at the moment these interested him but little. His mission, the sole object to be accomplished, must be carried out without delay. Austiline was calling to him in terrified accents; Oakes was coming on behind him to rob him of the satisfaction of finishing Anchor. To stop, even to pause, meant final submergence in the strange black sea surging upwards to engulf him. He was tired, so tired that even to think was torture.

Subconsciously he noticed that Anchor's and the doctor's rooms were open. He heard Austiline scream again, and wondered why the dickens she made so much noise. The farther he progressed towards the farther door, the farther it appeared to recede, the passage magically lengthening to infinity.

His breathing now rasped between his teeth and the automatic. Onward he lurched for years and years; and then, when the world had grown old and dead, he came to Austiline's door. Like a cat trying its claws on a wooden post, he clawed upward to the handle, turned it, and then the weight of his body sent the door flying inward.

The significance of Martin's facing and menacing Anchor was lost on Monty. He failed to note the crouching figure of Austiline, although he heard her urgent call. With a mighty, torturing effort he pulled himself up by the door-post, steadied himself as a man about to walk a wire, paused for a final tremendous mental effort, and, stiffly as a soldier on parade, marched the length of the room, halting only when he came to Anchor's rigid back.

The leaping inky sea was now lapping his mouth. The rising tide was beating his will to remain conscious. Knowing that it would overwhelm him before Martin could secure the millionaire, whilst he, Monty, covered him; knowing also that Martin would be beaten once his weapon wavered from the glaring eyes: there was but one thing left to do. He brought the butt of his automatic down on the back of Anchor's head.

Anchor collapsed.

"Lash him up tight, Martin, old son," he wheezed. "Tell Cotton, who is Oakes, that peace has been declared."

And then the flood engulfed him, and he fell on the prostrate figure of William J. Anchor.

* * * * *

Monty had many and strange dreams. Whispering voices sometimes came to him where he dwelt in darkness on a dead world. It seemed to him that this world was very small, and that if he moved it would turn over and precipitate him into an immeasurable void.

Although it was impossible for him to see it, he knew that not far away hung a gigantic curtain of black velvet: and it was from beyond this curtain that he heard the voices of Austiline, Mrs. Minter, Martin, Sir Victor Lawrence, and Mary Webster. While the others spoke of him, it was Mary who kept calling him. But how could he move from his dead world and past the velvet curtains?

He experienced no physical feeling whatever, unless the faint scent of attar of roses could be named one. He was trying to recollect, after a long sojourn on the small unstable world, where had he met before that alluring scent; when he felt the velvet curtain brushing his face, and, thrusting it aside, jumped off his planet and found himself lying on a bed. And he was looking straight into the rust-flecked eyes of Austiline Thorpe.

"Monty!" she breathed, her face gradually breaking into a tender smile.

"You ought to scorn a great big brute of a man like me for fainting like a—like a girl," he said, surprised to find how difficult it was to speak loud enough for her to hear.

"Hush!" With the touch of an angel she smoothed his pillow and raised his head so that he could drink some lemon-water. "I must get you your medicine now. I'll not be long."

He watched her almost run to the door, and when she disappeared heard her run along the passage. Smiling at her anxiety about the medicine, he lay there listening to the fall of water from the bore-head. Through the open window came happy excited cries of a small child, and in them he recognized the voice of Bubbles. Then fleeting footsteps ran along the passage to pause at his door. Slowly he turned his head. The thought of the coming medicine brought a shadow of a smile to his lips.

And when a woman entered, to stand regarding him with wide and misty eyes, he saw with a catch of breath that it was Mary Webster.

"Mary!"

"Oh, don't rise, Monty dear!" she cried, darting to the

bed, where she fell on her knees and laid her face beside his. "Oh, Monty! Dear, dear Monty!"

After a long while he said, with his usual touch of the unexpected:

"Where is my medicine, Mary?"

And, with tremulously happy lips, she answered:

"I am your medicine, Monty. Do you like it?"

"It is the Nectar of the Gods. But how do you come to be here?"

"Sir Victor Lawrence brought me. We have been here two weeks. Oh, Monty! I was afraid for you."

"Then how long have I been idle like this?"

"Three weeks."

"Jumping nannygoats! Tell me, my beautiful medicine, what has happened during those three blank weeks. Don't move your head, dear; I like that scent in your hair."

And so, cheek to cheek, she told him. He made her tell him the whole story.

"You see, Mr. Oakes happened to be at the Central Police Station at Adelaide one evening engaged with several experts trying to decipher a code message sent from a wireless-station at Mount Barker," she told him softly. "While there a man walked into the charge office below and said he had murdered a man up in the Adelaide Hills. He told them his name was Cotton.

"They believed his confession because the body of the man had been discovered. Mr. Oakes then hit on the plan of disguising himself as Cotton, going so far, he told me, as to glue each hair of the false beard and moustache to his face separately.

"He left the police station as Cotton. You know how he was picked up by one of Anchor's organization, because he says he told all of you about Cotton's affair when he arrived here. Mr. Johns, the Sydney detective, who was with Mr. Oakes, shadowed him to the bungalow at Glenelg, and saw him later on board a motor-boat.

"Mr. Johns, being unable to follow the boat personally, telegraphed to every station along the coast, and when the boat reached Port Augusta the police there didn't stop them, but let them go to the railway-station, where they booked to Marree.

"You see, the detectives had long suspected that there was in operation an organization to get murderers away. It was funny because, whilst Mr. Oakes would have it that the organization was directed from somewhere in the bush, Mr. Johns said it was in some city. Mother found that out from him soon after you left, and she told him what Bent Nose told you.

"So that, directly Mr. Oakes' companion booked to Marree, Mr. Johns telegraphed to the police at Innaminka, for information regarding the inhabitants in the vicinity of Lake Moonba. This house was the only one in a radius of eighty miles. The Innaminka police were ordered to be here on the Sunday following, and that day Mr. Johns arrived per aeroplane."

"Did he arrest Anchor?"

"Mr. Oakes had already done that," she said. "He had him, with Lane, Mallowing, and the girl Madeline Fox, locked in Dr. Moore's laboratory."

"Ah! And what of the others?"

"The others were dead."

"All of them?"

"Yes. Dr. Moore was found dead on his operating-table. They say you hit him too hard, Monty. Mrs. Jonas poisoned herself with strychnine."

"Poor soul! Well, go on, please."

"They took Anchor, the two men, and the girl Fox away," Mary continued. "They found records, Monty: written records in which were the names of all the chief members of Anchor's organization, the greatest and most far-reaching of any ever. And, Monty dear, it was you—you who overthrew it; although Mr. Oakes, of course, got most of the praise. He is a detective-inspector now."

"He'll be a detective-superintendent soon. He's a detective wonder, anyhow. What about Martin? Where is he?"

"He is coming back with Sir Victor Lawrence from Innaminka to-day. They've been practically living at the telegraph-office. When Martin first sent the story to the *Tribune* they thought it was a hoax. When they found it was not, Sir Victor decided to come up here himself. Martin wired me, too, about you, Monty, and I went off my head almost. I implored Sir Victor to bring me directly I heard he was chartering a 'plane. He gave me his secretary's place. Mother was frightfully upset, too."

"Poor Martin!" he sighed.

"Why poor? Is he not supremely fortunate?"

"Yes, maybe. He'll have a jewel of a wife, but a jewel he'll never see."

"Oh, Monty! Don't you know that when Mr. Anchor knocked him down the blow and the mental excitement restored his sight?"

"Honest?"

"Yes!" And she recounted the terrible scene of struggle prior to his entrance and final subjugation of Anchor. When she finished he sighed happily.

"Well, the clouds have rolled away, haven't they? Bubbles appears to be having a good time. What is he up to?"

"Do you mean Mabel Hogan's child?"

"Yes. My adopted son, Mary. Mabel gave him to me. She died that I might have him."

Rising, she looked out through the wide-open French windows. And then, slipping her arm underneath his head, she lifted him up so that he, too, could look. And what he saw sent a strange lump into his throat.

Over by one of the store-huts Mrs. Minter sat, half-buried in the deep sand. Bubbles, with a tiny spade, was busily covering her lank frame, shrieking with delight while he sent spadeful after spadeful over her. At a little distance, squatted upon his heels, was Mr. Minter, uproariously encouraging the youngster's efforts. Even from his bed Monty was struck by the wonderful joy on the weather-parched face of the selector's wife.

"I bet the boy will be spoiled," he said, when Mary lowered him again to the pillow.

"Let them spoil him," was her whisper. "Monty, don't you think Mrs. Minter could have him for good? We can all understand her tragedy, so we can all see how much she loves little Bubbles."

"Yes, she can have him, Mary. There is no one with a greater claim. I'm going to put the Minters on a small station well east in New South Wales, where it rains two or three times a year, at least. They are going to have a real beautiful home, which shall be Bubbles' some day."

"They will be deliriously happy, those three."

"They are not the only people who are going to be happy, Mary," he told her; and, seeing the look in his grey-blue eyes, she bent her head and kissed him.

EPILOGUE

IT was the end of April, and Monty Sherwood had taken his first short walk, leaning lightly on the arm of radiant Mary Webster. On their way from Marree were four hundred camels, chartered by the South Australian Government, which would return to the railway laden with William J. Hook's priceless collection of art treasures. Another fortnight would see the House of Cain dismantled, an empty shell, which finally no one would buy on account of its unexploitable situation.

The air exhilarated as wine; the sun was warm and the wind a caressing zephyr from the south. The rain had woven a carpet of brilliant emerald, and the sea of sand-hills which had formerly smoked and danced in the roaring winds of summer was now a mighty tossing sea of waving grass.

At the base of one of the huge green waves sat Martin Sherwood with Austiline, daintily chewing a wisp of spear-grass, at his side. A long pool of water glittered at their feet. When the woman removed the grass stem, she said softly:

"When are you going to ask me about Peterson's blackmail, Martin?"

"Really, I had forgotten all about him. Was he important? I was wondering if a sculptor could get the exact lovely curve of your cheek," he said simply. "But you remind me of a commission which the recent excitement caused me to forget." From his pocket he withdrew a foolscap envelope. "Inspector Oakes took this from the body of the blackmailer, and evidently it contains the secret he held over you. I think Oakes was very decent not to examine it. He said that, as the nature of the blackmail had nothing to do with the actual murder of Peterson, he refrained from so doing and entrusted it to me to give you."

"You open it, Martin," she ordered, with laughter-lit eyes.

A little surprised at her taking the matter so lightly, he broke the seal and disclosed a number of letters neatly pinned together.

They were letters, written by Austiline to her publishers, which had been stolen by Peterson, who had been a publisher's clerk. Martin read her urgent request to have the real identity of "A. E. Titchfield" kept a profound secret.

"But surely you would not have paid the blackguard two hundred pounds for these letters?" he said with wonder.

"I would have paid him a thousand," was her emphatic answer. "Oh, Martin! wait till you have met my dear father and mother. Such old-fashioned souls, but just wonderful." Suddenly she broke into a ripple of laughter. "When I take you home, dear, you bring 'A. E. Titchfield's' writings into the conversation and hear what my father has to say. Only my mother can calm him."

Placing the papers on the ground, he struck a match, and they watched them burn.

"I am always learning something about you, Austiline," he said.

"I'll take good care you do not learn all there is to know about me all at once," she said wisely. "Love requires feeding. Your love shall never grow hungry, nor yet ever be satiated."

.   .   .   .   .   .

Late in August, Austiline received the following letter through a firm of American solicitors. It was from Anchor:

"MY DEAR AUSTILINE,

"By the time you receive this the undersigned, in all probability, will be but a memory. I claim no tears.

"Respecting you as the only woman who declined my advances —therefore by love's political economy enhancing your value in my eyes—I do not want to be remembered by you at greater disadvantage than is necessary. No doubt you think I worse than dishonoured my promise to allow the Sherwoods to leave my Home on parole. I did my best to keep it, and would have kept it, but for unexpectedly adverse events.

"My hand being forced by the straying of the camels without which the Sherwoods could not set out, and by the imminence of a police raid, I had not only to hide my more conspicuous inmates (such as Lane and 'The Cat' and, alas! yourself) in the underground rooms, as was our practice during ordinary police visits, but also to dispose in like manner of the Sherwoods who would have welcomed and assisted the police. The Sherwoods I had been hoping to get rid of pleasantly and quickly before the coming of the police, but the straying of their camels made this impossible, much to my annoyance and regret. To prevent time-wasting argument, I therefore drugged them and had them taken underground and bound so that they could make no disturbance. My intention was merely to keep them thus in harmless security until the police had gone and the strayed camels had been recovered, and then to carry out my promise to let them depart in peace on condition of keeping our secrets. Moore I plainly forbade to operate on them; but as a sop to him I said he might test their nerve by expounding to them the sort of experiments he would like to subject them to. He appears to have done this only too convincingly, and Mr. Montague Sherwood's too hasty assault on him put it out of his power to explain. I therefore supply the explanation on his behalf, and trust it may enable you to think more kindly of Moore as an enthusiast in research and a martyr to science; and of myself as a man whose good intentions have been overborne by the *force majeure* of circumstances.

"As for myself generally, you probably think worse of me than you do of a certain British monarch whose record I have not nearly equalled. Had your inclinations been free, however, I am sure I should have been able to remove all difficulties and induce you to recall your first unconsidered if disinterested refusal. And I think neither of us would have had any cause to deplore the alliance.

"So convinced am I of this that I have taken steps to ensure that my various properties after my decease shall be placed at your disposal. While leaving you free to use these resources as you think fit, I should be glad if they could be applied, at least in part, for the benefit of outcasts of society—not necessarily always murderers, but such cases as Bent Nose, in whom you took so kind yet so practical an interest, and that delightful child of Mabel Hogan's, for whom indeed I was going to provide fittingly myself in due course; and those who, like yourself, have been endangered by purely circumstantial evidence. The funds that should come to you as I devise will be considerable enough to supply a conspicuous example to the world in the direction indicated, and the example once set will certainly be followed. I know that in heart and brain you and Mr. Martin Sherwood will be equal to the demands of such a trust, and I implore you to accept it.

"Sincerely,

"WILLIAM J. HOOK

"(*alias* ANCHOR)."

This letter was written when the plea of insanity, set up with legal ingenuity and backed by Anchor's wealth, had broken down. A day or two later he cheated the electric chair, as a last resource, by means of conia.

. . . . . .

In Australia, at the date of Anchor's letter, the public had exhausted the interest of the House of Cain. Lane, the glutton, was not hanged, since the law of Queensland dispenses with the death penalty. Mallowing, however, paid the uttermost price, because the State of Victoria still believes in the *lex talionis*. As for Madeline Fox, she is in safe keeping as a criminal lunatic.

Conspicuous and lasting interest, however, was shown by the intellectual section of the public and by the medical profession in the carefully compiled notes left by Dr. Walling, *alias* Moore. Although Dr. Walling did not originate the theory that murderers suffer from a brain lesion, he at least prepared the way for a procedure that eventually will become as familiar as the removal of the appendix. Humanity ever advances. To-day it regards the torture chamber with horror; to-morrow it will look upon legal murder with disgust.

. . . . . .

The brilliant morning of September 1st witnessed Princes Pier, Melbourne, crowded with people, waving and calling farewells to hundreds of others lining the deck-rails of the P. and O. steamer *Mongolia*.

The law had had its amusement with the farcical trial of Monty Sherwood for manslaughter, and was satisfied. He stood there, on the jetty, head above the crowd, carrying on his broad shoulder the flushed, excited Bubbles, whose little hands were entangled in half a dozen coloured streamers held at the other ends by Mr. and Mrs. Martin Sherwood on the liner's top deck.

At Monty's side, waving a handkerchief, was his wife, Mary. There, too, was the gaunt Mrs. Minter and her shriveled husband. Inspector Oakes, with never-flagging interest, watched the rows of faces looking down from the ship. Now and then he glanced at Bent Nose, who smiled at him crookedly but happily.

The ship was moving. The paper streamers broke one by one. Slowly it was pulled out into the fairway. Came Mrs. Minter for Master Frederick Minter, who scrambled willingly into her bony but hungry arms. Monty, looking down at his wife on their way to the train that would taken them to the city, said:

"Life! I love life, Mary."